MUFFINS AND MEDIUMS

MIXING UP MAGIC
BOOK FIVE

ROSIE PEASE

Muffins and Mediums

This is a work of fiction. Names, characters, organizations, places, events, and incidents are either products of the author's imagination or are used fictitiously. Any resemblance to actual persons, living or dead, or actual events is purely coincidental.

Editor: Paisley Press Books
Cover Designer: Melony Paradise of Paradise Cover Design

PAISLEY PRESS BOOKS
WEST WARWICK, RHODE ISLAND

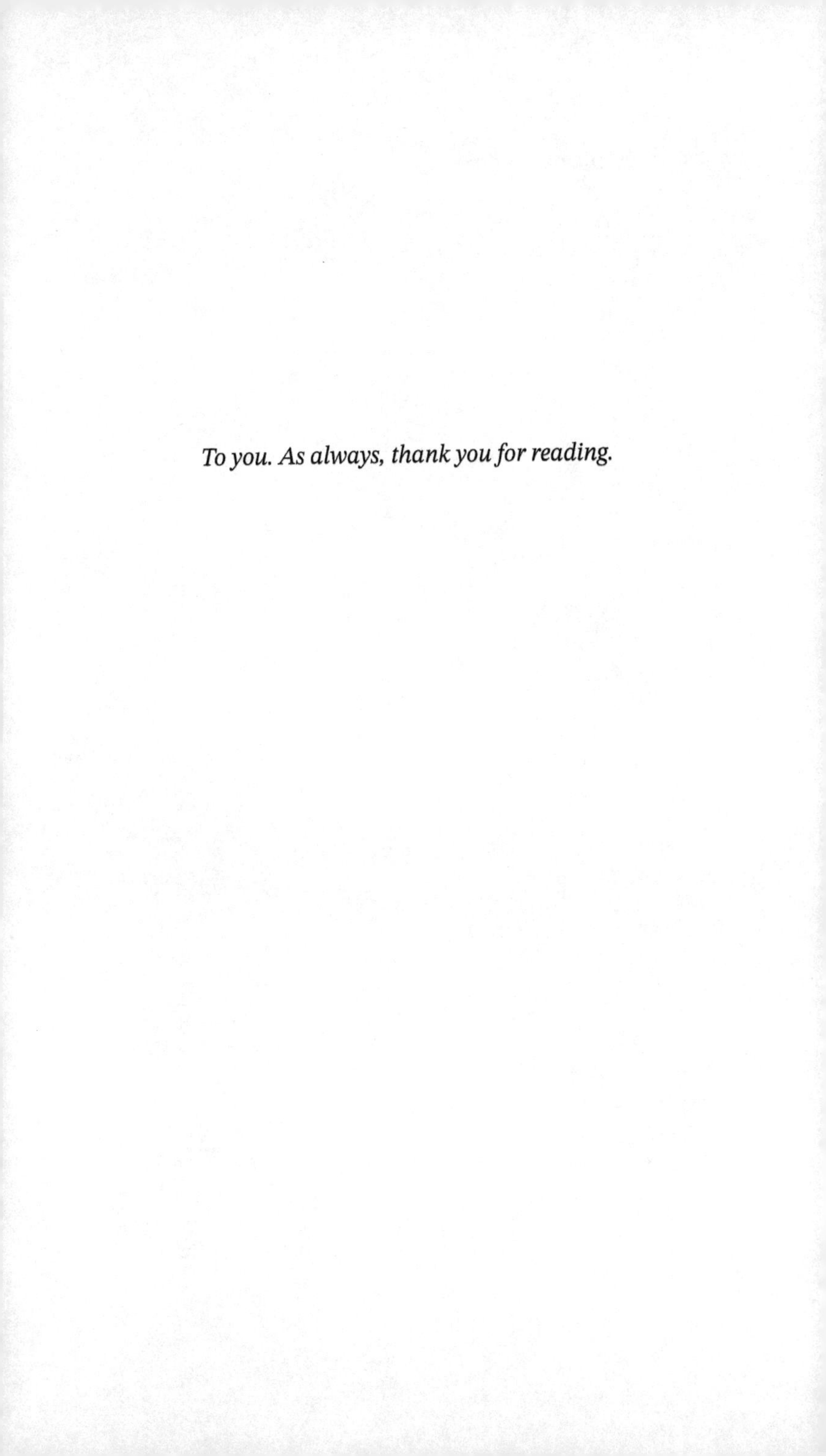

To you. As always, thank you for reading.

ABOUT THIS BOOK

After being courted by the local coven, my anticipation over meeting someone who could be like me builds. But that person is even closer than I think when she comes into my bakery asking me to find her grandmother. Or more specifically, her grandmother's missing ghost.

When she says her grandmother promised to be at her upcoming wedding, I agree to help her, but complications arise when I sense the bride is meant to be with someone else.

There are more tiers to this missing ghost case than there are on my cakes, and as the big day approaches, I can't help but wonder if one issue is related to the other. I've never been wrong about my matches, but there are some lines I won't cross, even when the groom makes veiled threats to keep me from getting involved.

With love, life, and the afterlife on the line, I must whisk it all and put my skills to the ultimate test. Can I give everyone their happily-ever-afters or will this be first time that everything doesn't pan out the way I hoped?

AUTHOR'S NOTE

Dear Reader,

Thank you so much for picking *Muffins and Mediums* as your next read. Maybe you're reading this book right after reading Potluck and Powers. Maybe there's been some time—or even a lot of time—between reading the two. The editing of this book took a backseat when the series was signed over to a small publisher and then over the following year as I prepped the previous books in the series for republication. If you've been following me since the start of that, you'll know that the books are back in my full control once again. But in a way, despite the wait for this one, it all worked out.

You see, this book is by far the longest in the series, and having to go over the four books leading up to this one in-depth the way I did and back to back meant that after the year-long break of finishing the first draft of this book and revising it, I went into it with a full and refreshed eye on the entire series versus trying to remember everything from the earlier books, some of which I hadn't looked at since my final proofreading passes of them a few years prior. It turned out to be a tremendous benefit, and I know this book is better for it.

This book is not the same book that would have come out originally. Although many things remain the same, the original book was darker and lacking some of the lightness that the other books have even in dealing with tough subjects. That's not to say that this one doesn't. It does. Without spelling it out but hopefully giving those who might need it a bit of a heads-up on content, you'll meet someone in here who just is not nice and another who is in a position because of that not-nice person that may seem familiar to some of you either because you've been in them or because you know someone who has been. Please, if you ever find yourself in a position like that, reach out to someone you trust or be the person that someone else can reach out to. This book does end happily, as all mine do, and if you find yourself in a similar position, I hope you get your happy ending too.

Enjoy your time back in Heartwood Hollow and discovering the new issues that Joanie faces in this book. You'll see some familiar faces as well as some new ones and will continue to discover secrets about them all as well as the place they call home. It really is one of my favorite small towns.

I love hearing from my readers. If you'd like to reach out to me, you can find me throughout social media @WriteRosiePease.

Happy reading!

Cheers,

Rosie

CHAPTER I

I vy shook her head, the end of her ponytail gliding across her shoulders as it swished back and forth. "It's missing something. I like it, but it's not quite there."

I looked down at the pint-sized sous chef. "What are you thinking?"

She grinned mischievously. "More sugar."

A laugh bubbled out of me. What seven-year-old didn't want more sugar? Then again, it was candy, so maybe she had a point. I tried a piece myself—okay, a second piece—and agreed with her. "Hear that, Bryan? More sugar."

"You got it." He scooped out another quarter cup.

Ever since Trudy, Sam's grandmother, had given me the recipes for all the candies she used to make in her shop, I'd been regularly experimenting on Wednesday afternoons, our slowest day in the bakery. Each of the bakers on my team, including the newest, Brittni, had been rotating one late shift to try their hand at candy-making. Although I still planned on hiring someone whose everyday responsibility would be making candy, I wanted everyone to see how they liked it and also to gain some understanding of the various confectionary processes. I'd made it a point to have everyone in the kitchen trained across disciplines, from decorating cakes to folding pastry dough to making the simplest cookie recipe. Candy would be no different. Besides, what if someone here excelled at candy far greater than someone I could hire? So far, it hadn't happened, but the experiment in rotating candy shifts had been worth doing.

Today we were attempting a recipe for peppermint wafers, and we had to add sugar "to taste." But whose taste?

That's where Ivy came in. One of Trudy's favorite things had been seeing the kids in town come into the shop and delight at her treats. Ivy certainly would have been among them back then. So on Wednesdays, she got dropped off by her babysitter after lunch to hang out with me, Sarah, and whoever else was working. Ivy would then be our taste tester and helper until her dad, Ken, arrived to pick her up. It had started out of necessity as her babysitter's sports practice had picked back up in anticipation of the school year starting, and Ken needed someone to fill in for a few hours as a result. Ivy and I had been getting along great since our initial misunderstanding when they moved here in April, so I was happy to offer Ken the bakery as an option. He'd agreed to it as a temporary measure, and although this was only our second week doing it, Ivy coming here had been working out so great that we'd decided to keep the arrangement even after Ivy went back to school on an as-needed basis.

Sarah popped her head into the kitchen. "Ken's here."

I glanced at the clock on the wall. "He's early." Although he was working shorter days for the summer to enjoy more time with Ivy, a trade-off of having to work events on some weekends, he was nearly a half hour earlier than expected.

"But we haven't perfected the recipe yet!" Ivy half-whined.

Not wanting to disappoint Ivy—or worse, have her go into a tantrum over that disappointment—I gave Sarah a small shrug before looking back at Ivy. "Send him on back. We can have two taste testers today."

Ivy bounced up and down, cheering, and didn't settle until her dad walked in.

He headed over to me and kissed my cheek. "Meeting finished early, so I figured I'd surprise you both." Then he mussed Ivy's hair. "How was your day, kiddo?"

"Good!" she chirped and took a deep breath.

Before she launched into a play-by-play, I told Ken to grab an apron. Although I was used to getting all sorts of things on my clothes when I baked, I'd hate to see his button-up and slacks get ruined by an errant drop of chocolate or caramel.

As he headed for the closet, Ivy started in on her description of the day's events as Bryan and I whipped up our next batch of peppermints. Usually Ivy would add an ingredient or two, but she was so thrilled to have the extra time with her dad that I didn't interrupt until it was time to taste test.

"Here you both go," I said, dropping a chocolate-coated peppermint wafer into each of their hands. "On the count of three."

The four of us lifted the candies to our mouths and then each took a bite.

Through a chorus of *mmm*s, Ivy said, "Much better. I think you've gotten it *to taste* now."

"Agreed," Ken said, popping the rest of his peppermint into his mouth.

I clapped my hands together in excitement. "Great! It's settled. We can let everyone know tomorrow morning that there will be a new item on the menu."

Bryan nodded, then began cleaning up the candy-making station we'd set up not too long ago. It made things even tighter back here, particularly in the morning with everyone in the kitchen while Brittni was training. Once Sam left for school, we'd get some room back. But if the candy-making continued to do as well as it had been, I'd have to consider some sort of alternative spacing.

I jotted the sugar amount we'd settled on in the margins of Trudy's grimoire. Thanks to a lull in ghostly activities and matchmaking crises, I'd written several notes in the cookbook over the last few weeks. My handwriting joined at least three others contained within the pages.

Since Chelsea and David's wedding, my run-ins with wayward spirits had been mostly routine, like seeing Arthur Miller in the park when I sat outside for lunch. The only surprise encounter with a spirit had been learning Cindy at the cider mill in Bug Creek had been a ghost the entire time I'd known her. But fortunately that discovery hadn't resulted in my needing to solve any great mystery. In fact, it had probably been my easiest one since all of this started, and I'd even gained a new community partner out of it, although we hadn't formally announced the business relationship.

That reminded me . . .

I slid the cookbook back onto the shelf of my workstation, where I kept it during the times we weren't actively using it. For weeks I'd been bringing it back and forth from my house to the bakery, feeling it was too precious a gift to leave behind, but lately it seemed to belong here more than at home. Especially now that we were selling candy to our customers. So today I was going to leave it here overnight and see how things went.

"Back in a moment," I told the three in the kitchen as I wiped my hands on my apron. Already deep in cleaning, Bryan grunted in acknowledgment.

Ken glanced up at me as I passed by. "Are we all done for the afternoon?"

"Just about. If you want, you two can take off your aprons and follow me." I continued into the bakeshop, followed a moment later by Ken and Ivy.

"How'd it go?" Sarah asked once we were all together.

"It was great!" Ivy chirped. "It's going to be on the menu tomorrow!"

"Wonderful!" Sarah's enthusiasm matched Ivy's. It was hard not to be swayed by the little girl's emotions. "I'll make sure to try one then." Although Sarah had been my original taste tester, she gladly gave the title to Ivy once she started hanging out here on Wednesday afternoons. Sarah had told me that she was worried about what the extra calories were doing to her figure and preferred to give up the trial sweets instead of her specialty drinks from Leafs and Grounds. Getting a tasty coffee had become a near-daily treat for her. And to think she'd once been avoiding them because the owner of the coffee shop, Gary, had a crush on her. I was pretty sure she had one on him too.

"I think we're finally getting the hang of this whole candy-making thing," I said.

Sarah nodded. "You're starting to get as much of a reputation for your peanut butter cups as your cookies."

It probably helped that my peanut butter cups were four inches in diameter, only a little smaller than my typical cookie. They were not your average peanut butter cups that came wrapped in a two-pack.

"And I don't mean just because of their size," Sarah added as if knowing what I'd been thinking, one eyebrow raised to hint at what she was insinuating. It made me wonder if her being my familiar created some sort of psychic connection to what I was thinking so we could be a more efficient team.

This wasn't the first time she'd practically responded to my thoughts.

Had it been anyone other than Ken and Ivy or my baking team in here with us, I would have rolled my eyes at Sarah's veiled comment. But everyone currently in the bakery knew what I was and what I could do. Ken had known since April. Ivy since May. I told the rest of my staff right after my gram visited in July. But Sarah had known all along, since before I even met her, although we had only formally been a witch and her familiar since the last full moon.

"Well, let me know if it goes beyond the usual." Rumors about me and my abilities were nothing new. They'd started almost as soon as I arrived. Partially because the small town always talked about its newest residents—Ken had quickly earned the moniker of "hot doc" when he first arrived because he worked at the hospital despite not being a doctor —and partly because my first match struck within a week of being here. By the end of my first year in Heartwood Hollow, two of my couples were engaged. That, plus the way my baked goods made people feel after eating them, gave people a lot to talk about.

Who would have thought the rumors about my being a witch would turn out to be true?

I sure didn't.

At least no one was talking about my ability to see ghosts. Then again, I kept that secret to myself as much as possible. Outside of Sarah, Lily, Ken, and Ivy, no one here knew. I hadn't even told the paranormal support group about that particular skill.

"So dinner tonight?" Ken asked, casting me from my thoughts. Behind him, Ivy pressed her hands together. I smiled as warmth spread into my cheeks at the sight. How could I say no to that?

"I don't see why not. I'll meet you at your place when I get done here, and then we can figure something out."

"All right." Ken put his hand on Ivy's shoulder. "How about we get out of here so Joanie can start wrapping up?"

Ivy grabbed her bag from underneath one of the tables, where she had tossed it when she got here. "Okay, Daddy. Bye, Joanie! Bye, Sarah!"

The two headed out the door, and once it was closed, Sarah turned to me. "Did you ever ask her about the missing crystal from your yard?"

I shook my head. "I haven't given it much thought, actually. It kind of went out of my head that night after getting the coven's invitation. I'll ask her tonight and get it while I'm there." The smoky quartz sphere was one I had buried in the front yard to cleanse and charge over the week after the full moon, per my gram's instructions. But when Sarah and I went to dig up the crystals, that one had been missing. Ivy finding it seemed like the most logical explanation. Who else would take it?

"Oh, Zeke called earlier when you were making the peppermints. I figured you wouldn't want to interrupt what you were doing with Ivy."

She was right about that. Wednesday afternoons were our time now. "Thanks. Did he say what he wanted?"

She shook her head, then ducked into the kitchen.

I grabbed the phone, realizing I likely already knew what he had to say. He'd been worried about not being able to find someone to help him at the Corner Bakery. His nephew, Tyler, still made an appearance occasionally, but he, like many others in town, would be going off to college soon.

Zeke picked up on the third ring while trying to stifle a yawn. "Corner Bakery. Zeke speaking."

His phone mannerisms had improved greatly since I'd

been forced to work there while my bakery underwent renovations. Before he'd just say hello, leaving a customer questioning if they'd reached the right place. "Hi, Zeke. It's Joanie."

"Wondered when you'd return my call." Clearly he wasn't fully reformed on his phone etiquette, but tired Zeke wasn't the Zeke I'd enjoyed working with and who would turn his bakery around.

I tried to sound cheerful. "How are you doing today?"

"Would be better if my only help wasn't leaving in two weeks."

"I hear ya. I'm losing Sam soon." And I still had to figure out a going away party for him.

Zeke let out a small snort. "But you've already gone and found someone else." He had me there. "And I'm sure with your candy expansion, you'll be looking to add more people to your staff."

Also right, but I wasn't going to pile onto his stress by confirming that I'd have another opening soon. "Well, Brittni was a special case. She came to a cookout at my house with cookies."

"That's a bold move." I could easily hear how impressed he was.

"So why were you calling?" Normally I wouldn't mind chatting with the other baker in town now that we were on friendly terms, but I wanted to start my closing routine so I could go have dinner with Ken and Ivy.

"You already answered my question. I was trying to figure out about your new girl. Find out if she applied and if maybe you had other applicants who you could let know I was looking. But since she magically fell into your lap, then I guess that's not in the cards for me."

"I wouldn't say magical . . ." And I knew a thing or two

about magic now. "She's one of Sam's friends, so he set up the whole thing."

"Well, if you do hear of anyone—"

"I'll send them your way. Have you thought about putting out a Help Wanted sign?"

"Bah! That's just one more thing I have to do. And I hate how those things look in a window. But I'll think about it."

"You have a good night now, Zeke."

Zeke mumbled a reply that I couldn't quite make out. Amongst whatever else he'd said, I might have heard "you too."

As I hung up the phone, the door opened, and in stepped who I hoped would be my last customer for the day.

The girl approached me with an uneasy look, her eyebrows pinched softly, and it appeared she was biting the inside of her lower lip.

I gave her what I hoped was a comforting smile. "Hi, can I help you?"

In a quiet voice that matched her nervous expression, she asked, "Are you Joanie?"

"I am." My gut was telling me that she wasn't here for cookies, although having one might make her feel better. I didn't recognize her from the paranormal support group meetings, but that didn't mean she was unaware of who I was thanks to the rumors that had circulated about me since moving here. "Are you okay?"

She nodded in short, quick movements before stopping herself and shaking her head. "I need help. My ghost is missing. Can you find her?"

CHAPTER 2

My heart stuttered, and I lifted my hand to my chest. "I'm sorry?" I'd guessed that she was here for some sort of paranormal reason by the way she'd acted upon coming in, but I hadn't expected it to be ghost related. Few people knew about my ability to see ghosts, and I would never have thought that they'd tell other people. It was my deepest secret, one that had cost me my best friend when I was a teenager after she refused to believe me. I swore then that I'd not tell other people and hadn't until recently when ghosts started interfering with my matched couples. "You said your ghost?"

"Well, not my ghost," she corrected, a nervous edge still evident in her voice. "It's my nonni's, my grandmother's. It's her ghost. She's dead."

"I'm sorry to hear that."

She gave me a small smile. "It's all right. She died several years ago, but now her ghost is gone, and I'm hoping you can help me find her."

I had two options here. Say I couldn't help her or see if there was something I could do to actually help her. But unlike everyone else who knew my secret, I didn't know this young woman. Could I trust her? But it wasn't like me to tell someone in need no. "What did you hear about me?"

"That you're special." She leaned in as if trying to tell me a secret. "That you're a witch."

I took a deep breath, feeling a bit better that my being a witch was all she knew. Since starting the paranormal support group here in town, I'd become more comfortable with the idea of people knowing I'm a witch. The people in the PSG all knew. So did everyone here at the bakery. Ken and Ivy too. And anyone else who wondered . . . well, I wouldn't deny it if they confronted me. Not that people did.

"Are you from the PSG? If you are, I'm sorry I don't recognize you." She could be new. We gained new members every meeting.

She shook her head. "I don't know what that is."

"That's all right, although maybe you'd like to come with me sometime." If she saw ghosts like me, she was as paranormal as they come. "But if not from there, then who told you about me?"

At that moment, the door from the kitchen opened, and Sarah poked her head through the opening. "Just checking in."

"We're good. I'm just chatting with . . ." I looked back at the girl. "Sorry. I never asked you what your name is."

"Erin."

Something in the kitchen clattered, causing Sarah to jump, and the scuffling of feet signaled Bryan's approach. But that wasn't the only thing that told me he was coming. A shockwave of vibrations coursed through me as if the noise was more like a sonic boom rattling up my toes and into my stomach.

Bryan pushed the door separating the kitchen and the bakeshop all the way open. "Rin? What are you doing here?"

Erin stifled a cry as they rushed to one another. I had no doubt the two were a match, and I wondered why they weren't together already. Bryan stroked Erin's hair with one hand, and she pressed her face against his chest as she held on to his shirt. "I couldn't take it anymore. I want Nonni back, and you told me if anyone could help, it would be your boss."

Well, that answered the question of who had told her my secret. At least the one he knew, anyway.

Bryan looked at me, an apologetic look on his face. "Joanie, I'm sorry. I know you trusted us with what you told us, but I've known Rin practically my whole life, and she's got this thing going on with her grandma's ghost. I didn't know who else to send her to, but I never expected that she'd come rushing on in here like this. I was going to talk to you about it myself. Introduce the two of you properly."

Despite knowing him for years, he surprised me sometimes. He had witty humor that didn't come out often, but he was good with one-liners and inside jokes. So much so that I wasn't sure exactly what his reaction was when I first confessed I was a witch and that the baked goods we sold had magic in them.

"I know you mean well," I began, addressing Bryan, "and what's done is done. I wouldn't have said no to helping, but I would have appreciated you coming to me first before you even mentioned it to her." I focused on Erin. She'd stiffened, and although she was still in Bryan's arms, she'd turned to give me her full attention. "That being said, I'm not one to refuse people who need help, especially in this area where I am uniquely qualified."

Erin's mouth parted, and her shoulders relaxed substantially. "Thank you. And I'm sorry. I didn't know who to turn to, and I've been grasping at straws for so long, and with the wedding around the corner, I had to do something. I can't not have my grandmother there on my wedding day."

"Wedding? You're getting married." My gaze shot to Bryan.

He held up a hand. "No, not us."

Erin laughed for the first time since entering the bakery. "Me? Marry Bryan? Oh, no. I've known him forever, and I love him, but no."

Bryan's eyes seemed to dim a little. It was obvious he cared for her, but I doubted she realized that. "She's marrying Travis Ellison in a few weeks."

Something about that name felt familiar, but I didn't know how. They weren't one of my cake customers, at least not that I was aware of. There were a few wedding planners I worked with and dealt with directly, so I wouldn't necessarily know who the couple was until the wedding day, but they usually came from out of town. Maybe Sarah would know. She handled the paperwork while I focused on flavor and design.

I nodded, catching sight of the clock as I did. Fortunately it wasn't time for me to meet Ken and Ivy yet. "Erin, why don't we go sit down and you can tell me about your grandmother and your ability to see her."

She pulled away from Bryan and walked to the tables, a bit more confidence in her step than had been there when she first walked in. Bryan moved to follow her, but I stopped him.

"Are you all set in the kitchen?"

"Uh, yeah. Just one last thing to clean up." No doubt it was whatever that had fallen when he realized Erin was out here.

"Can you head on back and let Sarah know she can leave

early today?" If I wasn't going to get out of here early, there was no need to keep Sarah late. I could easily clean up after my conversation with Erin. "I promise Erin and her secret will be safe with me."

"Oh, okay," he mumbled. He likely hadn't expected me to ask him to leave, but I wanted Erin to be free to talk without another's influence. And Bryan and their match were two major influences on her. He placed a hand on her arm and said something I couldn't make out.

She nodded. "I'll call you later."

He turned away from her and headed toward the kitchen, giving me a quick thanks as he passed. He may not have been happy with me at that moment, but he was glad that I was helping his friend—his match.

I pointed toward a seat with my hand as I returned my focus to Erin. "Please, sit." I pulled out a chair for myself as she sat down.

"Let's start at the beginning. Tell me about you and your grandmother. What's her name?" I hoped that mentioning her by name would cause the grandmother to appear. If Erin couldn't see her, maybe I still could. That would at least give us a starting point.

"Her name is Anita Esposito."

I glanced around the room, but nothing. She wasn't here.

"Now, before we get too far, I have to ask. Is it possible she decided to cross over and you're just not wanting to accept it? It can be—"

"Absolutely not." She shook her head vehemently. "She promised me that she wouldn't go anywhere until after the wedding."

"Okay. So she didn't go to the other side. Is there anyone else she could be visiting? Ghosts tend to go to whoever needs them at the moment. She may not have been able to tell you."

Again, she shook her head. "I mean, there's my mom. She's not in Heartwood Hollow anymore, but I see her often enough that if Nonni was around her instead, I'd have seen her. My grandpa and their son, my uncle, have both passed. I was her only grandchild. There's no one else, and I need her. I'm getting married. She's supposed to be here."

I nodded. "I understand it's very important to you. Weddings are a big deal. Trust me, I happen to know a thing or two about weddings."

That made her smile and seemed to ease the tension that had built up at my earlier suggestion of her grandmother having willingly crossed over.

"When did she die?"

"When I was thirteen."

"And did she become a ghost right away or did she come back during a time of need for you? What I mean is, were you always able to see her?"

She contemplated this for a moment. "Soon after. I kept seeing her out of the corner of my eye. At first I thought it was my grief playing a trick on me. Like a hallucination or something. It wasn't until I finally decided to acknowledge her standing there one day that she talked back and I realized she'd been there all along. It wasn't grief. And it wasn't my imagination. Nonni was a ghost."

"Did you ask her why she was there?"

"Of course I did. She said she didn't want to go. That she wasn't ready to cross over."

That wasn't uncommon. Back when I spoke to ghosts regularly, several had given me that reason. Most eventually came around.

"So that was how long ago now?"

"I'm twenty-five, so twelve years?"

I nodded. Although I'd always been able to see spirits,

thirteen was when the ghost activity had really picked up in my life, causing me to confide in my best friend about my abilities. But when she refused to believe me even though I'd given her proof, or maybe because of it, she stopped being my friend. Once that happened, I went to my mom for help. She then turned to my gram. The two of them did something to me that stopped the bad ghosts from being able to reach me, but my ability hadn't gone away completely. I still saw ghosts wherever they were. But only the good ones. And for the most part, they left me alone.

Talking to someone else who could see ghosts was a brand-new experience for me. I didn't know anyone else who could. At least no one I could talk to. One of my grandmother's older sisters, Pegee, had been able to see them too, but one day, she left. No one knew where she was. But that was how Gram knew as much as she did about my ability. What I wouldn't have given to talk to Aunt Pegee at the time.

But now, sitting in front of me was Erin. The first person who could do at least some of what I could. It was time to find out more.

Leaning in slightly, I laid my hands flat on the table. "Now, Erin, I have to ask. Do you see other ghosts?"

"Only my grandmother. Why?"

"Just curious. Wanted to see how strong your skill was."

She scoffed. "You think this is a skill?"

"Sure do."

"Well, I stink at it. If I didn't, I'd not be in this situation."

"You never know with ghosts."

"You sound pretty sure of that."

I smiled. "I'd like to think that I know what I'm doing." Something was holding me back from outright telling her that I saw ghosts too. "Helps give others a bit of confidence. Is it working?"

"A little." The corner of her mouth ticked upward. "I'm desperate to see my grandmother again. You could tell me she decided to possess the porcelain doll in my room and I would probably believe you because it would make me feel better."

I shook away the thought of a possessed doll. Creepy. Thank goodness that hadn't happened to me. "No dolls. I promise. And I wouldn't make something up just because. We'll get to the bottom of this. So, does anyone else know what you can do?"

She raised an eyebrow at me in an *are you serious* look. I understood perfectly. Seeing ghosts wasn't an everyday subject of conversation. More like the opposite.

Just then, Sarah opened the door between the shop and the kitchen to say goodnight. A moment later, the tingling sensation I'd felt since the moment Bryan realized Erin was in here began to fade. He must have left with Sarah, or Sarah was making sure that he was actually leaving. But back to the matter at hand . . .

"Well, Bryan obviously knows what you can do since he told you to come see me. But what about anyone else? Your fiancé? Your mom?"

"I told my mom when I first realized it was all real. It only made her sad because she couldn't see Nonni."

"The three of you were very close, weren't you?"

She sat back in her seat a little bit, seemingly comfortable with this topic. "We all lived together before she died. Mom and I moved into her house after my nonno, my grandfather, passed away. My dad had left my mom, and we'd been living in an apartment on Main Street. Nonni's house was big enough for all of us, and Mom got to save the money that had been going to rent. When Nonni died, she and I became even closer since I was the only one who could see her. Once Mom accepted what I could do, I was the go-between for them so they could talk."

"You said you're getting married soon. Did the relationship between the three of you change at all as a result of your relationship?"

"Well, sure. But I'd left for college first. Then Mom downsized, selling Nonni's house. Nonni followed me because, like I said, I'm the only one she can interact with. When Travis and I started dating, Nonni tagged along."

I could imagine. "So, does Travis know what you can do?"

"It's come up once or twice. I wanted to share that part of my life and my grandmother because she's such a presence. Or was . . ."

"Let's talk about that. When did she disappear?"

"I've been trying to get her back since the start of the summer. She stopped in briefly at my engagement party, and I haven't seen her since."

"Stopped in? I thought you said she was pretty much always with you."

"She used to be. But the more serious Travis and I became, the more privacy she gave us. There were some things I didn't want my grandmother there for, you know?"

"Let me guess. He's not into the ghost thing?"

"Well, it didn't send him running, which is good. Gosh, that makes him sound horrible. I promise he isn't. But you have to admit . . . it's a lot to accept, never mind understand it. So I stopped bringing it up, and Nonni stopped coming along."

"So overall, she was coming less and less frequently from the time you started dating Travis up until your engagement party."

"Well, yeah, but still regularly, and she always promised to come for the wedding. That never changed. She even told me that on the day of the party."

"Why not just take her at her word? That she'll be there."

"I wish I could, but she's been gone so long, longer than ever before, and she's missed so much. I need to know."

Part of me thought that perhaps Erin's grandmother could have been saving her energy for the big day. Another part of me wasn't so sure. Could she have crossed over? It was possible, but why leave right before a loved one's wedding after remaining here for so long?

Some might say it was a coincidence, the timing. And that didn't sit right with me. If I'd learned anything lately, there was no such thing as coincidences.

CHAPTER 3

"So you'll help me?"

"Of course, I will." I tried to give her a reassuring smile. "Might mean you need to hang out here at the bakery a bit more, though, give me time to get to know you and see if I can get anything from that."

Bryan would probably love the idea of her being around some more too, although if I couldn't fix her ghost problem, Erin would end up ghostless and marrying the wrong man. Not that Travis was a bad guy. I didn't know him. But I did know that he and Erin weren't meant to be together. My matchmaking tingle didn't lie, and it was never wrong.

She reached out and placed her hand over mine. Her eyes were rimmed with tears. "Thank you."

I flipped my hand over, allowing me to give hers a small squeeze. "We'll get this sorted. I promise."

She stood, letting her hand that had been on mine fall to her side. She pulled her purse over her shoulder. "You aren't mad at Bryan, right? I really didn't mean for him to get in trouble."

Shaking my head, I stood to meet her gaze. "Mad? No. But I did trust him with a secret and within a short time, he went and told someone who I don't know." It had only been a couple weeks since my confession to everyone here in the shop as we discussed how the Monday muffins they had made without me were different than those that got made while I was here.

"If it helps any, I haven't told anyone."

I smiled at her. "I appreciate that. And he's not in trouble—"

She let out an audible sigh. "Oh, good. He might not always be the best at showing it, but he really loves this job. Like we explained, we've known each other for years, and I can see the good it's done him. Settled him a bit."

"I'm glad to hear it, but I will have to talk to him about this."

Her shoulders dropped slightly. "Understandable." She took a step toward the door.

"Helps that he did what he did to help a friend." His match. But I couldn't say that.

She nodded, a small smile forming across her face. "I'll see you again soon." She seemed much calmer as she walked toward the door and left the shop.

I locked the door behind her. The bakery had officially closed ten minutes ago. All I had to do was finish cleaning and I could go grab dinner with Ken and Ivy.

I'd confided in Ken as much as I could over dinner and after Ivy had gone to bed. The conversation quickly morphed into one about how I felt about finding someone who also saw ghosts. We weren't exactly alike, Erin and I, but this was the closest I had ever been to someone who could remotely understand what I could do.

When I returned home after our meal, my answering machine was blinking with a message. I pressed play to listen to it as I made myself a cup of tea.

"Hey, it's Sarah. I know you're out right now and that you never check your cell anyway, so I am leaving you a message here. Wanted to check in on you after your chat with Erin. I swear I wasn't purposefully listening. She was a little loud when she first asked about her grandma. Hope it went well, but I'm more curious about how you are. Give me a call."

As I waited for the water to boil, I called my shop manager turned familiar. She picked up on the second ring.

"Hey," she said. "How are you doing with this whole ghost thing?"

"Honestly? It feels a little weird to not be the only one anymore. And I was just getting used to, well, everything else."

"I can imagine. It would be a little like me running into another familiar who wasn't someone in my family. I've never met another outside of my uncle and my grandfather. The rest of my family never got activated as it were."

"Did you know?" Sarah had grown up learning about the paranormal life in Heartwood Hollow as well as witchcraft so she could be a familiar if her witch—me—ever came along.

"About Erin? No. She probably never talked about it much beyond her mom and to Bryan."

"What about others?" In our few weeks of being witch and familiar, it wasn't information she had offered, and it wasn't anything I had ever asked, but now the timing was right.

"It's always been a possibility. Every once in a while,

someone who claims to be able to will come along. A psychic medium. A ghost hunter."

"Like those shows on TV?" Most of those seemed so fake, but I was open to being proven wrong. Occasionally one of the episodes seemed to yield something real.

"Yeah." The word had come out as a half-scoff. Seemed she didn't fully believe in them either. "Knoll's Grove had a paranormal investigation group for a while. Might still."

"Any good?"

"I don't put much stock in things done for entertainment value. One of them is Travis's sister, actually. She seemed cool back when we were in high school."

"Travis as in Erin's fiancé?"

"Yeah. You can probably catch their videos on their website if you're interested."

The kettle started to whistle, and I switched the burner off. As I poured the water into my teacup, I said, "I'll take your word for it. I still don't have the internet in the house."

"But I thought you took care of that with the crystals."

I jiggled the infuser basket inside the cup, catching the lavender aroma of the steeping brew. "Decided against it. I like my unplugged life here. It's nice. Quiet. I don't want to be connected all the time. Although you shouldn't have a problem if people call or text you. Or anyone else who stops by for that matter. Even Ivy should be able to do homework here with no problem."

The line went silent a moment. "You put all of that into the crystals when your gram came?"

"Yeah. She didn't say not to. Should I not have?"

"That's some pretty advanced stuff. Specific. You're doing way more than tapping into the usual energies of the crystals like protection or fortune."

I brought the teacup with me into the living room,

steeping leaves and all. "Figured I should ask for what I want. I didn't think about something being easy or difficult."

"Have you tried seeing if you get a cell signal?"

As I sat down on the couch, I raised my eyebrow at her skepticism even though she wasn't here. "You doubting my abilities?"

She chuckled. "Curious is all. It's always good to check your results."

"No one has bothered to call me, so I haven't tried." I set the teacup on the coffee table and stood back up, then walked around the end of the couch to the coat tree where I hung my purse. I pulled my phone out of the pocket where I kept it. "Battery's dead. Guess I'll have to check in the morning. Ken can get texts now, though." I plugged my phone into the charger cord sitting on the end table next to the couch.

"That's something, at least."

When I sat back down, Saffy jumped down from her perch on the cat tree Lily and her boyfriend John had made for her. She hurried over to join me on the couch.

"You want to hear what's really something?" I shifted my legs slightly to give Saffy more room to lie down once she finished circling.

"Something more than you've met someone else who can see at least one ghost?"

"Yeah. Erin and Bryan are a match."

This time Sarah was quiet long enough for me to think the call had disconnected. "You're kidding."

"I'd never kid about this." I blew across my cup, then took a sip of my tea.

"But she's getting married to someone who isn't Bryan."

"I know. This may be my hardest match yet."

CHAPTER 4

Bryan was waiting for me the next morning at the door to the kitchen. This was a first. He was never early. Never late either, really, more just right on time.

He gave me a hesitant smile as I crossed the parking lot. "Morning, Joanie."

"Morning. How are you?"

"I'm okay. Look, I wanted to apologize for what happened yesterday. No, not yesterday. Well, partially yesterday, but more in the way it happened than how it happened."

I'd never heard him ramble like this. This had to be because Erin was involved.

"Why don't we head inside and we can talk more."

He nodded, and I pulled my key out of my bag to unlock the door. I stepped inside, and Bryan followed, flicking the lights on behind me.

After putting our things away in silence, I leaned back against my workstation. "Like I said yesterday, I'm going to help your friend. No one should have to deal with that sort of stuff alone."

He nodded.

"And like I also said, I'm not mad, more disappointed. I trusted you with something huge in my life, and you went and told someone pretty much right away. What's done is done"—ugh, I hated sayings like that—"but I need to know that I can trust you with this secret from now on and that I'm not going to regret having told you. I need people I can trust on my team. *My family.* I told you this the day you started. We're family. This isn't just a boss/employee relationship."

He could barely meet my eyes, but he did before quickly looking away again. "I know. And I'm sorry. For all of it."

"You've been with me since the beginning, and you've never let me down before. Let's not start now. Can I trust you?"

This time he looked at me directly. Without hesitation, he said, "You can trust me."

"I believe you. "

"It won't happen again. Thanks, Joanie. And I don't just mean about this and Rin. I never really thanked you for giving me a shot back then. Not sure I deserved it."

"Of course you did." Although Bryan had been kicked out of his previous kitchen for alpha-like tendencies, I'd seen none of that here. He had a quick wit, but mostly everything he'd said had been jovial and boosted the morale of the team. Only after I'd confided in my team about what I could do did I worry about his jokes. But then I realized it was his way of making us all comfortable with the idea of my being a witch. That my baked goods were magical.

I walked over to him and even though he stood a good six inches taller than me, I put my hand on his shoulder. "And you've been a great member of this family ever since. I don't see that changing, okay?"

He nodded. "I won't let you down."

I lowered my hand and was about to ask him about his

feelings for Erin, to tell him she was his match, when Gina walked in. Although they both knew what I could do, I wasn't about to reveal his match with Gina here.

"Good morning," Gina said before stopping short and cocking her head to the side as she glanced at Bryan. "You're here early."

"Had to talk to Joanie about some magic stuff," Bryan replied with a shrug.

She tilted her head slowly back until her face pointed to the ceiling, her gaze still on him, before dropping it back to its normal position but said nothing. I didn't know what to make of the long expression and shook it off as Gina put her bag in the closet before prepping her workstation.

I hoped I'd get a chance to talk to Bryan soon to let him know about him and Erin. We were already short on time, and I'd barely begun to unravel the new ghost mystery on my hands.

Within minutes, Lily walked in right on time, and moments later, Sam arrived with Brittni, laughing and joking about something. No doubt they'd been carrying on like this since they started their trek to work this morning. I bet their neighbors probably weren't too keen on the early morning chatter as it carried through their open windows, though. Many in town had turned off their air conditioners for the first time in a while to let in the nice breeze overnight. It was still August, but the first hints of an autumn cooldown had begun.

"Morning, Joanie," Sam said in a sing-song voice.

"Hello, you two. Nice walk?"

Brittni nodded. "I think I might finally be getting used to these hours."

I chuckled. Although she'd said mornings weren't a problem for her when we first discussed her schedule, she'd still needed to adjust to the hours. For the first several days, she'd come in with a large coffee from home and had downed it by the time I made my morning deliveries. I should have planned ahead and saved more Monday muffins for her than I had.

"That's great! Well, come on, let's see what we can teach you today." I waved her over to my station as Sam walked to his.

We all got started with our work, falling into our usual patterns. Gina hummed between short bursts of conversation, Bryan beat a rhythm into the dough as he worked it—but never too hard to make it unusable—Sam and Brittni continued talking when I wasn't showing her something new. And there was something new for everyone today, well, except for Bryan.

Once I got back from the diners, I announced the plan for the day. "Tonight we have our last summer Stroll Along the Street, and we'll be highlighting our candies for the first time." They had still been too new last month to have a lot to offer at last month's event. "When Bryan's ready, I'm going to have him show you all how to make the peppermint wafers we experimented with yesterday. It was a big hit with my taste testers."

Sam snickered. "Everything is, Joanie."

The corners of my mouth curled upward as I shook my head using short motions. He wasn't wrong. Being a kitchen witch had its upsides when running a bakery. "We still had to try a few versions to make sure we had the perfect amounts of everything. You know how it is."

Lily glanced up from her workstation. "So what baked good are we pairing with it?"

"Glad you asked." I headed to the closet where I'd stored some new supplies for the shop this morning, then pulled out the new pans to show everyone. "I thought we'd give muffins a try."

Brittni hopped in place several times. "Mini-muffins!"

Even Gina seemed excited. "I haven't had those since I was a kid."

"Yeah," Bryan started. "Remember them being in those bags in the vending machines at school?"

I set the pans on the top shelf of my workstation. "These will be much better than those ever were. We're known for our muffins—"

"I'll say," Bryan quipped, a smirk on his face. It was good to have him back to his normal self after our chat this morning.

"But we've never really done any promotion of them at the Stroll because, well, our muffins are huge, and I have never felt right about giving people parts of something to try." Sure, I could have quartered them, but what was the fun in that? "With the mini-muffins, I'm hoping to give everyone a satisfying sample."

Bryan's grin widened. "Good thing Strolls aren't on Mondays . . ."

Gina turned to him. "Oh, can you imagine?"

"No one would sleep that night!" Sam said. Monday muffins—no matter the flavor—always gave those who ate them some pep in their step. The muffins would wake them up and get them ready to face the start of a brand-new week.

"Might be useful during a full moon," Gina added. "You know how this town gets."

Bryan snorted but said nothing.

That wasn't a bad idea. I wondered if I should save a Monday muffin for myself for the next full moon. Maybe one for Sarah too. We'd been invited to attend the next Moonshadow Coven meeting, happening on the full moon a week from now. Even though it would mean a late night for both of us, there was no way we could pass up the opportunity. They'd spent the entire week surrounding last month's full moon leaving presents at my house before sending an official invitation to the gathering. I'd seen dozens if not hundreds of invitations during my time as a baker, and this was one of the fanciest I'd ever gotten. The gold lettering almost glowed.

Both Sarah and I were looking forward to more hands-on experience with other witches. We were still so new to it all—me especially—and books could only teach us so much. Although Gram had been able to teach me a few things while she was here, the chance to learn from someone else who had magic was extremely appealing. And if I could find out more about me and what I could do and maybe why I could do so much . . . then all the better.

"Well," Brittni began, pulling me from my thoughts, "I think the mini-muffins are a great idea. A lot of people will be excited to see them, I'm sure."

"I'm going to do the peach muffins we'll be rolling out this weekend. They'll have some fresh mint syrup and honey too to play with the flavor. Sam, do you know how to peel peaches on the stove top?" He nodded. "Great! Once Bryan is done showing you all the candy, you can get started on that. Show Brittni how to too."

With that, we all got started on our next round of work. Bryan and the rest of the team on peppermint wafers, and me whipping up a batch of cupcakes and making a strawberry lemonade frosting while they were cooking. They were being picked up early by Drew so he could surprise his wife, Megan, for her birthday during the morning break at her office in town where she was a lawyer. My second couple matched here in Heartwood Hollow, they'd recently had a baby, and Megan had returned to work a couple weeks ago. It was sweet to see them doing so well. Not that I'd had any doubt. My matches had never been wrong.

Although, sometimes, they came at questionable times.

I glanced back at Bryan, hoping that everything would work out for him and his match.

CHAPTER 5

Lily returned later that afternoon to help me and Sarah set up for the Stroll Along Main Street. After her shift, Bryan would take over, and I was hoping that he and I could finish our conversation from this morning.

Sarah and Lauren were in the shop, ready to help any customers coming in after trying a sample at our table. I probably didn't need the two of them, but Lauren, like Sam, had college-related expenses coming up and was looking for any hours she could get. Fortunately, Lauren going off to school only meant a fluctuation of her hours since she commuted to and from Snowhaven. Sam, on the other hand, was going to be hours away from here at culinary school. I wasn't looking forward to losing him but was so excited for him at the same time. He'd do well in Baycliff. I'd liked it when I went to school there.

As Lily and I finished setting up, I glanced at her from the corner of my eye. Time with her was growing short too. Soon I'd be baking her a cake for her last day with us. She hadn't said anything yet, but it was coming. She was spending more and more of her free time up at John's furniture shop building things with him. I smiled at the thought of a dryad being a master woodworker. Who would have thought that would be the result of her match with John? Until their match, I'd had no idea about Heartwood Hollow's paranormal secrets. Me being a witch was only one of them. The town was full of paranormal beings and had been, likely since the town's founding.

And now new secrets were coming to light. Like that I wasn't the only one who could see ghosts in town. Okay, there was at least one other person and she could only see one ghost . . . but that was something.

"Hey, Joanie!" Whitney called as she and her boyfriend, Xavier, crossed Main Street. She'd likely just come from her photo studio next to Leafs and Grounds.

As they approached, the matching tingle from the couple grew stronger the closer they got. They were the fourth couple I'd matched in town, during my first holiday season with the bakery. I smiled at them as they stopped in front of the table. "How are you two doing?"

"Really good," Whitney squeaked as she stuck her left hand out at me. A diamond engagement ring flashed brilliantly on her finger.

"Congratulations!" I popped up from my chair and then ran around the table to give them both a hug. After a moment, I released them and took Whitney's hand to get a better look at her ring. It was a gorgeous square cut stone surrounded by smaller diamonds on a twisted band. "I'm so happy for you both."

"Well, we owe you for introducing us."

I'd been talking to Xavier at a business owners' Christmas event the first year the bakery was open. As soon as Whitney walked in, I could feel the match, so I made sure they met that night.

I waved Whitney's statement away in bashful dismissal. "You two were meant to be and would have gotten together eventually even without me." That's how it worked. My thoughts traveled to Bryan and Erin. At least I hoped my matches would continue to work that way.

"We're happy it happened when it did," Xavier said. "So thank you."

"We hope we can get you to do our cake," Whitney added, slipping her hand into his after I let hers go. "Of course! I'd be delighted. Stop into the shop and schedule an appointment with Sarah, and if you have flavor ideas already, let her know. I'll whip some up special for you to try. And be prepared to talk because I want to know all about his proposal."

"Will do," Whitney replied, and she took a step toward the bakery before stopping again. "Oh wow, look, Xavy. I haven't had mini-muffins in ages!"

I held my hand palm out to point to the basket of mini-muffins. "Please, both of you take one. They're peach."

Whitney grabbed the tongs at the edge of the basket and plucked one out to hand to Xavier and then one for herself. She popped hers into her mouth. "Oh, these are so good! Do you have any in the shop?"

"Not until this weekend. Wanted to try them here first."

"Hmm . . . Might have to schedule our tasting for then so I can get some while we're here." She glanced at her fiancé. "What do you think?"

He swallowed the bite in his mouth before answering, "What about a muffin wedding cake?"

"Oh! We could have a brunch wedding and do a whole spread of muffins, and maybe something like a bacon bar?"

He pulled her into his side for a hug and pressed his lips against the top of her head. "Bacon? You know the way to my heart. I love the idea."

Seeing how excited they were warmed my heart. "I can just as easily give you a muffin tasting too."

Whitney tugged on Xavier's hand. "Come on. Let's go schedule our appointment." She pulled him into the shop.

A few minutes later, they two strode out arm in arm.

"Thanks, Joanie," Whitney called with a wave as they turned to head up Main Street.

"You're welcome. And congratulations again!"

Next to me, Lily sighed wistfully.

"Once upon a time, that was not a noise I ever would have heard from you," I pointed out.

A smile played on her lips. "That was before John."

"Think that will be you soon?"

Her eyes widened. "It's only been a few months!"

I chuckled. "I've seen some pretty fast engagements around here."

"Now would be too fast for us." Her smile spread fully across her face now. "But someday . . ."

"Oh, most definitely."

At that moment, giggling caught our attention. I turned my head and saw Erin walking this way with two of her friends. They had coffees from Leafs and Grounds in hand. It was a good way to start the stroll since not everyone offered drinks at their tables. Soon I'd be getting my first shipment of apple cider from Bug Creek, and then I'd be able to offer tastes of that in little cups. The timing was perfect. Just in time for fall.

Lily blew a hard puff of air from her nose.

"You okay?"

"Yeah, just . . . never mind."

The giggling girls stopped at the table, and Erin gave me a small smile. Somehow I doubted her friends knew about our conversation yesterday. They likely didn't know anything about her ability to see her grandmother's ghost.

I smiled at the three girls. "Hello, ladies. How are you today?"

"Good," the two friends answered before diving for the mini-muffins.

"Hi Joanie," Erin said, then quieter, added, "Lily."

Lily nodded with a tight smile.

"These are so good," one friend said.

Erin reached for the tongs.

"You probably shouldn't do that," the second friend said. "You want to be able to fit into your dress. This time right now is crucial."

"That's right," the first friend added. "You don't want to get bloated and not be able to zip it up."

Erin's hand fell.

I'd never heard anything so absurd. These were supposed to be her friends.

"Well, I say she should do what she wants," Lily said from beside me. Annoyance was veiled only slightly by her plastered-on smile. "It is her day, after all. And besides, what's one bite *weeks* before the big day?"

Erin gave Lily a small smile. I believed I knew what was going on here.

"And haven't you all heard what they say about me? Do you think I'd let anyone get bloated by *my* samples? That wouldn't make much business sense now, would it?"

The two friends shrieked in delight.

"Well, in that case," one started.

"We'll each have another," the other finished.

I shook my head. "Only after the bride gets her first one."

"Go ahead, Erin," the first friend said as sweet as can be.

"Yeah, you really must try one."

Next to me, Lily tensed even more, although her saccharine smile remained intact.

Erin bent forward to grab the tongs once more, and I gave her a small wink.

"Thank you," she mouthed.

"Are these your bridesmaids?" I asked as a way to keep the girls' attention off Erin as she quickly grabbed a second muffin after popping the first one into her mouth.

"Two of them at least," the first one answered with a giggle. "She has six of us."

"Oh wow, that's a big wedding party." Not the biggest I'd ever seen, but plenty big for Heartwood Hollow. "All friends, or . . ."

"Most of us," the second one said. "There is Alice."

I didn't think I knew anyone by that name from Heartwood Hollow, although as Erin had proven, I didn't know everyone. "Who's Alice?"

"Travis's sister," the first explained with a huff.

Ah, the one Sarah had mentioned from Knoll's Grove. The paranormal investigator. Did she know about Erin's gift?

I kept my tone conversational but gave Erin a sympathetic look. "I sense some wedding drama." That was the last thing she needed.

"Alice isn't really for the wedding," Erin said. Her tone was subdued, almost sad.

"That's an understatement," the first friend replied. "She's been against your marriage from the start."

"I don't know why you even had to include her," the second friend added.

Erin shrugged. "She's family. Or will be."

"How could she not like you?" Lily asked. The surprise was evident in her voice.

Erin shrugged again, bigger this time. "I don't know.

Always thought she did. Then Travis and I got engaged."

The timing stuck out to me. "Maybe you two should talk over some cookies," I suggested. "Cookies make everything better. Even potentially awkward conversations."

One of her friends scoffed. I wasn't sure which one.

Erin seemed hesitant to answer.

"I'll throw in a few bloat-free muffins, and if you need a neutral place to talk, you can always come to the bakery."

Erin nodded, seemingly a little relieved I'd offered to do something, although I didn't know why.

"Stop in anytime," I pressed. We still had more to talk about anyway, but I wasn't going to add that. Her so-called friends seemed none the wiser about what was going on with her.

Nearby on one of the side streets, the sound of speaker feedback spread across the stroll-goers, making many of us wince from the squealing pitch. Fortunately it quickly subsided, replaced by an announcement that the band had finished warming up and would start its session soon. I'd forgotten they were adding that to this month's stroll.

"Oh, come on, let's go listen to the Howling Hellcats," one of Erin's bridesmaids eagerly suggested, grabbing Erin's arm.

The second friend spun away from the table without so much as a goodbye, but Erin gave us a small smile. "Thank you," she said quietly before being pulled away.

When they were out of earshot, Lily let out a loud sigh.

"Seems like there's a little tension there."

She huffed. "A little? Those girls hate me."

"I don't think Erin hates you."

"No." Lily's shoulders fell. "She doesn't. We used to be good friends, actually. Then she changed."

"Let me guess, Travis?"

She nodded. "I never liked him. Or those girls she was

with. They weren't even her friends until after she started going out with Travis."

I wondered again if she knew what Erin could do. Were they impressed with the ability or by the guy? "Does she know what you are?"

"No. But if I had told anyone, it would have been her."

"I wouldn't give up on her if you still care for your friend."

She turned her head and eyed me. "What do you know?"

I shrugged to feign innocence and glanced up at the sky. "Just call it a hunch."

"A witchy one or a ghosty one?"

I pursed my lips. "A little of both, maybe. But I can't say more than that."

"All right. Well, whatever it is, I hope you can help her. She used to be different before."

We helped a few more people on their way to the show, pausing our conversation temporarily. When it was just the two of us again, I asked, "So what can you tell me about Travis, or maybe his sister, Alice?"

"Alice was cool. A couple years older than us. Your age, I guess. She moved out of Heartwood Hollow right after graduation, but only to Knoll's Grove. I don't know why Alice doesn't approve of Erin's relationship, but I don't think it's because Alice doesn't like her."

"So what do you know of them?"

"They're a big name in town. They go back just as far as John's family does. Came here with the Dunmores, only as settlement support, not as part of the lumber crew. So they rose to prominence that way, helping to develop the town. But Travis?" She shrugged. "I don't know what he does. He was popular in school, but it wasn't like he did anything. No sports, no student government, not even all that nice. I never liked him. There was just something about him. I liked him even less after Erin dropped me in college because of him. Dropped all of her friends."

Her story reminded me of getting left behind by my ex-best friend, Ginny. Once I told her I could see ghosts, she stopped hanging out with me. Most of our friends chose her. I made new friends, of course, but the memory of being cast aside by someone I was close with still stung when I thought about it.

Bryan sidled up to the table with a simple, "Hey."

Lily looked pointedly at Bryan. "I amend my statement. Dropped all but one."

Bryan raised an eyebrow at her. "What are you two talking about?"

"Your lifetime crush. Wait, that's it, isn't it?" She turned toward me. "That's what you know. It isn't a hunch at all. Your matchmaker magic told you Bryan and Erin belong together."

Bryan stood there blinking, a glimmer of hope in his eyes. "Is that true, Joanie?"

Lily's mouth dropped open. "You didn't tell him?"

Letting my shoulders fall, I cast Bryan an apologetic glance. "There hasn't been a great time, and given the situation—"

"You mean that she's getting married?" Lily asked, giving me a look.

"It's a little more complicated than that," I replied, "but I can't say anything more than that. It's not my place."

She held her hands up in surrender. "Don't need to tell me. I get it. But you have to somehow stop this wedding and get Bryan and Erin together. Always thought they'd be great for one another."

A smile appeared on Bryan's face.

"Strong matches born from friendships are often felt by

those around them, even when they have no matchmaking ability. Sometimes you just know."

"Yeah, felt by everyone except the two people who are meant to be together." Lily lightly pushed Bryan's upper arm as he came around the table to relieve her of her duties.

I'd seen that a time or two as well. Usually all it required was a simple push, a "Hey, you two would be great together" to get them to consider it for the first time or a "You should ask her out" to give them a bit of encouragement.

But this was anything but usual.

Lily stood. "All right, I'm going to head out. Meeting John over by the band."

I nodded. "Quite the name. Howling Hellcats. They meet in junior high or high school?" The Howlers were the mascot for the junior high, and the Hellcats were the high school mascot. The possibility made sense to me.

Bryan sputtered a laugh. "Something like that." He seemed to be taking the news that he was Erin's match well.

After saying our goodbyes to Lily, Bryan and I sat down together at the table and helped a few passersby with samples.

When it looked like I'd have a spare minute, I turned to Bryan. "I'm sorry you had to find out that way, about the match with Erin, I mean. I wanted to tell you this morning, but Gina walked in and then we never got another moment alone."

He shrugged and opened his mouth to say something, but the speakers from the stage crackled to life once more. As people hurried to the stage, our table saw an influx of people, so much so that Bryan had to run in for our backup candy. Then once the band started playing, it became too loud to have a real conversation with him. We needed to talk—and soon—but it clearly wasn't going to be tonight.

CHAPTER 6

The band playing at the Stroll Along Main Street was the first and last for the event. At least in the way it had taken place. The concert drew most of the strollers away from Main Street, defeating the purpose of the event, and those of us who were too close to the speakers couldn't talk with those who had chosen to continue visiting tables. I'd even let Bryan go early from his shift, despite wanting to talk to him. It was pointless to try over the music.

And unlike yesterday, he wasn't the first one in the kitchen this morning, so we didn't get the opportunity to talk then either.

I'd need to make the time. Maybe he could stay a few minutes after the baking was done. I'd skip lunch if I had to.

But as it often did, life had different plans when it came to what it wanted me to do over my lunch break.

I'd just come from making my delivery at the inn and was riding my bike back down the long driveway when I pulled off to the side to let a car pass. Only it didn't drive by. It stopped, and the driver rolled down the window.

"Joanie?"

"Hi, Erin. How are you?"

She sighed. "I wanted to apologize for yesterday. My friends can be a little rude sometimes. They mean well, usually, but I don't do a good job at sticking up for myself—or others—when they get like that."

"You have nothing to apologize to me for. I had them handled. It was you they were rude to. I take it they aren't married yet." She shook her head. "Wedding stress will either make you eat or starve. They'll figure it out eventually."

Erin chuckled. "I'd rather eat."

"Is that why you're here? Are you going to one of Libby's teas?"

She nodded. "I'm meeting my mom and Travis's mom and sister."

"Alice?"

She nodded again, this time her mouth pursing to the side.

"You don't seem excited. Libby's teas are delightful. And I hear the scones and cookies are amazing."

That made her laugh. "Oh, I've come to many of the teas here. You make excellent food. Just not so sure about the company this time."

"Lily may have mentioned something about that."

She drew her lips to the side. "Not sure how much Lily knows. We'd already stopped hanging out when Alice's attitude toward me changed. Alice was fine when we were all in high school, not that seniors have much to do with freshmen."

Her comment made me think about how true it was for me and my cousin, Thea. We'd been close growing up until I started high school. She was a freshman the year I was a senior. Even though we were in the same school again for the first time in a few years, I barely saw her. Anytime we did see each other, our acknowledgment of one another was little more than a nod and smile hello. Then I'd moved for college, and our relationship was never the same. I understood why even more now. She'd always known she was a witch. I didn't. So could Alice know something about Erin?

I shrugged. "Maybe someone said something to her thinking you still did. You know how people talk around here. You ever try talking to Alice by herself to clear the air?"

She raised an eyebrow at me as she released a short burst of air through her nose. "Alone? No. She doesn't like me. Why would I go talk to her by myself?"

"Has your fiancé ever brought it up or talked to her about it?"

"He's the one who first told me. I was shocked at first. But the girls have all seen how she acts now."

"By girls, you mean your other bridesmaids?"

She nodded, and a warning signal went off in my head. I'd seen their behavior toward Lily. What if they had something to do with the whole Alice thing? Or what if her brother did?

"Does Travis have a good relationship with Alice?"

Erin shook her head. "Like I said, she was older. Into different things. Left home as soon as she could."

A car turned down the inn's driveway. I didn't have much time. They'd be needing Erin to keep driving soon. "My offer still stands if you think you'd be up for a little chat with her. I'd like to talk to her."

"You think she could have something to do with my nonni?"

I lifted back onto my bike seat. "Don't know, but the timing of her attitude shift seems odd to me. My gram taught me there are no such things as coincidences."

Erin glanced into her rearview mirror upon my movement. "I don't know if she'll want to go anywhere with me."

"But you could try. Bribe her with mini-muffins if you have to. I'll make sure to have some there for you just in case."

She nodded. "I can try." The car began to roll forward.

"Hope to see you later," I called as we parted ways. I continued down the driveway, passing the other car with two women sitting in it. I wondered if one was Alice. Guess I'd find out soon enough if Erin managed to get her to the shop.

It was close to closing by the time Erin walked through the bakery doors, followed by someone who I assumed was Alice. Her blond hair was streaked with pink, reminding me of Lily's hair back in the spring. Was that it? Was Alice—and therefore Travis—a dryad and didn't like the fact that Erin wasn't? It wouldn't be the first time I'd dealt with a paranormal being not approving of another's relationship because of who or what that person was. I hoped this wouldn't turn into another Bruce Malloy situation. He'd tried to ruin my bakery because of my involvement with helping a merrow and a selkie get married despite family skepticism and, in some cases, outright hostility. I shook away the thought. This could not become like that.

Erin smiled at me, although her face seemed a bit strained. "Hi, Joanie."

"Erin, good to see you again." I wiped my hands down my apron before sticking my hand out. "And this must be Alice. Hi, I'm Joanie, the sweets baker here in town."

Alice took my offered hand. "You had some great cookies at the tea today." Her smile seemed genuine and lacked the tenseness that Erin's had. Were Erin's beliefs about Alice not liking her or approving of her engagement unfounded?

"Why, thank you. I'm a big fan of them, but I'm biased," I said with a chuckle. "I like your hair. Pink is one of my favorite colors." I swooped my hand down toward the shop counter, highlighting the pink resin connecting the pieces of wood that comprised most of the countertop.

"Oh, thanks. I like to change it up regularly, much to my family's chagrin." She leaned in as if to tell me a secret. "I'm the rebel in the family."

Okay, so not a dryad. Lily's hair turned pink naturally in the spring to match the flowers in the trees she preferred to merge with.

Alice turned to Erin. "I will be dying it again the week before the wedding to match your colors. It will give you a chance to tell me if you hate it, and then I can get it stripped if necessary."

Erin shrugged noncommittally. "If it will make you happier about being in the wedding."

Alice sighed. "Don't be like that." She gave me an apologetic smile.

"Don't be like what?" Erin asked. "I know you don't like me."

Well, that was one way to start this conversation.

Alice's eyes widened. "What makes you think that?"

"Everyone says it."

Alice opened her mouth, closed it, then opened it once more, but nothing came out.

"Did you do something to my nonni?" Erin asked pointedly.

"Your grandmother? She's dead, isn't she?" Alice shot me a quick glance, and I pretended to organize the candy stand to give them an air of privacy. "How could I have done anything to her? I didn't even know you when she passed."

"I'm not talking about when she *died*."

A light seemed to go on in Alice's head, and she lifted her head slowly. "Oh . . . you're asking if I did something to her ghost, aren't you?" She looked at me again, and I nodded in hopes of letting her know I understood.

Erin put her hands on her hips. "Of course I am."

"I wasn't sure if you could sense her around you, never mind see her."

"Well, I could, but now she's gone."

This wasn't going at all how I'd hoped. I'd planned on easing them into the ghost topic, but I should have recognized Erin's stress about the situation, given how she had come to me the other day and her admitted unease of being around Alice.

At that moment, another customer walked in. "How about we go somewhere and talk," I suggested before greeting the woman who had beelined over to the pastry case and the candy on top of it.

"What do you mean by *we*?" Alice asked. "How does this concern you?" She didn't sound angry, more confused over my inserting myself into the conversation.

"Erin asked me for a little help with her grandmother since I'm in a unique position to offer some."

Alice was about to say something else, but I made an exaggerated show of darting my gaze toward the customer. "Where do you suggest?" she finally asked.

"We can sit in the park next door. It may seem out in the open, but there's a bench at the back where we won't be heard by anyone walking on the street." Unless things got heated, and I hoped they wouldn't. "Let me just grab Sarah from the kitchen." She'd been in the back grabbing the broom and glass cleaner when they walked in. I assumed she'd realized they'd come in and was giving us privacy despite likely listening in on the entire exchange. Once upon a time, her eavesdropping would have concerned me—Sarah had always been a gossip—but now that I knew she was my familiar, her curiosity and chatty nature helped in more ways than one.

"No need," Sarah chimed as she pushed into the shop from the kitchen, cleaning supplies in hand. "I'm right here."

"I am going to duck out with Erin and her future sister-in-law Alice for a moment if you don't mind."

"Sure thing." Sarah set the glass cleaner and rag on the back counter and leaned the broom against it before going to help the customer by the pastries.

Once she had scooted past me, I shuffled around the counter and pointed to the door with an open hand. "Shall we?"

Erin and Alice nodded, and the two followed me next door to Founder's Park. I directed the two women to the corner bench, then gave a small nod to Arthur and his dog, Bardi, who were on their usual bench taking a break during their walk. Arthur returned my greeting with a nod of his own, an eyebrow raised as he followed the three of us with his gaze.

Erin settled on the bench, and Alice sat next to her, while I took a spot on a cut log that had been placed nearby to provide extra seating. There wasn't a good group-sitting space out here otherwise, but at least it was quiet.

"So you could see my nonni too?" Erin asked, the earlier accusatory tone having left her voice.

Alice nodded. "I thought you knew what I could do."

"We never really talked about it," Erin replied, and I assumed *we* meant her and Travis.

"All ghosts?" I asked, unable to help but glance over at Arthur and his dog.

"Wait . . ." Alice began. "You too? Do you see anyone now?"

"Yeah, Arthur Miller and his dachshund," I pointed to them as they stood. Arthur tipped his fedora at us in farewell.

Alice waved at him before he walked away. "That was a weird one for me. I went to his funeral since he'd been a teacher of mine. About an hour later, I saw him out for a walk. It's usually not like that."

"No," I agreed. "Although there are plenty here who just go about their day as usual."

Alice nodded. "That's for sure. Knoll's Grove seems to be quieter. At least for me."

"Is that why you left?" Erin asked.

"That was part of it."

"So you didn't do anything to Nonni?"

Shaking her head, Alice said, "No. Although I can see and talk to them, I'm not capable of doing anything about them, except investigate of course. She seemed nice, your grandma."

Erin brightened. "Oh, she was. Very much so. That's why I'd like to see her again."

Together, Erin and I explained how she had gotten me involved.

"I'm sorry for not coming out and telling you that I could see ghosts too. It's not something I share with just anyone. You—and now you too, Alice—are the first people I've met who can do what I can in any way."

Erin dismissively flapped her hand. "Makes sense now why you knew what questions to ask. I just thought it was because you were a witch."

A small smile tugging at my mouth as I shrugged. "I'm sure that helps."

At that moment, a delivery truck pulled up in front of the bakery, but that wasn't uncommon. Sarah could handle it. I had more pressing matters here.

Erin turned to Alice. "And you don't hate me?"

"Hate you? Of course not. What gave you that idea?"

Erin was about to respond when Sarah came around the corner of the building. "Joanie, you're needed in the bakery. Your drink cooler has arrived."

"Coming!" I called. I'd forgotten that was being delivered today. Sarah returned to the shop as I stood. "Excuse me, ladies, but I must see to this. I hope this chat helped."

Erin looked at Alice. "Oh, it did." Her stress from earlier seemed to be almost completely gone. "Thank you so much."

"My pleasure. I'm going to keep working on finding out what happened to your grandmother. Alice, it was nice to meet you."

"Likewise," Alice replied. "I'd love to talk more about what we can do someday."

I nodded. "I'd like that. You know where to find me." I waved to the two still sitting on the bench before hurrying across the small park. As I turned the corner, they were still chatting, with smiles on both their faces. I may not have solved the mystery of where Erin's grandmother was, but hopefully I had set the two maybe future sisters-in-law on the right path.

CHAPTER 7

I couldn't wait to show everyone the new cooler inside the bakeshop the next morning. In a few hours, Zach from Bug Creek Cider Mill would be here with his first delivery of cider, part of my efforts to provide customers with something to drink that would allow them to remain in the shop to sit at the tables and eat their treats. I also had plain coffee and simple bagged tea. Good, quality stuff but nothing that would compete with Gary at Leafs and Grounds, so no freshly roasted beans or loose-leaf tea blends. I'd ended up going with the company whose tea I had tried when I chatted with my friend Chelsea's now grandmother-in-law, Greta, about the history of the merrow-selkie feud. It had been a blueberry aloe tea, and it was delightful. It would go great with the lemon-blueberry muffins I had in the shop this month, and the company's peppermint-peach herbal blend was the suggested beverage for the peach muffins that we were rolling out today after their successful debut at the Stroll Along the Street.

Suncraft Bakery had been in business for over four years, and things were really starting to take shape. I chuckled. It had taken me long enough, but the seatless, drinkless bakery had been exactly what I needed the first few years. This version would take me so much farther into the future. Who knew what would come next.

"Good morning," Lily said as she stepped into the kitchen, followed by Bryan a step behind her. Although Lily had always been the one to be early, beating everyone else in, I believed all of her time with John and his woodworking studio had changed this one thing about her. Now she was often just right on time, likely coming from John's place instead of her house around the corner.

I wouldn't have minded her being a few minutes late today, though, as that would have given me a chance to talk with Bryan. Now that he'd had some time to let it sink in, I wanted to see how he was handling the news about being Erin's match and the reality that his match was marrying someone else soon.

Within a few minutes, the whole team was here, and I pulled them all into the bakeshop and flipped on the light.

I swept both arms to my side to draw their attention toward the new drink cooler. "Ta-da!"

"It's here!" Brittni said excitedly.

"When is it going to get drinks inside it?" Sam asked.

"Hopefully before we open," I said, rushing to the case to plug it in. I needed to get it to temperature, although the cider would be delivered cold and ready to drink. "It will have cider and water. I'm waiting on one of those fancy multi-cup coffee machines too, but for now, a single pot machine will have to do. We also have an electric kettle for tea. You can set it for different types of tea too." Not that we had a huge variety of teas to worry about half of the temperature settings.

Sam smiled, although it contained a hint of sadness. "I'm glad I'm getting a chance to see it."

"I'm glad you are too. And you're going to get to see it every time you come home to visit too," I replied, turning to him and the rest of my team. Sam was moving into his dorm in fifteen days. Fortunately it wasn't my old dorm. Its resident ghost had been the reason I'd moved into my first apartment. He was a bit disruptive to say the least. It had all worked out in the end, though. Moving was how I'd ended up with my cat, Saffy.

Clapping my hands once, both to shake me from my thoughts and to get the attention of the team, I said, "All right, let's get to work." We all filed back into the kitchen to start our day. After the reveal of the peach muffins on Thursday, I had a feeling the morning was going to be a busy one.

And it was. Customers lined up to get the peach muffins as well as the rest of our new lineup. I'd disappointed Donna this morning by not bringing any peach ones to the diner, saying they were a bakery exclusive through the weekend. This revelation excited Walter and Paul who, although initially disappointed at not getting one today, now looked forward to peach muffins also being their Monday muffins. They convinced Donna that this was the best way to try a new muffin, and I promised her an extra one just for her.

The one thing I hadn't expected, however, was how well the mini-muffins had gone over on Thursday. Despite telling people Thursday that this was how I was making my samples for the Stroll only, several came in looking for mini-muffins of any flavor. They'd not been by on Thursday to try them, but word of their existence had spread.

"They *would* make a good addition to your shop," Sam commented as the fifth person to ask about them left the shop —not empty-handed, but without the mini-muffins. "Why not give it a try?"

After helping the next customer in line, I answered, "You

don't think it's too much of an addition? It's one more thing we'd have to make." Right now, I could do it with a full team, but with losing Sam soon and someone always on candy now, I wasn't sure if it was the best time to add something else to our lineup. Priding myself on knowing how much I needed to bake on a given day and thus having a sparse day-old goods shelf, I didn't want the mini-muffins to compete with our regular muffins and then end up with too much of one or the other come closing time.

Lauren finished pouring tea for the next customer as Sam handed the same person a peach muffin on a small plate to enjoy here in the bakery. "What if you only offered them on weekends? You could do one or two flavors a week. Maybe announce them somewhere ahead of time like how you did with the peach muffins."

"You mean online somewhere?"

"Well, that too, but I was thinking of something like a sign you could tape in your window or put on a chalkboard stand on the sidewalk." Lauren giggled.

"Although 'online somewhere,'" Sam added, using air quotes, "wouldn't be a bad idea."

They both helped out the next two customers in line as I rang them out. "You know how I am with technology like that."

Lauren gave me a look. "One of us could help. I bet Sarah would be happy to."

Sam stood from behind the case, a peach muffin in hand. "Or Brittni. She's helped her dad a time or two with things for the library back before they had a staff member handling their pages." He grabbed a pastry bag from the back counter and placed the muffin inside before handing it to our customer.

They had a point. "I'll have to ask them. Wouldn't hurt to get something like that running."

The morning continued with a steady stream of customers. Perhaps the only disappointment on my end was that the cider was late. Zach showed up right at lunchtime after Sam had left for the day and while Lauren was out grabbing something to eat.

Zach rushed into the bakery, a crate full of small cider jugs in his hands and a clipboard tucked into the crate. "My apologies, Joanie. I was all loaded up to go this morning, and when I checked the truck one last time, there was a flat. Had to get the repair guy from Knoll's Grove since the mechanic here was already on another call."

There was nothing I could do about it now, and no use making him feel worse than he already did. I didn't know Zach well, but he seemed like a genuinely nice guy, and I adored his mother—ghost or not. "Don't worry about it. You're here now. That's what matters."

"You got anyone in the back to help with this?"

I nodded, "Let me grab Bryan." Thank goodness he was still here. Maybe this would be my opportunity to talk to him.

"Oh, good." He let out a quick relieved breath. "I hate to do this, but I'm now behind on the whole day, so—"

"Say no more. Hang on one sec." I popped my head into the kitchen, where Bryan and the rest of the team were finishing the day's cleanup. "Bryan, can I get your help with something for a few?"

He stopped wiping down his station. "Sure thing."

A moment later, he joined me in the shop, where I introduced him to Zach. Together the three of us made quick work of unloading the truck. As soon as we were done and I'd signed the slip saying Zach had made the delivery, he was on his way again . . . for all of five minutes before returning to the store to pick up the baked goods I'd made for the Bug Creek Cider Mill snack bar. Our partnership was still very new. It hadn't even been properly announced yet as that would come at the memorial event for his mother, but I could already tell that working with the Bugs would be interesting. The way it started, by my finding out his mom who'd been helping me at the store had been a ghost since before I met her, had clued me into that.

Once Zach was gone again, Bryan and I were alone in the shop, finally giving me a chance to talk to him.

"About the other night . . ."

"Look, it's okay."

I shook my head. "I really should have told you up front that you two were a match. Or at least the next morning when you came to talk to me. I'm sorry."

Passing me a mini-jug, he nodded. "It's nothing I didn't know already. Not that I knew we were matched in the way you do it, but I've known for years that she's perfect for me."

"How are you holding up?" I placed the mini-jug into the cooler. "It can't be easy knowing she's getting married so someone who isn't you."

He shrugged, then handed me another cider. "If it's what she wants, who am I to stop her?"

"You think it's what she wants?"

"She's marrying him, isn't she?"

I raised an eyebrow at him. People married one another for plenty of reasons. Wanting to wasn't always one of them. "Does she know about your feelings for her?"

He let out a loud puff of air through his nose. "She knew at one point. Haven't said anything since she came barging into my apartment to show me her engagement ring. I was the first person she told."

"And how long ago was that?"

"Two years ago."

"And before that?"

"It was common knowledge back in high school. At least among my friends, and I'm sure a bunch of her friends suggested it. We even went to prom together." He shook his head. "She only ever saw me as a friend, though."

"She mentioned you've been friends a long time."

He passed me a cider. "Nearly our whole lives. Her grandmother, the missing one, lived next door, but Erin and I could see each other's backyards as kids too. We'd cut through our neighbors' yards to get to one another's houses. It was faster that way. Knocked on each other's back doors too."

The thought of Bryan as a little kid made me smile. "That's cute."

"Yeah, she was," he said, likely not quite realizing what I'd said.

As the door to the shop opened, Bryan nearly dropped the next mini-jug as he went to hand it to me. I didn't need to look up or ask what was wrong. I could feel it. The tingling sensation I got whenever my matches were near one another exploded into the shop. Despite growing up with the ability, I didn't quite know how it all worked. Sometimes I could feel the tingles build as the two people got closer physically. Other times, it wasn't until the two halves of a match made eye contact. My guess, for today anyway, was that Erin hadn't expected to see Bryan today but caught sight of him as she got ready to enter.

Bryan recovered the cider, clasping it between his hands. A wide, lovesick grin spread across his face as her posture straightened, her already happy-seeming demeanor getting just a bit brighter. Overhead, the bakery lights responded, increasing their shine to match the mood in the room.

"Hey, Bryan," Erin chimed as she strode into the room

and over to her friend. She plopped into the chair closest to him. "I didn't know you'd be here."

He glanced at the clock on the wall above the back counter. "Usually I wouldn't be, but I stayed behind to help Joanie load up her new drink cooler."

"Oh, that's so nice of you. You're such a good guy." Erin's grin threatened to grow even larger. "And drinks are just what this place needed. Hi, Joanie."

"Good to see you again, Erin." I slid the empty crate to the side with the other one we'd already emptied. "So what brings you in?"

"A few things, actually," Erin started. "One, I needed some time to kill before Travis and I meet up." The change in tone was slight, but as she sat here in the charged, tingly atmosphere in the bakery, the mention of her fiancé fell a bit flat compared to a moment ago when she'd greeted her match.

"But two," she continued, "I'm dying for another one of those peach muffins. Just don't tell Travis."

This time the shift in her tone was more noticeable, and Bryan picked up on it. "Is everything okay?"

"Huh? Oh, yeah. Everything's fine." She flapped her hand dismissively at her worry as she shook her head. "He, like my bridesmaids, is worried about me fitting into my dress. After yesterday's tea, I'm supposed to be eating salads from here on out . . . except for my shower tomorrow."

Bryan laughed at that. "You? Eat just salads?" He let out a breath of air between clenched lips, creating this funny sputtering sound.

"Hey!" Her mouth dropped open in false outrage, but her eyes still crinkled with happiness. Not done with her playact, Erin balled her hand into a loose fist and went to punch him in the arm but instead lost her balance and fell out of the chair toward Bryan.

He caught her, but the movement unsteadied him, and he ended up hitting the side of the cooler, knocking down several of the skinny, single-serve cider containers. Although they both laughed it off, I caught the seriousness of Bryan's semi-hushed tone as he said, "Salads? Does he even know you?"

Erin had no answer to that and avoided needing one by picking herself off the floor, using the chair she'd fallen off for assistance. She turned toward Bryan, her hand extended to help him up. They ended up inches apart, looking at one another, smiling and saying nothing before breaking into more laughter after a moment.

The butterflies in my stomach were fluttering hard enough to cause a tornado inside me. How could she not see that she was meant for him?

"Let me get you that muffin," I said, hoping even a few feet apart from the two would calm my matchmaking tingle. I stood and took a deep calming breath to center myself as I walked away from the pair and behind the counter. Stooping, I grabbed a peach muffin from the case, then stood. "On a plate or in a bag?"

Erin thought for a moment. "Plate. As long as Travis doesn't catch me eating it, I can pretend it's not mine."

"I can say I'm on break or something and that it's mine," Bryan offered.

"My hero." She looked at him. "Why are you so good to me?"

He shrugged, a slightly sad grin on his face. "It's just a muffin."

Oh, but it was so much more.

I stuck the muffin on a plate and then crossed the shop to set it in front of Erin.

"Thank you."

I smiled warmly at her. "I'm glad you're getting one. So what else brings you in? You seemed to be on a mission before you noticed Bryan here."

"Oh, that's right. I wanted to thank you for getting Alice to talk to me. I really don't think she did anything to my grandmother."

"Seems it was a big misunderstanding to me."

She nodded, unable to say anything due to the bite of muffin she was chewing. Bryan handed her a water from out of the case, which she took a sip from immediately. "Thanks," she told him before directing her attention to me once more. "It doesn't get me any closer to figuring out what happened, but it's not her."

"Did you say anything to Travis about your chat?"

She shook her head rapidly, arching a brow as if I'd said something ridiculous. "No. We don't talk about that stuff. I thought I'd mentioned that."

"I meant more that you and Alice seemed to be okay and that she didn't not like you."

Erin shrugged as she swallowed more muffin. "Figured I wouldn't bring it up at all. Alice said only the women in his family can see ghosts."

"So his mom too?"

"Yeah. No wonder he doesn't like talking about ghosts."

I quirked my head to the side. "What do you mean?"

"He's never told me, but Alice said that's why their mom left."

"It can be a lot to handle." And I should know. I thought about how I'd needed Gram's help as a young teen and how her sister Pegee left friends and family behind to escape the ghosts that she could see. "But their mom came back, right? You just saw her for tea yesterday." Maybe there was still hope for my aunt's return.

Erin shook her head as she cast her gaze to the floor. "That was their stepmom. Their dad divorced their biological mom soon after she walked out on them without a word. He was remarried a year or two later when they were still young, so she's mom to them. Now she's who they have left. Their dad passed a couple years ago."

The lights overhead dimmed, and as I looked up, curious if they had reacted to the story Erin was telling, I missed the fact the door to the shop had opened.

I did not, however, miss the heavy presence entering the atmosphere or the dulling of the matchmaking tingle between Erin and Bryan. I studied the gentleman entering the shop—polished shoes, pressed black pants, a burnt-orange polo shirt, a scrutinizing gaze, dark hair perfectly gelled back. This had to be—

"Travis!" Erin chirped, her tone one of genuine surprise, almost as if she'd forgotten about him coming to meet her here. She ran over to him, muffin abandoned.

Bryan stiffened, then gave Travis a quick nod before bending down to get two of the empty cider crates. He looked at me as he headed for the kitchen door. "If you need me, I'll be cleaning up in the back."

Travis had one arm wrapped possessively around Erin's waist that went tighter as Bryan turned toward her. "Good to see you, Erin. Travis."

"You too, Bry." She gave him a small smile. Although she'd used a nickname for him, I hadn't missed Bryan not using hers.

Bryan pushed through the door, and it swung closed after him. Travis remained staring at the door, as if daring it to open again, until Erin stood on her toes and kissed his cheek. "How was your day?"

Travis's demeanor shifted, and the room resumed its normal brightness. "Good." He kissed her forehead. "Why did you want me to meet you here of all places?" His next words were a mumble, but I could still make them out. "You know this isn't where we're getting our cake from."

I hadn't thought so.

"No, I know that, but I was thinking about the brunch at the hotel for the wedding party that morning. The girls really seemed to love the muffins when they tried them on Thursday, so I was hoping we could talk to Joanie and get a quote for her providing some for us."

His gaze honed in on the muffin on the table. "And I take it you like the muffins as well?"

Without Bryan to be here for her cover story, I stepped in, walking over to Travis and Erin. "No, it's mine. Forgot my lunch today, so I've been picking at it in between customers." He looked me up and down as I stuck out my hand. "Hi, I'm Joanie. The owner of this bakery."

Travis released Erin. "Travis Ellison. I guess it's a good sign that you eat your own muffins."

"Of course," I replied, plastering on a smile. "I wouldn't sell anything that I wouldn't eat myself."

It was only then that he took my hand and shook it hard once. I didn't like it. Something felt off about him, although I couldn't put my finger on what. It went beyond what I'd just witnessed of his behavior toward Erin, Bryan, and me.

When Travis released my hand, he didn't back away and instead scrutinized me with a slight squint. I wasn't going to give him the satisfaction of me stepping away first. After all, this was my bakery.

At that moment, Sarah breezed in. "Hey, Joanie. Thanks

for letting me have the morning off. I ran into Lauren on the way here and told her she was good to go home." She paused, then surveyed the scene she'd just entered. She cocked her head to the side. "Everything good here?"

That seemed to snap Travis out of it. He finally stepped back, and my fake smile morphed into one of relief. "All good here. After you put away your bag, think you'd mind talking to Erin and Travis here about setting up an order for muffins the day after their wedding?"

"Oh sure, sure." She turned to Sophia and Travis. "I can run you through the whole process."

It wasn't anything I couldn't have done myself, but as my familiar, Sarah would hopefully have some insight into what was going on after interacting with them. Erin was paranormal. So was Travis's sister and apparently his mother. But was Travis? Erin said he couldn't see ghosts, but was there something else he could do?

Sarah ducked into the kitchen and returned a moment later. "All right, let's get your muffins sorted."

Erin walked toward the counter immediately, but Travis hung back, instead approaching me once more.

In a low voice, he said, "I've heard stories about you. I'm not sure what you're doing or what you think you're doing, but you are not going to come between Erin and me, so back off."

I held one hand up to play innocent as I reached for the muffin on the plate with the other. Breaking off a piece, I replied, "Just helping out a customer with some muffins." I popped the piece into my mouth, then smiled, hoping it portrayed more confidence than I felt. My heart was racing. I hated confrontations. "They really are good. Some might even say *magical*."

"Travis, you coming?" Erin sounded slightly concerned as

she tried to get his attention. She cleared her throat, then chipperly added, "Sarah's going to give us some tastings, isn't that great?"

Travis's demeanor changed once more, becoming lighter as he turned toward his fiancée. "Of course, my love." He turned away, never sparing me a glance.

CHAPTER 8

I retreated into the kitchen, sure that Sarah was more than capable of handling things herself. Travis wouldn't try anything while we were all here, especially Erin.

Bryan was sitting on one of the overturned crates. I wasn't surprised to see him. My matchmaking tingle had never gone away, although it had dulled significantly once Travis walked in.

"You doing okay?" I asked him.

He nodded. "I think I should be asking you that question. You just had to deal with Travis."

"Eh, nothing I can't manage." I waved my hand in a dismissive fashion. At least I hoped I could manage it. The stuff I'd had to deal with because of Bruce Malloy interfering with my bakery was still forefront in my mind. I didn't want to go through with that again. Or worse.

Bryan stood up and craned his neck, no doubt trying to peek out the window from where he stood. "What did he say to you?"

"He thinks I'm up to something that might come between him and Erin." I raised my eyebrows at Bryan as I shrugged in a playing-innocent way. "I don't know about that. Would you say I'm doing something to come between them?"

Bryan chuckled. "I sure hope you are. I should have said something to her a long time ago. Joanie, I can't let her marry that guy. And for more than just because I'm in love with her. You saw all that, right?"

"I did. I even had to say that muffin was mine. She got enough comments about the extra carbs from her friends. She doesn't need it from her fiancé too."

"I'm sorry for leaving like that. I didn't want to make things worse by staying. He raises my hackles, and I can't get like that."

"Gotten you into trouble before, I take it?"

"Yeah." He didn't elaborate.

I'd never seen indications of his alpha-like tendencies while in the shop. I'd heard things, mostly when I first asked around about him when he needed a job, but I dismissed most of it as gossip.

"You and Erin were really cute together," I said to change the topic. "Not that I'm surprised given the tingling I get when you two are around one another. We'll get this figured out."

He smiled at me. "Thanks. And I'm sorry for whatever trouble might come your way because of it."

"What do you think he can do?"

Bryan shrugged. "Him personally? Not sure. But he knows people. Has a way of making things happen without it looking like him."

"We'll worry about it if the time comes. Right now, we have pressing issues that we *can* do something about. Like Erin's ghost."

"And stopping a wedding." He seemed to be filling with determination as he straightened, his shoulders back.

The tingling sensation continued to fade. "They're gone now. How about you head home or go for a walk in the woods or hit the gym. You look like you could hit one of those boxing things." I mimed the motion of jabbing my fist at something in front of me.

"Your form's not half bad." Bryan stood. "The mat was more my thing rather than a ring. Maybe I'll go wrestle a Hellcat." He laughed, and I raised an eyebrow at him in a questioning manner. That just made him laugh harder. "I sometimes help out with the high school wrestling team. One of my old teammates is now the coach."

I nodded slowly, taking him at his word but now wondering if there was something else to my broody baker that wasn't all human. There had been something about the way he'd said it. And hadn't there been something about hellcats in that folklore book? If the one about the tree monster had proven to be true and dryads were real, then why not hellcats too? Or had it been wolves? I made a mental note to head back to the library to check that book again.

Bryan removed his apron, then tossed it into the dirty laundry bin. "All right. You have a good rest of your day."

"You too. Go get those Hellcats. See you tomorrow."

He grabbed his keys from a drawer in his workstation, then headed out the back door.

I poked my head into the store. Sarah was alone, head buried in one of the cases. "How'd it go in here?"

As I entered the room, she stood, pulling an empty tray from the case as she backed up. "Well, they put in an order, although I'm not sure if I should enter it into the system or not. Guess that would be up to you and how you deal with this case."

I didn't want to get too ahead of myself, but I didn't like the thought of putting it in the system either. Almost like it would be a self-fulfilling prophecy, that I wouldn't succeed in helping Erin find her grandmother or in getting her together with Bryan. "Let's stick it in the book with the rest of them, but don't enter it. We'll leave a note in the register so we don't forget just in case."

Sarah nodded, then passed me the empty tray before sliding a binder out from under the counter. She tucked the order slip that she had left on the counter inside it, then returned the binder to its spot.

I placed the tray on the case next to me. "What do you think of him, Travis?"

"Rubs me the wrong way a bit. Always has." She slid the pastry case closed.

"Were you in classes with him?"

"I was a year ahead, and we never had classes together. Not even gym. But from what I know about him, he coasted. Probably could have done so much more if he applied himself."

"The others said he was pretty popular but didn't do much."

She scoffed. "Money can elevate some people if they let it. His sister was never like that."

"His sister sees ghosts." I hadn't had a chance to tell her yesterday because I'd told her she could go once the delivery of our new drink cooler was all set. We'd not hung out last night, and since she'd only gotten here today at lunchtime with Travis and Erin here, there hadn't been an opportunity.

She brushed back a few loose strands of hair. "I'd wondered. She always seems really into it on her show. I thought it was for entertainment value, but I'll have to give it a closer look now."

"We can make a night of it. I'd like to check out an episode or two." Thankfully my wired internet still worked, no need to mess with the wards for it. "Their mom saw ghosts too."

Sarah raised an eyebrow at me. "No way. Her too?"

"You didn't know that either?" I cracked a smile. "Your skills are slipping."

"Or I've developed them over time," she replied with a chuckle before turning serious. "What happened with their mom was years ago. Rarely talked about now, if you catch my meaning. I think I was only five or six at the time."

"What do they say happened? Surely it wasn't ghosts."

She shook her head. "They wouldn't have been the type to admit they're paranormal. I guess today they'd say she was depressed. But the story then was that she was so over-whelmed with everything that, one day, she just left. So it was really the ghosts that caused it, huh?"

"That's what Alice told Christie. My aunt disappeared entirely to escape the ones she saw. Gram hasn't seen her since they were teenagers. I still don't understand what Gram did to me exactly to help keep the bad ghosts away. I can't imagine what my life would be like if I could still see them."

Sarah nodded solemnly, but a grin formed on my face as the door to the bakery opened, shifting the bakery's atmosphere. It could only be one person. Turning, my smile grew wider as he and I made eye contact. "Ken! What brings you here?"

"Was on a mission for the hospital and thought I'd drop by to say hello." He walked over and I went around the corner to meet him halfway. He pulled me in for a hug, giving me a soft kiss on the forehead. "It's good to see you."

My shoulders relaxed as I breathed him in. He always smelled so good on days he had meetings around town, having added an extra splash of cologne to freshen up before leaving his office.

Sarah cleared her throat.

Over my shoulder, Ken said, "Hey, Sarah," as if he hadn't just been caught in a PDA with his girlfriend, whereas heat rushed to my cheeks. He added a bit more oomph to his squeeze before releasing me. "So who can't hide what?"

Some of the tension returned to my shoulders. "I'm still on that grandmother ghost mission I was telling you about. Seems the girl's fiancé's family has a ghost-seeing ability all of their own."

His eyes widened. "Oh, wow. More of them. How are you doing?"

"I'm more interested in what this could mean for my . . . client." Even with Ken, I tried not to name names when I could. Although he'd helped me time and again, I didn't want to involve him if I could help it.

He nodded. "So dinner later? Ivy's got a playdate, and her friends' parents have already said they're taking the girls to Dawg Pound for dinner."

"Oh, that sounds fun. What did you have in mind?"

He shrugged. "Don't know yet, but I'll think of something. Call me when you get out."

"All right."

He kissed my forehead once more. "Talk to you later. Sarah, good to see you again."

"Likewise." Sarah gave him a small wave, and he headed out the door. Once it was closed, she made a kissy face at me. "You two are really cute together, you know?"

"I do," I said with a happy sigh. "He's a really great guy. I'm glad he stayed with me after learning about what I could do."

She smiled, then opened the pastry case. "I may not be a matchmaker, but that guy's not going anywhere." She stooped to reach into the case.

"I sure hope not."

She straightened and cocked her head to the side. "You seem unsure."

"I know I shouldn't be, but this missing ghost matchmaker issue kinda has Bruce Malloy vibes, and it's messing with me." I told her about what Travis had said before she took over about the muffins. "Think it's something to worry about?"

She went to open her mouth once more, but a customer walked in then, one who didn't know all about my witchy secrets. We switched our topic of conversation to something that was a bit safer. Travis and his possible threat were forgotten in the afternoon's stream of business.

CHAPTER 9

"What do you think I should wear tonight, Saf?" I asked my calico cat as she sat between two options on my bed. "It's casual, but Ken has been busy with work lately, and I want to look nice." We were heading to a new Tex-Mex place that had opened up in Bug Creek. They didn't have many spots for restaurants there, their Main Street was maybe a quarter the size of ours, but it meant that they had high standards. It had to be good food.

Saffy turned her head to scrutinize both outfits. One was a pretty pale yellow, the same color as a dress I'd worn not too long ago but had felt so cute in, and the other was a more abstract fitted t-shirt design that I could wear with a plain black skirt that swished this way and that when I walked. After a moment, she flopped over onto the yellow shirt, exposing her belly. *Mrow!*

I reached for Saffy's stomach and gave it a quick scratch before pulling my hand away so she couldn't grab me. "Guess that settles that, then. Thanks for making my decision easier." The abstract shirt would have fewer cat hairs on it. "Plus, it will be harder to tell if I've dropped something on it." Always a possibility with me when it came to salsa, sour cream, or queso. Tonight posed the potential for all three.

Saffy rubbed along the yellow shirt. It was probably a good thing I hadn't laid the shirts out with the skirts. She would have flocked to the black one for sure.

"All right, let's get you fed before Ken gets here."

She rolled off the bed, landing with a hard thump, then peeled out on the hardwood floor and down the stairs. Silly cat. I still needed to get dressed.

By the time I reached the living room, I could hear the clinking of her empty food bowl. No doubt she was sitting there tapping it, protesting that it was still empty. She eyed me as I walked into the kitchen.

"Sorry. I hadn't meant immediately." I opened the cupboard where I kept her food and reached inside for the bag of crunchies. After pouring some into one of the bowls, I let her eat for a few minutes before adding a scoop of wet food to it. That guaranteed she wouldn't just eat the wet stuff and ignore the rest, only to complain she was still hungry when I got home. She'd still probably be hungry by then, but a treat would hold her over at that point. I swapped the second bowl with a fresh bowl of water. No one liked a drink with extraneous cat fur in it, although I was certainly used to finding the stray piece occasionally after she investigated whatever tea was in my cup.

Right on time, there was a knock at the door.

"I'll see you later, Saf." I shuffled out of the kitchen and across the living room, sliding my feet into my shoes as I opened the front door.

"Beautiful as always," Ken said, standing there looking handsome in a green polo and khakis.

"You're not so bad yourself." I grabbed my purse hanging

on my coat tree, then slung it over my shoulder. "Shall we go?"

"Let's." He opened the screen door for me, and I closed the wooden door behind me as I stepped outside. "But first, this." He let the screen door fall closed as he pulled me in for a kiss, this time on the lips.

"I could get used to those sorts of hellos," I said, tucking a lock of hair behind my ear. I'd opted to wear my hair down this evening. The humidity of mid-summer had broken, and it was one of the few times I didn't feel it necessary to get my hair off my neck. The hair fell right back in front of my face, and this time, Ken pushed it back.

"I could too. I like your hair down. It's pretty. Soft." He kissed my forehead, then stuck his elbow out so I could loop my arm with his.

"Thank you." We walked down the porch steps and along the flagstone path toward the driveway.

"Hullo there! Where are you off to?"

We both looked up and saw my across-the-street neighbor, Matt, waving at us. He'd been in his front garden and neither of us had seen him. Though with the hello from Ken, who could blame me? I had been a little distracted.

"Hi, Matt! Dinner. Mexican place in Bug Creek," I called back, waving as Ken did the same.

"I can't remember the last time I had Mexican." He wiped some sweat from his brow. "You kids have fun. Tell Miss Ivy hello for me."

"Will do," Ken affirmed with a nod. Ivy loved Matt. Had since the moment she laid eyes on him. It was sweet how she had warmed up to him so quickly.

Matt bent back down in his garden as Ken and I reached the car. Ken opened the door for me, and I slid inside. The humidity may have broken, but it was still hot in the closed-up car. The short drive from his house to mine hadn't given his car enough time to cool down. He got in his seat and started the car. As he flipped the AC on, I closed my door and rolled down the window to vent the hot air. As Ken drove away, I reached outside to give Matt another wave, and we headed for Bug Creek.

The AC was blasting, making it too loud to have much of a conversation on our way there, so we swapped glances and the occasional funny face with one another, our smiles growing wider with each look until I couldn't hold it any longer and broke out into a laugh. By the time we got to the restaurant, I was a giggling mess and needed a moment to collect myself before getting out of the car. Thank goodness I hadn't worn eye makeup, It would have started to run with the tears I had to dab out of my eyes.

Once we'd finally been seated on the restaurant's back deck, which overlooked Bug Creek, and had ordered drinks, Ken took my hands. "So what's going on with your case? It's more than just the fact others can see ghosts," he said, the word *ghosts* practically a whisper even though no one was sitting around us. "I could see your shoulders tense when I mentioned it."

"It's my client's fiancé. He . . . I don't know . . . kinda warned me to stay out of it." My face was pinched with hesitation as I waited for Ken's response. He didn't like me getting involved with things that could be dangerous.

Ken furrowed his brows. "He threatened you?"

"Yeah, kind of. I guess he wields some sort of power in town, but I don't know what."

In a hushed tone, he asked, "Paranormal power?"

I shook my head. "No. The normal kind. Connections. Influence. Money. That sort of thing."

"Who is this guy?"

I said nothing. It wasn't my place to reveal names, although Ken always seemed to find out by getting involved somehow.

"Look," he said, squeezing my hands, "I know you try to keep everyone's secrets, and that's honorable. I get it. But if you could be in trouble, I'd like to know who I have to watch out for."

"Travis Ellison."

"Ellison?"

"You know the name."

"Of course I do. They donate a ton to the hospital. Not Travis specifically, but someone in his family. They're very philanthropic."

"And here I thought you wouldn't know anything about them."

He smiled, looking pleased with himself.

"So do you think he's serious?"

Ken squeezed my hand again. "Don't know but I hope not."

I was quiet a moment as the waiter brought over our drinks, then took a sip to collect my swirling thoughts. A moment later, he returned with chips, salsa, and queso, then took our order. As soon as he left, I dove into the chips and loaded one up with topping.

Plop!

A chunk of tomato covered in goopy cheese landed smack on my shirt. Although I'd planned for this inevitability when Saffy helped me pick the shirt, I hadn't expected it to happen so soon.

Ken stifled a chuckle. "At least it's not salad dressing, right?" Our meeting in the hospital cafeteria hadn't been my finest moment, but his offer to help me up was how we'd gotten our chance to meet. Had I not fallen over a haunted brush, it may not have turned out like this. Me and him laughing over queso.

I couldn't help but grin at that as I grabbed a napkin and then wiped the food off my shirt. "See? All better." I pointed to the spot, barely visible over the design. I'd have had a hard time finding it if I hadn't just seen it.

His eyes twinkled with amusement. "That's why you wore the shirt, didn't you?"

"So you wouldn't be able to see it if I got covered in food?" I laughed. "You bet. I know myself. I'm always going to wear some of my meal."

Within a few minutes, Ken joined me in wearing some of his food. The queso landed close to the buttons of his solid-colored polo. Even after he wiped it off, the spot was noticeable.

"That's what I get for teasing you," he said, his tone maintaining his earlier humor.

"Or maybe that's what you get for wearing a single-color shirt. It's a canvas just waiting for paint—or cheese in this case."

He smiled, but then turned serious. "So back to this Travis thing."

I held up my hand. "I don't really want to talk more about it."

"I know, so I'll say only one more thing about it. I'm sorry your new friend isn't able to talk to him about what she can do." He reached for my hand, and I gave it willingly. "When you're with someone, you have to be able to share your whole self with them. I can't imagine being with you and not knowing all that you can do. We had a bit of a rocky start, but I'd never want you to feel like you had to hide this from me. It's part of what makes you Joanie, and I love that."

"It certainly keeps things interesting, huh?" I asked, not

missing the fact that he'd used the *L* word. Only he hadn't directed it to me exactly. We'd been together a few months now, but neither of us had taken that step. This was the closest. Was I ready for more?

"Well, it's never boring, that's for sure."

The waiter reappeared with our food, and as we dug in, several of the tables around us filled. Soon a band was setting up at the side of the deck, and they began playing music. I didn't know the words, but I loved the rhythm and ended up swaying in my seat through the rest of our meal.

Once we had finished eating, Ken stood, his hand extended toward me. I took it, and he helped me to my feet. I thought we were leaving, but instead, he pulled me close to him, placing one hand on my hip and maintaining his hold on my hand with the other. Although we didn't know the proper steps to anything, we danced for the next few songs, working up a little sweat and making me wish I had tied my hair up after all.

He kissed my forehead as one song ended and the singer took a moment to sip some water. "I scared you earlier, didn't I?"

"What do you mean?" I asked, knowing exactly what he meant.

"When I said the word *love*."

"What? No." I sputtered a raspberry for emphasis.

"I saw your face. You can't hide it as well as you think you do." He lifted my chin so I was looking right at him. "I'm not sure if it's the right time yet, but it's getting there. When I do say it, there's going to be no question as to what I meant. I won't disguise it with other phrasing. You'll know." He brought his mouth to mine, crashing our lips together. Too caught up in the moment, I had no worries about who was around us to see our PDA this time.

CHAPTER 10

The next morning, I was still reeling from the most amazing date I'd had, well, ever. We hadn't gone to grab Mexican expecting a live band or to dance, and I certainly hadn't expected that kiss, but it was, for lack of a better word, *magical.*

It made me that much more determined to help Bryan and Erin. Now that I knew what such a kiss was like, these two needed to be able to experience it for themselves with the person they were meant to be with. Each other. I could only imagine it would be that much better. I didn't know if I was meant to be with Ken—I sure hoped so—but the date had been perfect either way.

This morning, however, was not so perfect.

"Joanie, we might have a problem," Sarah said, poking her head into the kitchen.

I dropped the cookie dough I was working with back onto my table and wiped my hands on my apron. "What's up?"

"The town beverage board wants to talk to you."

"On a Sunday?" A beat passed before I followed that question with another. "The town has a beverage board?"

She gave me a half shrug. If she didn't know about it, this couldn't be good.

"Be right out." I hurried to wash my hands, then took a deep breath before entering the shop to muster up some confidence. Unable to delay it any longer, I pushed the door open and strode inside. Two men were standing by my drink cooler, and another was examining my tea kettle and coffee pot. "Good morning, gentlemen. I'm Joanie, owner of this bakery. How can I help you?"

The one closest to the counter walked over to me. "Morning." He held out an ID badge that displayed our town's seal on it. The words *Beverage Board* were printed boldly at the top. Below it was his name. The badge looked official, but I didn't know this Aaron DaSilva, and only recognized one of the other men as someone who worked at Town Hall. I'd have to talk to Courtney. "I'm here because you recently started selling drinks here."

"Just within the last week or so. But I have all the proper permits. I've technically been allowed to since I opened here a few years back but hadn't until now. Is there a problem?"

"We got a report—"

"A report from whom?" I'd been down this road before.

He glanced at his clipboard. "I'm not at liberty to say."

I crossed my arms. "Okay . . . So what did this report say?"

"That you're beyond the scope of your original victualing license."

"I'm not selling anything I shouldn't be."

"The cider, ma'am."

Ugh, *ma'am*? "It's apple cider. Straight from Bug Creek Cider Mill. I've partnered with Zach Bug. You can call him and see that everything is on the up and up. I only sell four types of drinks here. Coffee, tea, water, and cider. No sodas, no alcohol. Nothing that would compete with anyone else in town."

"You have establishments two doors down—"

"That sell special coffees at their sit-down restaurants, and before you mention it, I've already cleared my selling drinks with Gary at Leafs and Grounds. I even allow people to bring their drinks from there to here if they prefer something beyond what I offer. I can assure you, I've checked with everyone up and down Main Street, and I'm not stepping on any toes."

The man nodded, and I caught one of the others over by the cider jotting something down on a tablet.

I sighed. "Am I going to be able to sell my drinks here while you head back and file your report and see that whatever this is has been a misunderstanding?"

He shook his head, actually seeming a bit remorseful. "I'm sorry. Rules are rules. My hands are tied. But if it is as you say, then there should be no problem."

Well, at least it wasn't my whole shop like last time. "I understand. But I'm leaving the cooler on. I'm not going to lose product over this."

The man nodded again. "Only rule I'm here to give is for you to not sell it. I see no problem in preventing it from spoiling." Thank goodness for that. "And hopefully this has been a big misunderstanding and you'll be able to sell everything again once it's sorted. Good day to you."

"I'd say thanks for coming in, but . . ."

The man looked around. "Maybe another time. My kids would love some cookies."

I smiled at the man, the first genuine one I'd given since stepping foot into the kitchen. "I hope you do that."

He turned and waved at the two men standing by the

drink cooler to follow him. The three headed out the door, then got into a car sitting parked just outside the entrance.

A loud sigh escaped me, taking with it all my bravado. This hadn't been a major confrontation, but I didn't like any kind. The events surrounding the health inspector were fresh in my mind, and with this coming so soon after Travis's warning, I was left uneasy.

Sarah reached into one of the cases. "Why don't you sit down for a minute. You're looking a little pale."

I made my way over to a table. She came around the counter with a lemon ricotta cookie.

"Thanks. I'll be fine after this. Cookies make everything better."

"So you keep saying." She eyed me before turning toward the window. "I've never heard of a beverage board. You think they would have been involved before you started selling anything to drink."

I took a bite of the cookie. "You think Travis had something to do with this?"

"Maybe."

"Do you think he's involved in the other thing?"

"Erin's grandmother?"

I nodded, my mouth full of cookie once more. "Yeah. Erin's certain he has no abilities. And I doubt Alice is involved. So there has to be someone else. But someone different from us."

"You mean someone who could make ghosts go away?"

"Yeah. I can only help a ghost move on if they wanted to. There's no forcing someone who doesn't. I tried back when . . ."

"Say no more. You don't have to get into it right now."

"So what other sort of paranormals are there? Mediums? No, they can only talk to them like me. *Maybe* see them.

What's the name of something that can control ghosts? Does that exist?"

Sarah took the seat next to me. "Only thing I can think of is a necromancer."

That term I was familiar with thanks to some of the books I'd read. "I thought they could only raise the dead."

"That they can do that too, but they raise them to command them. I would imagine that a strong one could command ghosts who were around even if they didn't raise them."

"Are there any in Heartwood Hollow?"

She shrugged. "I think it's time to call in help and give my grandfather a ring."

I popped the last of my cookie into my mouth. "Please tell him you're on a time crunch and don't have time for his riddles."

"I will. Not sure that he'll comply, though." She chuckled, she studied me as I ate more of my cookie. "Good. Your color is coming back."

I gave her a cheeky grin. Or at least I hoped it came off that way. "I told you that cookies make everything better."

"I never doubted that, or you for that matter, even when you doubted yourself." She pulled out her cell phone, and I took that as my sign to head back into the kitchen. Hopefully Vince would be able to help us—and soon.

CHAPTER 11

W hen the door opened shortly before closing, I didn't
know what to make of the person walking in. Travis.

The lights remained neutral, not darkening like yesterday. And Travis's demeanor seemed pleasant if not a bit hesitant as he looked around my shop and approached me.

Although I suspected that he had something to do with the so-called beverage board, I didn't know for sure, and I had no reason to be rude to him but all the reason to not be rude to him too. I didn't want to make things even more difficult for Erin during what was a stressful time for anyone being so close to her wedding, never mind having issues with ghosts.

He gave me a small smile. "Hello again."

I returned the smile. So far so good. "Hi, Travis, how are you?"

His gaze darted away before looking at me once more. Unlike yesterday, it held no evidence of malice or ill-will. "Good. Look, could I maybe talk to you somewhere in private?"

I glanced at Sarah.

"Please," he urged. "It won't take long."

"Sure thing." I stepped out from behind the counter and held my hand out toward a table. "Have a seat."

Sarah gave me a pointed look and said, "I'll be in the kitchen if you need me," before beelining for the door. No doubt she'd eavesdrop as soon as it closed.

"Thanks, Sarah," I called over my shoulder as I followed Travis to the table closest to the window. He sat with his back to the window, and I took the seat across from him, my back facing the bakeshop. "What can I do for you?"

"I wanted to apologize for my behavior yesterday. It was unwarranted. I get a bit jealous when I see Erin with other guys, Bryan in particular. They go way back, much further than me in college, and I always thought there was something there. Surprised me when she agreed to go out with me." He chuckled. "Even more when she agreed to a second date and then finally to officially being my girlfriend a couple months later. I'm a really lucky guy."

I smiled at the man who was close to gushing about his fiancée. This was what I wanted for Erin, someone who loved her. There was, of course, still the issue about her being matched with Bryan, but my worries about Travis's behavior yesterday were lifting.

"So when I came in here yesterday and saw the two of them together, I panicked. I'd never be able to do anything to Bryan if things got heated." He flexed his arm. "I mean, look at the difference between me and him, but all of that worry and frustration with myself over my jealousy was immediately at a spilling point. And then I took it out on you. I shouldn't have, and I'm sorry."

I opened my mouth to say something, to let him know that I'd accepted his apology, but he was quick to continue.

"But I'm still worried." He scrubbed at his face with both

hands before clasping them together and letting them fall back to the table. "Look, I've heard things about you around town, and if Erin's coming to you, it has to be ghost related."

He looked to me for confirmation, and I nodded. It did no good to lie. Travis let out a resigned sigh.

"Thought so. I'm not sure if you know my family's history with ghosts. My mother could see them, and it ruined her life. I was forced to grow up without her as a result. I don't want Erin to face similar issues. And I don't want to lose her to the dead like I lost my mother."

I wasn't going to outright tell him about me and my abilities, but I wanted to let him know I could relate. "It sounds like my aunt went through something similar to your mom. She ran away and hasn't been seen in years."

His eyes widened with surprise.

Now it was my turn to apologize. "Sorry, Erin may have mentioned that part to me."

He nodded. "Glad you understand where I'm coming from. I'm only interested in protecting her. I'm not the bad guy."

"I never said you were."

He nodded again. "I know. It's me projecting again. That I'm going to be made to be the bad guy because I can't help her solve her problems. But it's not wrong to ask for help, so I thank you for trying to get her grandmother back. It's given her comfort these last couple days, and I think that's helped ease some of the wedding stress. It's part of why we hired a wedding planner in the first place. I don't want Erin to be so stressed. I want the world for her because she's my world."

A phone rang in the kitchen, momentarily drawing my attention away from the conversation. Travis loved Erin. Even if he could have, he wouldn't have done anything to Erin's grandmother knowing it would have stressed her out. My only hope now was that Vince would have some information for his granddaughter about necromancers.

Travis coughed, and I turned back to face him. "Sorry about that."

He waved me off and pointed to his throat as he coughed again.

"Are you okay?"

Through more coughing, he said, "Swallowed spit down the wrong pipe."

I stood. "Let me get you some water." I hurried to the cooler and pulled out a bottle. Returning to my seat, I handed it to him.

He took a large sip, then another, draining half the bottle before setting it on the table. "Thanks." He cleared his throat. "What do I owe you?"

I waved off his question. "Nothing. Can't sell it, but they never said anything about giving it away."

He raised an eyebrow as he tipped his head toward me slightly. "Who's they?"

"The town's beverage board."

"Since when do they have a say over bricks and mortar establishments?"

"What do you mean?" His question gave me hope that this morning's events had all been a big mistake.

"Let me amend that. Establishments that don't serve alcohol. But they also deal with outdoor pop-up events like beer and wine tastings at our festivals or if the breweries do any special events closer to town. They'd have no reason to come here unless you started selling alcohol."

"The only alcohol I've ever had in here is by special request to put in baked goods or when I do a very rare Irish creme, ale, or white Russian cupcake." They were delicious, but I had to put an age restriction on them because of the alcohol in the frosting. And it disappointed the kids when I had to say no, which I hated to do.

He pulled out his phone. "That doesn't sound right. Let me put in a call. My family regularly deals with them at various functions."

"Oh, I couldn't ask you to do that," I said at the same time wondering if it could really be that easy.

He smiled. "That's the thing. You didn't. Please. Let me. For Erin."

I gave him a single nod, hope blooming inside me. "If you think it will help."

"Worth a shot." He picked up his phone and keyed a few things on the screen before placing it to his ear. "Hey, it's Travis. How are ya?"

It didn't escape me that both of my issues right now hung in the balance of a couple phone calls.

"Good. Hey, I'm standing in the bakery here in town . . . No, the other one. Suncraft Bakery . . . Yeah, we're having her make muffins for our guests at the morning-after brunch. Erin loves them, and whatever makes her happy, you know? Anyway, I'm calling because your guys put a stop to her being able to sell drinks today . . . No. No, she's got all the licensing and isn't selling alcohol of any kind on the premises . . . Cider. Sure. Apple cider. Not the hard stuff. Fresh from Bug Creek. I'm staring at the labels of the bottles she can't currently sell . . . Yeah . . . Okay, got it . . . I'm sure. It happens. All right, I'll talk to you later, bud, thanks." Travis lowered the phone from his ear, pressing his phone's screen.

"So . . . what did he say?"

"You are free to sell everything you have."

I pressed my hand to my chest as I let out a relieved sigh. A smile played on my lips. "Thank you."

"Seems someone keyed in the update you sent Town Hall

incorrectly or they interpreted it wrong or something. Either way, they thought by cider, you meant hard cider, which then put you on the radar of the beverage board since that's their arena. And that was why they were out here today."

"I appreciate you making that call."

He smiled, letting out a light chuckle. "And I appreciate that you had water here when I needed it. I'm sure it would have gotten straightened out on its own, but you know some things take time around here. I'm glad I could help speed it up for you."

"Can I get you anything else while you're here?"

He shook his head. "Aw, no, but thanks. I only came in to apologize for yesterday." Then he eyed the case. "Actually, you know what? Let me get something for Erin. I know she thinks she needs to lose a couple more pounds so her dress fits her just so, but she's perfect the way she is. Always has been."

We walked toward the cases and he pointed to a caramel- and chocolate-dipped whoopie pie, one of the gooiest, most frosting-filled things in here. I smiled at him. If this couldn't prove to Erin that she didn't have to worry about her figure, nothing would.

"And a toffee crunch square for me." He pointed to the candy display on top of the case next to him.

"Sure thing." I bagged up both treats, then rang him up. He put all his change in our tip jar, more than covering the cost of the water I'd given him. I passed him the bags.

He held them up. "Have a good rest of your day, Joanie."

"You too, Travis. Thanks for coming in."

He waved over his shoulder as he headed out the door.

Once it had closed, Sarah poked her head into the shop. "So that seemed to go well."

"Yeah, it did." She came back into the bakery, and since

she'd been on the phone, I explained the misunderstanding that had happened with the town's beverage board.

She put her hands on her hips. "I'm relieved that it got cleared up quickly. Having some pull in town can come in handy sometimes. Guess he's in the clear for having caused the trouble in the first place then, huh?"

I nodded. "I think he's in the clear for all of it."

"All of it?"

"Yeah. I don't think he would have done something to Erin's grandmother even if he could have."

"Well, that complicates things." She pursed her lips.

I turned toward her. "Things not go well with your grandfather? Did he not know of a necromancer?"

"Oh, he knew of one. Only one. They're rare, possibly even rarer than someone with multiple powers." She eyed me, her chin so close to her chest that had she been wearing glasses, she would have been looking over them at me.

"Shouldn't that mean the odds are in our favor?"

She breathed hard out of her nose. "Not sure that's how odds work."

"But he knew of one. That's a good thing, right? Can he put us in touch with them?"

She shook her head. "He can't."

"Why not?" The earlier bubble of hope I'd had popped.

"He's dead, and last I checked, while necromancers can raise the dead, they can't rise from the dead on their own."

"That's probably a good thing," I replied, unable to keep myself from grinning at my comment, "but what are we going to do now?"

CHAPTER 12

As I locked the shop, a familiar voice chirped my name. "Joanie!"

The voice was quickly followed by the pounding of tiny feet on the sidewalk.

I turned to greet Ivy. "How are you? It's so good to see you."

She wrapped her arms around me. "It's good to see you too."

"Where's your dad?" I asked as she let me go. Heartwood Hollow was a safe town, but Ken wasn't one to let Ivy run around unsupervised.

She pointed behind her. A moment later, Ken stepped out of the gift store a few shops up, the one with the tumbled stones that I kept meaning to get her a few of.

Which reminded me . . .

"Hey, I have a question for you." She looked up at me with wide eyes. "A couple weeks back, you didn't happen to take a brownish-gray crystal sphere from my yard, did you? It would have been buried in the garden."

Ivy didn't hesitate when she said, "No." She wrinkled up her nose. "What's a sphere?"

"It's a ball." I held my hands a few inches apart from one another. "The one I'm missing is about this big."

She shook her head. "I know better than to take things without asking."

"You're a good kid, that's why." I smiled down at her.

Ken caught up to us then, and he kissed me softly on the forehead, sending warmth through my system. This was much more in line with his usual hellos, not that I expected anything different in front of his seven-year-old daughter, but I thought I felt something just a little bit more behind this one. Or maybe I was reading too much into it after last night. For being a matchmaker, I still fell into the same traps that many people did, overanalyzing things in my own relationship despite my telling others not to do it. If anything, it showed just how much I couldn't use my matchmaking powers on myself.

"Hello," Ken said, offering his free arm to me.

I slid mine through his. "Hello, yourself. How was your day?"

"It was good. Got to take Ivy out to breakfast with some of her friends and their dads. Went on a boat ride down the river with them all."

Ivy bounced on her feet. "It was really fun!"

"It sounds fun. You both must be tired."

Ivy shook her head. "Not tired. Hungry. Do you want to go to Dawg Pound?"

I glanced at Ken, who looked at me with a hopeful expression.

"We were going there next. I was hoping you'd join us."

"I would love to."

The three of us walked past the little park next to the

bakery and across the street to the local hot dog restaurant. The restaurant was cute, dog themed, and featured pictures of dogs in local animal shelters looking for homes. There were a few others around the region, and the pictures were updated weekly when there were adoptions.

We settled into a booth by a window after ordering our food. Ken preferred this particular one because it had the fewest photos. As much as he loved Dawg Pound, he worried that his resolve would one day break and Ivy would end up with a dog after spotting one she couldn't live without in a photo.

"So how was your day?" Ken asked me.

I filled him in on everything that had happened from being told I couldn't sell my drinks to Travis saving the day. "So I think I had him all wrong," I concluded. "Sounds like he's being protective of her, although a bit over protective, which is why he came off so strongly."

"Probably used to getting his way. Still, I don't like that she can't talk to him about what's going on with her."

"I agree with you on that part. And she's still matched with someone else, so I'm not going to ignore that either. I'm just glad to rule him out of the other thing."

He pinched his lips together, clearly reluctant to say what was on his mind.

"What? Do you think he's still involved, or do you think I should ignore that they're not meant to be?"

He held his hand up. "Nope, neither of those things." His gaze darted to Ivy, happily eating her cheesy hot dog.

Message received. Considering Ivy knew about the paranormal world and had just listened to everything I'd said, I was curious about what he had to tell me that he couldn't say in front of her.

After a quick stop at my house to feed Saffy, I headed to Ken and Ivy's house to spend more time with the two of them, which quickly morphed into spending time with just Ken when Ivy ran outside to play with one of her friends down the street.

I sat next to Ken sipping tea as he caught up on the day's news, but once that was over, he turned to me. "About what I wanted to tell you earlier but couldn't . . . it's about Erin."

"What about her?"

"Are you sure she's being entirely truthful with you about her abilities?"

"I have had no reason to doubt her, why? Are you saying she's been making it all up? We're a little past the age of make-believe." And even then, if someone Ivy's age came to me and said they saw ghosts, I'd believe them because I had been able to back then.

He shook his head. "Just the opposite, actually."

"What do you mean? That she can do more?"

He nodded. "Exactly that."

I sat up a bit straighter. "Why wouldn't she tell me, especially after I told her what I could do?"

He shrugged. "I know you want to see the best in people, but I think she's hiding things from you."

"Why?"

He sighed. "One of the dads today mentioned how he'd spent yesterday getting fitted for a rental tux for his friend's wedding. Based on what they were saying and what you've told me, it became pretty obvious he's in Erin and Travis's wedding. One of the other fathers said something about how he hopes their kids don't have the same issues that Travis's mother and Erin did. Apparently, she used to go around saying she could see ghosts as a kid, and they were making fun of her for it."

"Wait, so you're telling me Erin can see more than just her grandmother?"

"Going off what you told me about when her grandmother died? Yes. This happened before that."

"I need to go talk to Erin." I stood, teacup in hand, and took the last sip of my drink.

Ken followed my movement, turning to face me as he stood. "You still want to help her?"

"Of course. I may not like what she did, I may not like what this could mean, but I offered my help. Something is going on with her grandmother's ghost, that's real. She deserves the opportunity to tell me the truth. The whole truth."

He took my teacup from me and set it on the coffee table before pulling me in for a hug. "Do you want me to come with you?"

I shook my head. "I'll be okay. Besides, you have Ivy."

"She's playing with a friend."

"For how long? Until the streetlights come on?"

He nodded. "That's the rule."

"And I can't guarantee you'll be home in time. The days are already growing shorter." I lifted onto my toes and gently kissed his lips. "Thank you for offering. I'll talk to you later."

CHAPTER 13

I called Bryan on the walk back to my house, asking him to get Erin. He didn't hesitate and said they'd be right over, one way or the other. Within fifteen minutes of me getting home, Bryan and Erin were knocking on my door.

"Come in, come in," I said as Saffy scrambled to get a closer view of the people she'd stared at through the window.

Bryan held the door so Erin could walk in first. "Thanks, Joanie."

"Well, thank you for coming so quickly."

Erin wiggled her fingers as Saffy sniffed her fingers. "What's this all about? Bryan didn't say much, just texted me to meet him along with your address."

I held my hand toward the couch. "Why don't we all sit down and we can talk."

They both nodded, and as Bryan tried to let Saffy sniff her, saying "Hello, kitty," her tail poofed. She didn't hiss or growl, but she took off toward her cat tree and climbed up to the highest perch.

Weird. She'd met him once before back when I had everyone over after the bakery had been wrongly shut down by the health inspector. She hadn't acted this way then, although I didn't remember him acknowledging her. She had stayed near Lily, Ken, or me, but Lily had been her favorite, likely because Lily could turn her arms and legs into trees so Saffy could sharpen her claws. But this wasn't how Saffy usually greeted guests, not even Ivy, who was still a little overbearing sometimes with how much affection she wanted to give my cat. Saffy would either run out of reach but stay in the room or run upstairs into my bedroom. But poofing up? Never. Outside of being startled, I'd never seen such a floofy tail on the calico. She never gave Erin a second glance after Bryan said hello.

"Would either of you like some tea?" I offered, already on my way toward the kitchen.

"Oh, yes please," Erin said at the same time Bryan shook his head.

I stopped at Saffy's cat tree. She nudged my hand, seemingly calming down, but she wouldn't stop looking at my two visitors on the couch. "What's got your attention, Saf? It's just Bryan, you know him, and that's his friend, Erin. They need my help like how Lily needed my help. You remember Lily."

She looked at me then and slow blinked.

"That's a good girl." I scratched behind her ears before stepping into the kitchen. The kettle was already full of water, so I turned the knob for the burner underneath it and then prepared two cups for tea.

As the water boiled, I asked Erin how she liked her tea before putting it all onto a tray. Milk and sugar for her, honey for me.

Once the water was hot, I poured it into both cups, then brought everything out into the living room. The tea could steep out here while we chatted.

Saffy was no longer poofy, and although she'd put her

head down, she was still intently staring at the couch. "Silly kitty," I told her as I passed by.

I set the tea tray onto the coffee table, then nodded to Erin. "Green cup is yours."

"Thank you." She immediately added a spoonful of sugar and a splash of milk. Swirling it all together, she asked, "So what's going on?"

"I learned something tonight that I wanted you to confirm as it could have a major bearing on everything."

She perked up at that, a hopeful look in her eye.

"No, I haven't found your grandmother yet," I said with a shake of my head, "and I'll continue trying, but I have to know why you're keeping things from me?"

Bryan looked at her, head tilted in question as her eyes went wide. She sat straight on the couch. "Keeping things from you?"

"I heard you were made fun of as a kid for claiming to see things—people—who weren't there." She deflated at this. "Why didn't you tell me you could see ghosts aside from your grandmother when I asked?"

"You didn't tell her?" Bryan asked. I hadn't noticed until then that he'd been holding her hand as they sat on the couch.

She pulled her hand out of his and ran both of hers through her wavy nearly black hair. "I didn't think it mattered. It's been years since I could. My problem is with Nonni. She's the one who's gone. She's the one I want to talk to." Erin lowered her hands, letting them fall to her lap with a small thwack on her thighs.

Bryan gently picked up the hand he had been holding and took it in both of his. "But if that knowledge could help her help you, why not tell her? I told you she was safe. That you could trust her."

She sighed, the sound coming out as one of disappointment and defeat. "I know." She looked at me. "I'm sorry. I didn't think it mattered. It was a long time ago, and I can't really do it anymore."

I gave her an understanding smile. "It all matters, but I get it. I don't go around telling everyone about what I can do, that's for sure. It's only recently that I've told anyone outside of my mom and gram." I explained to them how telling my childhood best friend about my abilities had ended the friendship and caused me to lose the friends she kept after our breakup.

"At least you didn't get made fun of for weeks on end. It only stopped after school ended for the year. Everyone thought it was *so* funny." She looked up at Bryan with big doe eyes, a soft smile on her face as she used her free hand to press his cheek. "Except for this one here. He's always stuck by me."

It was a small movement, but I caught how Bryan leaned into her hand for a split second. The gesture nearly broke me, seeing how he reacted to the show of affection. Added to the butterflies in my stomach, I wanted to ask her how she couldn't see how the perfect man for her was right there, sitting by her side, the one who would continue to stick by her even as she married another. If it got that far once I found her grandmother.

Instead, I asked, "Does Travis remember that this happened?"

"I assume so, but he's never brought it up." She was quiet a moment. "I don't remember him making fun of me, though given the situation, it probably wasn't funny to him either. If only I'd known at the time."

I nodded, torn between mentioning what Ken had heard and keeping it to myself. Even if Travis didn't know, didn't remember, or didn't care, it seemed his friends did. But that knowledge wouldn't help Erin at all, so decided to stay quiet about it. "And there's nothing else that you should be telling me? Anything could help me."

Avoiding my gaze, she shook her head. "No. There's nothing else I could tell you. I just need to talk to my grandmother. Please say you'll still help me." She sounded so sad.

I smiled at her, not that she had looked at me again yet. "Of course I'll still help."

Her shoulders relaxed at my confirmation. Bryan pulled her toward him, wrapping his strong arm around her back. She melted against his side, and the butterflies fluttered up a storm inside me. Had I known them as kids, I imagined I would have been able to feel the matchmaking tingle even then. That's how solid it felt.

Erin closed her eyes, and Bryan leaned his head against hers before giving her a small squeeze. "Thank you," he mouthed to me.

I nodded.

"Erin, do you have anything that belongs to your grandmother that I could borrow? Sometimes that helps. I've been able to feel spirits who are connected to objects before."

She finally looked at me. "I don't have anything on me, but I can bring something by tomorrow. Would that be okay?"

"Absolutely."

After another few minutes, Bryan and Erin left. Saffy beelined for the couch as soon as I had closed the door behind them. She sniffed all over the couch, especially where Bryan had been sitting. I expected her to settle down once she was done, reclaiming the spot to leave her scent and fur all over it once more, but instead she pawed at the blanket Bryan had sat on, pulling the portion of it that had been on the back of the couch onto the cushion. Not done there, she continued to wrestle with it until the blanket landed in a heap on the floor. She glared at me as I attempted to put a perfectly good blanket back on the couch.

"Okay, okay," I said, bringing the blanket up to my nose. It smelled fine to me, but maybe he had gotten a dog or something and Saffy was picking up on it. "I'll wash it."

As she settled on the de-blanketed couch in her usual spot, I brought the blanket over to the little door in my wall. I opened it, then pushed the blanket into the space, dropping it down the laundry chute. By the time I'd closed the small door and walked to my closet for a spare blanket, Saffy had fallen asleep.

"Silly kitty," I told her not for the first time this evening as I joined her on the couch with my tea.

I wasn't sure if I could get Erin's grandmother back, and that worried me. Hopefully getting something that belonged to her would allow me to concentrate my efforts. But even if I failed at helping with the ghost, I needed to help my latest match.

CHAPTER 14

Something was bugging me. The thought wiggled its way into my brain as I had that first cup of tea after Erin and Bryan left, then stayed there through the second, lingering until I fell asleep. And it was still there the next morning when I awoke.

I tried to figure out what it was as I walked down to the bakery that morning, but unfortunately nothing came to me.

The morning started as normally as Mondays did. They were always a little busy as people came by for Monday muffins, the breakfast treat guaranteed to give you an extra pep in your step . . . at least when I helped make them. We'd learned that for sure a couple weeks back. The magic-less muffins on the one Monday I'd ever taken off had been the talk of the town, sending new rumors about me being a witch throughout Heartwood Hollow. I'd learned to live with the rumors. If anything, they brought in business as people had to see if these claims were true for themselves. And since the magic-free Monday, a few had come in asking for two muffins just in case I had changed the recipe and reduced "whatever I added to them" that made them so good.

Brittni arrived with Sam, a black poster board in hand. "I brought in the sign you asked me to make," she said, an excited smile on her face. "Want to see?"

"Of course, I do!" She walked over and gave me a peek. "This is great. Really. Let's wait until Sarah gets here, and then we can do a big reveal with everyone."

A few hours later, I waved Brittni into the front, and everyone followed to see what she'd created.

She unrolled the poster board, laying it out on the table. "Ta-da!"

"This is gorgeous! So much better than I could do." At the top of the poster was the logo for Suncraft Bakery, a sun rising over a muffin, a spin on what I now knew was the symbol for the Suncraft Coven. But she'd added a floral border to the rest of the top and trailed it down the sides, incorporating more baked goods and even a few symbols that pertained to witchcraft hidden among the vines and leaves. This would certainly add a bit more credibility to the rumors in town, but it was time for me to embrace them even more than I already had. Just wait until they saw my ideas for decorating come Halloween in a couple months.

"Thank you so much!" She beamed. "I went with a black one so that when you wrote on the window, the words would really stick out."

Gina nodded once slowly, realization dawning on her. "Oh . . . I was wondering why you wanted a paper sign and not a chalkboard one. You're not writing on it."

"Exactly. Be right back." I hurried into the kitchen to grab a window paint marker from the closet, then rushed outside. On the window in front of the poster board, I wrote: *You asked and now we're doing it. Coming next week. Mini-muffins! First flavor: Peach!* In smaller letters, I added: *Available Thursday through Sunday.*

I turned around to find my team behind me. "In all honesty"—I put the cap back on the marker—"it will probably be something we do every day once school gets rolling, but this is a good start. There will be a new flavor each week."

"It will be great!" Sam said enthusiastically before adding in a less excited tone, "Too bad I won't be here to see it take off."

Brittni patted his back. "But you will get to see it every time you come home."

"I know," he said with a sigh. It was clear his nerves about leaving for culinary school had kicked in. I knew how that felt. We'd all miss him here, but he was going to do great things at school. But first, we were going to send him off in Suncraft Bakery style. He just didn't know it yet.

I put my hand on his shoulder. "Brittni's right. And we'll be just a phone call away."

"We can always wake you up real early so you can chat with us in the mornings. We'll put you on a video call or something," Brittni offered.

That seemed to cheer him up. He had no idea yet that his studies would often involve him getting up just as early as he usually did to start classes. They weren't all like that, but the morning ones were. I had several friends during college who would take a nap between their first and second lab classes of the day if they didn't have regular classes scheduled during that time.

After we admired the sign for a moment longer, I clapped my hands once. "All right, everyone, back inside. We still have work to do." As everyone started to file into the shop, I pulled Brittni aside. "I definitely think you have some under-utilized art skills. I'm going to put you on a special cake-decorating project later this week, okay?"

She nodded, a beaming smile across her face. She and Lily could tackle Sam's cake together. It wasn't like I could have him decorate it.

One more detail figured out for the surprise party on Friday. Only a few left to go.

CHAPTER 15

Close to lunchtime, the door to the shop opened, and I had to chuckle. Once again Erin was coming in as Bryan was in the shop, this time helping Sarah and me load the second round of baked goods into the cases. Their match kept bringing them together.

"I've brought something that belonged to my nonni," she said in lieu of a greeting, "but can I just say how excited I am that you're going to start selling mini-muffins? And once I don't have to fit into my wedding dress, I'll be able to eat them."

So much for Travis getting through to her about his not worrying over how she looked.

"Rin, you can afford to eat a mini-muffin of two. You told me she said they didn't have calories, remember?"

She raised an eyebrow at him. "Joanie may be able to see ghosts, and she may be a witch, but there is no magic that will prevent such delicious baked goods from having calories." Erin smiled at me apologetically. "Sorry. I do appreciate you telling my friends that so I could try them."

I held up my hands. "No apologies needed. It's not like I've had them tested to affirm those claims."

"Yet," Sarah added from behind the case next to Bryan and me. "It might be something worth investigating at some point."

Probably not a bad idea. I had once seen a calorie-calculating machine on a trip for school when we went to a food science lab. Now they made much smaller versions, even some for the at-home user. I didn't want to know how many calories I consumed on a regular basis working here, but I was sure I knew someone who had one that I could use for the sake of science . . . and magic.

Erin pulled something out of her front pocket on her pants. "Anyway, here. I wanted to give you this." She dropped the tiny object into my hand. A single earring. "I had the stone from the other one made into a necklace to wear for the wedding. My something blue. I'd have worn them as earrings, but they're clip-ons, and well, you see it, don't you?"

It was a little gaudy. Definitely square in costume jewelry territory. More something I'd expect Ivy to play dress-up in than for anyone to wear out and about. The luster of some sort of brassy metal possibly once coated with gold leaf had dulled, and tiny clear crystals surrounded a larger blue stone that had lost some of its shine. I wasn't adept at identifying crystals by their energy fields alone—I bet Gram could—but the clear stones seemed like quartz of some kind, not diamonds, and the blue one I got no signature from at all. Holding it up to the light, I wondered if it was faceted glass.

I closed my hand around the earring. "I bet the piece you turned it into is beautiful."

She nodded. "It really is. Kinda ironic, though, that I'd use something of hers for the wedding."

"Why's that?" With how connected she and her grand-mother were, I didn't find it ironic at all.

"She never really liked Travis or his family."

Bryan let out a small snort, which he tried to cover by sliding the pastry case closed.

Ignoring him and maybe distracting her from realizing his reaction to her comment, I pressed Erin more on the issue. "Alive or as a ghost?"

She shrugged. "The family? Probably both, but she never met Travis before she died. She told me shortly before we got engaged."

Beside me, Bryan tensed. No doubt he had something to say over the matter. I'm sure I would have had I been in the same position. To me, that would have been a big red flag.

"Is that part of why you want to talk to her before the wedding? To see if she still feels the same way?"

She glanced toward her feet as she toed the floor. "Part of it."

This time, I placed my hand on Bryan's shoulder, hoping he'd get the message that he shouldn't say anything. It wouldn't help right now. He was too tense.

"And the other?"

"I want to know that she's proud of me. Of who I've become."

Bryan's shoulders sagged, and this time I gave him a small pat. He took the hint and stood. "Of course she'd be proud of who you are now." He walked over to her and put a hand on each of her shoulders, stooping slightly so he was eye level with her. "Look at all you've accomplished. You graduated in the top ten of our class and put yourself through college. Now you're back here and successful."

She looked up at him finally, a small smile on his face. "Thanks. I needed that."

That reminded me of how much I still didn't know Erin. "What do you do?"

"I'm a physical therapist over at the nursing home. I love old people. They're cute, and I think they remind me of my grandmother. She'd fallen down the stairs when I was a kid, and I used to help her with her exercises. That's what got me into it."

"That's wonderful. I may not have met her yet, but there's no doubt in my mind about her being proud of you." I held up the earring. "And hopefully this will help me get a hold of her. Thank you."

"Thank *you*." She glanced at the clock on the wall. "Now I should get going. I still have to grab lunch before my next appointment."

"Care for some company?" Bryan asked, turning to me. "If that's okay."

"Absolutely," I replied.

Before I could say more, Erin said, "You're buying this time." She looked past him to me. "Thanks again, Joanie. I'd be lost in all this without you."

I waved goodbye to the two of them as they headed out the door. Once they were gone, I opened my hand to look at the earring in my hand once more.

"What are you thinking?" Sarah asked, closing the case she had been restocking during Erin's visit.

"I don't know how I'm going to do this," I confessed, shifting my worried gaze to her. "There's no energy signature in this earring. At all."

"Well, it's not haunted like the other objects you've helped with have been." She walked over to take a closer look at the piece of jewelry.

I shook my head. "I've always been able to feel some sort

of residual energy if it was something someone who has passed owned."

Sarah made the motion of putting something in a folder and then closing a cabinet. "Filing that piece of information away for later."

"Sorry. Should have told you." Compared to everything else I could do, this was so normal to me that I forgot it wasn't to others.

She waved off the comment. "Don't worry about it. So you don't feel anything with that?"

"I feel nothing. It's like it wasn't even hers." I looked at my shop manager turned witch's familiar. What could erase someone's energy so completely like this? And how was I going to use the earring to help me without that energy?

CHAPTER 16

"What else is on your mind," Sarah asked as she sipped on the coffee she'd brought back after lunch. "You seem distracted."

"I am." The earring combined with the nagging thought from earlier clouded my lunch break.

"Not worried about tomorrow's coven meeting are you?"

"You had to remind me, didn't you." I cracked a smile at her to let her know I was kidding. Despite everything else going on, I hadn't forgotten about meeting the members of the Moonshadow Coven tomorrow.

"Thought it could take your mind off things for a bit. Maybe you're thinking too hard about everything else and it's keeping you from seeing the answer."

She had a point. "What do you think I should bring? I always used to give Gram cookies to take when she met with the ladies."

"I'm a firm believer that the way to win anyone over is through their stomach." She eyed me. "Especially when you're literally a kitchen witch. Bet they'd be fascinated by your culinary magic. And if you're so worried, just make them like you by putting it into what you bake."

I put up my hand. "I will never use my magic to make someone feel any differently about a person than they already do. No love potions—or cookies—for me, thanks." That was the last thing I needed, to have my work as a matchmaker complicated by people running around under love spells.

"Got it. But you could add friendliness or open-mindedness into them, for sure. Or maybe make some for you over your nerves about meeting so many people at once. I know they're all interested to meet you."

My eyes widened. "What do you know? Did Vince say something?"

She averted her gaze up toward the ceiling over my head in an attempt to look innocent. "He may have mentioned something about their excitement over the possibility of a Sunevall joining their ranks, but we figured that anyway based on the invitation. Everyone knows your name."

"Yeah, but now it's confirmed. Oh gosh, maybe I really do need to make cookies."

Sarah put her hands on my shoulders. "Breathe. Shake it loose. It will be fine."

I nodded. "I'm making cookies. There are sun and moon cookie cutters around here somewhere."

"Don't stress yourself too much over it. I'm sure they'd even like your leftovers from the day-old stuff."

Leftovers . . . Left . . .

"Sarah, that's it!"

"What's it?"

"The thing that's been bugging me."

Her face brightened as did the lights in the room. "That's great! Spill."

"It has to do with Travis's mom."

"What about her?"

"Something Travis said doesn't quite add up."

"What did he say?"

"He said he *lost* his mom. But everyone else, including Alice, has used the word *left*."

"She wasn't around for his childhood. Maybe that's what he meant? More that he lost the chance at growing up with her around?"

I nodded. "Maybe . . . but people also say *lost* when someone has died. That's a lot more common. Surely Erin or Alice would have said so if she had."

"Then what happened to her?"

"I think there's more to this story than what I've been told."

Sarah picked up the phone and started to dial.

"What are you doing?"

She held out her finger in a one-minute gesture. "Hey . . . Yeah, I'm at the bakery . . . Got something I need your sleuthing skills on . . . Records on a Helen Ellison who last lived here in town about twenty years ago . . . Anything. Change of address. Name changes. DMV records. Unclaimed property . . . Everywhere. We're trying to track her down . . . Thank you. I'll see you tonight for dinner."

Sarah hung up the phone. "Jill's looking into it. She knows her way around all that sort of stuff thanks to her work."

"Good idea." I made a grabby hands motion and pointed to the phone. "I'll call Steph."

It only took half a ring before she picked up. "Joanie! What do I owe the pleasure?"

I laughed. "It's me who's going to owe you." I quickly explained the situation. "Sarah's got Jill helping with various vital records, but if anyone can dig up other sorts of info, it's you. Think you can help us?"

"That family knows how to bury a story as well as they know how to create them, but I will certainly give it my best shot." She clicked so loudly on the mouse the noise carried through the phone. "I'll call you when I have something."

"Thanks, Steph. Talk to you soon. Say hi to Alex." We hang up and I return the phone to its cradle on the back shelf before turning to Sarah. "If anyone's going to find something, it will be one of them."

CHAPTER 17

As if the day could get any stranger, just before closing, a young woman I'd never seen before walked into the bakery. She seemed to know who I was, though.

"Joanie, right?" she asked as she walked toward me despite Sarah standing a few feet away.

"Yes . . . and you are?"

"I'm a friend of Alice Ellison's. She sent me here with a favor."

My stomach twisted. "What type of favor? I only recently met Alice." I shot Sarah a questioning glance. Her eyes were wide, and her brows raised. She didn't seem worried about this favor, more like curious and maybe a bit excited. Her demeanor calmed my nerves somewhat.

The brunette crossed her arms. "She told me about what you can do."

So much for trusting Alice with my secret. How many people had she told?

I matched her stance. "And what does she think I can do?"

The young woman's gaze darted to Sarah. "I'd rather not

say in front of others."

"I trust Sarah with my life. There's nothing you can say that she doesn't know."

Sarah stood a bit straighter, the lights brightening once more. I'd never confessed that to her before, but it was the truth.

The woman shrugged. "She told me you can see and talk to ghosts. Is that true?"

"Does Alice usually say that sort of thing about people?" I was starting to sound like Sarah and her grandfather, Vince, when they wanted me to figure out the answer to things by myself.

"Well, considering she can do the same thing, it's not something she makes up about people." The young woman, probably a couple years older than Brittni and Sam but maybe not as old as Lily or the rest of my team, placed a hand on her chest. "I can't see them myself, but I talk to them through the aid of machines."

"Machines?"

"She's a paranormal investigator," Sarah explained.

The girl nodded proudly. "Sure am. I run investigations with Alice."

A wave of relief shot through me. "Sorry, I think we may have gotten off on the wrong foot." I held out my hand as I came around the counter. "You already know this, but I'm Joanie, owner of this bakery."

"Becca," she replied, taking my hand in hers. We shook as she said, "I live out in Knoll's Grove with Alice and our roommate, Cole. He's great at the historical research stuff that we sometimes have to do out on the road when we go to cases."

"Cases?"

"Yeah, our paranormal investigations."

"Gotcha. That is one part I'd be no good at."

"Well, Alice had to go out of town for a few days"—

It seemed like too much of a coincidence to me that Alice would leave right after finding out I was looking into the disappearance of Erin's grandmother's ghost. Alice's being gone just bumped her back onto my suspect list.

—"and she was hoping that if we got called on an emergency case nearby that you might be able to step in and help us investigate."

"Me? Investigate?"

"You know, like they do on the shows." Sarah turned to me. "Looks like we should make a plan of checking some out sooner rather than later. There's a pattern to them all, some historical research, a walk-through with the owners of the supposed haunted property, followed by the investigation. Even the hokey ones follow the same method."

"Hokey?" Becca repeated. At first I thought Sarah had insulted her, but she chuckled. "Some are pretty fake, but what makes our team unique is that many of us are special. Most people are like you or Alice, not that all of you can see ghosts, but there's some sort of supernatural skill there. One of our guys can even smell ghosts."

I glanced at Sarah. "Okay, now that I can't do."

Her shoulders lifted. "That's a new one to me as well."

Becca leaned against the counter. "So what do you say? Chances are nothing will happen, but it's nice to know that we have backup if it's needed." She looked at me with such eagerness that it made it hard to say no.

"One question. What are the chances that they are bad ghosts? I don't want to have to put myself in that situation." I didn't want someone unprepared to deal with them to be in that situation either, though. Like a scared homeowner. Could I face a bad ghost to help someone else? I believed I had my answer.

Becca shook her head. "In all honesty, most of our cases don't result in actual hauntings. It's usually stuff like high electromagnetic frequencies or something. It's rare to have real ghosts."

I sighed. "All right. But truly, only in an emergency. I do not want to make this a regular thing. You do this mostly at night, right?"

She nodded. "It's when things are most active and everything else the quietest."

"I like my sleep." Needed it was more accurate. How would I be able to investigate and then head to the bakery right after? That was more than a Monday muffin could fix.

That made her chuckle. "I think we all like our sleep. You should see us crash after an investigation."

Despite my uneasiness over the situation, both the ghost hunting and Alice being gone, I liked this girl. "Was that all?"

"From Alice, yes. But I'm on another mission. She eyed the case. Cookies."

Now it was my turn to laugh. "That I can help you with."

After we loaded up a box with nearly a half pound of cookies, Becca went on her way, one hand already pulling a cookie from the box by the time she turned onto the sidewalk.

"What do you make of that?" I asked Sarah as I started to consolidate the few remaining cookies onto one tray.

"It could be fun. I might want to tag along if you get called out on any investigations."

I shook my head. "Not that. I meant Alice going away. Now I can't talk to her."

Sarah *hmm*ed in agreement. "Why not call you herself to ask for this favor? Seems a bit convenient, don't you think?"

"Agreed." But was her sudden departure enough to land her back on my list of people who could have done something to Anita? I wasn't sure.

CHAPTER 18

Tuesday. Finally. A real day off. I woke up late. Six in the morning. Still too early for some, but not for me. On any other day, I'd already be making my muffin deliveries to Double Aitch and Olde Templeton.

The morning saw me on my couch with Saffy curled up at my feet as I drank tea and read a book. I had things to do later today, the least of which was not the coven meeting tonight during the full moon, but for now, I was calming my nerves over attending the esbat in the best way I knew how.

When the afternoon came, I grudgingly slipped out from under the blanket that Saffy refused to move from. The blanket was the spare from the closet still. The one she had thrown off the couch was in the dryer that had been done for a couple hours. Now that I didn't have to do all of the bakery's washing here at my house, I'd grown a little lax in my own. No one but me was here to mind if my blankets and towels didn't come upstairs still warm. Saffy groaned as I stood, causing me to chuckle. Okay, maybe Saffy cared that they weren't warm, but I didn't want her all over my clean laundry, anyway.

It didn't take long for Saffy to follow me once I headed into the kitchen. "Time for a treat before I head out, Saf." She stared at her dish before looking back up at me as if she had been expecting more. "Not today. I'll be back before dinner with plenty of time to feed you, but then I'll have to go out again. I have my coven meeting tonight."

She straightened, tilting her head just slightly.

"I know that I've been embracing all of this witchy stuff lately, but this makes it all the more real, you know? I'm Joanie the kitchen witch . . . and probably a whole lot more." I dug out two tuna catnip treats for her from the container in the cupboard where I kept them and then dropped them in her dish. "I'm not afraid to admit that I'm a bit nervous. So I'm going to make some cookies because they make everything better."

She seemed to nod once, connecting with my gaze for an instant before dropping her head again, this time to her dish and her treats. Once the treats were gone, she'd be hyper for a little while, then turn into a stretched-out kitty puddle either on the back of the couch or on her cat tree.

With her munching away, I finished getting ready, then left the house. My first stop: Leafs and Grounds to pick up lunch. On a normal Tuesday, I'd usually have called Courtney to meet me or stayed and chatted with Gary for a while, but I was on a mission. Lunch in hand, I walked to Founders Park, and instead of going to my usual bench, I deviated and plunked myself next to Arthur Miller and Bardi.

I dove into my bagged lunch and pulled out my panini. When alone, it was always good to look busy when talking to ghosts. People found it strange when they caught someone talking to thin air. Ken had suggested I get some sort of wireless earbuds to make it look like I was talking to someone through that, but then I wouldn't have been able to hear the ghosts as well. I'd just have to take my chances.

"Afternoon, Arthur. How are you doing, Bardi?"

Arthur turned to me inquisitively, while Bardi took one look at my lunch and pawed at my leg. To my knowledge, ghosts didn't and couldn't eat, so instead of breaking off a piece for him, I reached down and scratched between his ears for a moment before rubbing my leg just above his head for show, not that I could see anyone looking at me.

"Miss Joanie, a pleasure. Saw you talking with Alice Ellison the other day."

"She told me she can see you."

He nodded, removing his hat and placing it on his leg as he did. "Doesn't talk to me like you do."

"About that."

"You mean Alice?"

I shook my head. "Not exactly. So she can see you, and obviously I can see you. I've recently learned that there's someone near here who can smell ghosts."

He chuckled at this. "I didn't know we smelled. Do we, boy?" He looked down at his dog, who was still staring at my sandwich.

"Are there any people around here in Heartwood Hollow that could make you do something? Like against your will? Even so much as to force you to leave?"

He thought a moment. "I'm clearly still here, so I haven't run into anyone like that, thank goodness. And I don't get those, what do you kids call them nowadays, *vibes*, from anyone, but it could be that they are hiding their abilities or in some way not acknowledging our presence, much like a certain someone we know used to." He eyed me over his thick black-rimmed glasses. We'd discovered recently that before word about my abilities had spread among the ghosts in town, the majority of them hadn't known I'd been able to see them unless I'd reacted to them in some fashion.

"So what you're saying is you might not know someone could assert their will over you because they haven't tried." Much like how I never knew anyone in Heartwood Hollow was anything other than human until they told me or I saw it with my own eyes. I didn't know if I'd ever get used to watching someone walk out of a tree after they'd just been a part of that tree.

Arthur nodded. "That's exactly what I'm saying. I will reach out to some of the chattier ghosts and ask if they've heard anything. Someone like that could be dangerous. For all of us."

"Thank you. I appreciate that. And stay safe." I didn't want him to be forced to leave—or worse.

"Oh, I will." He placed his fedora back on his head, then stood. "You take care of yourself too, Miss Joanie. You've been getting involved in all sorts of things lately."

"And this isn't even the half of it," I said with a chuckle, but I wasn't about to elaborate on my preparations for my first coven meeting. "You have a good rest of your walk."

He nodded once more before giving Bardi's leash a gentle tug. "Come on. Let her eat her sandwich in peace." With a small whine, the dog turned away from my panini and followed his owner.

I reached into my lunch bag to fish out my chips, and by the time I'd opened the bag, unleashing the smell of salt and vinegar, Arthur and Bardi had disappeared.

CHAPTER 19

Inside the bakery's kitchen, I dug through my drawer of cookie cutters, looking for some that could elevate my standard sugar cookie to Moonshadow Coven standards, not that I knew what those were. But I knew I had suns and moons somewhere in this drawer. The sun had come out at the end of the school year as part of my "enjoy your summer" designs, and the moons I'd used last Halloween.

After a few minutes, I finally found them. Leaving all the others I'd pulled out on Bryan's workstation for him to organize tomorrow, I gave the sun, crescent moon, and standard round cookie cutters a quick wash before sitting them on my table. Then I pulled out everything I needed for a large batch of cookies—how many people were in this coven, anyway?—and got to work.

It was always so strange working by myself in the quiet of the bakery. I'd been back here plenty of times alone, but someone was always in the shop, and if they weren't, it was because it was the end of the day and I was busy cleaning, not baking. Being back here alone to make something by myself was a rarity. It had happened most recently when I got so excited about receiving Trudy's candy grimoire that I had to come try a recipe right away. Before that, it hadn't happened since my first Christmas when Libby asked me to bake for her holiday tea service.

Cookies had always been one of my favorite things to make. Something about rolling the dough flat was cathartic to me. After I'd mixed all of the ingredients by hand—no need to get one of the big mixers going for these—I got lost in the process of using the rolling pin to even out the dough to a quarter of an inch thick. The dough nearly covered my entire table, so much so there was no room for the baking tray. I had to put it on Lily's station.

When I couldn't cut any more cookies out of this dough flat, I worked it back into a ball, then rolled it out once more. I didn't want to overwork the dough and have too hard of a cookie, so after cutting out what I could, I made a few fiddle-fern cookies out of the scraps rather than roll the dough out once more.

By the end, I had two full trays. I popped both into the oven and then gathered ingredients for royal icing. I had just rotated the pans in the oven when there was a knock at the back door.

Who could it be? Why would anyone be knocking on the door when we were usually closed? No one could see inside the kitchen to know I was back here. Curious, and a little cautious, I approached the door, but it opened before I could reach it. In the split second before seeing who it was, I second-guessed my decision to leave the door unlocked. But when I saw Bryan's sheepish smile, I brought my hand to my chest and took a relieved breath.

"I didn't mean to scare you," he said, coming all the way into the bakery. "Guess I should have called first to say I was stopping by, but I know how you don't like the phone. I tried your house first, but you weren't there. Your car was still in your driveway, though, so I figured you couldn't be too far, and once I saw you weren't at Leafs as I passed by there, I figured I'd check here next."

"Why were you looking for me?"

He shoved his hands in his pockets. "I was wondering if you'd had any luck yet with Rin's nonni. Tell it to me straight. I can help you break the news to her if it's bad."

"She only brought me something to use yesterday."

"So you've gotten nothing from it yet?" He leaned against the wall as if deflating slightly.

I shook my head. "To tell you the truth, I feel nothing in it. Not even residual energy." I drew my lips to the side. "If she hadn't told me they were her grandmother's, I would think they weren't hers or that she'd fully crossed over, her energy completely dispersed, no possibility of contacting her. But Erin says it's not possible, so I'm giving her the benefit of a doubt. I'll try charging it tonight in the full moon."

"And if that doesn't work?"

"Then we'll figure something else out."

"Do you think someone could have done something to her?"

"It's possible. How well did you know her?"

"Anita was my neighbor when I was a kid, and she took my rambunctious family in stride. She even taught me to cook," he explained as I rushed to the stove to pull out the two trays of cookies. Phew, perfect. "That's how I first met Erin. I'd even sleep over Anita's house when Erin stayed over. Well, me and two of my sisters."

"I didn't know you had sisters."

"Oh, yeah, three actually." Bryan smiled. "Two brothers too."

"Wow. So were you friends with Erin first or were your sisters?"

"Three of us were a package deal. One is my twin sister, and the other is less than a year younger but was still in the same grade at school."

I had to stop myself from commenting again. He'd never really talked about his family in all the years he'd worked here. I guess I'd spent so much time emphasizing how we here at the bakery were a family that I hadn't learned enough about everyone's actual families. I was always willing to listen, and some were more willing to talk than others, but Bryan wasn't one of them. Sure, I knew his favorite mid-morning snack and what he thought about this summer's latest blockbuster, but nothing that was too below the surface. Now that he knew he was at the center of one of my matches and a pivotal player in my latest ghost mystery, it seemed he was opening up more.

"That's great. So you obviously knew her pretty well." When he nodded, I continued, asking, "Do you think she could have crossed over?"

He sputtered an exhale. "What? No. Anita would never miss Erin's wedding, even with her not liking Travis."

"Did she ever tell you why she didn't like him?"

He looked at me as if I'd said something silly. "Anita was already dead when they started going out, but it's not hard to guess. He'd shower her in gifts. Flaunt his money. Any time he'd get her something, Erin told me her nonni would comment that it was too lavish or not to Erin's taste, that the Erin she knew didn't even like whatever it was. I have to agree. He tried changing her from day one. I couldn't stand it. Still can't. My sisters called her out on it. She chose him over them."

"But she stuck with you."

He gave me a sad smile. "I should have spoken up too, but I saw what was happening with the rest. I hoped I would be the one she turned to when he tired of her. Guess that didn't happen. But I didn't want to lose her—couldn't lose her. Soon enough, I guess it will happen, anyway. Travis won't allow our friendship to continue."

"I'm still working on it. On everything. Don't give up hope."

"Thanks, Joanie." He surveyed the kitchen as if realizing for the first time that I was back here working. "Do you want any help with anything?"

I pointed to his workstation. "Made a mess of your table looking for cookie cutters. If you want to take care of that now, you won't have to do it in the morning. I have to finish making some royal icing to decorate the cookies that are in the oven, but that's all I'm doing."

"What are you making cookies for?"

"I have a coven meeting, and don't laugh, I'm nervous." I added a few tablespoons of meringue powder to the confectioner's sugar I had already measured out before Bryan got here.

"Covens . . . that's something witch related right?"

I nodded. "It's what you call a group of them. They're meeting tonight for the full moon. It will be my first time going."

"I didn't realize there were that many witches around."

With a laugh, I replied, "I didn't either. I'm so curious about them all."

"Trying to make a good impression by filling their stomachs?"

I dumped the warm water I had at my station into the bowl before turning to him, smiling. "Absolutely." Then I grabbed out my hand mixer from my drawer and beat the mixture for several minutes until stiff peaks formed in the icing.

When I turned off the mixer, Bryan, who'd waited nearly ten minutes to speak, asked, "You know they're going to love you, right?"

"I don't need them to love me. I just want them to like me."

"But everyone likes you."

I tapped the bottom of the bowl against the tabletop a few times to help the air rise. "I can think of one person who doesn't."

"Travis," he stated without hesitation.

"No, I was thinking about Bruce Malloy. Why would you say Travis?"

"Because of what happened the other day."

"Ah, I never filled you in on what happened next." As I iced the moon cookies with a solid coat of white, I explained to him how Travis had solved my problem with the beverage board the next day.

He pulled his lips to the side. "That's all well and good, but I don't trust him. He just as easily could have created your problem too."

I divided the remaining icing into two bowls. "You really think he would do that?"

"It would fit his style. He tries to win people over like that. This is just like the gifts. He bought Erin a laptop once."

"That's a nice gift," I said, adding yellow food coloring to the larger portion of icing.

"Yeah. Her other one broke." I heard him walk up behind me, and he put his hand on my shoulder, then turned me to face him. "Joanie, he broke her original computer first. She thinks it was an accident, that he spilled his coffee all over it, but I saw it. He doesn't know I did. He poured coffee over the edge of her computer and then onto the table, making it look like he knocked his cup over accidentally."

"How did she not see this but you did?"

"We were at Leafs. This was before the expansion, so there was only one bathroom. I was in it. She was waiting to use it. I saw it happen on my way back. He never saw me. I was pretending to straighten the collar on my shirt as I approached the counter to order another coffee. Pretty sure I was only allowed to hang out with them because Erin had convinced Travis I was into one of the baristas at the time. I wasn't, but if that's what kept me near Erin, then so be it."

I took a moment to process everything that he had just told me. "Wow."

"I know. It sounds a bit far-fetched, but I swear it's true."

"And you never told Erin this?"

He shook his head. "Travis bought her a new computer that night. He was her knight in shining armor. She never would have been able to afford another computer at the time. Even if I had told her, she wouldn't have believed me, and I was afraid of losing her as a friend, remember?" When I nodded, he continued, "Please be careful, and don't put too much faith in the guy. If anyone was going to do something to Anita's ghost, I'd put money on him."

"Do you know something about him that could help?"

"You mean if he's like you? Never seen anything. But he's the only one who'd have any desire to get rid of her."

"What about Alice?"

He raised an eyebrow at me. "His sister? Why would she even get involved?"

"To help her brother?"

"Doubt it. They never seemed that close. Just please. Be careful, okay?" After I said I would, he pointed to his work area. "I'm finished with the cookie cutters. Do you need my help with anything else?"

"Nah," I answered with a flick of my wrist. "Only have these few to flood yellow, then I'm going to pipe some designs on them all. I've got it."

"All right, I'm going to head out, then. I'm glad I caught you."

"Thanks for that information. I appreciate it."

He turned to head out the door but stopped and looked over his shoulder. "And, Joanie?"

Already working on making my suns yellow, I glanced up at him.

"Don't worry about tonight. You'll be fine." He smiled.

And with that, he left the bakery, leaving me with my cookies and a lot to think about.

CHAPTER 20

About two hours later, I had just finished boxing the cookies when I heard the door again, this time the front. With how the energy shifted, I knew it could only be one person.

Sarah poked her head into the kitchen moments later. "I figured you'd be here. You want to drive together?"

"That would be great, but we don't even know where we're going yet. Not even your grandfather would tell you."

"He said he would if he had to." She held up an index card with familiar gold lettering on it that seemed to glow even under the fluorescent lighting of the kitchen. "But now we have an address."

"Where did you get that?"

"Delivered to my house. You probably got one too, but seeing as you are here . . ."

I checked the back door to make sure it was locked. "Point taken," I said when I came back into the main part of the room and grabbed the cookies. "So where is this *covenstead*?"

"It's a short drive, but not too far. But we should head to your house first, maybe grab some dinner. We have time. You should check to make sure your card doesn't mention bringing anything." She turned back into the bakeshop, one box of cookies in hand.

I followed her with the other box, flicking off the kitchen lights before I left the room. "Do you have to bring anything?"

"A white candle. My guess is it's part of their ritual tonight after the *esbat*."

"Esbat?"

"That's what you call a coven meeting. Then there are the *sabbats*, which are the meetings for rituals. Based on your invitation, this is both. One right after the other." She held the front door open for me. "So how many cookies did you make?"

I crossed the bakery, answering, "Batch and a half. Plus some extras. Think it will be enough?" I stepped through the doorway.

Once I had cleared the landing, Sarah locked the door. "Considering they weren't expecting you to make any cookies, I'm sure whatever you bring will be more than enough." She pointed to her car. "There's plenty of room in the trunk."

Royal icing was a time-consuming process requiring a couple hours to fully set, but the results were worth it. I'd used the time to clean up my area and put away the cookie cutters Bryan had organized. So as I loaded my cookies, I had no worries about them shifting during the drive and smudging or transferring their designs to the undersides of other cookies.

It was a quick drive back to my house. As Sarah had suspected, there was an invitation waiting for me at my door, tucked into the corner of the screen.

Leaving the cookies in the car, we walked up to my house, and I grabbed the envelope. Once in the living room, I lifted the wax seal of the Moonshadow Coven and released the flap. Inside the envelope was a card like Sarah's.

Sarah made herself comfortable, and Saffy jumped down from her top perch to come say hello and get some attention from her. I plopped down next to them and read the card.

It gave me the same address I had seen on hers and told me to bring a white candle as well, but at the bottom was a separate note. *We thank you in advance for the cookies.*

"How did they know?" I whispered.

Sarah eyed me as she scratched Saffy's neck. "How did they know what?"

I flipped the card toward her. "They know about the cookies."

"Well, as to the cookies, it wouldn't surprise me if there's someone in the coven who is psychic and can predict the future. Or they just know you."

She had a point. "So what do you want for dinner?"

We settled on tuna melts using a rye bread I had picked up from Zeke's the other day. It was one I could have made, and would have made a few months ago to avoid going to The Corner Bakery, but now that Zeke and I were on good terms, I liked checking in on the occasionally curmudgeonly baker. He was truly an okay guy who didn't handle stress or the lack of sleep well.

The cheese had come from Cheese Louise on Main Street. Although she was mainly a restaurant with many cheese specialties, she did have a case of cheeses for sale. This Havarti dill was one of my favorites, and she always called to let me know when she had more in stock.

"You nervous?" Sarah asked as we cleared our dinner plates from the table.

"I was, but I think the baking today helped. It would be nice to be a part of a coven that's so close by, but if I don't fit in, there are others. Even if I have to go home for, what did you call them? Sabbats?"

Sarah nodded, handing me her dish for me to put in the sink. "You can even find virtual coven meetings nowadays and be with people from all over."

"How does that work?"

As I washed the dishes, she explained the process of sitting in front of a computer screen with a camera to watch and sometimes partake in ceremonies. "Sometimes the cameras are focused on people's individual altar spaces where a ritual will take place, but it's not always possible."

Scrubbing the pan I'd made our sandwiches in, I glanced over my shoulder at her, guilty that I hadn't thought about her possibly wanting an altar space or to be part of a coven. "Do you want an altar?"

"I've thought about it." She shrugged slightly. "But let's see how tonight goes first. I'm your familiar, but it doesn't mean I have to do everything you do if it doesn't fit me. But I have been enjoying the virtual meetings I've been going to. Grandpa Vince wasn't against any of us practicing, especially as I got older, but he's always wanted us to follow our witch's lead, and that meant not establishing too tight of ties to the local coven before our calling in case that wasn't wanted by our witch. Like if you wanted to go home to join your gram's coven instead. That's what I would do."

I put the pan in the dish rack, then grabbed a glass jar I had set out earlier. I filled it up, then turned to her as I capped it. "But you were called later than the others. Surely he would have relaxed things beyond a certain age."

She laughed but then rolled her eyes. "I'm now the example. If anything, he's doubled down on these sorts of things because one can never know when our witch might find us. He's encouraging both of my cousins to travel more. They're older like me, and I think he's hoping they'll find someone along their journeys from place to place."

"That sounds fun."

"Oh, it is," she confirmed as we walked into the living room, the jar of water firmly in my hands. "Grandpa sends my younger relatives on all sorts of trips. He used to send me until he thought I was too old. Then you came along. Now he's offering to pay for my older cousins again. Kinda jealous about that."

"Is that your way of saying you want a vacation?"

She laughed again. "A vacation might do *you* some good, and these are places that would benefit you too. Places like Stonehenge and others along ley lines. Fascinating places. Even Danvers, Massachusetts, where the famed Salem witch trials were held."

"And he just finances these trips for fun?"

"Well, he has us study them, determine for ourselves what sort of powers they might have. Really, he's hoping that our witches may be drawn to these places with they themselves being magical."

"I went to Salem as a kid for a class trip once, but sorry I never went to other magical places. Could never afford it." Well, I could have had I not wanted to start up a bakery. I was sure the small trust fund my grandfather had left would have made for one amazing vacation had I wanted it. There had never been any strings attached to it. But it went toward the house and the bakery instead.

She held up a hand. "It's okay. You found me eventually. Here. In this magical place. Rescued me from a life as a bank teller. Not bad for some—Rachael loves it—but it wasn't for me."

"You'd make a good travel buddy."

She gave me a cheesy grin. "You know it. I bet the snack game would be better with you, though."

"Speaking of snacks, how about we head out to the coven-stead and maybe get these witches their cookies as a pre-meeting snack?"

She answered me with a firm nod.

I grabbed my bag. "See you, Saffy," I called. Too busy eating her dinner in the kitchen, she didn't answer me. She was probably already licking every last drop of the tuna water I had left her. It was an extra special treat.

Sarah pushed the screen door open and stepped out onto the porch. "With the way you talk to her, no wonder your gram thought Saffy was your familiar."

"She had other reasons, but I can't blame her," I said as I followed Sarah outside. "Saffy is pretty expressive."

Sarah closed my front door as I placed the jar of water on the small table by my porch swing. Here it would sit overnight in the moonlight to charge. At the last second, I reached into my purse and pulled out the earring Erin had given me. I placed it next to the water. If I was wrong, and the central stone wasn't plastic, the full moon would hopefully charge it the way it had my crystals last month.

"Good idea," Sarah said, as she came up beside me. "Ready?"

As I ever would be. "Let's go."

CHAPTER 21

We turned down a dirt road just past the town line and drove between a hayfield and a cow pasture, heading closer to the woods and the river. As we curved around a gentle hill, we came to an old barn. Several cars were parked outside. They ranged in make, model, age, and condition, giving me no clues as to anything about the makeup of the witches aside from anyone and potentially everyone.

"This must be the place," Sarah said.

"Don't know what else it would be," I quipped, taking in the unassuming barn as I stepped out of the car.

As we started to walk toward the barn, I recognized one car from the library parking lot. "That's Emily's." I pointed at the blue coupe, a wave of relief flowing through me because I already knew one of the people inside. "I wonder if Brittni will be here."

"Brittni from the bakery?"

I explained how I'd seen her wearing a necklace like mine. "Emily got it for her."

"I wonder what her mom thinks about that."

"Who is her mom?" I asked at the same time someone shouted at me from a car pulling into a spot between two others.

"You're here! Finally!"

I turned toward the familiar voice. "George?"

My elderly neighbor whose backyard mine butted up against waved at me from the window of his son's passenger seat.

I turned to Sarah. "Did you know?"

She smiled. "Of course, I knew. He's been friends with my grandpa for years."

George stepped out of the car and waited as Nathan got out from the driver's side. The two approached me, and George's eyes grew wide as he spotted the boxes in my hands.

He elbowed Nathan. "She brought treats. I told you she'd bring treats." To me, he asked, "What did you bring?"

"Yes, Dad, you were right," Nathan said, looking up at the sky. His father's sweet tooth knew no bounds.

George rubbed his hands together, still eyeing the boxes.

Realizing I hadn't answered him, I said, "Cookies. But you have to wait until we get inside and you can show me where to put them. That way you'll get the first one."

"Better make it the first two." He winked at me.

Nathan let out a little groan. "Dad . . ."

"Okay, fine. One. But if there are any left after the esbat, they're mine."

I giggled. "He drives a hard bargain, huh, Nathan?"

"Like you wouldn't believe."

George struck up a conversation with Sarah as she took him by the arm toward the barn.

"Can I hold the cookies for you?" Nathan offered, holding out his hands.

Feeling he was asking to be nice just as much as to have

something to do with his hands, I passed him the boxes. "You never told me you were witches."

"I never really could before. It's not something we tell just anyone. Besides, before a few months ago, would you have believed me if I had?"

He had a point, and I shook my head. "So are you magical, too, or normal witches?" As soon as the words were out, I clapped my hands over my mouth. How could I just blurt that out?

"You have got to work on your delivery," Nathan said with a chuckle. "All witches are magical. But in the way you're thinking, yes, we have magic. Well, Dad more so before. Still has some powers, but it's never been the same since the accident."

"Accident?"

"He wasn't always like this."

"So his . . . behavior isn't because of a medical condition?"

"It masks as one, but no. He is the way he is because something went wrong with a spell. I don't know what. He either won't or can't tell me what he did. I wasn't here at the time, but it's why I moved back. Got to keep him safe, especially when he tries to do magic."

"Will he be okay?"

"Here? Sure. Everyone watches out for him. But it wasn't safe for him at home alone."

I placed my hand on his arm. "It was really good of you to come home. Even more now that I know."

He stopped and smiled at me. "Thanks. I've wanted to tell you. But like I said, you wouldn't have believed me. I had hoped . . . Nah."

George and Sarah had continued walking and were now several feet ahead of us. But still, I lowered my voice, when I asked, "Hoped what?"

He sighed. "Had hoped that once you knew the truth, I'd stand a chance with you. But that was before Ken, and I can see how great you are together. Does he know?"

"About all of this? Of everything? Yeah."

"Good." He nodded. "Good. That's the way it should be. You shouldn't have to hide anything of what you are with anyone you love."

I let that sink in a moment. It was what Ken had said, too, about Erin not being able to be her true self around Travis, reminding me of a big reason as to why the two didn't belong together and she and Bryan did. "I don't," I finally answered. "Not anymore."

With that, he nodded, and we resumed walking toward the barn in companionable silence.

CHAPTER 22

The barn was old. It surprised me by having electricity. Lights dotted the beams in the ceiling, the cords visible overhead. Hay still poked out from the loft, and I wondered if it was still used as a working barn of some sort when it wasn't being occupied by witches. Farming equipment—an old tractor and some manual tools—stood at the ready in the back corner. In the main front room, wooden benches were set up in rows punctuated by the occasional tree stump for additional seating. Off to the side was a table, and Nathan beelined for it. He set my cookies down and pointed to several thermoses already there.

"The metal ones are hot coffee and hot water. There's tea in that basket over there, probably some hot chocolate packets too. These thermoses have milk, juice, and I'm sure the lemonade will be here soon."

"So I'm not out of place with my cookies? Phew."

"Not at all. We're witches, not robots. We still eat." He chuckled. "A lot."

I eyed the rest of the table where there was pasta salad, a leafy green salad with some of the freshest looking tomatoes

I'd ever seen cut in half in a bowl on the side, and some rolls set out next to deli meat.

"Why did I make dinner first?"

"Rookie mistake. Sarah wouldn't have known to tell you either."

"So what type of witch are you?" I asked him as I opened the boxes of cookies.

"Tech witch. It's a lot of fun. Computer-related stuff is my specialty. I can do it anywhere there's a good Wi-Fi or satellite connection. That's what made it so easy to come home."

"He's lucky to have you."

"I'm lucky to have him too."

At that moment, George and Sarah came up behind us. George clapped his son on the back. "Excuse me. One of those is mine."

Nathan moved over to allow his father access to the box of cookies. "One, Dad. One."

We were soon joined by Emily. The usually reserved librarian gave me a hug. "It's so good to see you here." She touched the pendant hanging at her neck. "Welcome to the Moonshadow coven."

I turned to her. "Thank you. I'm happy to see another friendly face."

She took my hand. "Come on, let me introduce you to a few people who are already here."

I grabbed Sarah's hand and pulled her with me.

Emily took us around to several people, introducing us to more and more as others continued to arrive. Many had been my customers since the day I'd opened and were excited by the cookies I'd brought. Some were from Knoll's Grove and even as far away as Snowhaven and Astoria, including someone I recognized.

I smiled at the librarian who had helped Rich, Ashley, and

me that day we showed up to do research on the Astoria Fair and stumbled on a key piece of evidence. "It's good to see you again, Gloria."

"You as well. I'm sure Wayne would be happy to hear that I ran into you. Everything going well with what you'd come in for?"

"Absolutely. Thank you." In reality, it couldn't have gone better. Rich and Ashley were happily living together now.

She smiled. "I'll let him know. Do stop in again if you're ever in the area."

I nodded, and Emily pulled me away to meet someone else.

As the space got fuller, I began to worry that my cookies wouldn't be enough, but when I glanced at the food table across the barn, I saw the offerings had multiplied. "Next time, no dinner," I told Sarah.

Emily laughed. "Oh, you'll never go hungry at one of these."

"So is Brittni coming?" I asked. "She told me you got her a pendant."

Emily shook her head. "Doubt she'd be able to get away for one, but I've given her a website where she can find a virtual coven if she so desires."

"I wonder if it's the same one I've been participating in," Sarah said.

We continued walking around, and as we drew near the food table again, I recognized another face from town placing three pizza boxes at the last empty spot. "Larry?"

He turned. "Hello, Joanie. Sarah," he said with a nod in her direction.

"I didn't realize . . ."

He smiled. "We come from all walks of life. There's no

bright beacon over our heads that says *witch*. Although I'm sure that would make some things easy."

Elizabeth, one of my shop regulars, stopped next to him. "Well, if you're an aura reader like I am, there kind of is."

He smiled. "Yeah, guess you do sort of have that, don't you." He turned to me. "This is my sister, Elizabeth."

I hadn't known they were related. "It's good to see you again. How is your job going?" A few months ago, she'd come bursting into my shop to tell me she'd gotten the position at the senior center.

"I love it there." She held up one of the moon cookies. "These are awesome. Very appropriate for the evening."

"Thanks."

Elizabeth grabbed Larry's arm. "Come on. Let's grab a seat." She dragged him away, leaving Sarah, Emily, and me alone.

I turned to Emily. "So is there a high priestess for this coven?"

"Of course there is." She glanced at her watch. "Should be here any minute now. She's very punctual."

A figure appeared in the doorway.

"Ah, there she is now."

CHAPTER 23

A hush fell over the space, one of those magical moments where everyone in the middle of their own conversations drew a breath or paused, creating a silence. In school, we would then laugh about it happening, finding it funny that there was any silence in a group of kids even when we were supposed to be silent. But in this moment, it felt weighty and significant, and we turned toward the door. But the timing was perfect, and as the high priestess stood at the entrance to the barn, I wondered if she had some magic that had created the moment.

Although she was dressed in a flowy mustard-yellow robe with a simple silver circlet around her head and a Triple Goddess Moon pendant around her neck, this wasn't how she looked on an average day. I recognized Clara, who lived down my street, instantly. I didn't know her well, but we'd always been friendly, and everyone knew her for her colorful outfits. She loved the holidays especially, when her dressing for the occasion extended toward her house and yard as well. She even decorated a statue of a dog in her front yard, a tradition started by her husband.

Stay, the dog statue, had been stolen a few years back just before Christmas. Fortunately he had been found and returned. After that, Clara cemented him in place. He wasn't going anywhere. Living down the street, I'd come to enjoy the dog's various costumes and how the kids in the neighborhood had their pictures taken with him.

I never would have thought that Clara would be the high priestess of a local coven. Larry's words came back to me about how witches hid in plain sight, and I felt thoroughly put back in my place. He was right. They—we—were like anyone else in Heartwood Hollow.

The silence continued as Clara made her way to the front of the room.

Emily pulled on my arm and showed me to a seat at the side of the room. "You and Sarah can stay here until you've decided if you want to join the coven. You'll be able to take part in our discussions as well as any full moon rituals and weigh in on things because we listen to all voices, but you won't be able to vote on anything right now," she whispered. "Although, I don't think we're voting on anything tonight. I'll come find you after." She smiled at us, then found a seat closer to the middle of the room.

Sarah put her hand on top of mine and gave me an excited smile. "Are you ready?" she whispered.

"I thought your grandfather was coming."

She glanced around the room. "He's supposed to be here." She shrugged, then turned her head back to the front as Clara cleared her throat.

Clara raised both of her hands. "Well, it looks like we are just about all here. I'd like to take a moment and thank our guests for coming, Joanie Sunevall and Sarah Stohl." She made no fanfare out of it, no indication of the mystery that had surrounded my invitation to tonight's gathering. Perhaps it was like the PSG where they didn't tell others what they could do outside of those who were in the same circle.

"We do thank you for the cookies," she continued. "As you can see, we like to eat, and they are a wonderful addition to our Sturgeon Moon table."

"That they are," another voice whispered through a bite of food as the owner of that voice sat next to me. A second person crossed in front of me and sat on the other side of Sarah. She turned to the individual, and out of the corner of my eye, I could see her hugging her grandfather. But who was next to me?

I turned. "Matt?"

He smiled knowingly at me. "Weren't expecting me, were you?"

I shook my head. "I wasn't sure who to expect."

He patted my leg. "We'll talk more later." Then he focused his attention on Clara.

I looked at the room once more. Trudy, Sam's grandmother sat in the back of the room as did several other Heartwood Hollow elders. I thought back to how Vince had told me that there were paranormal beings at the town's nursing home who needed a place to meet because not all of their caretakers knew what they were or would understand if told. I imagined the nursing home residents here now were much like that, witches who Vince helped take to the coven meeting. With this being a spiritual way of life or religion for some, the nursing home had to let them come, the same way they allowed everyone else to attend their respective services in other locales throughout town.

"Good. Now we're all here. I'm so happy to see all of your faces again so soon after *Lughnasadh*," Clara said, smiling. "The Sturgeon moon is the last before the Harvest moon next month and *Mabon*, the autumn equinox, soon after that. We are already underway with our preparations, and I hope you can be here for the festivities."

Clara pulled a smudge stick from under the altar and lit it with a white pillar candle already burning on top. The smudge stick caught, and she held it ablaze a moment before blowing out the flames and letting it smoke. She blew on the smoke, sending it out above those sitting in front of her, then she turned to do the same behind her then to her right and left.

"The four points of a compass," Matt explained as Clara faced us all once more and then in a clockwise fashion walked around the room blowing more smoke.

The smell was unlike that which I had used to cleanse my house. I breathed in deep, taking in hints of rose, thyme, and something else I couldn't put my finger on.

"I call upon the moon, the Sturgeon Moon, the Green Corn Moon, the Lightning Moon. Shine down upon us and cast your energy on our circle. We give thanks for the bountiful fish that swim in our river at this time of year, the abundant crops that will feed not only us but our animals that we will rely on this winter, and the energy that you cast down upon the earth. May the light of the moon shed truth on that which has hidden in the shadows and release us from any negative energy as we enter the darker days toward winter. May it restore hope and put some fears to rest. May we realize all that we have been working toward this month."

Finally Clara completed the circle. "So mote it be."

"So mote it be," the others repeated.

Caught unprepared to join in with everyone, I quickly followed with a "so mote it be" of my own.

Clara set the smudge stick still smoking in a metal bowl on the altar. It was then I realized the cloth looked just like mine. Did everyone in the coven have one? Or maybe just a select few. Perhaps those who were paranormal?

Clara pulled a stack of papers out from under the altar. "As with every full moon, please write down those things you need to release this month. Those things not under your control. Your doubts. Those fears that still need to be dealt with. Anything that could be affecting you negatively from unkind words said to unkind deeds."

Gloria stood from her seat in the front row and took the stack of papers from Clara, then took one for herself and passed the rest in two piles to those sitting on either side of her. Movement in the middle of the room drew my attention as Emily pulled out a large bag of pens and sent it through the group for anyone needing one. Those who had both began to write or sat a moment in contemplation before setting pen to paper.

Eventually, the paper and pens made their way to me, one coming from Matt, the other from Sarah.

"Go on," Matt encouraged as he handed me the bag of pens, "do what she says."

I nodded and handed him the rest of the paper before turning to Sarah to give her the pens. She already had one as did Vince, unsurprising for a former newspaper editor and his granddaughter. Vince passed the bag back to someone sitting in the central area.

Sarah started writing immediately, Matt too, but I took a few moments to study the paper. Handmade with specks of flower petals and herbs among the pulp. I could make out the bits of rose as well as a small sprig of thyme, corresponding with the smudge stick used tonight.

But what to write . . . What did I have to release?

First to come to me was the negativity surrounding Bruce

Malloy and any of the guilt I harbored after falsely accusing him of murder.

Then I wrote down my doubts about myself and this path. I was finally here and embracing what it meant to have magic. I acknowledged my regret of having been so oblivious to it all before a few months ago, making others wait on me. Like Sarah. I glanced at her. She was done writing. What had she written? I hoped I was doing right by her and that she didn't mind having such a novice at this all. As if she could feel me watching her, she cast me a glance and smiled as she pretended to peek at my paper. I teasingly stuck my tongue out at her as if I'd caught her cheating on a test and blocked her view with my hand before smiling back at her. We'd be fine. Thank the Goddess for her.

Next I wrote down the beverage board and the fear I felt that I could have faced with another shutdown to my business. It hadn't happened, and I needed to let it go.

Last I wrote down Erin's grandmother's name and the fear I had that I wouldn't be able to help. If I could release that fear, maybe an answer would come to me. I was going to ask for help tonight and didn't want to hinder that aid by being afraid.

Finally, I felt I was done, so I set the pen down on my lap and turned over the paper so no one else could see.

As if she'd been waiting for me, Clara spoke once more. "All right. Now fold your paper in half. We'll come back to it at the end of the night. Let's move on to the next order of business."

And business it was. Who knew that covens had budgets for things like ceremonial preparation? They talked of what they would do for their fall fundraiser, and I remembered how Emily had sold candles last year at the library. The smell had been so wonderful I bought three, keeping one for myself and giving one each to Mom and Gram. Now that I knew my cousin, Thea, was a craft witch, I wondered what they all had thought of the gift since she made candles. I flipped my paper back over. I had to let go of that which I didn't know before.

After the business was complete, Clara asked, "Who would like to report on their personal growth over the last month? Who has seen improvement on something they released during the last full moon? Or perhaps something that has blessed you since the new moon?"

A few spoke. Someone else read a poem they'd written.

"Now as I mentioned before," Clara continued, "August's moon is about the celebrating of abundance. Is there anyone here with something they are so abundant in that they are willing to share with the rest?"

A woman stood, and I recognized her from one of the stalls at the town farmers' market that I went to on the weekends when I could steal myself away from the bakery for a few minutes around lunchtime.

"I have more tomatoes than I could begin to know what to do with. Even with high demand at the markets right now, it's more than we'd be able to sell before it goes bad. Got boxes out in the truck. Please come take what you need. If you had any with the salad, you know what you're getting."

Someone else stood and said that they'd taken in a stray cat who had kittens and were looking for a home. "Every witch needs a cat, right?"

The farmer who'd offered the tomatoes chimed in. "We could use another farm cat."

Then one of the vet techs here in town offered his services to get them all fixed during the clinic the vet ran in conjunction with the humane society. By the end of the discussion, every kitten was spoken for.

Including two by Matt.

"It's time," he told me after offering to take in a pair, sight unseen, in a few weeks.

When no one else spoke up, Clara moved on. "Now for the next order of business. Is anyone in the coven in need of anything? You've seen what we can accomplish if we all work together."

Someone asked if anyone had books that they would like to get rid of so she could replenish her craft supply and make things from the pages. I thought of the paper flower bouquet Ken had given me. Hands shot up to answer the call, even Emily's who said the library had a few discards that were too damaged to put out in the used book sale. Based on everyone's offers, the girl was going to be stocked for a long time to come.

A woman I recognized from a birthday party of one of Ivy's friends a couple months ago stood up. "I'm a new troop leader this school year, and I'm wondering if anyone might have ideas or could host my scouts on a fun trip. Nothing long, maybe an hour or two one afternoon or a weekend day depending on what you can handle. There are only seven of them."

The farmer stood up and offered for them to come pick pumpkins in the fall. Someone else offered to teach the kids how to milk a cow.

I raised my hand, then stood once I was called. "The kids are welcome to come to the bakery. We can either make cookies or I can have some ready to decorate. It's up to you."

The woman smiled at me and clasped her hands together. "Oh, they would love that!"

"Stop by the shop sometime, and we'll pick a date."

She nodded, then unclasped her hands but kept them pressed palms together.

I felt called to mirror the motion.

We sat, and the esbat continued until all needs were, at least in part, satisfied. It reminded me of a town council meeting. But unlike the council meetings, there was no need to put something on next month's agenda before it could be discussed and no vote on whether something had merit. Here everyone acted immediately.

I liked it.

"Is it always like this?" I whispered to Matt as someone sat down after their request had been granted, pausing the conversation for a brief moment.

He nodded and replied softly, "Mostly. Especially the esbats. No one goes without if someone can help. The good we put into the world comes back to us threefold, you know." He chuckled. "Might be why you see some of us jumping at the chance to lend a hand."

"So since you got two cats, does it come back sixfold?"

Matt smiled as Clara, who had been silent for most of the needs and abundance portion of the night cleared her throat once more. "Now for the card draw."

Larry's sister stood, a deck of palm-sized cards in her hand.

As she made her way to the front, I leaned toward Sarah. "She sees auras too, so does this mean she has multiple powers?"

She shook her head. "Not in the way you're thinking."

"As I was preparing for tonight's esbat, I found myself called to one of my tarot decks that I bought because it was fun but don't use all that much. Baseball Tarot." A few chuckles rose from the room, but Elizabeth continued unde-terred, shuffling the cards as she stood behind the altar. "Per-haps not a typical subject one thinks of for tarot cards, but it's fitting for August. The game of summer. It's a standard deck of seventy-eight cards, so those of you who are already familiar with the cards should have an understanding of what I'll pull."

She stopped shuffling, then grabbed the smudge stick from the bowl sitting on the altar. She waved the herb bundle over the cards, then set it back into the bowl before placing her hand on the top card.

"Let this card guide you this month." She flipped over the card and then held it high in the air. "The card is The Lovers, reversed."

"Reversed?" I whispered to myself.

"The Lovers, when upright, mean partnership, union, or duality, but in reverse, it indicates a lack of harmony, one-sidedness, or imbalance. Reflect on this in your life. Yes, for some it may be a literal lover or romantic love. Could someone be putting more into a relationship than the other? Is it you? If it is, why?"

Immediately I thought of Erin and Travis. Did this relate to them because Erin wasn't meant to be with Travis and thus the lovers—she and Bryan—were out of balance? Or was this card not about a romantic relationship but instead somehow related to Erin's grandmother being gone and Erin feeling like she lacked inner harmony?

"Or perhaps this could be a business partnership or something else in your life that was once a passion project that now doesn't mean as much to you as it once did," Elizabeth continued. "The time has come to reevaluate. Do you need to reinvest in that relationship or should you thank it for having come into your life and then send it on its way?"

"Thank you, Elizabeth," Clara said as she stepped back up to the altar. "Your readings are always very insightful. Let us all take a moment to reflect, and when you are done, please take out the slips of paper that you filled out at the start of the esbat for the release."

Mine still sat on my lap, and I unfolded it to read one more time.

Clara swooped her arm up, hand pointing toward the open barn door. "Let us gather outside. As we always do for the full moon, we're going to take that which we need to release and send it away in the candle flame."

As we waited our turn to go outside, I asked Matt, "Why didn't you ever tell me?"

"That I was a witch?"

I nodded.

He gave me an understanding smile. "Come now. Would you have believed me?" It was the same question Nathan had asked.

"She sure wouldn't have a couple months ago, that's for sure," Vince said from behind us. "Think she was barely believing in anything back then."

I sighed. "You're right. I wouldn't have fully. But coming from you, Matt, I think I might have. At least a little."

He patted my arm. "Enough to humor an old man, at least."

I found myself telling him something I often said to Gram, "You're not old."

Next to us, a woman cackled. I turned to find Trudy standing with Clara, leaning on her for a bit of support. "Oh, he's old, all right."

Warmth spread through me at the sight of the woman, and a smile grew across my face. "Trudy, It is so good to see you again. *You* being here is not surprising at all."

"My grimoire give it away?"

"Maybe . . ."

She chuckled. "Now come here and give me a hug and help warm these old bones." She released Clara's arm and took a step toward me, her arms open.

I walked toward her and then wrapped her in a hug. Her many layers, even in the nighttime heat, made her feel soft and pillowy.

Matt snickered. "I noticed how you didn't tell her she wasn't old."

Beside us, Clara snorted, and a hearty chuckle escaped Vince.

Trudy, still hugging me, jiggled with laughter. "There's no denying it for me, I'm afraid."

"You've always been older to me," Matt said.

Trudy released me from the hug, then took Clara's arm once more as we resumed walking to the exit. She shook her head. "Only by a few years."

Matt stepped aside to let us all go through the door before him. "Seven. You're seven years older than me."

"And you've never let me forget it."

I looked between the two of them. Now that we were outside, it took me a moment in the dim light, but there it was in the shape of their eyes and cheeks when they smiled. "You two are siblings!"

"Sure are," Matt replied.

"As am I," a new voice from behind me said. I turned and a woman a few years younger looking than Matt stuck out her hand. But there was no denying the relation. "The name's Betty. It is so nice to meet you finally and have you here. Thank you for keeping my brother well-fed. Goddess knows I can't do it."

"You're not a kitchen witch," I confirmed as I took her hand in mine.

We shook hands, and she answered, "Far from it."

I glanced at Trudy. "But you are."

"Sure am, but I hung up that hat some years ago."

I nodded in understanding. "Does Sam know?"

She shook her head. "His father was never into this sort of life. Doubt his mother even knows what I am."

"So could he be a kitchen witch like how I was before I knew what one was?"

"No. He's skilled in the kitchen, but there's more to it than just that, as I think you know."

That I did, though that wouldn't stop Sam from having a wonderful career in the food industry.

I looked at Matt. "So what are you?"

Matt chuckled. "We'll have more time to talk about that after. I know Clara wants to get started with this month's release so we can move on to the next stuff."

Trudy dropped her hold of Clara's arm, and Clara made sure she was all set before stepping back from the group. "I look forward to talking more with you shortly," Clara added to me. Then she raised her arms in the air so everyone could locate her under the moonlight as she spoke, louder this time, "All right, everyone, gather in a circle."

Using me as support, Trudy guided me to the forming circle. We stood with linked arms as the others took up spots next to us. Betty on Trudy's other side, Matt next to Betty, then Sarah on my other side, and Vince next to her.

Clara stood in the center, her arm extended as Emily came out from the barn. She held the smudge stick with one hand and the bowl it had been sitting in, in the other. She passed Clara the smudge stick first, and Clara took a white candle out from somewhere, a back pocket maybe. I didn't think it had appeared out of thin air, although I didn't know what type of witch she was. Could some witches do that?

"If everyone could take out their candles and their papers, we can begin," Clara announced.

I pulled my candle out of my purse, and Sarah did the same. She seemed giddy with expectation, much like she had the night she'd helped Gram and me bury my crystals in the front garden, excited to finally participate in something witchy after all this time.

Clara held her candle to the smudge stick and then blew on the ends of the stick to make the small embers flare. It took a moment, but it caught the candle wick. She righted the candle, then passed the smudge stick back to Emily, swapping it for the bowl.

"As we have guests today, I'll explain the process." She spent the next few minutes discussing how everyone would light our candles and then the papers. "Once done, I will smudge the ashes of everyone's papers and send them away on the wind, scattering them once and for all."

She brought her lit candle to Emily's unlit one, and it caught immediately. The two women returned to the circle's perimeter, inserting themselves among the rest of us. Emily used her candle to light Elizabeth's next to her. As Clara held the bowl, Emily set her paper on fire. It flared yellow, then took on a hint of green, and even pink before settling back to the color of a normal flame. When it had burned about half-way, Emily dropped the paper into the bowl in Clara's hands before taking it from her.

As she did, Elizabeth lit her paper on fire, and the process continued more than a dozen times over before it was Sarah's turn. With all the solemnity in the world, her face now blank of the earlier excitement, Sarah placed the candle against her paper. She held it for only a moment before dropping it into the bowl Vince was holding. He passed the bowl to her, and she turned to me with it, her paper still very much ablaze inside.

She widened her eyes at me in encouragement, her excitement returning, and I brought my candle to the paper, thinking in my head about what I had written and letting those thoughts drift up with the smoke rising from my the flames nipping at the paper, flaring pink and green like it had done for all the others, crackling and letting out a small pop as the edge of the slip was consumed. I wondered if something in the paper caused the colors, the flower petals perhaps, or maybe something I couldn't see so easily —magic.

My paper was over half burned by the time I let it fall into the bowl. Sarah passed me the bowl as Trudy lit her paper.

She didn't let her paper stay lit for very long before dropping it in the bowl, and as she took it from me, she winked at me over the firelight.

Behind her, Betty lit her piece of paper, and I steadied Trudy as the old woman turned to her sister with the bowl. Once Betty took the bowl from her, Trudy leaned against me once more, and the release ceremony continued, the bowl chasing the lit candles and papers around the rest of the circle. I smiled as Nathan and George took their turns, and I realized then that I'd been living next to witches—several of them—since moving into my house a few years back. Had its previous owner been a witch too? Is that why the house had felt perfect for me from the moment I saw it even though I didn't yet know what I was?

Trudy squeezed my arm, almost as if knowing I was about to spiral toward thoughts I'd meant to release. "Just be in the moment," she whispered.

I turned and gave her a small smile, mouthing "Thank you." She patted my arm and looked back toward the circle.

After several more minutes, the bowl had made its way around the circle, and everyone's faces appeared to glow thanks to the candlelight.

Clara lit her paper and cast it into the bowl after letting it burn for as long as I had. Then she took the bowl from the person next to her and stepped back toward the center of the circle, bowl in one hand and smudge stick in the other.

She walked in a small circle, waving the smudge stick over the ashes of our once slips of paper.

"Repeat after me. I invoke the power of the full moon."

All together we said, "I invoke the power of the full moon."

Clara continued in a circle as she spoke and we repeated in unison. "I release those things that held fear and doubt . . . I release those things that limited me, that hold me back . . . I release that which I believe to be obstacles on my path to my purpose . . . I release those things that aren't mine . . . I release those things that no longer serve a purpose in my life . . . I release that which seeks to do me harm . . . I release relationships that hinder me . . . I release my regrets, holding on to the lesson but letting go of the feeling . . . I send them into the wind and banish them into the night."

She waved the smudge stick over the bowl one final time, then staunched the tiny embers remaining on the stick with a few gentle taps on the inside of the bowl.

The far side of the circle opened wide enough to allow Clara to walk through it. With the bowl in her hands, she thrust her arms out.

In the light of the moon, I could see flecks of ash catch in the light, others darkening the scene beyond as a gust of wind —the first we'd had the entire time we'd been standing out there—blew, drawing the ashes away. Clara tipped the bowl over to pour out the last of the ashes, then righted it.

She removed something from under her cloak, but it was small enough that I couldn't tell what it was from this angle. "What's she doing?"

Trudy lay her head against my shoulder. "She's using moon water from last month to wash out the bowl."

Thankfully, I didn't need to ask what that was.

After a minute, Clara returned. "The esbat has ended. Remember, some things will remain in limbo this month, just as there are still crops in the ground whose outcome is not yet certain. Goodnight, everyone."

Trudy lifted her head, tapping my arm with her hand once more. "And that's my cue to bid you a good night. I take it you're staying to sleep under the stars?"

My eyes widened. Me? Sleep under the stars? Tonight's activities had quickly become more than I'd bargained for.

CHAPTER 24

"I—I didn't sign up for any sleepover under the stars."

Trudy chuckled. "No one is sleeping under the stars. Well, some might, but that's not what I mean."

I nodded as understanding took over. "Oh . . . It's code. Not everyone knows about the other sort of magic," I whispered.

She pressed her index finger to the side of her nose, then pointed toward a large 15-person van close to the barn. "Right you are. Now, help me over there." The van's door was already wide open. Matt and Vince stood on either side helping people get inside. Sarah was there too, chatting with her grandfather.

As we began walking, I asked, "Did you used to stay to sleep under the stars?"

"Oh, most certainly. But as I've said, I retired from that life a while back. I'm sure I still have a trick or two, but I'm content with leaving that life behind. I've passed on my grimoire, and I hear you're doing wonderfully."

"It's been a lot of fun bringing candy into the shop. Speaking of, might you want to come by soon? I don't know how getting you out of the nursing home works, but I want to have a going away party for Sam and would love for you to be there."

We stopped at the door to the van, and she turned to me. "You just let me know when, and I'll make sure I get there. Wouldn't miss anything for that boy." Once I agreed, she pulled me in for a hug. "You have fun."

"Thank you." I helped her into the van. She was the last one, so once we said goodnight, Vince closed the door.

I turned to him. "You help them get here every month?"

"Sure do. It's a bit easier of an explanation than the other thing, but I'll make sure those who need it get to that too."

"Let's do it." I glanced at my familiar. "Tell Sarah whatever you think would be best and we'll make it happen."

As Sarah and her grandfather said their goodbyes, I turned to Matt. "Are you leaving?"

He shook his head. "I'll get a ride home from Nathan and George." He stuck his hand toward Vince. "Good to see you again, my friend. Thanks for the ride."

Vince grabbed Matt's hand, and the two shook. "Anything for you. You know that."

"You're welcome to come over anytime."

They dropped each other's hands, and Vince nodded. "I know."

Matt clapped him on the shoulder as he took a step toward the barn, where a few others had already gathered. I followed him.

"Hasn't been to the house since Henny died," Matt said quietly.

"He was her familiar, wasn't he?"

Matt nodded, and a small sigh escaped. "He was."

"So what are you?" I asked to change the subject.

"I figured that would be obvious."

"You've known me for how long now?" I said with a look. "You should know I don't pick up well on those things. I've been magical my whole life and only finally came to that realization four months ago."

Sarah came up next to me then. "And she had me hinting at it since she got here too." She gave me a cheesy grin.

Matt chuckled. "Well, you must have some guesses."

"You're not a kitchen witch." That much I knew.

He threw his head back in laughter. "No, Trudy got all of the cooking magic. Neither Betty nor I were any good at it."

"Was Henny a kitchen witch?"

He shook his head. "No, but she kept me well-fed all the same." He patted his stomach.

"The only other thing I can think of is a green witch. You have a lovely garden, but admittedly, I don't know all the types yet."

"And that is what I am. Nothing makes me happier than being in my garden."

"I still need to have you come help me with mine."

"Plenty of time for it still, though we're going to be looking at fall flowers soon and prepping for the spring."

"He'll have your garden in shape in no time flat," Betty said as she walked up to us and took my hands. "It is so good to meet you. I've stayed away so as not to slip and pressure you to join us before you were ready. And Sarah"—she continued, turning to my familiar—"it is so nice to have you amongst us as well. We're thrilled for you after all this time. So how about we all head out back?"

I nodded, looking at Sarah, then Matt, and finally toward the rest of the group beyond. Nathan and George. Clara. Larry and Elizabeth. Several others from town that I knew by face but hoped to get to know by name. Then a few more who I assumed lived out of town.

"Are there more of us?" I asked as we all headed toward the woods.

A narrow path wound between some trees and opened up onto a clearing by the river. Tree stumps surrounded a firepit already set up for a small bonfire.

"Of course," Clara replied. "You already know Trudy. Vince still joins us from time to time. He's not magical, per se, but he knows all about us in the same way that Sarah will soon. But others come when their time allows. Not all are witches in the spiritual sense. I do hope you'll consider joining the coven, but if this path isn't for you, I understand. It might be a bit selfish on my part. A great Sunevall in our coven? So wonderful. Inviting you to a coven meeting, however, was probably the easiest way to get you to one of these extra meetings."

Everyone took up a spot on the stumps or cut logs around the firepit, but no one moved to light the fire. Maybe it wasn't meant for us.

"You could have been a little more forward about it," I admitted. "Leaving me mysterious gifts was maybe a bit over the top. Worrying almost if I'm being honest."

Clara frowned. "We hoped it would intrigue you enough to actually come."

"Who brought it all to my house? I never saw." I turned to my across-the-street neighbor. "Was it you, Matt?" He had the best view of my house to know if I was in the living room where I could have spotted him.

He shook his head. "I'd have been caught before making it back to my yard."

That ruled out my other neighbors too.

"It was me," a soft male voice said.

"Larry?" Sarah and I said in unison.

He nodded with a smirk.

I chuckled as I remembered being surprised about him delivering Chinese food one day instead of pizza. "I thought you meant for all of the food places in town. Didn't realize that comment extended to mysterious gifts from the local coven."

"I deliver *everything*."

Over the next couple of minutes, a few others joined the circle. I assumed these were who Clara had meant by those who had magic but weren't Wiccan. But with the light of the moon obscured by trees, I couldn't see faces well enough.

Betty cleared her throat. "Let's get this fire going." Instead of striking a match to light the smallest tinder in the bundle of logs and sticks, she brought her hands close to her face, palms up and fingers extended toward the firepit. She sucked in a deep breath and blew out. The fire caught instantly, roaring as if it had been going for quite some time.

The warmth of the fire reached my front. "Wow . . ."

"Show off," George said with a laugh, looking at Matt. I envisioned them as younger men, joking around with one another and teasing Matt's siblings.

"Really?" She seemed disappointed. "I thought snapping would be too much."

"It would have been more of a surprise," Matt said, "but this added a lot of dramatic flair."

"I thought it was wicked cool," I assured her. "So you're a fire witch?"

A smile crossed her lips. "Not just that."

My heart jumped with hope, and Sarah stiffened beside me. "You have multiple powers?"

She shook her head. "Not quite, but close. I'm an elemental witch. Didn't you notice the wind? I controlled the air to sweep through and blow the ashes away when Clara emptied the bowl."

"Now that you mention it, yes. So water and earth too?"

She nodded and waved her hand. At once, a small waterspout formed on the river and sent drops of water toward Matt and George. Most landed just short of them, I assumed on purpose, but some spray reached their faces.

Matt wiped the water off his face, saying nothing, likely accepting the retribution from his younger sister for the earlier jab at her abilities. George, however, looked up at the sky.

"Was it supposed to rain tonight?" He turned to Nathan. "I thought you said it wasn't."

Nathan's shoulders slumped slightly. "Late night must be getting to him."

Betty nodded in understanding. "I shouldn't have."

Nathan held up his hand. "He would have appreciated the gesture. Somewhere I'm sure he still does. We won't be out much longer, Dad."

Conversation continued for a while. Maybe George's response to the water had tempered the evening, or maybe this was always how the nights under the stars went, but outside of Betty's show of magic, there was little magic done or talked about. It almost seemed that tonight was more about me getting to know them.

Nathan, George, and Matt were the first to leave. When Betty yawned sometime later, followed by Sarah, then me, the rest of us decided to leave as well. Betty extinguished the fire, removing all the air from around the flames and the fuel until it died, casting us in moonlit darkness once more. We said our goodnights in the parking area in front of the barn, and then Sarah and I climbed back into her car to head home.

"Do you need help with anything else because of the moon tonight?" Sarah asked as we got close to my house.

I shook my head. "Thankfully we took care of the water after dinner. I think I'd be too tired to do anything now."

Oh, good. She yawned. "Expect tea from Leafs in the morning. I know we can technically make our own in the shop now, but Leafs has that something extra."

"You mean Gary?" I giggled.

Sarah's mouth parted a moment. "Oh, tired Joanie is spicy Joanie. I like it. Okay, fine, yes, it's Gary."

"About time you admitted it."

"Figured if you can admit that you are a witch now, I should admit that I like him." She pulled up to the front of the house.

"Tea sounds good to me, thanks." I opened the car door. "Thanks for driving. Sleep well."

"Likewise." Almost as an afterthought, she added, "I hope charging the earring tonight works."

I did too.

CHAPTER 25

That night, I had one of those dreams where I wasn't sure I was dreaming until I woke up. It felt so real. I'd woken up in it and saw a ghost I'd only recently seen in pictures. But there was no denying who it was. Erin's grandmother, Anita.

In my dream, I sat up upon hearing a noise, and when I looked around, there she was standing at the foot of my bed. It wasn't the first time I'd been visited at this hour. Kate, the ghost I'd helped back in April, had woken me up in the middle of the night too.

"Hello," I said when I spotted her. "I was hoping you'd come. Charging your earring must have worked."

But like with many of the ghosts I'd met recently, Anita couldn't talk. I would have assumed ghosts could in my dreams. They were mine, after all.

When she said nothing and just politely smiled at me, I pressed on. "Where have you been? Erin's been missing you. You disappeared."

Her smile morphed into a frown as she raised her hands to shoulder height, palms facing up in a shrug.

"You don't know where you've been? You didn't cross over and come back because of the energy boost?"

She shook her head.

Although the full moon shining into my room had cast everything in a bluish hue, Anita was blue. Not just shaded by the color. Ghosts had always been just as solid as any living being, which made it hard to determine if someone was a ghost by looks alone. It was why I'd been surprised a few times over the years. Like with Arthur Miller and Bardi or Cindy at Bug Creek Cider Mill. But Anita was semi-translucent, something I rarely saw outside of fictional representations of them.

Now that I was awake, I wondered if maybe it was my dream causing the translucence, but even in the dream, I must have been thinking something was off about her appearance. It was enough to make me ask, "Are you really here?"

She puckered her lips while puffing them out and bobbed her head left and right. Then she lifted a hand so it was flat in front of her and wobbled it back and forth.

"You're here but you're not?"

She nodded, and a small smile crept back onto her face as if she were pleased I'd understood.

The closest I'd seen to this sort of ghostly appearance was when we were trying to release Kate from the hairbrush she was anchored to. Daniel, another ghost who was helping us, nearly faded out of existence by lending his energy to help the woman—the ghost—he loved. But he'd flickered and faded. Anita was stable.

"Is there something preventing you from being all here?"

Again Anita nodded.

"Do you need help?"

One solid nod this time.

"Where are you?"

She shrugged.

"Did someone do something to you?"

She nodded yet again, this time her nose wrinkling. Whoever it was, she didn't like them. But then again, I wouldn't like whoever was preventing me from walking around free as a ghost either.

"Who?" I hoped this could be the key to it all.

Nothing. She was gone. Blinked out of the room as if she'd never been there.

That was when I woke up.

For a few moments, I sat there disoriented as I thought I'd been awake the entire time. Willing Anita to be here, I looked around the room as if my dream would repeat itself in real life this time. But after several minutes, I realized she wasn't coming. Or wasn't coming back. It had felt so real. People regularly claimed to be visited by those who had passed on in dreams, so why not me too?

I pulled my legs out from under Saffy. She grumbled at the disturbance but settled down again as I sat up to slide my feet into my slippers. I'd not slept enough, but if I tried to go back to sleep, I'd end up more tired than I was now. At least I had an extra Monday muffin waiting for me at the bakery and the promise of more tea from Sarah.

I headed downstairs and into the kitchen. The tea from Sarah was still hours away, and I needed some now for more than one reason. The caffeine would help wake me up and clear my head, and I hoped the warmth would erase the chill I'd woken up with despite the warm August night.

As I set the water to boil, I realized the cold I was feeling had to be another sign of having been visited by a ghost. They were always colder, but I could only assume this would be how one being in my dreams would affect me. I'd never been visited like that before, even back when I was dealing with bad ghosts, and I hoped to not experience it again. I'd had dreams before with people in them who were no longer here, but those had all been pleasant. Sometimes the replay of a memory. Other times something completely fictional. But they left me happy, even if sometimes a bit sad too. But the biggest difference between them and last night was that I'd known who those people were when they were alive and knew it was a dream upon waking up.

I was not closer to my answers than before, even after finally making contact with her, or rather her with me. Charging the earring under the full moon last night had to have done the trick. But everything that had transpired worried me. Who had done something to her? Where was she now? And what had that usage of energy done to her?

The kettle started to release steam, so I pulled it off the burner before the whistle could blow. It surely would have woken Saffy. Someone in this house deserved to sleep through the night. Even if that someone was a cat who slept most of the day too.

I poured the water into my cup over my infuser basket full of grapefruit tea. The strong black tea would help wake me up, and the grapefruit would add the bit of zing that I currently lacked.

As the tea steeped on my kitchen table, I sat and watched the steam rise from the cup. Seeing the rest of the kitchen through the vapor reminded me of how I could see through Anita, and as I blew across the mug, dispersing the steam, I thought of how quickly she had disappeared.

It was like how the other ghosts had reacted to the wards Mom and Gram had placed around the house that I didn't even know about at the time. How Daniel couldn't cross them and had to wait on the porch when Rich came inside. And how the brush trapping Kate had immediately dropped to the ground when it tried to cross the threshold and head outside. The brush had been floating through the living room, and as soon as it hit the ward, it was as if the energy snapped, disappearing completely. Kate had retreated so far inside I was afraid we'd lost her.

It had taken days to draw Kate back out of the brush—and two seances. We didn't have that sort of time for Erin's grandmother, but we did have an object now.

I took my tea and headed outside. Then I sat down on the porch swing and took the earring in my free hand. It still didn't feel like anything was attached to it in any significant way. Possibly a result of Anita expending too much energy during her visit. But the longer I sat with it in my hand as I rocked in the swing, the more it felt like it had at least once been owned by her.

It wasn't much, but I'd take it.

CHAPTER 26

The morning walk to the bakery did little to wake me up as the dream that wasn't a dream clung to me. As soon as I flipped on the kitchen light, I grabbed one of the spare Monday muffins. By the time I was done, the rest of my team was arriving and I was already starting to feel more awake.

Bryan looked at me as he arrived with the others, his eyes full of hope, and asked, "How did things go last night?"

"It was an interesting night." That was true for everything about last night, perhaps just a bit more so from my dream-time visitor than the esbat and the meeting of the magicals.

He nodded in semi-understanding as he placed a mixing bowl on his station. "They liked your cookies?"

"They did. There was a ton of food."

"Good." I knew I had to tell him about my quasi-dream, but with everyone here and already busy with our morning prep, it wasn't the right place. And how could I explain what had happened with Anita when I had no answers from it?

A few minutes past two, Ivy popped into the shop, chirping a loud "Hello" to announce her presence. Not that she needed to say anything for me to know she was here. The lights almost always brightened when she arrived.

"Hi, Ivy!" I chimed back, happy to see the little girl who had been absent from my life the last few days. I hadn't seen much of her father either, and I looked forward to him picking her up later. "It's good to see you. Ready to make some candy?"

She bounced on her toes. "I sure am!"

"Great! Well, you know where everything is in the back. We're working with Lily today."

"Oh!" She clapped. "We haven't worked together yet."

I wasn't going to burst her bubble and say this might be the only time it would happen if Lily left like I expected her to. But until that time came, she was still one of the team and that meant a turn in the candy-making rotation. "Head on back. I'll be right there."

She nodded once and then, with a wave, half-ran to the swinging door between the shop and the back. "Lily!" she yelled excitedly once she likely made eye contact with her. They'd met a few months back when Ivy played a pivotal role in solving the mystery of the north woods and the dryads who had disappeared there. And to Ivy, that made Lily one of her best friends. Ivy had a lot of them. There wasn't a person she'd met who she didn't like. She'd probably even melt Zeke's heart at The Corner Bakery, although he was a softie in disguise as long as he had enough sleep.

Sarah gave me a knowing smile. "Have fun back there."

"It will be fine."

At least until we all got a little hyped up on sugar.

I pushed my way into the kitchen, where Lily had already set up the ingredients and supplies we needed to try various flavors of butter mints. Although we had made peppermint wafers last week, I wanted to try a few new flavors that weren't in Trudy's grimoire in addition to the mint. The easy base recipe would lend itself well to lemon, orange, and other citrus fruits that were perfect for summer.

That meant a lot of taste testing today.

"You're really going to like this one today, Ivy," I told her as she tried tying an apron around her. She'd gotten the ties overlapped and made the first twist, but hadn't been able to knot it, instead trying to tuck the strings into her back pockets to secure it. As I tied it for her, I continued, "The main ingredients are powdered sugar and butter."

"Oh, yummy!" She squirmed in place as I tightened the knot on her apron, likely trying to keep herself from clapping like she did when excited.

Lily *mmm*ed from over by the stand mixer where she was already dumping cups of confectioner's sugar into it. "My thoughts exactly. Hey, Ivy, how about you bring me over the butter?"

Ivy skipped over to Lily and the two began a lesson in baking math. "If you need one stick of butter per four cups of sugar, how many sticks should you put in if I just added twenty-four cups of sugar into the bowl?"

The little girl stuck out her thumb and counted one before extending her fingers out and counting two, three, four as she folded her fingers into a fist. After reaching two on that hand, she repeated the process again and again starting with her other hand until she'd arrived at the answer.

"Six!" she finally chirped.

"Great job!" Lily and I said in unison. If Lily was still here, I'd have to have her help me with the scouting troop that was going to come visit. She was a natural teacher, and I think she'd be a great mom if that was something she wanted to be.

We helped Ivy cut the sticks into one-inch chunks, and after she added the butter to the mixer, Lily flipped the switch. The mixer came to life, and over the next few minutes, it creamed the sugar and butter together, forming a soft dough.

We split that dough into six sections, one for each flavor, then moved to Lily's worktable with the first chunk. We split that into six again, and we each took one. I grabbed the bottle of peppermint extract sitting with the rest of the supplies, then because this recipe called for adding flavor "to taste," explained how each of us would add drops of oil into the dough, one more than the person next to us. Me one, Ivy two, and Lily three. We'd work the extract into dough, then cut pieces of each to try. If one worked, great. If not, we'd add enough drops to get four, five, and six drops per section and try again. Hopefully, one of those would prove to be a winner.

Fortunately we settled on three drops making the buttermint with the best balance. We tried four to be sure, but it proved to be just a bit too strong.

So we moved on to spearmint, followed by the various citrus flavors, and then cinnamon at Ivy's suggestion. With each winning combination, we either adjusted the rest of the dough to match—easy if we had to add flavor—or put it to the side. The too-strong dough was still edible but wasn't something I could sell. It would end up as snacks for us back here, although with the way Ivy insisted on multiple pieces to be sure of winning flavor ratios, Ken was going to end up with a very sugar-high child when all of this was done.

I certainly wasn't going to stop her from eating her fill. That had been my one condition when I offered to watch her. These were pleasant visits with no restrictions on sweets.

Ken walked into the back as the three of us were cleaning up the kitchen. "Hey, you three." He came up to my side, then kissed the side of my head above my ear. Quieter, he said, "I've missed you."

"I've missed you too." I leaned into him, careful to not get anything on him. Unsurprisingly, I was covered in stuff.

"Dinner?"

Before I could answer, Erin burst into the kitchen, Sarah close on her heels.

CHAPTER 27

"What did you do?" Erin asked.

From behind her, Sarah mouthed, "Sorry," but I waved her off. If Erin had come in like this, then it was important.

I focused on Erin. "I don't know. What did I do?"

"Travis didn't say, but he's furious with you."

My mind immediately went to the phone calls Sarah and I had made. "We *may* have tried to find his mom."

Erin's mouth dropped open. "You what?"

"We were hoping we could talk to her about what she can do." I glanced back at Lily and Ivy. "Why don't you two head out front. You can bring Sarah a sample of things to taste."

"Okay!" Ivy chirped. She and Lily quickly put a few of the finished buttermints onto a plate.

Ken followed them to the door. I thought he was going to leave, but he didn't exit the kitchen.

Once the door swung shut, Erin let out a long breath. "Okay. I know you were only trying to help, but why?"

"We were trying to figure out more about her powers. If somehow she could have done something to your grandmother from where she is to keep her son from possibly getting hurt by someone else who sees ghosts. If you can't see your grandmother, problem solved."

Her eyes raised slightly as if searching her brain for a thought. After a moment, she asked, "You think she could do something like this?"

"I honestly have no idea. It was a long shot. But that's why we tried to locate her. Someone had to have done something. We already decided it's not Alice, and since Travis can't even see ghosts, then it can't be him. We were grasping at anything we could, but no luck."

She nodded in understanding. "So did you have any luck getting a hold of my nonni? Did the earring help?"

I explained what had happened overnight. "We might need to do a séance. But if we do, we'll need more than just the earring, since the energy signature isn't strong enough.

"I can get some other things, no problem. Would a photo help?"

They typically didn't have an energy signature to them if they were just of the deceased, but "It wouldn't hurt."

Erin pulled her wallet out of her purse, then slid a photo out from a protective sleeve. "I had a copy of this made for the memorial table at the wedding. This is Nonni and me when I turned thirteen." She frowned. "She didn't make it to my fourteenth birthday."

"Thanks. I'll take really good care of it."

At that moment, Ivy came back into the kitchen, and I saw just how dim the lights had gotten in the shop. "There's a man here looking for you, Joanie. I don't like him."

It could only be one person.

"Thanks, Ivy. Why don't you hang back here with my friend?" She didn't need to be exposed to whatever Travis would say or do once he saw me. I looked at Erin. "Let me see what he wants first, please. He may not know you're here."

She nodded, although she looked like she was ready to see him and say hi as if he was completely fine, and judging by the lights, he was definitely still unhappy.

Once Ivy stepped clear of the door, I pushed through into the kitchen, then plastered a smile on my face. "Hi, how can I help you?"

Despite the darkness in the room, something noticed by Lily, who was looking up at the lights, there was only so much Travis could do or say with Lily and Sarah in the shop with me.

His hands balled into fists. "Just who do you think you are?"

My smile slipped. "I'm sorry?" I said at the same time Sarah said, "Excuse me?" Out of the corner of my eye, Lily's mouth dropped.

"Where do you come off trying to fill Erin's head with hope about all this ghost stuff? I thought we were on the same page with that."

"Would you like to sit down?" I hoped the movement would give him a moment to calm down.

"I'll stand." He crossed his arms. "Answer the question."

"I'm not filling her head with anything," I assured, taking on a calm, placating tone, and put a smile back on my face.

Lily moved behind Travis so that he couldn't see her. She made a look as if she was wondering if she should step in. I waved my hand by my side, palm facing the floor, to dismiss the offer. She nodded, but I noticed her hand had turned to wood. I didn't condone violence, and I didn't think Lily would instigate anything, but it was nice to know my feisty dryad friend had my back if I needed her. She glanced toward Sarah.

"If I'd realized how serious she was about this missing

ghost nonsense again, I would have gotten her the right sort of help. Certainly not sent her to some baker to indulge in her fantasies."

His answer wasn't what I'd been expecting at all. I had assumed this was about their mom. That he'd found out I was digging into her whereabouts. But Travis hadn't brought his mother up at all.

Nonsense? Fantasies? "I can assure you that I am concerned about Erin, but our paths to helping her over these concerns seem to be vastly different. You seem to want to ignore her worry, but if I can help her locate her grandmother—"

He barked out a derisive laugh. "You can't locate her. She's gone."

I tried again to make him see reason. "But if she says she could see her—"

"I know what people say about you, but don't tell me you actually believe that." He scoffed.

"Wouldn't you want to do everything in your power to help her just in case what she claimed is true?" My voice shook more than I wanted it to.

"She's not coming back."

"You sound sure of that." I cast a glance at Sarah, who stood next to the phone.

"Because it's ridiculous." He scrubbed at his face, then thrust his hand into his pocket.

Quietly, I asked. "But what if it's not?"

"Do not go putting hopeful thoughts into her head about this." He stepped up close to my face and held up his index finger. "If you want to help, you'll tell her it's not possible. She needs to let this go. Her grandmother is *gone*. There's nothing you or she can do about it."

I was about to open my mouth in protest when Travis

spun on his heels. I felt the air from his movement across my face. He stormed out of the bakery, one hand clenched back into a fist, the other still tucked into his pocket.

Ivy burst through the door from the kitchen, Ken immediately behind her. She ran up to my side. "Joanie, are you okay?"

Ken wrapped me in a hug. "I should have come out here."

I shook my head against his shoulder. "It's good you didn't. Besides, you had Ivy to think about."

"Daddy wouldn't let me come out here. I would have given him a piece of my mind." Her brow was furrowed, and her voice low. The look and sound reminded me of the incident regarding the blueberries that she'd believed were raisins the first time I watched her.

I stepped out of Ken's embrace. "Your daddy did the right thing. And see? I'm fine. Nothing happened." I gave them both a reassuring smile before glancing at Lily and Sarah. "I'm fine. Where's Erin?"

"Still in the back."

"Let me go talk to her." I crossed the room to the kitchen, finding Erin only a foot or two into the room. "How much did you hear?"

She looked a little panicked as if I'd just caught her with her hand in the cookie jar. "I swear he's a really good guy. He's just angry right now. The ghost stuff sets him off and so does stuff about his mom. And well, you kinda brought both to the forefront."

So she hadn't heard everything or else she would have known that his mom never came up in the discussion. "What are your plans for the rest of the evening?"

She raised an eyebrow at me as if confused by my changing the subject. "I was going to head home and cook Travis and myself dinner."

"But nothing's cooking right now, right? You've not done any prep?"

She shook her head. "Why?"

"Well, you were right. He is angry, and I'd feel more comfortable if you didn't go home right away. Give him some time to cool off." Was he always like that when angry? "How about you come to my house and we can hang out. Maybe order a pizza." And hopefully I could get her to realize that Travis, while I'm sure had some nice qualities occasionally, was not the one for her. Then it would be up to Bryan to prove that *he* was.

Erin sighed. "I'm trying to fit into a wedding dress next week, remember?"

"Trust me on this one." I cracked a smile. "The pizza is amazing, and if you're still worried about your dress after dinner, I know of a tea that will help with any sort of bloating from fast food." It had been one of Miss Susan's blends. It had been popular with a lot of people in high school. I didn't know the complete recipe, but I was sure I could get it close enough that it would do what I needed it to if I put enough intention into it.

She brightened. "I haven't had pizza in ages."

"You haven't tried Mama's, then, have you?"

She shook her head. "I've really wanted to. I keep saying after the wedding."

"Well, come on, we can go to my house and then call in an order once you've checked out the menu."

She nodded. "Okay."

"Can I have pizza too, Daddy?" Ivy asked from behind me.

I turned back around, not realizing until that moment that Ivy and Ken had followed me into the kitchen. A weight settled in my chest. I'd forgotten all about Ken wanting to grab dinner.

Ken glanced at me before looking at his daughter. "That sounds great, kiddo. How about you and I actually go eat at the pizza parlor tonight?"

"Sorry," I mouthed to him, then drew my lips to the side.

He held up a hand to let me know it was okay, and I gave him a small smile. I'd have to make it up to him. I really had wanted to get dinner and spend some time with him.

"Yay!" Ivy chirped and bounced in place, the events of the last several minutes seemingly forgotten. "I love their bread."

"Who doesn't?" Lily said, matching Ivy's enthusiasm, as she walked up behind the young girl. Lily held her hand out to Ivy. "Let's go pick out something from the case for dessert."

"Okay!" Ivy twirled around on her heels, half jumping in the process, then grabbed Lily's hand. The two walked back out into the shop.

When the door had closed again, I went to Ken and hugged him. "Thank you for understanding."

He kissed my head. "Don't worry. We can always get food tomorrow."

"It's a date," I said before telling Erin, "Give me about five minutes and then we can go, okay?"

"Take your time."

I walked Ken out of the kitchen, then said goodbye to him and Ivy. Once they were out of the shop, I turned to Lily and Sarah. "Any chance you two would be good closing up for me?"

"Sure thing," Lily said at the same time as Sarah nodded.

I pressed my palms together the way I had done at last night's coven meeting—had that really been only yesterday? Suddenly it felt like longer ago—and said, "Thank you."

Sarah leaned against the counter in front of her and studied me with concern. "You okay?"

"Yeah, just gonna spend some time with Erin."

"Is she going to be okay?"

"Yeah. Figured we could give Travis some time to cool off from whatever that was."

"Be careful," Sarah warned. "This fluctuating attitude of his is giving me some weird vibes."

"Me too," Lily said.

Me three.

CHAPTER 28

Erin and I settled on the couch, plates full of pizza, a box of garlic knots, and cheese fries sitting on the coffee table in front of us, and tea at the ready. My nighttime usual, and the anti-bloating blend I'd mentioned to Erin earlier. Saffy lay behind us, paying Erin little mind. It had to have been Bryan that she'd reacted to so strongly the other day, though I still had no idea why.

Usually I wouldn't eat something so greasy in the living room, but tonight was an exception. I wanted Erin to feel comfortable when we talked. The kitchen table would have been too formal, too serious—and while it was serious, I didn't want her to feel cornered or think I was lecturing her. If she'd pushed friends away for Travis the way Bryan said she had, then she'd have no problem doing so with me.

I blew across my pizza slice. The last thing I wanted was to burn my mouth on the first bite. "So how did you end up with Travis, anyhow? You went to school here together, but you weren't together then."

Already starting in on her tea, she nodded, then swallowed. "It started during a long weekend in college, actually.

We didn't go to the same school, but we ended up at the same happy hour in New York City. Total coincidence. Bumped into each other, quite literally. It was nice to see a familiar face a few hours away from home, even if he barely remembered who I was at first. We weren't friends in high school, although I knew who he was. Everyone did. We had a couple of classes together over the years, so I jogged his memory a bit."

"But didn't you all go to elementary school together? You, him, Bryan, Lily?"

"Believe it or not, but Heartwood Hollow has sometimes been big enough to require one and a half classes of the same grade." She cracked a grin. "We didn't always have the same teachers even back then. Add in the kids from Bug Creek for high school and those who transferred in from other towns for the vocational tech programs, and it was easy to lose track of people."

"So did you two hit it off right away or . . ."

"Yeah." Her grin turned wistful. "As soon as he remembered me, he asked me out for coffee. Said it was nice to connect with someone from home. I felt the same. Coffee turned into dinner. That turned into dinner the next night. Lunch that weekend." She took a bite of pizza, the cheese pulling away in one long string. "It was just a quick subway ride between our campuses, so whenever we ended up with more than an hour to hang out, we did. Then when his roommate moved out for the summer, Travis asked me if I wanted to move in since we were both going to be there for internships. I jumped at the chance to not stay in the dorm."

"And let me guess"—I smiled at her happy memories— "you never moved out?"

"Not until we came back to Heartwood Hollow together."

She sipped her tea. "We can afford so much more here than there."

In an attempt to hide the seriousness behind my next question, I dipped a fry in a glob of cheese stuck that had accumulated in the corner of the box. "And it's still good between you?" I popped the fry into my mouth.

Her brow furrowed. "Yeah, I mean, we're getting married. Of course it is."

So much for me trying to be nonchalant about it. "Has he ever been like this before?"

"He's just stressed, that's all. We both are with the wedding."

He'd said as much about her being stressed, but him? "Didn't you hire a planner?"

She sighed. "Yeah, but Travis likes to be hands on with everything, so he's still involved. The planner is more of a go-between. She made a lot of connections for him. He didn't really have any in this industry."

"Not even with the various fundraisers his family has organized over the years for the town?"

"He doesn't deal with that sort of stuff." She bit into her pizza slice.

Huh. Then how did he know about the beverage board? "What does he do?"

"He works in an investment firm," she said, then took another sip of tea. At this rate, I'd be making her more soon. "Manages the whole stock portfolio for his family and their various endeavors. He's good at what he does. How else do you think his family lives like they do and gives so much to charity? I promise you. He's a good guy."

"You heard what he said though, right?"

She dismissed the comment with a wave. "He was upset, and it just came out. Like I said, he doesn't like the ghost stuff. He'd never do anything to me. He loves me. I've never wanted for anything since being with him. I wouldn't be with him if I didn't love and trust him."

"And there's no way that he could be putting on an act about the ghost stuff? I get the whole mom thing and how he worries about you over your abilities, but—"

"No way." She shook her head. "I think he's jealous if anything."

"Jealous?" I bit into a new slice of pizza.

"Yeah. Alice was telling me the other day how as a kid he used to try to talk to the ghosts she saw all the time. Sort of one of those things where, when she was doing it, he'd attempt it, but it never worked. You know, pretending to be able to do it, too, so he wouldn't be different from his older sister and his mom. But none of the ghosts ever paid him much attention. Alice was a go-between if they ever did want to interact with him, which wasn't often. They didn't have some relative coming and checking in on them like how it was with me and Nonni."

Now it was my turn for tea. It had sat long enough to cool down. I drank as she continued talking.

"He tried the same thing with my grandmother when I finally told him what I could do. I caught him once trying to talk to her once, but he had no idea that she wasn't in the room at that point. She'd followed me into the kitchen."

She set her plate on the coffee table. "It wouldn't surprise me, if after losing his mom and growing up with Alice and her abilities, that finding out what I could do reignited his desires to see if maybe he had developed his powers late or something."

When my cousin and I were little, she tried to talk to a ghost I could see. She was younger than me and had lost the ability already. Nearly everyone has the ability to see and interact with ghosts until toddlerhood. Some, like me, don't ever lose it. But I hadn't realized it wasn't normal for people my age to see them until then. She was upset she couldn't do something that I could, and I didn't want to make her feel bad, so I stopped talking about it. I didn't bring it up again for years. It wasn't until I couldn't handle the ghosts coming to me when I was a teenager that I revealed what I could do. Mom thought I had outgrown the ability years before.

I reached for another fry. "And you don't think he could be hiding abilities from you?"

She half snorted. "I live with the guy. There's little he could hide from me."

At that moment, the phone rang in the kitchen. I stood and went to answer it. As I reached for the handset, I checked the caller ID.

The bakery. This couldn't be good.

CHAPTER 29

I glanced at the clock on the wall. It was already an hour past closing. "Sarah? Is everything okay?"

"Yeah . . . nothing I can't handle, but figured I should let you know now versus telling you tomorrow." The hesitation in her voice gave me pause.

"Okay . . ."

"One of the lights in the shop exploded."

"The ceiling lights?"

"One of the tubes."

"You should have called earlier."

"I knew you were dealing with other things. Lily stayed to help clean up. We're just about done."

I peeked out into the living room. Erin was eating another slice of pizza. Good for her. "I'm going to swing by. You know how good I got at looking at the lights when we first opened."

She laughed. "Yeah, you took out the shop ladder to get right up there with the electrician. Don't think he'd had that happen before."

"Gotta be prepared to do anything and everything when you run your own business." From day one, the lights' fluctuating brightness had been a concern. By the time I got onto the ladder to see what the electrician was doing, frustration had taken hold. He had come out three times to figure out what was wrong with the lights in the shop, and each time, he found nothing wrong.

Now that a few years had gone by, I'd noticed a pattern of it happening when emotions ran high in one direction or the other within the shop. "I'll be over in a few minutes. You call the building manager?"

"He was next on the list. You deserved to know first."

"I'll give him a call on the way over. Can you call the electrician and schedule a time for him to come in and check it out again? It's been a while."

"You really think he's going to find something this time?"

I chuckled. "No. Probably not, but it will make me feel better all the same."

"All right. See you soon."

We hung up, and I walked back into the living room.

Saffy eyed me expectantly as Erin wiped her mouth. She set her napkin onto her plate. "Everything okay?"

"Should be, but I need to head down to the shop for a bit." I grabbed my purse off the end table and slung it over my shoulder. "Are you okay staying here by yourself?"

"I can go, it's fine. It's been a couple hours now."

"Maybe give it a little more time just in case. I can call Bryan. I'm sure he'd come by."

She laughed. "Are you trying to find me a babysitter? Trust me, Bryan is not the person you want babysitting anyone. He's more the type to need one, not be one."

"Something tells me there's a story there." At any other time, I'd love to hear it.

Her laughter grew louder. "There are a lot of stories."

"Still. If you want the company . . ."

"Nah, it's okay. Gives me a chance to eat another slice of pizza." As if to ensure she'd stay, Saffy slid off her spot at the top of the couch and sat on Erin's lap. "See? I won't be alone."

Taking that as a sign, I nodded. "I'll be back as soon as I can. Don't worry about putting away leftovers." Not that there were many. "I'll take care of it later."

"Thank you, by the way. For the pizza. It's delicious."

I knew she'd like it. "I'll make you more tea when I come back."

She smiled. "I'd like that. See you later."

I slipped my feet into my shoes, then headed out the door.

As soon as I reached the sidewalk, I dug my cell out of my bag. It wouldn't have worked any sooner thanks to the wards around the house. Maybe. I wasn't sure if the wards would consider this to be an emergency situation and allow my phone to get a signal inside.

I searched for the building manager's number in my contact list, then pressed the call button.

"Isaac, here. How are you, Joanie? It's a bit late for you to be calling. Everything okay?"

"I'm sure it is, but I wanted to let you know we're having Russ come by to inspect the place. One of the light tubes exploded this evening while Sarah was closing, and I want to err on the safe side."

He let out a long sigh. "You need anything?"

"Nope. I'll stop at the general store to pick up a new tube. Still know what kind I need. If they don't have it, I'll have Sarah grab one from the hardware store before she comes in tomorrow morning. They open early."

"So glad you're on top of things. Good luck with the electrical inspection. You know the drill."

"Sure do. I'll forward you the report for you to look at."

"And call me if you run into any trouble."

The door to the shop stood open, so I walked inside. The middle of the room was darker than the rest thanks to the busted tube. "Will do. Thanks, Russ."

"Take care, Joanie."

"You too." I lowered my cell, clicking *end call* as I did. "Drats, forgot the bulb."

Sarah was sitting at one of the tables, looking at something on her phone. "Lily offered to run and get one. She should be back soon."

"Great. Thanks." I looked up at the light in the ceiling. "So what happened?"

"It just exploded." Sarah put her phone down and shrugged. "No warning."

"And you're okay?"

She held up her hands palms out, then showed me the backs. "Perfectly fine. Probably want a new broom just in case. Those pieces get tiny."

I nodded. On the rare occasion we broke something in the kitchen—we didn't use a lot of glass—the shards were chunky with the occasional sliver. This sort of glass resulted in the opposite when broken. The bits were closer to sand. Not to mention the mercury and phosphor in the tubes as well. "Call Lily. She can grab one across the street."

Sarah picked her phone back up as I continued staring at the light. A quick call to Lily and we were on our way to getting a glass and element-free broom.

When Sarah clicked off her phone, I said, "Light probably couldn't handle the strong swing it had today during Travis's visit today."

"I'd never seen it so dark."

"It wasn't even that bad the last time when he practically threatened me. And then there was no reaction the day he came in to apologize. It was just normal. There's something weird going on with him."

"Jealousy does make people do weird things. If he's spent a lifetime living around those or hearing about those with these abilities, I could see it. Can't say I wasn't jealous of my uncle and grandfather getting to be familiars as I was growing up."

"Yeah, but you'd never be like Travis."

She scrunched up her nose. "Goodness, no. But I also got to grow up with a whole family of people hoping to have a familiar someday. It wasn't just me. You think his dad could do anything?"

"Erin said the men don't have abilities in his family."

She shook her head slowly, her lips drawn to the side. "You'd think his dad would have helped him to understand."

"Maybe he was too wrapped up in other stuff. Not everyone's parents are there for them. Look at Ivy and her mom. Or me and my dad. I don't even know mine."

"At least Ken is an awesome father from everything I've seen and what you tell me. And she has you now too."

"I don't know about that." I had no idea what I was doing when it came to Ivy.

"You're great with her. You should see the way she looks at you when she comes here on Wednesdays."

My cheeks grew warm. "Thanks."

At that moment, Lily rushed into the shop. "I was just getting ready to check out when you called. Luckily I knew where the brooms were. The lightbulb wasn't as easy a find. That place can be a maze, and then they had to send someone into the back."

"Thanks, Lily." I studied her up and down. "And you're okay? No glass?"

She shook her head. "I was in the kitchen when it

happened. Heard the sizzle and pop and came running into the shop."

I spun on Sarah. "You didn't tell me it sizzled."

"It buzzed like how the lights do sometimes when we first turn them on. It got louder for a second and blew. I'll make sure to mention it to Conner when he comes in the morning."

"Thanks. Remind me to forward the report to Russ when I get it."

She nodded, a proud look on her face, and glanced at Lily. "We got it all handled. Even remembered to open the door for ventilation because of the potential for mercury vapor."

I remembered how worried I'd been when we first opened about the lights breaking because of how the brightness fluctuated. Everyone had gotten a lesson on what to do back then if it happened. Once I started to believe that maybe the lights reacted to moods, I stopped worrying about it so much.

"You really didn't need to come," she added.

She had a point. "Need? No, but you know me. Thank you both for taking care of it."

Lily gave me a small smile. "Not a problem. But if you don't need me anymore, can I go home now? I'd told John I'd meet him for dinner."

"Absolutely. Go on. Go."

She handed me the fluorescent tube but kept hold of the broom. "I'll go swap this out with the other and take that one to the dumpster on my way out." With that, we said goodnight and she left.

After Sarah and I carefully removed the broken ends of the fluorescent tube and installed the new one, we both headed home too.

But when I got inside my house, Erin wasn't there.

"Saffy, you were supposed to keep her here," I said as she

looked up at me, barely opening her eyes. "I knew I should have asked Bryan to come watch her."

Saffy seemed to take issue at the mention of him—or maybe it was the thought that I didn't think she'd done a good job. With what almost sounded like a huff, she hopped off the couch, then strutted toward the kitchen. I followed her.

On the table was a note.

Took care of wrapping up the pizza and fries. I don't care for fries reheated, but I figured if anyone can make them taste good, you can.

I'm heading home to grab another picture of my grandmother and a couple more of her things. Maybe one earring isn't enough, but something else could be. I'll bring them by tomorrow.

Thanks for the food and the chat.

Don't worry about me. I'll be okay.

See you soon.

Erin

CHAPTER 30

Arthur waved me over to the park as I headed for work the next morning. He and Bardi were hours early for their usual walk. I'd never seen him break his schedule, not for the weather, not even when he had helped me with the mystery in the North Woods. As a result, I'd always thought he was one of those spirits bound by routine. Apparently I was wrong.

"Morning, Miss Joanie." He nodded slightly. "Got some information for you."

"Good morning. You didn't have to break your routine for me. I'd have seen you later."

He looked at me over his thick-rimmed glasses. "I may keep a routine, but you do not. This is the only time I know you're going to be out here for sure."

"Does anything happen to you for breaking your routine?"

"To me?" He shrugged with a slight shake of his head. "I just like them. Helps me keep track of time passing. But I'm not bound to them like some. Don't know if they could break them. Haven't seen it."

Until I'd met him and talked to him a few months ago, I wouldn't have believed that. But he'd proven to be every bit of an intelligent ghost. Sort of like Cindy at the cider mill. Intelligent in that she could interact with me, but kept to a daily work schedule as if alive. She, however, had thought she was still alive.

"Have you always known you were dead?"

"Sure have, and if this is a conversation you want to have, we can chat about it another day."

Right. He had a point. "Sorry. You said you had information for me?"

"I asked some of the other ghosts in town about people who might be able to make them do things, and well, let's just say the gossip doesn't change any in Heartwood Hollow just because you're dead. They don't know of anyone with that ability around here. One's been dead for years now, but that's it."

"That's what Sarah's grandfather said too."

"Vince is a smart man. Thought you should know this too. That man you're looking into . . . Some of the ghosts remember how he used to pretend he had powers when his sister was around. But that's all it ever was. Pretend."

I sighed. That confirmed what Erin had told me at least. "Thanks, Arthur."

He patted Bardi's head. "Sorry it isn't much help."

"Might not be much, but it's something. Can rule out his doing anything to Anita."

"I hope you find out what happened to her. Anita was a lovely woman. Knew her from town all those years back. And then after I died too. Always kind when I saw her around with her granddaughter. She'd sit with me sometimes after her granddaughter started needing more space." He glanced at the bakery. "Now you go on and get about your day or else you're going to have to get everyone coffee because you're late."

"You really do know my routine."

He chuckled. "Like I said, the ghosts talk. Have a good day now, Miss Joanie."

"You too, Arthur."

Bryan and Lily were already waiting for me when I got to the back door.

Before I could say good morning, Bryan asked, "Have you heard from Erin? She was supposed to call me yesterday and didn't."

"I already told him about what happened Wednesday afternoon," Lily offered.

Bryan's expression was almost pained. "And that makes me more worried."

As I dug for my keys and unlocked the door, I explained what had happened and that she left while I was dealing with the broken light.

"You should have called," Bryan said. "I would have come."

"I thought about it," I began as we shuffled into the kitchen. "But she said she didn't want a babysitter. I can understand that but still can't help but be a bit disappointed that she left."

"She's a little headstrong." He seemed almost proud.

Lily chuckled. "That's saying something coming from you."

The comment lightened Bryan's mood significantly.

He put a hand to his chest as if wounded and said, "That hurts," before breaking into a smile. "But seriously. She is. And if she left you a note to say that's what she'd do, that's what she's going to do. Still, it's not like her to call or text me in the evening."

Lily grabbed a mixing bowl from the shelf. "You really talk to her that much?"

"Sure I do. She's my best friend."

"I can't imagine what this is doing to you." Lily returned to her workstation. "You stuck with her when the rest of us didn't."

"Can't say I blame you. She didn't make it easy."

She shook her head as she scooped a cup of flour into the bowl, avoiding his gaze. "Not so much her. Her new friends. I hope things work out for you two."

She wasn't looking to see Bryan's small, sad smile. "Same," was all that he could manage.

I patted him on the back. "Well, I'm working on that." And as the rest of the team arrived, I could only hope that we would have just enough time to pull everything off.

But first things first. Sam's going away party was in a few hours, and I had to keep him distracted. Fortunately for that, I had a plan.

"Morning, Sam," I said as I walked up to his workstation. The thought that it wasn't going to be his after today nearly stopped me in my tracks.

Sam gave me a look that said he understood. "Morning."

I pushed the feeling away. This was supposed to be a happy occasion. "Ready for your big day?"

He groaned slightly as he answered, "No, I still have so much packing to do."

I chuckled. "Not that big day. I mean today."

His eyes widened. "What?"

"I have one last thing to teach you before you can officially go to culinary school. Well, I guess it's more like a final exam." He continued to stare at me. "You're doing the lunchtime deliveries today. Solo."

CHAPTER 31

Making solo deliveries was a big step in one's path to having a bakery. But little did Sam know, he was also delivering his own cake.

Although Erin's lack of communication and then realizing this was the start of saying goodbye to Sam had tempered the beginning of the day, as the morning went on, it became hard to keep from bursting with excitement over the surprise.

"I arranged the slips in the order of delivery," I said, handing him the few slips of paper. "Most of the accounts are squared away already, but you're going to have to get the second payment for the cupcakes from the historical society."

He nodded, staring at me with a serious intensity as if I'd entrusted him with state secrets.

"You've got it handled, I'm sure of it," I told him, turning him to the door. "And to go easy on you, we've already loaded the bike trailer." Really, I'd needed to make sure that he kept his hands off the cake until the last minute just in case. There was no identifying information on the box, but I was taking a risk having him deliver it. It was the only way I could ensure his family and Todd would get here without him noticing.

"How much of a solo delivery is it if I didn't do all of this?"

"You all help me get the bike ready, which means you already know how to do it. The deliveries themselves are your final test."

He hopped onto the bike. "I can't remember the last time I rode one of these."

"Well, it's like they say. You don't forget how." I giggled. "It's just like riding a bicycle."

He shook his head slowly, his gaze turning up to the sky, before closing his eyes as if embarrassed for me.

I gave him a cheesy grin. "You're going to miss my terrible jokes, admit it."

"Of course I'll miss *you*," Sam started. "I don't know what I would have done without you here. Might not have even pursued a career in baking. Gosh knows I wasn't going to approach Zeke about an internship."

"He probably could have used you."

"No doubt. But I *needed* you."

My chest tightened, and my eyes had no doubt turned glassy, one step away from welling with tears. I was probably going to miss Sam more than the other way around. "Okay, go now before I cry. Libby hates when people are late. Which for her means on time."

He took off on the bike and turned up Founder Street to start his deliveries.

As I walked back inside, I clapped once to get everyone's attention. "All right, anyone who can, please help Sarah with decorating." We weren't doing much, just a few things to make the space a bit more festive. Lily, Brittni, and Bryan headed into the shop as Gina wrapped up the last of her cookies.

I grabbed the phone off the wall. "I'll be out to join you in a moment," I said, already dialing.

"Hello, Riverview Bed and Breakfast, Billy speaking."

"Hi, Billy. It's Joanie from the bakery. Libby around?"

"In the kitchen already. Let me forward you."

"Great thanks."

The line muted a moment before ringing again. Libby picked up on the second ring. "Libby here."

"It's Joanie. Wanted to let you know that Sam has left the bakery and will be heading your way soon. He has a delivery at the historical society, then another at the law office at the top of Main Street, but those won't take long."

"And you want me to stall him a bit, right?"

"Yes. His parents are picking up Trudy from the nursing home, and I want to give them ample time to get her here."

"Can do."

"Show him how you like to load the trays. Give him a history of tea services. Whatever you need to."

"Got it. I'll put him to work in the garden."

I stifled a snort. "That would take fifteen hours. I only need fifteen minutes."

"Fine, fine, fine. He can dust the teacups," she quipped before breaking into giggles. "I'll see you on Monday. I hope you have a wonderful party for dear Sam. Such a sweet boy."

"Have a good day, Libby, and thanks for doing this."

We hung up, and I walked to the closet to grab the box of general party supplies I had in there. I brought the box into the shop, where my team was in full swing. Brittni was putting a new sign on the window using the window chalk. Closed for a Special Event. If anyone came to get something, they'd see we were busy. They could come back later. They'd understand. I didn't want anything to interrupt Sam's party.

Todd was already here, helping his sister hang a banner on the back wall. Large blue and yellow letters, colors of the culinary school Sam was going to, alternated to spell out CONGRATULATIONS! Lily was arranging centerpieces on the small tables at the side of the room. Bryan had dashed across the street to the general store to get helium-filled balloons. Sarah and I set to work blowing up those I had in the box. Gina taped them along the counter and on the shelves.

A few minutes later, the door to the shop opened, and in walked Trudy with a little help from Sam's dad. Behind them was Sam's mom.

I hurried over to Trudy, and we greeted each other with a warm hug.

"It's so good to see you again. Did you have fun sleeping under the stars?" she asked of the meeting after the coven's esbat.

I nodded. "It was fun meeting everyone and getting to see what they could do. Already looking forward to the next one."

"Good. Good." She let me lead her to a table, and I helped her sit down.

Next, Sam's parents came up to me. I'd seen them several times over the years since coming to Heartwood Hollow, more since Sam had started working here, but we'd never really talked. It had always been little more than a quick hello or an update on how Sam was doing with his internship back when he was doing this for school credit.

His mom hugged me. "Thank you so much for doing this for Sammy. I know how much he adores you, and he's going to be thrilled that you've put this together."

"Well, I adore Sam too, and he's part of the bakery family. It wouldn't be right to not send him off in our own way."

After Sam's mom let me go and stepped back, his dad gave me a quick hug. "You've done so much for him. I can't begin to thank you."

"You don't have to thank me at all," I said, stepping out from his embrace. "I'm happy to do it. You have a great son."

"We do," Sam's mom agreed as his dad wrapped an arm behind her. She glanced at Todd before looking back at me. "I don't know if he'd be him without you, though. You gave him a place where he felt comfortable, and I think that helped him with everything else."

I nodded understandingly. "I'm happy I could provide that for him. And he's done the same for me."

His mom smiled and looked around the shop. "Is there anything we can do to help?"

I shook my head. "We're just about all set."

They each took a seat at Trudy's table, and Todd joined them a moment later once he was done hanging the banner.

Bryan returned soon after with an overwhelming number of balloons. "If I weren't me, I'd worry about floating away with all of these," he said as he struggled to corral them into the shop. They kept jostling one another out of place and back outside. I rushed to help him, not wanting any of them to get loose from the bundle and take off. I pulled a few toward me, and that seemed to help, and after a few more seconds, Bryan and all the balloons were through the door. He and Lily then arranged them so that they were obscuring the window near in front of the table seating. I didn't want Sam to be able to see his family and Todd first thing when he got back.

Several minutes passed before I felt the matchmaking tingle unique to Todd and Sam.

"Sam will be here in about two minutes," I announced.

"How do you know that?" his dad asked.

I gave him a knowing smile before looking at Trudy. "Oh, just a hunch I have. Time to get into your places."

Right on time, Sam arrived. He pulled up to a stop on the sidewalk before removing a piece of paper from his pocket. Sam looked at the slip, at the number on our door, and then back to the slip. He quirked a brow as he looked through the window at Sarah and me attempting to look busy behind the counter.

Sam grabbed the cake box out of the trailer, then pursed his lips and squinted at me as he pushed through the door. He stopped in the doorway.

"Hey, Sam," I said with extra chipperness in my voice, hoping to distract him away from seeing his family. "You have a problem with an order?" I came around the counter, nearly tripping over a hiding Brittni as I tried to avoid stepping on Lily's foot as she hid crouched in the corner.

He looked at the slip once more. "The address says the delivery is here."

"Let me see." I took the box from him and the slip, making a show of looking at it. "Well, it's correct."

"What do you mean?"

"Surprise!" we all shouted in unison, jumping out from our hiding spots or rushing up to him.

Overhead the lights surged, a test of the new light tube we'd put in there. Thank goodness it held. Now *that* would have been a surprise.

Sam's hands flew to his face as his mouth dropped open, and his knees almost buckled. He squatted before standing back up to take hugs from his parents, Todd, Brittni, the rest of the baking family in a group hug, then me, and finally Trudy.

"You did this for me?" he asked, holding on to his grandmother.

The tears from earlier welled in my eyes once more. "Surprise, Sam. We couldn't let you go off to college without doing something for you. So here we are. This is your graduation slash going away party."

He looked to his dad, who came to take Trudy's arm, and Sam rushed toward me, his arms open wide for another hug. "Thank you so much."

"Sorry I had to make you deliver your own cake. It was the only way I could get you out of the bakery so you wouldn't suspect something."

"It was smart. You know that door isn't soundproof. I would have picked up on something."

Todd laughed. "Well, you didn't pick up on the balloons or the signs we made you, silly."

Sam took in the shop. "Wow. Look at all of this. I can't believe you did all this."

Brittni bounced on her feet. "You want to see your cake?"

"Of course I do. Explains why you wouldn't show me what you were working on." Since she started here, she'd been eager to show him everything she was learning how to do.

I brought the cake to one of the tables. "Lily, will you go grab a knife and a server?"

She scooted into the kitchen, then returned a moment later with them.

Sarah pulled a stack of plates from their spot on the back shelf. She walked back around the counter and placed them next to the cake box.

When we'd all gathered around the table, Sam lifted the box top to reveal a cake covered in things that made Sam, Sam. A painted abstract background with fondant sculptures of all of Sam's favorite things ranging from music notes to a Pride flag to baking tools. Brittni had even made a beanie that looked just like the one he always wore no matter the weather.

Sam's jaw dropped. "This is amazing! I don't know if I can eat it."

"Well, I'm hungry," Bryan said, "So I can if you can't."

Everyone laughed at that

Lily held the knife handle out to Sam. "Would you like to do the honors?"

"You bet," he said, taking the knife and expertly cutting into the cake. He placed the first slice on a plate and onto the table, then cut into the cake again. He passed that slice out and continued to do so until we all had a piece.

After eating, Sam opened up presents the baking team had bought him. They weren't much, but I knew he'd appreciate the extra baking tools.

Next, he opened the card everyone had signed. Several gift cards fell out, sliding onto the table.

As he picked them up, he must have seen the names on them. He tilted his head to the side.

"I may have a few contacts left at school. and had them pick these up from places right around campus. You're going to learn a ton about cooking, and you'll be practicing a lot, but there are going to be times when you won't want to cook. So I hope this gets you through the first little bit until you find your favorite spots to eat at."

Sam's mom pressed her hand to her heart and looked at me warmly. Trudy nodded her head slowly once.

"This is great!" Sam said excitedly. He flipped through the plastic cards once more. "Pizza, sandwiches, Chinese food, Indian, burgers. Wow! And I know if you've gotten these, then the food has to be good."

I chuckled. "At least they were when I was there." It had been six years since I'd graduated. "But I doubt anyone who helped me would have let me get you something from a place that had slipped."

"Thank you. Really. I love it."

"They all know to be on the lookout for you too. And some of those are food trucks."

His eyes widened with excitement, and he hopped up from his chair, then rushed over to me for another hug. "You're the best."

I squeezed him extra hard. "And you are too. You're going to do great things."

After he let me go, he went around to everyone once more to give them hugs.

"So I hope you liked your party," I said as he sat back down. "I know it wasn't much—"

"It was perfect."

I smiled, then turned to make sure I could see everyone. "Some of you have other things to get to, I'm sure, so once you're done eating, don't feel like you have to stick around. We're done baking for the day, and I know most of you have already cleaned up."

Gina looked at Sam. "We took care of your area too."

Lily chuckled. "Didn't feel right to throw you a party and then make you clean up afterward."

Sam's dad placed a hand on his son's shoulder. "We can put the cake in the car so you don't have to walk home with it. He does get to take home the cake, right?"

I smiled. "Of course."

"Oh, good. It was delicious. I try not to eat so many sweets, the byproduct of growing up with a candy maker, but I think I could eat the rest of this myself."

I laughed. "Well, you know where to find me if you want anything."

He stood. "Thank you." Then he helped Trudy stand as his wife took the cake. "See you back at the house, sometime, Sammy. I assume you'll be out with your friends for a while."

Sam nodded.

"It's a nice day. Enjoy it."

Sam said goodbye to his parents as I hugged Trudy once more. "Guess I'll be seeing you regularly now."

She nodded. "At least until it gets too cold for the barn."

Maybe Vince could convince her to go to the new paranormal support group we were putting together. Even though she'd retired from the magical life, I was sure she'd enjoy the socialization with others like her, especially if it were somewhere warm.

Sam took Trudy's arm. "I'll be right back." He helped her to the car, staying outside until the car drove off. Then he hopped on the bike that was still parked outside and turned it around. A few minutes later, he reappeared in the shop from the kitchen. It was just Sarah, Todd, Brittni, and I now.

I glanced up at him from where I was wiping down the tables. "Thanks. You didn't have to do that."

"Of course I did. I had to finish the job."

"Everything did go okay, right? Libby didn't give you a hard time?"

He shook his head, a smile playing on his lips. "Nah. She's very particular about her tea trays, though."

"Everything has its place."

"Oh! And at the lawyer's office, your friend was there. The one Bryan likes."

"Erin?"

"Yeah. I didn't get all of what they were saying, something

about ship conservation? I don't know if I got that right. The receptionist was trying to hurry me out the door."

Whatever it was didn't sound good. "Thanks, Sam. I'm sure I'll hear all about it soon."

He nodded, then gave me another hug. "Thanks again for my party. And all the gift cards."

As Sam stepped back, Todd came up behind him and put an arm around his shoulder. "Hope you'll save some of them for when I come visit."

"Me too," Brittni added, as she squeezed her head between theirs, throwing her arms over both their outer shoulders.

Sam turned, forcing the others to as well. "What? No, those are all mine. Gotta find out what's good before you both get there." He laughed.

Done wiping the tables, I jokingly shooed them away, rag in hand. "You three have fun. See you tomorrow, Brittni . . ." And then it hit me. "Sam?"

He glanced over his shoulder, then dropped his arms from around his Brittni so he could face me.

"Will I see you again before you leave?"

I could practically see him looking at his mental to-do list. After a moment, he answered, "I'll stop in for something for the road."

"Good." I smiled weakly, fighting back tears. "I'm not ready to say goodbye today."

He walked toward me, arms already outstretched for a hug. I stepped between them, and he wrapped them around me. "It's only a see you later. I'll be back for every break. I'll probably need the shifts too." He pulled back so that I could see his face and cracked a smile. "I'm a poor college student now, you know."

I chuckled at the comment but followed it with a big sniffle. "You can have all the shifts you want. I'll be looking forward to it."

"Thanks, Joanie. For everything." He gave me a quick hug before he resumed his earlier position with Todd and Brittni.

Sam and Todd waved with their free hands as Brittni struggled to maintain her position in the middle as they walked to the door. It proved impossible for them all to fit through at the same time, but much laughter ensued as they tried to make it work.

Wiping my eyes, I followed them to the door, then after they left, I erased the sign saying we were closed as Sarah wrangled the balloons so they weren't all blocking the window.

She tied several balloons together. "What do you think he meant by ship conservation?"

I pulled the bunch I had to the corner of the room. "I have no idea, but with the way things are around here, I'm sure we'll find out."

CHAPTER 32

S arah and I had almost finished cleaning up the shop from Sam's party when Becca came back to the bakery. The moment I saw her, I thought I was about to be asked to go on a paranormal investigation in Alice's place. I had yet to hear if she had returned from wherever she was on her conveniently timed trip.

"Hi, Joanie," Becca said, a hesitant smile on her face. Her gaze flicked to Sarah, then back to me. "Got a minute?"

"Sure." I motioned to the tables. "You want to sit?"

She pinched her lips to the side. "No. It won't take long. It's about Alice's future sister-in-law."

Instantly, I was on edge. "Erin?"

"Yeah. Something strange happened earlier, and it's been eating at me ever since. Alice isn't back yet, or else I'd have gone to her, but I *know* she's friends with some of your bakers and that you've talked to her, so I figured you were the next best option."

Sarah stepped around me. "I'll be in the kitchen."

Once the door closed, I turned back to Becca. "Okay . . ."

She took a deep breath. "Well, when I'm not working on

216

the investigations, I work nights at the hospital. Keeps my schedule regular. Anyway, I was driving home after my shift and saw Erin trying to start her car. I ended up giving her a jump and got her on her way, but it was really strange. I remember her from school. She didn't seem like herself at all, and I could tell she'd been crying."

"Did she say why?"

"She was really worked up, more than what I thought was normal for a car issue. More like this was the thing that finally broke her down. I asked if she and Travis had a fight. I mean, what else could it be?" If only she knew. "She didn't say no, but she wasn't denying it either."

I held up a finger. "Give me a second." I popped my head into the kitchen. "Bryan? Can you come out here?" Thank goodness his running to get the balloons earlier had prevented him from cleaning up his space, keeping him here after the others had left.

My voice must have given something away. Sarah met my gaze and gave me a reassuring nod. She'd be listening once the door closed.

Bryan followed me back into the shop. "Becca?"

She smiled softly. "Hey, Bry. Long time."

He looked at her, genuine confusion on his face. "Why are you here? What's going on?"

I placed my hand on his arm. "It's Erin."

His shoulders tensed. "What about her?"

Becca took a tentative step forward. "I ran into her this morning. She was upset. Really upset."

"Travis?" He balled up one of his hands into a fist. It almost looked as if he had gotten bigger somehow.

"She didn't say, but you might want to go check on her. I think she could use a friend."

"Where is she?"

Becca shrugged as I said, "Try the law office. Sam mentioned seeing her there during his delivery." Bryan met my gaze as he took a steadying breath, and I nodded. "Go. Call me if you need anything."

Without another word, he sprinted out the front door.

Becca scratched at her forehead as she glanced out the door. Bryan was already nowhere to be seen. "You know? Back when we were in high school, had that happened, Bryan would have broken something. His hand against a wall, probably. Or the wall. He's a big dude, and would never hurt a fly, but when his family is threatened, he doesn't always think so rationally. Even just for the possibility of someone hurting Erin. Being here has been good for him. He's grown up."

"You seem to know a lot about him."

Becca shrugged, still looking toward the door. "Long story that we don't have time for." She turned back to me. "Thanks for talking with me."

"Thank you for coming to tell me. I've been worried about her."

She sighed. "I have no idea what Erin sees in Travis. Especially with my brother standing right there waiting for her."

She was Bryan's sister? One of them, anyway. I didn't call her on it. I doubted she realized what she had said, and besides, she was right. We didn't have the time.

CHAPTER 33

E rin stormed into the shop an hour later, Bryan following close behind.

"Stressed?" she shouted as if she were already mid-argument. Based on Bryan's face, perhaps she was. It wouldn't have surprised me if she'd been ranting about whatever it was for a while.

"Erin, what's going on?" I asked, trying to direct her attention to me so I could get the full story.

She threw her hands in the air. "Travis filed for conservatorship because"—she made air quotes—"'the stress of the wedding has gotten to me' and he's worried about what I might do."

"What!" My mouth dropped open. What Sam has said now made sense. Ship conservation. Conservatorship. Got it. "How is that even possible? You're not married yet. I thought only family members could do that."

Her breath came out part heavy sigh, part sound of disgust. "That's only in some states. Here it's any qualified adult. And usually it would take a while, but I gave him power of attorney a few years back when I was going on a week-long trip for school. He was going too, although he did it for fun, not a class. He suggested it as a safety precaution should anything happen while we were gone."

Sarah blinked rapidly as if having a hard time processing what she'd just heard. "What about your mom?" I wondered the same.

"It would default to her if something happened to the both of us." She shrugged. "It made sense at the time. We were together already, and he would have been there to make immediate decisions should that have been needed. I'd not thought of it again until now. But now he's using that to fast-track this entire process."

Now Sarah's mouth had dropped open. "That's so underhanded!"

"How did you find out?"

"I won't name names because the person still has ties to town, but an old friend works in the law office he uses in the city. She called to give me the heads-up. Hadn't talked to her in years. You were right about me giving some of my friends another chance. Same with Becca. Once she jumped my car, I drove down to Main Street to get my own lawyer. You better believe I am fighting it."

I didn't really want to ask the next question, worried she hadn't thought that far ahead yet, but it had to be asked. "And what about the wedding?"

"Oh, I am not marrying him while I'm trying to fight him to prove I'm fully capable of making my own decisions. No thank you. The wedding is off." She sighed. "I don't know how we can recover from this."

Part of me wanted to tell her flat out to forget repairing her relationship and that she should break up with Travis completely, but I was sure her friends had once done the same. If she'd not listened then, pushing her in that direction if she wasn't willing to go could cause her to put walls up and shut me out. Then we'd definitely be lost. Her. Bryan. And her grandmother. Right now, though, I still had hope for all of them.

Instead, I reached into the case and pulled out a cookie, then handed it to her. A cookie wouldn't solve her problems, but it would help her start to feel better. "Erin, how about you stay at my place for a while? Maybe some time away from Travis will help clear your head."

She took the cookie from me and immediately broke off a piece, listening but likely not ready to commit.

"I have the space," I pressed. "And we seem to be about the same size, so I have pajamas and clothes for you to wear tomorrow. Or we can go get your things. Whatever you need."

"I don't want to impose."

"You won't be. I offered. And maybe having you there could help me with your grandmother."

That was all it took. "Okay. I'll do what I have to if it means getting Nonni back. Thanks, Joanie. I promise it won't be long. I don't feel right going to my mom's and involving her in all of this. Especially since I never told her about Nonni."

I grabbed my purse from under the counter. "Let me give you a key so you can get in."

Erin raised an eyebrow at me. "You lock your house?"

Bryan turned to her, "She even locks her bike."

"I'm not from here, remember? Sam's going to come home locking things up too. Just you wait." I dug out my spare key, then tossed it to her. "Here."

"Is Saffy going to be okay with the bags coming in and everything? I don't need to put her in another room or anything to keep her from going outside, do I?"

"Saffy? Outside?" I shook my head. "It's never been a

worry. She'll probably sleep through the whole thing. Although you kind of freak her out a bit, Bryan."

"I'll keep my distance. It's her space. I'm not trying to encroach."

I thought a moment about what would smooth things over with my cat. "In the lower cupboard next to the sink in the kitchen is the container where I keep her treats. If she gets bothered, just throw two of those in there and she'll be your best friend."

"Might do it anyway. Since Erin's staying with you, I'll probably be over once or twice."

"Sounds good. Let me know if you run into any trouble. If not, I'll see you at the house."

Erin was sitting on the couch when I opened the door, a timid smile on her face and dark circles under her eyes. This was the first time I'd seen her not looking completely put together. Even when she'd first come to me looking for my help, she'd been perfectly coiffed and dressed.

I hung my bag up on my coat tree. "How about some tea?"

"I'd like that, thanks."

A few minutes later, I returned with a full tea tray with two mugs of steeping tea and a snack. She took the cup from me before I set the tray down in front of us on the coffee table. I sat next to her, and Saffy, who had been on the back of the couch wiggled in between us.

Now that the heat of anger had left her, she didn't seem ready to talk about what happened. No doubt she was still processing it. And judging by the looks of her, emotionally exhausted. I'd hoped we'd be able to try a seance to summon her grandmother tonight, but we could wait a night. Erin needed to rest first.

"Can I ask you something?"

"That depends." She blew on her tea. "Sorry, that came out wrong. I just don't know if I want to talk about . . ." She waved her hand out in front of her, flapping it randomly.

"It's okay. I get it. And we don't have to. It's about Bryan. He seemed surprised to see Becca when she came into the shop. I know they're siblings, but he didn't tell me that. More she let it slip."

"They haven't spoken in some time. It's sad really. They'd been so close." She took a sip. "We all had been."

"What happened if you don't mind me asking?"

"It started when Bryan's parents got divorced, but that's not my story to tell as far as the two of them. As for me and her, part of it was that she moved with her mom so I didn't see her as much, and the other was, well, Travis."

I nodded. "It's hard being in a relationship and maintaining friends."

"Especially when your friends don't like the guy you're with." She scoffed, and Saffy headbutted her. "Guess I should have listened."

"I'm sure it's not too late to get your friendship back. All of them."

Erin scratched Saffy's neck. "Doubt it. People don't like to be dropped like that."

"They might surprise you. Like Becca today and your friend who called you from the lawyer's office."

"I'd only be able to get some of them back if Travis and I broke up." A tear fell down her cheek.

"Maybe that's true, but I bet if you talked to others, they'd understand. Just something to think about."

"I have a lot of thinking to do."

CHAPTER 34

The next morning, Bryan got to the bakery early again. Really early. But unlike recent mornings, there was no tenseness in his shoulders, and he looked like he'd slept.

"Keep showing up like this and I'm going to get used to it," I said with a smile.

He chuckled, a low grumbly sound. "We get so busy, it's sometimes the only chance I get to talk to you."

I unlocked the door to the kitchen, then pushed it open to let him in. "It's good to see you. How are you doing after yesterday?"

"Much better. Thank you for taking Erin in. She's safe with you." He headed for his workstation and stored his keys and wallet inside one of the drawers.

"You'd like her to be with you, though."

He spun to face me. "Sure do, but that wouldn't be the best option for her right now. Will be the first place Travis looks for her."

"Why's that?"

"Becca and I helped Erin grab some of her things before she went to your place yesterday."

"You saw your sister again. That's good." I passed him a mixing bowl.

"You know she's my sister?"

I took a mixing bowl for myself and grabbed a spatula. "She may have let it slip when she was here. I don't think she'd meant to."

He shook his head. "Probably not."

I headed to my station to set up for the day. I wasn't going to pry.

Finally he spoke up. "You don't want to know what happened?"

"Of course I do"—I turned and leaned against my table—"but I wanted to see if you'd offer before I asked."

"I'm a hellcat."

All the buildup for that? "Uh, yeah. I know. You were on the high school wrestling team."

"No, Joanie. I'm a *hellcat*. A real one. I can shift at will."

"Oh . . . Okay. I didn't realize we had those here. Is that why Saffy's weird around you?"

"Yeah. It makes animals a little funny." He studied me a moment, one eyebrow raised. "You seem to be taking that really well."

"The last few months have been quite something." I pointed to my head, extending and bending my finger repeatedly. "Witch, remember? One who is a matchmaker and can talk to ghosts too. So how does all of that play into what's going on between you and your sister?"

"My parents got divorced. Mom went to a new pride. Dad stayed. So did I. My sisters did not. I had a chance at being alpha. Still might. I wasn't going to give that up." He shrugged. "Maybe I should have."

Alpha? I'd read enough books to know what an alpha was. That explained several things I'd learned about Bryan over the years, starting with his losing the job he had before coming here.

"I'm a firm believer that everything happens the way it should and for a reason. As my gram says, there are no coincidences. It's all brought us here to this moment."

He nodded but didn't seem certain.

"You going to keep talking to your sister?"

"I hope so."

I gave him an encouraging smile. "She'll like that. I don't know her beyond talking to her yesterday and the other day, but I get the feeling she misses you."

"You talked to her the other day?"

I nodded. "Not about Erin, though. And I had no clue she was your sister then. She does some pretty cool stuff."

"Is that all you're going to tell me about them?"

I shook my head in an exaggerated, almost teasing motion. "You should ask her about her current hobbies. That's all I'm going to say."

"Thanks, Joanie. I don't really know how to go about talking to someone I haven't in a few years. Maybe I'll start with that."

"Start with what?" Gina asked as she walked into the kitchen with Lily.

"Cookies," Bryan answered quickly.

She eyed him skeptically. "But you usually do the muffins."

I cleared my throat. "With Sam gone now, we're doing a bit of shuffling," which was true. "Get out of our comfort zones a bit. How about you make the muffins?"

"Sounds good to me." Gina had always been open to making anything. She liked it all. Even the things that blurred the line of what I wasn't supposed to make per the town council's rules. That reminded me, I still needed to ask Zeke about baking with more savory fillings.

Brittni arrived a moment later, and as I helped her get situated at her solo station, we all fell into a rhythm. Although Sam was already missed, the mood in the kitchen felt lighter than it had in days.

Erin stopped by the bakery around lunchtime carrying a to-go bag with the Leafs and Grounds logo on it.

She plopped the bag onto one of the tables. "I usually head home for lunch, but I didn't want to impose any more than I already am and disrupt your cat's schedule. I know how they're creatures of habit, especially at mealtime."

"Aww, you could have. You're staying there. It means you can come and go as you need to." I chuckled. "Though it was probably a good call. Saffy wouldn't have left you alone until you fed her, and she doesn't need it."

Bryan stepped out of the kitchen. "We're all set back there, Jo—" His eyes lit up as he caught sight of Erin. "Hey, Rin. What did you bring me?"

"You're favorite." She pulled two containers out of the bag and set one in front of her and the other across from her.

His face softened. "You're the best." My matchmaking tingle swirled into my stomach at the reaction.

Erin smiled as she sat down. "My thanks for you helping me get some of my stuff yesterday."

Bryan pulled the seat out across from her. "You do not need to thank me for that. And my offer still stands. You say the word and I'll move it all again to my place. Travis has already driven by to see if you're there. It would be safe now."

Erin peeked over at Bryan as she chewed. "Glad to know

we threw him off the scent like we thought we would, but have you seen your apartment?"

Bryan crossed his arms in mock indignation. "Hey . . . what's wrong with my apartment?"

"It looks as if it's been ransacked by a pack of wolves." She smirked.

He raised an eyebrow at her.

She tossed him a knowing smile. "What? I thought it was more clever than calling it a pigsty." She looked back at Sarah and me. "Total bachelor pad."

Bryan gave her a look. "But wolves? Really. And it's okay, I told Joanie already."

"I know, I know. But it really is that bad." She laughed. "I thought cats were supposed to be cleaner."

Sarah cleared her throat. She looked absolutely confused. "Well, none of you told me."

Her comment seemed to catch Bryan off guard, almost as if he'd forgotten she was there. Maybe that was how she was so good at finding things out. She sort of blended in and people talked about things right in front of her even when she wasn't purposefully eavesdropping. Perhaps hiding in plain sight was a familiar's superpower.

I turned to Bryan. "I trust Sarah with my life. She's my familiar."

He gave me a serious nod before looking back at her. "I'm a hellcat. A shapeshifter."

Sarah scrunched her face and flapped her hand in a dismissive wave. "Oh, I knew that already. Thought I was missing something big."

Bryan's mouth dropped open, and Erin burst out laughing. I shook my head slowly. Of course she already knew.

"How?" Bryan finally asked.

"I know a lot more than any of you think I do." She'd told

me the same once. "The signs are pretty obvious. Well, to someone who knows what to look for."

Bryan continued to stare at her, his mouth still slightly open. "Huh," he said after a moment, shaking his head as if to clear it.

That sent Erin into another round of giggles. After the stress of the last several days, it was good to see her laugh. I wondered how much she laughed with Travis. Seemed it happened all the time with Bryan.

The two had their lunch and then went on their way, but not before I promised Erin that we would try to summon her grandmother through a seance later that night.

CHAPTER 35

It wasn't until I could see my house that I knew something was wrong. But the raised voices coming from the front yard alerted me to someone else being here as well. And Travis didn't sound happy.

Fearing my approach would only make it worse, I didn't want to come up behind him and make him feel boxed in, especially in my front yard, so I detoured. My backyard gate popped open, almost as if it were beckoning me inside that way. And who was I to argue? There were no such thing as coincidences.

I stepped into my kitchen, then crossed into my living room. Erin was on the couch. Tears of frustration and sadness rolled down her cheeks. Saffy, her tail poofy, was staring out the window. Bryan stood at the door, his arms crossed.

An almost growl rumbled through him, sending Saffy running to her cat tree. "Erin is not coming outside to talk to you."

"I demand to speak with her," Travis shouted back.

"She's not someone you demand to speak with like she's some manager and you're an unhappy customer."

"She's my fiancée and I want to talk to her."

That seemed to spur Erin into action. She charged to the door. "You are NOT my fiancé," she yelled as she pushed Bryan back a step.

I crept to the window and peeked out, lifting the edge of the curtain slightly so Travis wouldn't see me. Not that he was looking in my direction. His entire focus was on Erin as she yelled.

"You do not get to file for conservatorship on someone who doesn't need it without repercussions."

He held his hands out in front of him at his sides. "I just don't want you to do anything stupid regarding your finances."

"I'm not going to do anything stupid."

"You're still on this ridiculous search to find your grandmother's ghost. What's your next step if a baker of all people can't help you? Fork over your money to a purported psychic?"

Erin crossed her arms. "I'll do what I need to, to find Nonni."

Travis pulled something from behind him, then held up the sheet of paper. "Well, you don't get to make that call. This statement says that I do."

She huffed. "Well, I'm having an injunction filed."

"And until that happens, what I say goes. Now let's go home."

If Erin had been a dryad, she would have sprouted roots right through my floor. "I'm not going with you. If you think I am, then you're sorely mistaken."

"Don't make me come get you."

Who did he think he was talking to? A petulant toddler refusing to come out of one of those ball pits at a kids' arcade? Ken and I had recently taken Ivy to one in

Snowhaven, and even at nearly eight years old, she'd loved playing in the ball pit with her friends.

But if Travis thought that he could just come inside my house to remove her, he had another think coming.

I let the curtain fall back across the corner of the window and whispered, "You don't have anything to stop him yet?"

She turned toward me and stepped away from the door. "Hopefully soon. Megan said she'd have it for me at the end of the day." She sighed. "I'm really sorry he's out there like that."

I held up a hand. "No apology needed. Let me see what I can do."

Bryan had resumed his place in front of the door, his hands now on his hips presumably to block Travis's view even more. He didn't look as imposing as he had with his arms crossed. As I shifted one of his arms so I could get in front of him, I saw Travis had come up closer to the house.

"I'm going to have to ask you to leave now."

His head shifted back in surprise. "I didn't realize you were home."

"So me not being home would have made your behavior okay? Erin has refused to go with you, and as the owner of this house, I say she's free to stay here as long as she wants no matter what that paper you have there says."

At that moment, an ambulance, fire truck, and police car pulled up in front of the house. The EMTs were first out of the vehicles, and I waited anxiously for the police officer. One of my neighbors must have called.

Finally, Seth and his partner, Oliver, stepped out of the car. Thank the Goddess.

They stopped at Travis first, speaking too quietly for me to hear, but Travis pointed to the house and then tapped on the paper he was still holding. He handed it to Oliver as Seth glanced at me standing at the door, his gaze darting between me and Bryan.

I gave him a slight wave but didn't smile, and instead raised both my eyebrows as I dropped my chin toward my chest and drew my lips to the side.

He held up a finger in a one-minute gesture.

Travis was still talking, his hands raising and lowering with his palms up as he pled whatever case he thought he had. Finally, it seemed like he'd had enough.

"Well, go get her, will you?" He turned to the paramedics as if hoping to find a more sympathetic audience with them. But they glanced at the two officers.

Seth held up his hand as if telling them to stand down. Then he and Oliver approached the house, leaving Travis in the middle of the yard.

"Joanie, is everything okay in here?" Seth asked.

"It would be a whole lot better if Travis stopped harassing my friends."

"It just you three in there?"

I nodded. "Erin's staying with me for as long as she needs to. How about you both come in and we can fill you in. I'd have Erin come to the door, but I think that would set Travis off again."

Bryan and I stepped aside so Seth and his partner could come in. It was then that I noticed Matt standing on his porch, arms crossed. The neighbor to his left was on hers. Guilt gnawed at me for their evenings being interrupted by this. At one point, something like this would have embarrassed me too—I didn't want the attention, and certainly not like this—but now that I knew pretty much everyone living around me was a member of the local coven, their stares felt less like ones of judgment and more of concern or protection. As if they were watching out for me . . . one of their own.

"Is it okay to offer you tea if you're here on official business? Are you allowed to sit, or do you have to stay standing?" Seth had come to the house numerous times with his girlfriend, Courtney, but he'd never come here before in uniform.

"I wouldn't say no to water, actually," Oliver said. "It's a hot one, and the AC is on the fritz in the car. Kinda makes me want to stick my head out the window."

Bryan snorted, and for the first time since I'd gotten home, I saw him with a smile on his face. "It would suit you."

Oliver seemed to be unfazed by the comment as Seth shook his head slowly, his eyes closed.

"Seth, do you want water?"

"Nah, I'm good."

I looked at Bryan, who shook his head, then headed into the kitchen, flipping on the burner under the teapot. It would do Erin some good to have something calming. Me too. With that started, I filled up a glass of water for Oliver. I returned to the living room as the tea water heated, to keep him from having to wait.

Erin was in the middle of her explanation. Most of it I knew already.

"And once Joanie left, I thought more about what she'd said, and although she'd offered me her pajamas to use that night, well, I have mine that I prefer. And really, I thought he'd had enough time to cool down, so if he had, then great, I'd stay home. If not, I'd come back here for the night.

"When I got to the house, Travis seemed annoyed but calmer than he had been when he was at Joanie's bakery. We talked for a few minutes, and I decided I'd stay. But he never came to bed that night, and he was gone when I woke up. He clearly was still mad at me, and when my car wouldn't start, that was the last straw. I broke down." She took a calming breath. "I have every right to be upset over what happened."

Seth glanced up at her, pen now still. "Mr. Ellison said that you claim to see ghosts and that's why he's filed for conservatorship."

She leveled her gaze on Seth. "Even if I did, that doesn't necessarily mean I can't take care of myself. There have been stranger things said about other townspeople that have turned out to be true."

Now it was my turn to snort. When both officers turned to me, I shrugged. "What? It's true."

Seth and his partner shared a look that I didn't understand.

Seth directed his next question to Bryan. "And where do you fit in all this?"

The whistle on the teapot let out a shrill bird tweet, and as I turned to take care of it, I heard Erin explain, "He's my best friend. He offered to help me get some of my things from the house today because I wasn't going to go alone this time. I wasn't naïve enough to think that Travis wouldn't try to stop me again." A second later, she continued, "As you can see, I was right about that."

"Joanie, can you come back in here?"

"Be right out." I finished pouring the tea, then carried both cups back to the living room. Erin readily accepted the warm cup. "Still needs a few minutes to steep."

As I sat back down, Seth asked me, "So how did you get involved in all of this?"

"Erin's one of my friends, and she came to me with a problem that I could help her with." I pointed to the ceiling. "I have another bedroom up there that barely gets used."

Seth nodded slowly as if knowing that what I'd said wasn't the whole story. But it wasn't anything I wanted on record, and this was not how Courtney was going to find out about what I could do.

I blew across the top of my tea mug. Barely done steeping, it was still too hot for me to drink.

Erin took a sip of her tea, wincing, I assumed, at the temperature. "So are you going to make me go with him?"

"She has a lawyer," I added in case that hadn't been mentioned. "The paperwork is coming."

"The paperwork is here," a voice announced from my kitchen. A moment later, the back door shut, and Megan strode into the room.

Bryan visibly relaxed, though maintained his stance. "Way to make a dramatic entrance."

She cocked her head, then smiled. "Gate was open, so I figured someone saw me coming and opened it or something."

She didn't know that my gate seemed to have a mind of its own with letting people in. Nor did she need to. "We're glad to see you."

Megan plopped down next to Erin on the couch. "I have the injunction here. It doesn't void his petition for conservatorship, but it does stop his ability to act upon it while we fight it."

"Mind if I see that, Meg?" Oliver asked, holding his hand out.

Megan leaned forward and thrust the paper out at him. "Happily."

He took the document, then stepped back to Seth so the two of them could look at it together. After a moment, Seth spoke, "To answer your question, Erin, no, you will not have to go with him."

She let out a large sigh of relief, then glanced at Megan. "Thank you. You made it just in time."

I looked at Seth. "Now what can be done about the uninvited guest in my front yard? I presume he's still there."

Bryan glanced out the front door. "Oh, he's still here, all right. The rescue and fire truck are still out there too. What sort of resources is he wasting because of all of this? "

"We never gave them the all-clear," Oliver answered. "They stay until we tell them to go, and had we assessed that she needed to go, they would have been able to take her."

Seth pressed a button on the walkie on his shirt. "All right, everyone. You can clear out."

"Clear out? What does that mean?" Travis said loud enough so we could hear him, frustration still evident in his voice. Whatever answer he got, we couldn't hear, but it didn't satisfy him. "What? I have the order right here!"

"Seth, please." I didn't know what the rules were for touching officers on duty, but I placed my hand on his arm. "Get him to leave."

A devious smile crossed his face before it settled into a more professional, neutral one. "Are you wanting to press charges?"

"I'd prefer not to," I responded with a shake of my head, "but if forced, I will. He has no right to come on my property, especially not once I've already asked him to leave."

"Darn. Might'a been nice to see him get in trouble for a change," Oliver quipped. Seth tapped him with the back of his hand. "What? It's true."

Seth bobbed his head to one side in acknowledgment of this. Then he stood. "Doesn't mean we can't spook him a bit and let him think you are. Even he knows he doesn't want to get slapped with a trespassing violation. I hope you can put this behind you for the night and have a quiet rest of your evening. He won't be able to bother you again while you're here."

Erin scoffed. "We'll see about that. He doesn't like being told no."

Seth stared at me. "Joanie, you call me anytime if he comes back. I mean it. Even in the middle of the night."

I nodded. "Thanks, Seth. Tell Courtney hi for me."

"Be prepared for her to call if I do that."

I held up a hand. "I'll call her first so she's not surprised when you talk to her. But truly, thank you."

Bryan moved out of the way so Seth and Oliver could leave.

As he continued to look out the door once they were gone, Erin and I peeked out the window. The EMTs and firemen were already settled in their vehicles, the engine pulling away and the ambulance running, waiting to follow.

The officers approached Travis. We couldn't hear what Seth was saying, but Travis did not like whatever it was. "What!"

Seth said something else, then lifted a hand and made a turn-around motion.

Finally Travis nodded, and he headed for the sidewalk. "This isn't over!" he yelled once he'd reached the concrete.

Erin slumped back onto the couch. "Of course it's not."

I placed my hand on her shoulder, patting it gently. "But it is for tonight."

Looked like we'd be able to have our seance after all.

CHAPTER 36

"Joanie?" Matt called from outside. "Are you all right?"

I stood. "Back in a minute."

Bryan pivoted toward the couch as I stepped away. If anyone could comfort Erin, he could.

Matt was with two of our neighbors. Clara put her hand on her chest as she saw me. "Oh thank the goddess, you're all right."

"Yes, I'm fine. Thank you."

"Why was Travis Ellison going on like that?" Matt asked.

I stepped down into the yard so I wouldn't have to talk as loud. "He's been bothering a friend of mine, so I'm letting her stay with me for a few days until she can figure out her next steps."

The neighbor who lived next to Matt, Dolores, bit her lower lip. "I hope I didn't cause any trouble by calling the police. I was just so worried. You've always been such a quiet neighbor. I was worried this was due to your new affiliations."

I released a hard breath. "You thought this because I'd come to a coven meeting?"

They all exchanged a glance.

"But nothing like this has ever happened to any of you in the time I've been here."

"Well, people know not to bother with us now," Dolores started, "but you're young, and that man and his family haven't been the nicest to those who are—"

"Let's say *different*," Clara finished for her.

"Despite being different themselves," Dolores added.

Even Alice? "But his sister—"

Matt shook his head. "There are exceptions in every family."

"Got more of her mother in her," Dolores agreed.

"You knew her mom?" I realized quickly how silly that question was in a small town like this. "Of course you did."

"Nice woman. Shame what happened to her."

"What do you mean? I thought she left."

"We have our suspicions," was all that Dolores replied. Even with Sarah's and my digging into where she'd gone, this was the first time anyone had said anything different than that she'd left. A knot tightened in my stomach.

Clara turned to face me. "You're good to protect your friend like that. Be careful and if you need anything, we have your back."

"You're one of us now, and we wouldn't let anything happen to you," Dolores added.

Matt smiled warmly. "Always been one of us. Before you even realized it."

I took Matt's hand and gave him a big hug, then one to Clara and to Dolores. "Thank you all."

The three dispersed back toward their homes, but as Dolores reached the sidewalk, she made a circular motion with one of her hands, then followed it with a few swooping motions and a zigzagging of her other hand. She smiled at me. "That should help."

Pressing my palms together, I inclined my head in thanks, then she turned back around and continued across the street. I waited until I was sure everyone was inside before heading back into my house.

Bryan sat on the couch, his arm wrapped around Erin as she rested her head against him. Her eyes were closed.

"I'm sorry if I've made trouble for you with your neighbors," Erin began. "Maybe I should just rent a room at the motel in town for a few nights."

"Aw, there's no trouble with them. They'd all come out to make sure we were okay. They're good people." Who didn't seem to like Travis, although I didn't need to add that to the conversation. It wouldn't help. "And I'd never tell you to go to a hotel when I have the space available. It's money you don't need to spend."

"And considering I don't have much right now, thank you." She sniffed. "I spent a lot on the wedding."

Bryan pulled her closer momentarily for a side hug. "I'm sure you'll be able to get some of that back."

For her sake, I hoped so. Right now, I wanted to take her mind off of it all. "Can I make you two something for dinner? I don't have a TV, but I can put on some music or something for background noise and hopefully help you clear your heads a bit."

It looked like Erin was about to object, but Bryan said, "I could eat." Then he poked Erin in the side. "You could too. And now you don't have to worry about fitting into that dress anymore."

I had to keep my mouth from dropping, but Erin's did slightly. Here I was trying to steer away from the whole canceled wedding topic, and he was charging through it. His comment seemed to snap her out of her funk, though. Instead of sending her into another worry spiral over the cost of the dress or about not being certain if she'd still need to fit in it, she laughed.

Erin grinned wickedly. "Joanie, I want something bad for me. Gooey, cheesy, buttery, full of fat and sugar, you name it. Bry's right. And minus the other night with the pizza and fries, I've not eaten anything I like in months because of that dress."

I smiled. "I think I can handle that."

"And I don't want any of that tea you'd offered me the other day either. I don't care how much I bloat." She turned to Bryan. "And maybe we could have ice cream later?"

Bryan's eyes met mine in a silent plea, as if he didn't want to say no to her, not because of the ice cream but because needing to leave the house for it.

But that was a problem I could fix. "I can go pick some up. I need to talk to Lucy about next month's special dough flavors, anyway. You can give me an order and go pick it up for you both."

"Ice cream that comes to me?" Bryan stretched both his arms and put them on the back of the couch. "I like the sound of that."

Erin pushed him teasingly. "You like any food that comes to you."

I chuckled, happy to see her smiling. "All right, let me go get dinner started."

As I cooked a quick macaroni with homemade cheese sauce, I heard other voices coming from the living room that weren't Bryan's or Erin's. I poked my head in and saw the two cuddled on the couch. Bryan was holding his phone up for the two of them. Must have been some sort of video because it wasn't music. My wards should have prevented him from getting any sort of signal, but maybe this qualified as an emergency. That had been my one exception as I established

242

my wards last month. Good to know there was a bit of leeway in what *emergency* meant.

I smiled at the sight of the two of them. This was how it was supposed to be. The matchmaking tingle left no doubt about it.

When dinner was ready, I called them to the kitchen. "Sorry to disturb you two, but I figured this would be easier to eat at the table."

As they crossed the living room, I grabbed a lighter from my drawer and then lit the candle at the center of the table. It was surrounded by a few crystals—citrine, apatite, and carnelian—all meant to help with digestion and other food-related issues. And besides that, it was pretty.

Erin entered the kitchen first. "Oh, that smells good,"

Bryan was only a step behind her. "Try having my sense of smell and knowing what was coming as she made it. I can't wait." He tapped at his phone before shrugging and then slipped it into his pocket. Emergency over.

I'd never thought about what being a shifter would do to one's senses in the human form. The whole idea was still so new to me. "That strong, huh?" He nodded. "How do you survive working in the bakery?"

"Like anything, you become nose blind. Only have to adjust when you make something new like the candies you've been trying out."

I wanted to ask if there were smells that bugged him more than others. Saffy didn't like mint or citrus things. Would he prefer to avoid working with those in the future?

But before I could, Erin pointed out, "There are only two plates here."

"I'm going to head out for a bit. Like I said, go talk to Lucy. I'll grab something while I'm gone. This is for you two. Sit. Destress. Spend some time together."

Whereas Bryan looked excited, Erin asked, "Are you sure? I feel like I'm kicking you out of your house."

"I offered. And I'm happy to do it. Talking to Lucy was something I'd hoped to do anyway, but with Sam's party today, I ran out of time." Truthfully it was that after the cake, I didn't want to be further tempted by ice cream. I still couldn't go in there and not get ice cream.

She nodded, then looked back at Bryan with a smile as she handed him a dish. "Thanks, Joanie."

"You two have a good dinner. Call me if there are any problems."

CHAPTER 37

I pulled my cell phone out of my bag as I reached the sidewalk, then watched as it found service, its bars increasing as I walked further down the street.

My first call was to Courtney, who I hadn't talked to in a few days. "I saw your boyfriend today," I started when she asked me how I'd been. We talked all the way toward Main Street and we still weren't done by the time I'd reached the ice cream shop, so I continued to Founders Park and sat on one of the benches. It was good to talk to one of my best friends, but a weight settled in my stomach as I realized there were parts of me, even just parts of my afternoon that I couldn't tell her about because she didn't yet know about me. Now wasn't the time. I'd been saying that for a few months now, hadn't I? The next time we were in person, I'd have to let her know and accept whatever the outcome was.

"Can we please get together soon?" Courtney asked. "The four of us or just a girls' night. I love seeing you for lunch when you can escape the bakery long enough, but I have not seen you outside of that since the potluck, and I had to share you with everyone else."

"I would love that. Let's meet up for lunch in the next day or two, and we can plan something. I want to see how all of this with Erin works out before I make too many plans, but hopefully she'll be back on her feet next week." And not heading down the aisle.

"Sounds great. I'll pop into the bakery and whisk you away." She laughed. "Get it, whisk you away."

I closed my eyes and shook my head at the pun. "That was a good one."

In the background, a door opened and then closed a moment later, followed by the sound of keys softly hitting something hard. "Hey, honey, I'm on the phone with Joanie," she called out. At a normal volume she said to me, "Seth's home. I'm gonna let you go and get his side. You always leave out the good parts."

My inability to tell her everything often left my stories a bit disjointed. "Sorry." I meant it more than she knew.

"I love your Joanie stories, don't worry. All right, I'll see you soon. Bye."

We hung up, and when I looked up from putting my phone away, Arthur and Bardi were heading this way.

He tipped his fedora as he approached. "Hello, Miss Joanie. Heard you had some trouble at your house today." At my questioning look, he continued, "One of the afternoon dog walkers saw it happen and spread the word around."

As I explained the situation to him, Arthur grew increasingly concerned. His brow furrowed, and even Bardi pawed his leg to check up on him.

When I was done, he said, "Let us help you. We've been keeping a more vigilant eye on things since you mentioned there might be someone who could make us do things. We'll keep a lookout for him too. If he shows back up at your house when you aren't there, we'll come find you."

That wasn't a bad idea. "And you don't mind?"

He shrugged. "What are a few afternoons in an eternity of an afterlife?"

"It could be dangerous for you. We still don't know what happened to Anita."

"All the more reason we should be involved. I'll spread the word and we can figure out who has the power to shift their routes and schedules. You know that I can, but it might be a stretch for others."

"I'll take all the help I can get. And do be careful. You need to be here for football season."

"Wouldn't miss it. I think they've got a chance this year." He quirked a grin. "Anyhow, I'll make sure someone is at your house as soon as possible. Have a good night, Miss Joanie."

"You too, Arthur. Enjoy your walk."

With that, he turned away from me and resumed his walk.

I stood, grateful that the ghosts would now be on the lookout. I couldn't be with Erin all the time. Neither could Bryan. I hoped their dinner was going well. And speaking of dinner, a sundae while I chatted about ice cream flavors sounded like a very good dinner to me.

CHAPTER 38

"Can we try again tonight?" Erin asked. "Just because it didn't work last night doesn't mean it won't tonight. I got better sleep, so my energy should be better."

I shook my head. "I don't think it was a matter of our energy not being enough. She didn't show, not even a flicker of the candlelight. That's never happened before. I don't think she has the energy on her side."

Erin slumped further into the couch. "So what do we do?"

I didn't have a good answer for her, but I was saved from telling her that when someone knocked on the door.

Bryan offered to get it. He'd barely left Erin's side except to come work at the bakery, having fallen asleep on my recliner last night after we'd unsuccessfully attempted to reach her grandmother via a séance. I suspected that after we were done baking for the day, he'd waited for Erin outside the nursing home where she worked, so it was no surprise that he'd followed her back here.

"Um, Joanie? There's no one here."

I came out of the kitchen with two cups of tea. "Are you sure it's not Ivy?" I asked. We were expecting her and Ken to come over with some pizza from Mama's. "She likes to hide behind the bushes. Especially when she beats her father here. She thinks it's funny."

Bryan turned around, a confused look on his face. "I checked. Nobody's here."

Erin started to laugh as she came up behind him. "That's because you can't see them. What you are looking at—or not looking at in your case—is a ghost."

It wasn't lost on me that Erin could see Arthur Miller standing on the porch.

I headed toward the door. "Good to see you again."

"Mind if we talk outside?" Arthur asked. "I can't come in."

"Absolutely." I handed Erin her cup of tea. "You're welcome to come outside. Then you can join in on the conversation."

She looked at me a moment, but then understanding dawned on her as she truly processed who—and what—she had seen outside. "I would like that, thanks."

Bryan's gaze darted between the two of us. "Okay, now this is a bit weird."

I shrugged, a wry smile on my face. "Welcome to my world."

He stepped away from the door to let both Erin and me outside. Erin settled on the porch swing while I leaned up against the railing. Arthur stood in the middle of the porch, the leash in his hand extended so that Bardi could sniff along with the bushes. I'd only seen Bardi in the park, and it was fascinating to see the dog acting so much like, well, a real dog as he investigated this new-to-him area.

After a moment, Bryan joined us outside. "Figured my sister would get a kick out of hearing that I had a conversation with the ghost." I'd been meaning to ask him if he talked to her again. Guess that answered my question. He sat next to Erin, and not knowing where to focus, he looked back and forth between her and me.

"Wanted to update you for the day. He stuck around the house all evening and for most of the day, with one exception being that he showed up to the nursing home this afternoon but must have seen our friend here." He pointed to Bryan, and we all turned to look at him.

"What? Is he saying something about me?"

Erin nodded, a playful smirk crossing her face. "Not going to tell you what, though."

"He is on the move again now," Arthur continued, drawing our attention back to him, "which is why I popped over to talk to you."

With a sigh, Erin said, "Guess that means I should go back inside. No telling what he'd do if he actually saw me. And I was enjoying this too."

Arthur gave her a sad smile. "I was enjoying this myself. It's been nice talking with you. I do hope that this helps you find your grandmother. As I told Miss Joanie before, she was a good woman. Knew her back when we were both alive. Don't know why anyone would want to do something to her."

"I don't either." She stood and studied Arthur a moment. "Thank you for the update."

As she placed her hand on the doorknob, I said, "You could always go into the backyard if you want to be outside. He won't be able to see you as long as you aren't up on the steps."

She waved her hand behind her in acknowledgment but said nothing and went inside.

Arthur turned to me. "I do hope I haven't upset her."

"She's dealing with a lot."

He nodded as Bryan said, "I'll go make sure she's okay."

Once Bryan was inside, Bardi came up on the porch and sniffed all around where Bryan had been.

"He's different, isn't he?" Arthur asked as he watched his little dog.

"Yes," I replied simply. It wasn't my place to say more, even to a ghost.

"Never realized how different this town was until after I'd died. Who would have thought? Not me. I was a regular human. Maybe that's why I'm a ghost now. Now I can get my turn to be different." He chuckled. "Now, now, I haven't forgotten there are dryad ghosts and all that. Humor me."

The more I talked to this man, the more I liked him and wished I had been in Heartwood Hollow back when he was alive. The idea of him passing on someday made me sad. I should have talked to him when I first realized he was a ghost. Until him, I'd kept my distance from the town's ghosts, but maybe that could change. Especially now that they were helping me and potentially risking their afterlives to do so.

"Joanie!" an excited voice chirped out the open window of a car. Ivy waved excitedly as Ken turned into the driveway.

Arthur chuckled again. "I'll let you go now. The next patrol should be here any moment."

He poofed out of sight, and a moment later, the car's engine stilled. Ivy barreled out of the car and came charging toward me, forgetting to close her door.

"I—" Ken called before dismissing her with a flap of his arm. Once Ivy got going, there was no stopping her. Ken shut his door, then walked around the car to take care of Ivy's before going to the trunk and pulling out three pizzas and a bag of sides. Likely garlic knots and fries. They'd quickly become our favorite, and Erin had really liked the fries the other night too.

Bryan had heard them coming and stepped outside to

help Ken with the food. He brought it inside, giving Ken the opportunity to kiss me hello.

"You waiting out here for me?"

I shook my head. "You had good timing. I was just finishing up a conversation with Arthur."

Ken nodded. "Hello, Arthur."

Both Ivy and I giggled. "He's not here anymore, Daddy."

"And how do you know that, kiddo?"

I was curious about the answer too.

"Because I scare the little hot dog." A few weeks back, that was how I'd described Bardi to her. She'd grown curious about the ghosts I knew and said it was her duty as a guardian to know more about them.

"Did you see him, Ivy?" I asked, wondering if Heartwood Hollow was having an effect on one of its newest residents.

She shook her head with a frown. "No, but you said the doggie is Saffy sized, and I scare her sometimes."

"Well, I don't think you scared him. They left as you were getting out of the car."

Ivy brightened. "Oh, good."

"Excuse me," someone said from behind me, making me jump. I turned to find the ghost of a middle-aged man holding a bowler hat in his hands. He wore a vest and an unbuttoned jacket. "Sorry to have startled you."

"I know you," I said, "but I don't know your name."

"Bernard, Miss Joanie."

"We danced together one night down by the river. I remember. You spun me around."

He nodded. "I do love to dance."

I glanced at Ken over my shoulder. "At the time, I'd had to pretend that I'd tripped. You didn't know what I could do then."

Ken raised an eyebrow in question, but then it seemed to dawn on him. "Our first date."

I smiled at him before turning back to my ghostly visitor. "What brings you here, Bernard?"

"Arthur said to come straight away if there was any sign of Mr. Ellison heading this way, and well, he should be here soon."

"Thank you. I appreciate the advance notice."

"It's not that much of a notice, I'm afraid," a second ghost —this one the young teen from the 1800s that I'd occasionally see on the swings at the park—said. She pointed. "There he is."

I turned, as did Ken and Ivy. Travis's eyes widened and then the steely look of determination settled across his face. Thank goodness Erin was inside.

"Excuse me, I need to handle this."

I scooted around Ken toward the porch steps.

"Time to go inside, Ivy," Ken ordered, the screen door opening.

Ivy huffed. "Daddy . . ."

"Now, kiddo."

She stomped inside as Ken and I crossed the yard to meet Travis. "You're not welcome on my property."

He pointed to the sidewalk. "Not on it. I demand to see Erin." His voice was already elevated.

"She doesn't want to see you."

"Then let her tell me," he stated flatly. "Erin! Erin, come out here! Talk to me!"

The screen door opened once more. I fully expected either Bryan to have had enough and that he was coming out to deliver a message or for Erin to have given in to his commands. As much as she'd said she'd called off the wedding, she still loved him in some way, even if she was hurting right now.

It was his love for her that I questioned.

However, it wasn't Erin, nor was it Bryan. "You see here, mister I don't know your name, but this is not how you deal with things," Ivy said sternly with her pointer finger extended. "You've made her cry. Yelling doesn't get you anywhere. You should try being nice."

I stared at the little girl. Where did she get this stuff from?

"You just got told off by a seven-year-old," Ken quipped.

Travis glared at him as Ivy said, "I'm almost eight!" as if that made it any better.

I expected Travis to continue yelling, but he chuckled as he looked at Ivy. Then he sighed long and hard.

"The little girl's right," he conceded, his words coming out soft as he directed his gaze toward me. "But Erin needs to hear me out."

"And she doesn't want to right now," I replied. "This isn't the way to go about any of this, and you know that."

He nodded. "I'm sorry." With that, he turned away, and the three of us watched him until he turned the corner down the far side of the street.

As we headed back across the yard, Bernard popped in front of us. Unable to see him, Ken and Ivy each took an extra step, stopping only when they realized I wasn't moving.

Bernard took his hat off before addressing me. "He appears to be heading back toward his house."

"Maybe the walk will help cool him down some more." He'd probably stewed over things on the way here, but Ivy's chastising had cooled him down real quick.

Bernard nodded. "Edith and I are still on schedule to watch him."

"Edith? Is that the young girl's name?"

"Sure is. We'll let you know if anything changes." He placed his hat back on his head, then disappeared once more.

With Bernard gone, I resumed my walk across the yard, Ken and Ivy a half-step behind me.

We'd just finished cleaning up after our pizza dinner, and Saffy—after many treats as bribes—was playing on the floor with Ivy and Bryan, when there was a knock at the door.

I opened it, and everyone in the room behind me fell silent as if they were collectively holding their breath while waiting to find out who it was. "Edith?"

"He's left his house. This time by car. He doesn't seem mad, but I think he's on his way here."

I thanked her, and she smiled at me, then turned around. She disappeared before she reached the stairs.

Before I could turn around and warn the others, Travis was pulling up in his red sports car. He'd either sped here or it took ghosts some time to poof from one place to another. I didn't know how it worked.

"It's Travis," I said quickly. Closing the wood door would only set him off, but I certainly wasn't going to give him an opportunity to easily get inside, so I locked the screen door. If I heard him out, maybe he'd leave.

Travis turned off the engine and then stepped out of the car, but he came no closer to my yard than the sidewalk. His chest expanded with a deep breath, then he slowly let it out again. As he did, his shoulders fell slightly.

Finally we made eye contact, and the corner of his mouth lifted slightly. He walked several paces across the lawn before stopping a safe distance halfway to the house.

"I mean no harm," he said calmly once he was close

enough for me to hear him. He held his hands up at chest height, showing they were empty save an envelope in his right hand, and he lowered his head a tad in deference. "I'm no good with speaking. I let my feelings take over, and we can see how well that has gone. So I wrote it down. Please, give this to Erin and tell her I love her."

I nodded. "Leave it on the bottom step. If she wants to get it after you're gone, she can."

It appeared he was going to say something, but then he nodded, setting the envelope where I'd indicated. "I under-stand. Thank you, and I'm sorry for any trouble I caused you." He did an about-face, then walked across the lawn and got back in his car. A moment later, he started the engine and drove off.

As soon as we could no longer hear the car, Erin bolted from her seat on the living room chair and went outside for the letter. She plopped down on the swing and then tore open the envelope. Tears were already falling as she started to read, some landing on the paper.

I turned away to give her some privacy and then joined Ken on the couch. Ivy had resumed playing with Saffy, but Bryan sat cross-legged, his head back as he stared at the ceiling.

"She's going to take him back, isn't she?" he muttered.

I hoped not, but that wasn't my call. "It's her decision."

He sighed, likely resigning himself to that possibility.

Several minutes later, Erin came back inside.

Bryan's gaze bounced from her face to the letter in her hands and back to her face. He probably wanted to say so much to her but settled on, "Long letter?"

She shook her head. "I read it a few times."

"Well, what did he say?" Bryan asked at the same time as I said, "You don't have to tell us what he wrote."

"I for one want to know what he said," Bryan replied with a shrug.

Erin and I both shot him a look.

"I want to know too. I can keep a secret," Ivy said proudly. That she could. Better than Bryan actually.

Erin wiped her eyes with the back of her free hand. "He apologized. He expanded upon a few of the things he'd said before, about being afraid of losing me, and how the feelings are overwhelming."

I handed her a tissue from a box on the coffee table. "He shouldn't be taking them out on you, though."

"And he knows that. That's partly what he apologized for. That this on top of the wedding has been making him stressed and snappy." She dabbed the corners of her eyes with the tissue and sighed. "Can't blame him for being stressed. I mean, look at how I've been."

"Maybe it's a good thing that you called it off. You can have some time to decompress," I started.

She nodded. "He still wants to marry me, ghost stuff and all, but said I can take my time to decide if that's what I want."

I smiled at her, wanting to at least seem supportive even if I thought getting back together was a bad idea. "You're welcome to continue to stay here as long as you need until you figure out what you want."

Erin shook her head, reminding me of when I'd first offered to have her stay. "I couldn't ask you to do that. You've done plenty for me already. Thank you, but no. I know what I want to do. Bryan, will you take me home?"

My heart hurt for Bryan, even more when I saw his facial reaction shift to hide how her decision had affected him. He nodded, but he wouldn't look at her. "Sure."

"Thanks. Let me grab my things. I won't take long." She headed upstairs.

Bryan turned toward me and shrugged. Despite this setback, my matchmaking tingle hadn't wavered.

"I'm sorry, Bryan. As much as I want you two to be together, it's still something she needs to realize for herself. You can't force someone."

He nodded. "Especially her. She'd just push me away. That's what happened with everyone else."

Everyone . . . "Didn't you say her grandmother didn't like him?"

"That's what she told me."

"So what if Erin pushed her grandmother away like she did her friends?"

Bryan cocked his head to the side as if considering it.

"Do you think she would have done this?" I asked. It was the one possibility we hadn't thought of yet.

Bryan shook his head. "No way. She may have asked her grandmother for some space, but she'd never have made her leave. And besides, had she done it, she wouldn't be freaking out now because of it."

I didn't want to believe that she'd done it purposefully. "Even if it were accidental? She may not have meant to and is trying to get her back."

Bryan drew his lips to the side but nothing as the top step creaked from upstairs, signaling Erin's return.

CHAPTER 39

The next day, Alice came into the shop, making a beeline for me as soon as we made eye contact. "I wanted to thank you for covering for me while I was gone."

"Where were you, if you don't mind me asking?" Her being gone just in time for everything else to happen had been pretty convenient.

She smiled as if she had a big secret. "I'm not supposed to tell, but seeing as you helped us out, and I'd like to be able to call on you again, I will. I met with a production company."

"Oh, wow, that's neat. What for?"

She eyed me as if I were dense, one eyebrow raised. "For the ghost hunting. What else would it be for?"

I gave an exaggerated shrug. "I don't really know what else you do outside of investigating. Could have been for that. What do you do? I know Becca works at the hospital."

"She did say you two talked a couple times," she said without answering my question. "I'm glad she's on speaking terms with her brother again. Goodness knows I have problems with mine, but Bryan has always seemed like a good guy. Divorces can get so nasty, can't they?"

Nodding, I thought of Ken's custody worries. I could only imagine how being shifters would introduce new complications to an already difficult time.

"Speaking of my brother," Alice continued, "thank you for taking care of Erin too. Becca filled me in a bit on what happened. I can't believe my brother would do such a thing. It just bugs me, you know? Like, would he have done the same thing to me if I had stayed around? I can do the same things that Erin can."

That reminded me of our new theory from last night. "About that, do you think you'd be able to send a ghost away if you wanted to? Even perhaps accidentally?"

"Me? No. I don't have that skill, and I've tried purposefully. The ghost just laughed. We actually got the laughter on tape. It was pretty cool. If you want my opinion, I don't think someone could just do it by accident."

"Yeah, I didn't think so either. The accident part, I mean. Thanks."

"No, again, thank you. I know we didn't end up needing you for an investigation, but it was nice to have someone here who could have helped out just in case."

"I'll admit I'm glad nothing happened. My schedule was already jam-packed, but it sounded interesting."

"You should tag along some night. It's a lot of fun, and it feels good to help people who need it. Might as well use the skill I was given for something positive, right?"

I nodded. That's how I felt about helping my couples, and now that I knew I could put spells in my baked goods, I felt similarly about being able to help anyone around town with a treat or two. My thoughts turned to Rachael. What would have helped her with her morning sickness a couple of months ago had my ginger scones and cookies not done the trick? Monday muffins and lucky cookies were one thing, but I'd done something really good for her.

"I might just take you up on that," I finally said. The late night, early morning combination would be worth it at least once to see what investigations were really like.

"It would be great to see your skills in action. From what I understand, you have more than one."

I arched my brow. Who would have told her? Erin? Someone from the PSG?

She pointed to the cases. "I've heard the rumors of what your treats can do. Hoping to get a few things boxed up, too, if you don't mind."

"Absolutely." I turned to the back counter to pop an empty box together. Setting it on one of the cases, I asked, "What can I get for you?"

I'd just finished ringing her out when Sarah got back from lunch, two drinks in hand. She was sipping from one of them, not paying attention as she crossed the shop. "Grabbed you a chai. Should already be cool enough to drink." She looked up as she held my cup out to me. "Oh, hi, Alice."

"Thanks," I said at the same time Alice said hello. I took my cup, then stowed it on a shelf under the counter before sliding Alice's box of treats to her. "Good to see you again."

A smile formed across her face as she picked up the box. "I'll be in touch."

CHAPTER 40

When Matt called to say he needed to reschedule our usual dinner on account of his needing to pick up his new kittens, I couldn't say I wasn't relieved slightly. It had been a long few days. But that didn't stop me from having Ken and Ivy over. They were my comfort people and just as happy with takeout as with me cooking. We'd finished our sandwiches from Cheese Louise a little while ago, and now Ivy was with Nathan and George in the yard behind mine helping them weed the garden.

Ken chuckled as he peeked out the back window, coffee mug in hand. "Can't get her to do it at home, but she's more than willing when they suggest it."

"Of course she'll help them. She adores Nathan. Plus, George offered her cookies. They're not mine, but who doesn't like a cookie you can wear on your finger as you eat it?" Honestly, he probably could have skipped the bribe.

We headed into the living room where I sank into the couch with a cup of tea as Ken sipped his coffee. Like him getting a kettle for when I went to his house, I'd recently purchased a coffee maker for him. Nothing fancy, but it did the job.

Ken settled next to me, and he pulled out his phone to play some music. We'd been dating for a few months now, but our lives had been so busy, sometimes in very weird ways—and that was probably an understatement—that we still had a lot to learn about one another. Tonight was music.

"These songs got me through high school," he said, hitting the play button. The chords of alternative music filled the air. We listened for a while. Occasionally, being the same age, I'd know one of the songs.

"And this is—"

There was a knock on the door. I peeked out the window but couldn't see who it was from my spot. I could see who it wasn't, though.

"Ivy?" Ken mouthed.

Standing, I shook my head. "She wouldn't knock. Besides, she'd come in through the back."

When I opened the door, I was surprised to see the person on the other side. "Larry, what are you doing here? We didn't order any food."

He smirked. "Not delivering food. I'm also a courier for legal documents. I deliver everything, remember?"

Legal documents? "For me?"

"No. Is Erin here?"

I shook my head. "Come inside a moment?"

He stepped aside to allow me to open the door, then walked in once space allowed. "Ken." He nodded politely.

Ken waved. "Larry, how are you?"

"Can't complain."

"What do you have for Erin?" I asked. "Is she in trouble?"

Larry shrugged. "I only deliver the papers. I don't read them."

"Did they come from Megan?"

"Not from around here." He flipped the folder around in an attempt to read the name. Instead, he dropped it, scattering the papers between us. He sighed, dropping his head momentarily. "Can't say I've done that before."

I stooped down to help him pick up the papers, catching sight of a few keywords that made me pause, but I pretended not to see them. Until I talked to Erin, I couldn't know for sure what it all meant. "Looks like the pages are numbered, at least."

As he straightened the papers, I caught sight of the law office's name. They weren't from Megan and they weren't from her firm, so they weren't from Heartwood Hollow.

"Why did you come here looking for Erin?" I asked.

"I thought she'd be here."

"Not for the last couple days. She went back to her place."

"Huh . . . Didn't feel like anyone was there. Not even Travis."

"Feel?"

He wiggled the fingers on his free hand. "Locater."

"Now it all makes sense."

"Exactly. And I've never been wrong." His brow furrowed. "At least until today."

"How strange. I'm certain she's there." But for his house to not feel like him? What was Travis up to? "Do you want me to give her a call?"

He shook his head. "Nope, I'll find her. Thanks, Joanie. Enjoy your night."

"Good luck," I told him as he turned around so he could open the door.

He stepped outside. "Thanks." Then he headed down the porch steps and toward his bike, tucking the folder back into his leather satchel.

"That was . . . different," Ken said.

"Yeah." I plopped down next to him. "It was."

"You look deep in thought. You have a line . . . right. There." He pointed next to my eyebrow. "I don't see that one come out all that often. What did you see when you picked up the papers?"

I was still trying to wrap my head around what I'd seen, wondering if it had anything to do with what was going on now. But how could it? If I understood what I'd seen correctly, Erin likely didn't know.

"Erin has an inheritance. A big one."

CHAPTER 41

I tried calling Erin that evening, but she didn't pick up. I called her a few hours later and still nothing. The next day too. Her phone hadn't rung any of the times I'd called. More like the connection would be made, but it would crackle before dropping without ever ringing.

It was too early to call the next morning, and worry swirled in my gut all the way to the bakery. I needed to ask Bryan if he'd heard from her. Of course, he wasn't waiting for me today. I knew I'd get too used to his being early.

Gina was the first one in. "Bryan says to check your phone."

I dug through my purse to find it. Hopefully it was charged. I clicked the side button to check, and the screen brightened. One new text from Bryan.

Not going to be in today.

He wasn't one to take the day off for no good reason, but with everything going on, I wasn't going to pry. I did have a question for him, though.

Okay. See you tomorrow. Have you talked to Erin at all? I

tried calling her last night, and her phone was all weird. Never went through.

I hated to ask. He'd been trying to give her space after she went back home with Travis.

Yeah. The wedding is back on. It was a rough night. That's why I'm not coming in.

You take care of yourself. Call the shop if you need anything.

Thanks. See you tomorrow.

I slipped the phone back into my purse and unlocked the door to the kitchen.

"That's what calling your cell was like when I would try you on that before I started calling your landline first," Sarah explained later that morning when I mentioned it to her as she took a tray from the cooling rack.

"It was?"

She nodded, then headed over to the kitchen door, pushing it open with her hip as she faced me. "I'm sure it was the same for anyone else trying to reach you."

I followed her into the shop. "But Gram used crystals to interfere with the signal— Wait, do you think something like that could be going on at Travis's house?"

"Truthfully, he doesn't seem the crystal type, but there are other ways to block cell signals." She set her tray on the far case.

That reminded me of what Larry had said. "And what about people signals?"

"Meaning?"

As we loaded the case with our first couple of trays, I

explained what Larry had said about not feeling Erin's presence at Travis's house. Or Travis's for that matter. "If there are wards to keep ghostly energies outside, and ways to mess with cell signals, are there ways to keep the energies of living people inside?"

"Not sure. I'd imagine they'd almost be the same thing."

I pushed the cookies forward on my tray to make space for more, giving myself more time to think. "But let's say whatever's going on there does have to do with Erin's grandmother. If she was in the house, how would Erin have not found that out by now?"

Sarah shrugged, then scooted behind me to head back to the kitchen for another tray. "Maybe she's in the basement? They can be kinda creepy."

"I go in my basement all the time," I said, filing through the door behind her.

"Yeah, but you're one of the few I know who uses yours regularly. Both of them. Between regular storage, food storage, and laundry, you're down there multiple times a day. Of course they aren't creepy to you." This time she passed me a tray, and I led the way back into the shop.

I unloaded the cookies from my tray onto the one already in the case. "I need to order takeout."

Sarah quirked her head. "Okay . . . not sure I follow."

"I have to talk to Larry about this. Should be the easiest way to get a hold of him. Good thing I'm heading to Ken's tonight."

CHAPTER 42

When Erin breezed into the shop later that afternoon, I didn't know whether to throw my hands up in relief or put them on my hips. "Where have you been?"

She looked at me as if she had no idea what I was talking about. "At Travis's."

"It's been days. I was getting worried."

"We've been busy. Our wedding is this weekend." Right. That was back on again. "With everything that's been going on, not to mention having work done on our kitchen, we got a little behind on prep work." She walked toward the case but didn't look into it, no doubt feeling unable to eat treats again because of her dress.

"Who redoes their kitchen the same week as their wedding?" Sarah asked as she wiped down part of the window display.

Erin sighed. "Wasn't supposed to be still going on this week, but you know how contractors can get behind. I wanted to postpone, but Travis wanted to be able to show it off to his family and friends. So they're rushing to get the job done. Finally got the countertop installed the other day."

Sarah looked like she was about to say something more, but I quickly changed the topic. "Did Larry get a hold of you?"

"Yeah. Had to go pick it up at work this morning." She shook her head lifting one shoulder. "Don't know why he didn't just try Travis's house yesterday. He knows I live there."

So he hadn't told her he'd had the papers since Monday? Interesting.

Her gaze drifted toward the muffins before darting back to me. "Wait, how did you know he was looking for me?"

Without mentioning the when, I explained that he'd heard she'd been staying with me. "I tried calling you."

"You did?" She looked confused, and that worried me. She should have seen the missed calls.

I glanced at Sarah across the room and thought back to what she had said, about trying to call my cell phone when I was at home before she switched to calling my landline. I didn't recall ever seeing missed call notifications then either. So maybe whatever was preventing energies from being read from outside Travis's house and blocking the cell signal was crystal related like at my house.

I'd have to ask Gram about it if I couldn't figure it out on my own. "Yeah," I replied to Erin, realizing she was looking at me expectantly, "but he found you, so it's all good."

"Yeah, could be really good. I have an inheritance. So weird."

"You do? Is that what he wanted to see you for?" I wasn't technically supposed to know already, so I pretended this was news to me. "That's great. From your grandmother?"

A wistful smile grew across her face. "From Nonni and my nonno." Then she huffed hard through her nose. "Course, I can't access it until I'm thirty, but give me another five years, and oh my goodness, I can't even imagine."

"Isn't Travis fairly well off?" Sarah asked as she wiped down the tables.

"Sure he is"—Erin spun to face her—"but I've never had any real money of my own. It will be nice to finally contribute financially to our relationship more than I've been able to. Won't that be great?"

As Erin turned toward me once more, Sarah gave me a look that told me she was thinking along the same lines as I was. Money was nice to have, but it did not make a relationship and certainly shouldn't be the focus of one.

"Of course, I've always enjoyed being spoiled by Travis," Erin continued, "but it will be nice to do the same for him now too. I've never been able to afford much in the way of surprise presents or fancy dinners out."

"Speaking of presents," I asked, "what should I get you as a wedding present? Do you and Travis collect anything? Crystals perhaps?"

"Crystals?" She giggled. "I find a lot of them pretty, but Travis would never go for that unless they were crystal wine glasses or something like that. Crystals of the rock variety aren't his taste. Not sure what he'd think about having any on display in the house anywhere."

"Well, what sort of thing does he decorate with?"

"You know? He collects boxes."

Sarah coughed on a chuckle. "Boxes?"

"Yeah, small ones. Usually wooden. Often ornately carved or painted. You know how some people get magnets when they go places as souvenirs? He gets boxes."

Travis didn't strike me as the magnet type. "That sounds neat. So what does he do with them?"

"He's got shelves of them in the hallway leading from the kitchen down to his office and the bathroom. Oh, you should have seen it. One of the contractors banged into a shelf while doing work and knocked some of the boxes off. You should have seen Travis. Threatened to call off the whole job if they weren't more careful."

"Oh, wow. Was anything damaged?"

"There was a chip in one of them, but nothing I couldn't fix. Good thing he doesn't keep anything in them, though."

"Yeah, lucky break, I guess." Both Erin and Sarah chuckled in response. "So what can I get you?"

"Oh, I'm just here to make sure everything is still good for the muffins at brunch the day after the wedding. Didn't want the order to have gotten dropped with the on-off nature of everything going on."

I gave her a reassuring smile. "No worries. We got it." I still hoped we wouldn't need to make the order, but time was running out.

CHAPTER 43

Ivy gave me a big hug when I arrived at her house that evening as she scooted out the door to play. "We're getting Chinese food," she said excitedly. I chuckled. A few months ago, she would have turned her nose up at it, requiring Ken to make her a separate meal. But we'd since found something that she liked. Pad Thai. She liked anything with a hint of citrus.

"Well, that sounds great. I haven't had Chinese in a while."

Ken and I quickly said hello before calling in our order. We then settled on the couch to wait for our food.

Ken put his arm around my shoulders. "It hasn't been just us in a while." He was right. Not since our date in Bug Creek. I wouldn't mind a repeat of that. He rested his head against mine. "How's everything been going lately?"

"Bryan didn't come into work today."

"I feel bad for him. He's a good guy. Ivy enjoyed making candy with him last week."

"I can't imagine what he's going through."

"I have to admit, though, I'm glad Erin left your house."

"You are? Why? Did she say something to you? Was she not nice to Ivy?"

"Oh, no, she was plenty nice." He shifted and moved his arm so he could take my hands. "This is more about Travis and what could have happened if we hadn't all been there. I support you, I do. This sort of stuff worries me, though. More so with the custody hearing soon. If Kelly's lawyer got word of Ivy being around any of this . . ."

My heart clenched, and I squeezed his hand. "Before you say anything else, you're right, and I'm sorry. I didn't think of the consequences. I wouldn't ever purposely do something to hurt your custody case. If something like this ever happens again, I'll help whoever find someplace that's safe to go to that isn't my house."

"Thank you." He pulled me toward him and pressed his lips to mine. It had all the makings of a kiss that would have rivaled the one at the restaurant the other night, but then Ivy burst in.

"Food's here . . . eww." Ivy darted into the bathroom to wash up for dinner as Ken and I pulled away from one another in laughter.

Ken stood. "Guess I should grab that."

I put my hand on his arm to stop him. "Let me. I need to ask Larry something."

Ken met my gaze in confusion before pulling out his wallet. "Here. I didn't tip on the card."

I stood and kissed his forehead. "I can get that too."

Larry smiled widely at me as he approached with the food. I waved from the doorway. "Good to see you again."

I opened the door, and he stuck out the food. "Likewise."

Ken came up from behind me. "Let me take that."

Larry handed him the bag. "I should be thanking you. Slow night."

Perfect. "So does that mean you got a minute?" I asked.

"Sure do. What's up?"

Ken walked into the kitchen with the food as I ticked my head to the side. "Have a question for you about your abilities."

He stepped inside. "What about them? I'll have you know they're people specific. Can't find lost lottery tickets or missing remotes, so if you're looking for something like that, I'm afraid I can't help you."

I chuckled. "No, nothing like that, though good to know. I admit I'm curious about what everyone can do. But this is about how you couldn't find Erin the other night."

His brow furrowed. "Ah, that. Not my finest moment."

"Has it happened before?"

He shook his head. "Closest to it is when there's a weakened energy field and I find someone not quite alive anymore."

"Do you mean ghosts?"

He raised an eyebrow at me. "No. I didn't. I meant the couple of times I've discovered that people have passed, but that's a story for another day."

"Oh. I'm sorry."

He shrugged. "Comes with the territory. You're the first person who's ever jumped to ghosts, though, and now I have questions for you." As my eyes widened, he continued, "But that's also something for another day. Might explain a few things."

My pulse quickened. "About me?"

"No, about me." Okay, phew. Larry studied me a moment. "So why did you want to know if my not finding someone has happened before?"

I explained the situation to him as best I could, leaving out the ghost talk. He'd probably find it interesting given his comments, but he was right. Another time. "So something was obviously messing with your ability to do what you do. But I'm wondering if you know what could have done it?"

"Not a clue. Sorry."

Drats. I'd been afraid of that.

"Okay, well, thank you for that info. I appreciate it and your time."

"You're welcome. Like I said, slow night." At that moment, his phone chimed with *Mamma Mia* in the voice of a famous popular Italian video game character. Larry chuckled. "Or not. That's Mama's letting me know they have an order for me to deliver."

"Do you have a sound for each takeout place?"

He nodded. "Makes it easy to know where to go without having to look."

"Smart."

He grinned proudly. "Thanks. Enjoy your dinner."

"I will. Thanks for bringing it over and thank you for your time. Say hi to your sister."

"She liked seeing you again."

"Likewise."

Larry turned around, then opened the door and left.

"You know Larry's sister?" Ken asked as he came back into the living room.

"You do too," I said, shutting the door. "Elizabeth from the senior center."

"Where'd you see her?"

"Coven meeting."

"Oh, that's right. Tell me how that went."

I followed him into the kitchen, where I filled him in on what had happened there while we ate. Ivy listened with fascination.

"Daddy, can I be a witch?" she asked between bites once I was done.

Ken half choked. I doubted he'd been expecting that question. "If that's something you want to explore, I guess it doesn't hurt to learn about it." He turned to me. "Were there kids there?"

I shook my head. "Neither of them." Ivy looked at me, her eyes big as if silently begging me to say something to throw my support behind the idea. "But I can ask if any do regularly." Not that she needed kids around her to enjoy herself. She'd be thrilled with Nathan and Matt being there, not to mention everyone else who would fall in love with her. They always did.

Ken nodded, and Ivy raised her hands in triumph, sending the pad thai that had been on her fork flying.

Later that evening, Ken and I sat on the couch as Ivy enjoyed the last rays of sunshine outside. Every day it was getting darker just a little bit earlier.

"You mentioned it a little earlier, but how is your custody case doing?"

"It's out of my hands right now." He sighed. "My lawyer said to keep doing what I'm doing. Kelly wanted Ivy to visit, but she didn't have a place for her to sleep when she first made the request. She converted her walk-in closet to a small bedroom with a futon, but now I guess she's just so wiped out from the pregnancy, so things are up in the air."

I reached out and then squeezed his hand. "So it's a no news is good news situation?" I didn't, and really couldn't, understand the situation, but I wanted to support him. If that meant finding a small silver lining for him, then that was what I'd do.

He gave me a small smile. "I guess. I'd hoped to get the visit over with before school started back up. It wasn't easy uprooting her world in the middle of April. Finish one school. Spend all of April break moving. Start a new school right after that with your life in storage. We lived in a hotel for a week before the house closed."

I hadn't known that about the hotel.

"She's doing great now, and I'd like to keep it that way. I don't want to interrupt her life any more than I have already," he finished.

"Well, I hope everything with your ex's health is all right, but I can only imagine how much harder it makes things for you. How much does Ivy know?"

"I don't want to worry her. You know that will only give her a tummy ache. She knows her mom would like to spend time with her, but I'm not so sure how much she's looking forward to it. She's more excited about being a big sister." He let out a big sigh. "I hope that doesn't sway her too much when she's asked where she wants to live. My lawyer said to expect that question."

"I'm sure she'll want to live with you. A new sibling is exciting, but that won't make her forget who's been there for her. You're giving her a great life."

"Thanks. I'm sure it helps that you're a part of it." He tucked a stray strand of hair behind my ear. "She loves being a part of your magical world. I do too."

This time, I pulled him in for a kiss.

CHAPTER 44

Erin rushed into the shop. "I think I'm in trouble."

"Trouble?" I'd been lost in thought over yesterday afternoon's candy recipe and how many variations of truffles were too many that the sudden focus on her made my shift in concentration slower than intended. I shook my head to reset. "What's going on?"

"Travis." The simple statement felt loaded. Had she finally realized he wasn't the one for her? "He got mad today when we were talking about the wedding. He mentioned wanting a prenup, which has never come up before, and then he started talking about life insurance policies."

"Plenty of people take life insurance policies out on their spouses," Sarah said, casting me a sideways glance, giving me the idea that she was trying to get Erin to say more.

She set her bag on a table, then plopped down into the chair in front of it. "Oh sure, but did we have to talk about it all of a sudden when trying to figure out seating arrange-ments? And to bring up the insurance right after I told him I was hesitant about the prenup? The timing was all wrong."

I came around the counter and approached her. "I'll admit it's a bit late, but it's good to talk about these things."

"He had both already written up. As if he'd been planning this for a while. Call me a little cautious after the whole conservatorship thing. I told him I wanted to run it by Megan. That's when he got mad, and that's when I left."

I sat down across from her. "That was a really smart move on your part."

She leaned her elbows against the table, arms up and hands supporting her head. "Was it? Like Sarah said, these are pretty commonplace for people getting married."

"Him getting mad isn't," I said softly. Now was as good a time as any to ask what had been at the back of my head since feeling the match between her and Bryan. She'd had multiple opportunities to see that he wasn't right for her, and then some. "I don't want to come across as sounding insensitive, but are you sure you want to marry him?"

She sighed. It came out long and shaky. "I . . . I don't know anymore. I need time to clear my head. And Megan needs to go through those papers. I brought them with me. But I didn't bring anything else. Is there any way I can stay with you tonight?"

A big part of me wanted to say yes, to let her stay in the guest bedroom at my house again, but I couldn't. There was a bigger part of me that had to consider Ken's concerns for Ivy and his custody case. I wasn't going to do anything to jeopardize my pint-sized candy chef's ability to stay here.

Shaking my head, I said, "It's not an option tonight, sorry. What about Bryan's?"

"And make Travis even more upset?"

She had a point. I glanced at Sarah. It didn't feel right putting her on the spot, but what choice did I have?

"I'd have to ask Jill."

Right. And how would that work with Jill being a fairy? I couldn't let her secret be put in jeopardy either.

The lights flickered, and I looked up. Great. Now something weird was going on with them again too, and Russ had given the electricity a perfect bill of health. I never had asked the upstairs tenants . . .

"Wait. I have an idea."

I jumped from my seat and rushed over to the kitchen door. Glancing back at them, holding my finger out to tell them one minute, then stepped into the other room. As soon as the door was closed, I grabbed the receiver from the phone cradle on the wall and then dialed. The door wasn't thick, and I was sure Sarah would be able to hear me if Erin couldn't, but in case I didn't get the answer I was hoping for, I didn't want my face to give it away. And I'd be given a few moments to think of another plan.

Russ picked up the phone on the second ring. "Please don't tell me it's your lights again."

"No." I wouldn't tell him about the flickering just now. "That's all good. Did Tim move out like you said he was going to?"

"Sure did. Turned in his keys on Saturday."

"It's not been rented back out, has it?"

"Nah. Why do you ask?"

"I have a friend in trouble who needs a place to stay. Probably won't need it for more than a few days, but she—"

"What kind of trouble?"

"Relationship trouble." I crossed my fingers that he wouldn't say no but not everyone wanted to get involved with other people's relationships.

"Is she in a safe spot right now? Do you need help getting her out of wherever she is? I have the PD on speed dial."

"If you count the shop as safe. She's not in immediate

danger, but she's got nowhere to go. I'm sorry to ask, but you know the motel prices around here this time of year."

"All right, let me see what the boss says, and if not, I'll talk to the missus. Corey left for college last week, so we have a room."

"Thanks, Russ. I really appreciate it."

"Don't mention it. You go take care of your friend. Talk soon."

I'd only managed to walk back into the shop to give Erin an update when the shop phone rang. Sarah picked it up, and after greeting the person on the other end, handed the phone to me. "That was quick."

"Hello?"

"I'll be by with a new set of door knobs shortly," Russ said. "Usually we just hand over the set of keys, not that anyone uses them, and that's that, but as soon as I mentioned why you were needing the space, I was told to change out everything."

"Thank you so much, you didn't have to go through all that."

"It's no trouble. More important that we keep your friend safe."

I glanced at Erin. "Do you need to know who it is for any sort of contract or lease?"

"Nope," he said, swallowing the *P* a little. "Your word vouching for your friend is good enough. Best not to keep any record of it so no one can find her but those who need to know."

A smile crept along my face. "Thank you so much. I'll see you when you get here."

"I'll call you when I'm out back and you can meet me. If your friend is in the shop, I don't want to see her."

"You got it." I hung the phone back up. "Well, I found you

a place. I can't guarantee it will have anything, not even a bed, but no one will know where you are except for you, me, and Sarah."

"Where?"

I pointed up at the ceiling. "Empty apartment. Building manager is meeting me out back in a few with new door knobs for extra security. There are two other apartments up there. Shared hallway, but a private apartment otherwise."

Erin smiled slightly. "Might be a rough night, but I'll take it."

"We have an air mattress I can go home and get," Sarah offered. "Some sheets. Maybe some pajamas?"

"Yes, please."

"And I can head to the general store to grab things like a toothbrush and toothpaste to get you through the night. And how about you call Megan? You can meet her here if you want her to look over those documents. I'm sure she'd come to you given the situation."

Erin pulled her phone out of her purse. "Good idea." Then she glanced at her phone. "What do I tell Travis?"

"Honestly? The truth. You can't go into a marriage lying to him, or him to you. Tell him you're meeting with Megan to go over the documents he gave you and that you're spending the night somewhere else. That you need time to think. You don't have to tell him where you are, though. That would negate the whole us trying to keep where you are a secret. Given his record, he'd try to find you to sway you."

"Do you think he's lying to me?"

"I don't think he's being entirely truthful to you if he won't say why he wants these things now. Like you said, the timing of the two, when they've never been discussed before and with everything else going on . . . It doesn't feel right."

She nodded with a sigh. "Okay. Mind if I step out to call?"

I pointed at the door. "Feel free to use the kitchen. There's a bathroom to the left that you can use if you want even more privacy."

She stood, lifting the strap of her bag onto her shoulder and holding the phone with her free hand. "Thanks," she said as she crossed the room toward the door.

Before she was back from her calls, Russ had called to say he was in the back parking lot. I peeked into the kitchen. Erin's muffled voice was coming from the bathroom, so I crossed the room and headed outside.

Russ greeted me with a large bag dangling from one hand, and he held a toolkit with the other.

"That looks like more than a doorknob," I observed. "Tim leave the place a mess or something?"

"Nah," Russ started as he headed up the steps to the second-floor landing. "The missus told me to pick up some things for your friend while I was getting the knobs. Figured your friend wouldn't have had much time to pack if at all."

It warmed my heart that people who didn't know Erin would do something like that out of kindness.

"Thank you. We were just talking about how she didn't have anything."

"Don't mention it. We helped our niece in a situation like this once, and she'd needed the same."

I followed Russ to Tim's old apartment. The last time I'd come here was back in April when Rich lived with him. Beyond that, I'd only been up here once before shortly after opening the bakery to ask the tenants if they were having weird issues with their lights. But no, the apartments had checked out fine.

Russ unlocked the door, then pushed it open. "Sorry the apartment doesn't come furnished or anything like that. But I guess your friend will be able to get some stuff in case this is going to turn into something longer term."

I *mmm*ed in agreement as I looked around the living room before adding, "I hope it doesn't come to that."

"This won't take me long." He kneeled on the floor beside the door. "Don't gotta do it often, but it's simple enough."

"Thanks again." I peeked into the first bedroom. It overlooked Main Street. I'd loved living on this street when I first moved here, getting to peek out on the small town hustle and bustle below. My apartment had been only a few buildings away from this one, making my commute to the bakery quick and easy.

As I moved on to the next bedroom toward the back of the apartment, I thought of the added privacy this room provided. Probably a better option for Erin given the situation.

Next I checked out of the bathroom and swung through the open kitchen on my way back to Russ. "Did you happen to bring toilet paper?"

He pointed. "All in that bag."

I grabbed the bag off the floor and brought it to the bathroom, then set up the toilet paper in the holder, a toothbrush and toothpaste tube next to the sink, a cheap shower curtain on the tension rod above the bath, and small bottles of soap, shampoo, and conditioner along the edge of the bathtub. It wasn't much, but with the air mattress from Sarah's, Erin would be comfortable here at least for the night. We'd see what tomorrow would bring.

"It's all set," Russ called, the first two words coming out more like *sall*. I returned to him at the entrance to the apartment. He was already packed up, the new doorknob in place.

We headed downstairs and said our goodbyes, and he

hopped into his old pickup, starting the engine as I walked back into the kitchen.

Erin appeared to have just stepped out of the bathroom. Her eyes were wet, and her entire face appeared damp. She rubbed her hands on her skinny jean capris.

"The hand towels are behind you when you're looking in the mirror," I said, not mentioning her face at all. There were few reasons she'd need to splash water into her face right now. "It's cramped in there." Probably the one thing I didn't like about the layout of the kitchen. We needed a bigger bathroom, but the space had been too small to expand it in any direction.

"Oh, thanks." She leaned back into the room and grabbed one.

"I have the keys to where you'll be staying. There's a supply of toiletries, but not much else. I'll have Sarah run and grab the air mattress in a little bit, but let's get you up there first." She dabbed at her face with the towel, and then I led her outside and up the stairs to the second-floor apartments. "There are two other apartments up here. Quiet tenants. I doubt you'll even run into them, but they're good people. No one you should have to worry about."

She nodded as I passed her the keys, and she slipped one into the knob to unlock it. "You know? Under different circumstances, I would be excited for this moment. I've never really lived alone before. Always had roommates of some kind." She pushed the door open and stepped inside.

"Do you want me to come in?"

She shook her head. "It's okay. I'm going to give Megan a call now and see when she can meet me to go over these papers. Then I need to figure out what I'm going to say tomorrow if I don't go back to the house. I told Travis I'd let him know one way or the other. Guess it all depends on what Megan has to say."

I reached out and put my hand on her upper arm. "One thing at a time. I'll see you later." Giving her an encouraging smile, I let my arm fall, and she closed the door as I turned to walk back downstairs to the shop.

CHAPTER 45

Although it wasn't Monday, Matt still came over early as he always did to help me set up for dinner. It was the first time having Matt over since I'd learned he was like me. Magical. There was so much I wanted to talk to him about, but I had two main missions tonight. See if he knew anything about blocking energies from being read from outside of a house and ask about a kids' coven for Ivy.

I greeted him at the door. "How are you doing, Matt?" I opened the door for him. "How are the kittens?"

"I have a confession to make," he said as soon as he stepped inside.

"Did you not get the kittens?"

He held out his arms. Tiny scratches and claw pokes dotted both. "Oh, I certainly did. Those rascals. I forgot how sharp kitten claws can be. They climb all over me."

"Then don't tell me you can actually cook . . ."

He chuckled. "Never burn it on other nights, though maybe that's because dinner consists mostly of your leftovers. Must be part of the magic."

"You think?" I turned and led him into the kitchen.

He reached up into the cupboard where I stored my plates. "I wouldn't be surprised. Your abilities are rather striking in that regard."

"I do give them to you with the hopes that you'll eat well." I grabbed one of my frying pans, then set it on the stove. "It feels good to be able to talk to you about this sort of stuff. Strange too."

He *mmm*ed in agreement, but then in one big rushed statement said, "I do have a real confession to make."

"Oh?" This time when he said it, I couldn't help the slight tightening of my throat, and when I turned to look at him, he was looking down and wouldn't meet my eyes.

He placed the dishes on the counter. "The first time I came here was a bit of a ruse." He held his hands out slightly in front of them, palms up. Empty-handed, reminding me of the day when he'd come to my house hoping he might get a plate of dinner after burning his.

"Everyone in the coven knows I am a terrible cook," he continued, "and with you owning a bakery and the rumors that had already started, they all assumed you were a kitchen witch. That evening, you were making a delicious garlic bread to go with the stuffed shells, and you could smell it outside the house. We'd been wanting to invite you to the coven even then, but you'd never seemed remotely aware of what you could do. They sent me here to check you out essentially. Then when it appeared you didn't know anything about what you were or witchcraft in general, we held off."

"And it took you all this time because it took me all this time."

He nodded, still not looking at me. "But you were so warm and inviting—and your food was delicious—I wanted to keep coming back for you. Witch or not."

I turned away from him and tried to figure out exactly

what I wanted to say as I pulled spices out of my cupboard and let the pan heat up. Part of me didn't know if I should feel upset because he'd come here almost as a coven spy, but I'd liked him immediately and was happy to have a regular dinner guest. I scooted around him and dug into the refrigerator for the steak and peppers I'd bought on the way home.

Finally I settled on, "You'd make a pretty decent spy, you know." I said nothing more while I seasoned the steaks.

"Gardeners overall are fairly unassuming. You'd be surprised what I've seen or heard over the years out in my yard. Course, most of us are all from the coven around here, so either I already knew what I'd heard or their secrets are safe with me." I glanced back at him, and he pressed his lips into a tight line. "Are you mad?"

I dropped the steaks into the hot pan. "No. I wasn't mad at Sarah for holding out on me all this time about her being my familiar. Or my family about establishing the wards around my house. I can't fault the coven for being curious or you for not telling me the entire truth before now." After they'd gotten a good sear, I flipped the steaks. "Besides, I've always enjoyed Mondays because of our dinners."

He let out an audible breath, then quirked a grin. "Good."

"I have a secret too." Might as well tell him everything.

He returned to the counter and then opened the drawer with the silverware. "Oh?"

"Just the serving utensils. We're doing fajitas," I said so he wouldn't pull out more than necessary.

"I already guessed that from the tortilla press."

A single laugh escaped me. "That's not the secret. I'm more than a kitchen witch. I have my mother's matchmaking skill, and I can see ghosts too. Gram says I'm fairly skilled with crystals, so who knows what else I can do."

"Wow. That's pretty rare."

"Do you know anyone in the coven who can do that?"

"Closest is Betty, but as she explained to you, it's not so much as multiple powers but the ability to control multiple elements."

I removed the steak from the pan to let it rest, then sliced the pepper, before adding that into the pan where the steak had been. Then I excused myself to my basement for an onion.

When I returned a moment later, Matt asked, "That wasn't what you wanted to ask me about, now, was it?"

I shook my head as I placed the onions on the counter. "I have two questions. First, are there kid witches?"

"Numerous coven members have kids, but they don't often come to the esbats. They're welcome to, of course, but they typically wait until they are older to come regularly."

As I removed the skin from the onions, I peeked at him from the corner of my eye to watch his reaction. "Ivy asked me. Said she wants to be a witch."

His smile grew so much that his eyes wrinkled even more at the corners. "You should bring her and Ken to the Equinox festivities. Plenty of kids."

"I think she'd like that. She's gotten very curious lately after finding out about me and more of the town."

"The town?"

There was no way he didn't know that there were other paranormal beings in town. He was old enough to have known Sandra who'd confirmed that merrows and selkies were aware of one another. And Kim, a fairy, knew of the dryads. And Bryan had recently said that he was aware of wolf shifters. And if his wife had been Vince's witch and he knew everything . . .

"You know. That we're not all . . ."

"Human?"

I sighed with relief knowing I didn't have to tiptoe around my wording. "Yes. That."

"How much do you know?"

"The hellcats were a new one to me last week. Same with the wolves, although I had my suspicions. But dryads, merrows, selkies, fairies, trolls? Since May. And there I was worrying that I was going to be different because I was the only witch in town."

He snorted. "Hardly."

"Does everyone know? All the witches?"

He shook his head. "The older ones know more. Guess we've kept it from the younger generation for safety. I probably know more, though, given Vince's way of finding things out. Used to hear him tell Henny lots of things."

"Spy," I said with a chuckle, giving him a knowing look.

He shrugged. "Not that they were concerned with me knowing. The merrow-selkie relations put a damper on things. The dryad disappearances did so even more. Eventually everyone kept what they were hidden to keep themselves safe. I'm not sure that it works. What if something comes in threatening the town? How will those who don't know about us understand?"

"We have a support group now."

"I heard. That's good of you to get it out in the open. If you ask me, that's what we need around here."

"So I know you're a green witch, but obviously you know a thing or two beyond that." That comment made him laugh. "So what do you know about wards?"

"Like the ones on your house?"

"Kind of. Maybe. I'm not sure." Whatever wards were around Travis's house might have been completely different than mine.

"I know someone who does. Can I make a phone call? Do we have time before Ken and Ivy get here?"

As I pointed at the phone on the wall, I glanced at the clock above it. "We should."

He shuffled over to the phone and then picked up the receiver from its cradle. After dialing, he waited a moment for the person on the other end to answer.

"Hi, it's Matt . . . Yeah, I'm at Joanie's house . . . Monday dinner. She's got a wards question that I think you'd be better at answering . . . Thanks. See you soon." He'd barely hung up the phone before there was a knock at the front door. "That will be her."

I rushed to answer it, wondering how anyone could get here that quickly. "Clara?" Stepping aside, I opened the door so she could come inside.

She smiled as she entered the living room. "You have a question about wards?"

"I do. You know about them?"

She nodded. "My specialty." She pressed her fingers against the door jamb. "Good. Solid. You did well with these."

"Thanks. My gram helped."

She nodded. "Aside from your last name, feeling the wards go up around your apartment when you first got here sparked a serious interest in you and your abilities."

"Please, come into the kitchen where we can talk more." I swept my arm in front of me to have her lead the way. "You're welcome to stay for fajitas."

"Oh, I just might. Matt's raved about your dinners for years." She settled into one of the chairs and I offered her tea. While the water boiled, I sliced an onion and threw it in with the peppers. Once I set her steeping tea in front of her with some honey, she asked, "So what is it you wanted to know about wards?"

"Well, I know about the ones that keep ghosts outside, like mine do, but are there any that could keep things inside? Say one that would block any energy from being traceable outside?"

Her eyes widened. "Ghosts? I might need you to rewind a bit for me."

I glanced at Matt, and he gave me a small reassuring nod. He trusted her. I could too.

So as I finished cooking the ingredients needed for the fajitas, I told her all about me, but as I moved on to more recent events, I skipped over elements, avoiding names and status as something paranormal whenever possible. "So then someone was trying to find my friend, but it didn't seem like they were where they were. Like the whole house lacked any sort of energy signature."

"This would be easier if I had a bit more context so I'm not guessing at things. Names would help."

I pursed my lips to the side. "I try not to reveal other people's secrets."

"I respect that. Well, I assume Larry's involved if your friend needed to be found. No need to avoid his name. As a member of our group, I know all about him. He's the only locator in town."

I nodded. "He felt my friend more strongly here than where she was, but she'd left here a couple days prior. Said it didn't seem like anyone was there at all. Her or her significant other." I hadn't wanted to say *fiancé*. There were a lot of couples in Heartwood Hollow, but fewer were engaged.

After a moment of contemplation, she added, "There's only one who I knew of who could put wards on someone who could completely erase something's presence. But she's been gone for years."

Matt looked at her in question at the same time I asked, "Who?"

"Helen Ellison."

I raised an eyebrow. "I thought she could only see ghosts." Being able to do both would have given her multiple powers.

"Ghosts? Her?" Clara shook her head. "That was Oswald. Her husband."

I let out a small gasp. "This changes everything." And someone—or someones—was lying to me.

Both Clara and Matt cocked their heads to the side in opposite directions.

"How so, Joanie?" Matt finally asked when I didn't elaborate.

"It's Travis's house," I confessed. "The one with the wards. Wait, what do you mean by she's gone? I thought she walked out on her family. I know it's been years, but . . ."

A sad smile crossed Clara's face. "She didn't walk out as you say. She disappeared. We didn't have a locater back then. I think Oswald made up the story of her leaving so it would be easier to explain."

"How is that easier? Making his kids think their mom left them willingly?"

She shrugged. "I didn't say it was a good decision."

"So how are the wards on Travis's house if she's been gone for so long?"

"Wards don't just break because a long time has passed. Not for someone like Helen. Someone would have to do something to them."

"Like the ones Gram established for me did when I invited a ghost inside my house."

"Exactly." Her smile turned wistful. "Oh, please do let me know the next time your grandmother comes to visit. It would be great to see her again. I'm so jealous that Matt and George got to spend time with her at your cookout."

"You know Gram?"

She nodded, and we followed the tangent about how the two now-older women met years ago during one of Clara's family's trips to Sunny Valley. As she spoke, Ken and Ivy arrived with chips, salsa, and tortillas. We all sat down to eat as Clara started the story over for a very curious Ivy.

Halfway through dinner, Matt turned to Ivy. "I hear you want to be a witch."

Her mouth dropped open, and she glared at me. "You told Mattie?"

"Now, now," Matt started. "She only asked me anything because she knew that I'd have the answers."

Ivy's head whipped back towards Matt, and her voice rose an octave as she nearly shrieked, "You're a witch?"

He nodded, a proud smile crossing his face. "Sure am, Miss Ivy."

She leaned forward, her hands pressed against the table on either side of her plate. "But I didn't think men could be witches. I thought you were all wizards or warlocks or something."

He chuckled, clearly enamored by the little girl. "Some may prefer those terms. But we're fine with being called witches too."

She sat back in her chair and considered this for a moment before nodding. "So what's the answer? Are there kid witches?"

"There are," Clara answered, "but they don't typically come to the meetings." She explained more about the several kids she knew, saying she'd get in touch with them and their families. And by the time dinner was over, promises had been made for Ken and Ivy to attend the upcoming equinox cele-brations.

Ivy had always been an excitable kid, but by the time she'd left, very late for her and Ken because her requests for "one more question" about witches and witchcraft were always granted, she was near bursting with anticipation. And we still had nearly a month left until then. I had a feeling the questions were only going to grow in number for the curious little girl, but maybe teaching her would help me too.

CHAPTER 46

At seven thirty the next morning, I answered a knock on the kitchen door. I didn't need to open it to know who it was. Even if I hadn't expected her at some point this morning, the tingle I got from her and Bryan's match was an immediate giveaway. It was so strong it had even clued me into when Bryan was within range on his way here this morning despite Erin being on the floor above me.

"You're sure it's okay if I meet with Megan in your shop?" she asked as I opened the door wide enough for her to come in.

"Absolutely. Shouldn't you be getting ready for work, though?"

She shook her head. "Took the whole week off for wedding prep. If there even will be a wedding at this point."

"Well, at least it gives you the opportunity to meet with Megan."

She shrugged noncommittally. Stepping further into the room, she said good morning to everyone and stopped for a few moments to chat with Bryan. He hadn't seemed surprised to hear her voice and didn't rush to ask what was going on, so I assumed they'd talked last night once she was settled.

I led her into the shop and then flipped on the lights. "I'll leave the blinds down as we prep for opening while you two are in here talking so no one can see you."

"Thanks. Travis didn't take time off except for the day before the wedding, so he should be at work by now, but who knows after last night. He called again after you left to say how a *real* lawyer should go over the paperwork with me and that his would have been happy to do it. Funny how all of that makes me want to keep my lawyer all the more."

"Good thing Megan is as real as they come. She's great, isn't she?" I'd first met her when I needed a lawyer to help me file the various licenses and contracts to get Suncraft Bakery up and running.

"She really is. And she's local. Trav's lawyers are people from out of state. You think they'd be meeting me here?" She made a face.

Shaking my head to answer, I slid open the case where we had a few things left over from the day before, then began bagging them up for the day-old shelf. I'd always been good at guessing exactly how much I'd need on any given day, but I purposely made a couple extra for those who might need the discount the next day.

"Are you going to mind me coming in and out while Megan's here?" Not that she had much of a choice if she wanted to use the shop, though I knew it wasn't typical for meetings between lawyers and their clients to have other people around.

Erin shook her head, then pulled out the papers from her bag. "You do what you need to do. I'm just grateful for the space."

As she settled in to read, I headed back into the bakery to

finish everything I needed to do before Sarah got here to set up shop for the day.

I glanced at the clock. Almost an hour until she was due in. Plenty of time. And now that Brittni had her own work-space, we were both able to move that much faster. The kitchen felt weird without Sam, but it comforted me that he was probably already up and working in his kitchen class-room now too.

For the next forty minutes, I alternated between deco-rating cookies and frosting cupcakes, whatever had cooled on the rack. As much as everyone in the bakery could do anyone's tasks, we specialized in various areas, and with Sam gone and Lily likely on her way out, I had to reacquaint myself with some of the jobs I did less often. I'd forgotten how fun and creative it could be as I stuck a lemon slice that we'd candied right here in the bakery and a candy straw—not made here, but I wanted to learn how—into a pink lemonade cupcake.

Erin stuck her head into the kitchen, asking, "Is it okay if I unlock the door to let Megan in?"

"Absolutely."

She ducked back out of the room.

I thought of how I should probably go greet Megan and lock the door behind her. With the windows down, there was no way to see who else was around. I looked down at my workstation and my hands. Frosting smeared the back of one hand, but other than that I wasn't too bad. Still, I'd have to—

"I'll go make sure it's just Megan coming in," Bryan offered, already coming out of the bathroom from washing his hands. "Don't want Travis to use this as an opportunity to get inside to see if Erin's here. There's no way he doesn't think you're involved."

"Thanks, Bryan. You read my mind."

He stepped out of the kitchen, returning a few moments later. "There was no one else on the sidewalks. I checked. Should be good now."

Wiping my hands on my apron, I nodded. There were two cookie trays left to decorate, and then I'd head out there myself to start loading up bakery cases.

Sarah was unlocking the door as I pushed my way into the shop, a tray of Bryan's muffins in my hands. Beyond a quick good morning to Erin and Megan as she walked in, Sarah paid no attention to them as she headed into the kitchen to store her bag and grab a tray to help load cases.

No doubt she was listening, though. I was too, wondering what Travis was up to with those documents. As much as I knew Erin and Bryan were meant to be together, I didn't want Travis to be a terrible person no matter the outcome of his relationship with Erin. She had to have seen something in him originally, even if no one else did. I always tried to hold on to hope and see the good. But sadly, aside from his helping me out with the town's beverage board—if he didn't cause the problem in the first place—I'd seen little proof that he had much good in him.

A lot of the legal stuff went over my head or seemed fairly self-explanatory. Nothing really stuck out to me, but perhaps that was why I hadn't had any interest in becoming a lawyer.

"The timing of the prenup is a little questionable in my opinion, but it happens," Megan explained. "As you can imagine, there aren't a lot of them done in Heartwood Hollow. The life insurance is common, although few think of taking care of it when they're young. I see older couples, or couples once they have kids to consider, that sort of thing. I doubt Drew and I would have had one as early as we did if I hadn't seen what happened to people without them."

"So you think this is all fine?" Erin's voice held an edge of uncertainty.

Megan pressed her lips into a tight line. "Well, I didn't say that. There are a couple issues I have. First, although it is a plus that he's telling you about the policy, if he's going to take life insurance out on you, you should do the same for him. There are major red flags if he balks at that idea."

"I can do that, for sure. But what else is there? You're still making a face."

"It's the way this one thing is worded." I popped my head up over the case as Megan plopped one of the stacks of papers flat on the table. She pointed to something in the middle of the page. "Everything you have or are entitled to."

"What's that mean?"

"For many, that would be like if they won a big lottery while married. He'd want a part of your yearly annuities even if you got divorced. The wording also appears in wills in case an adult child passes before their parent. If the deceased would have inherited something had they outlived their parents, the deceased's heirs would then be entitled to the inheritance instead. Obviously, this isn't a will. But the idea still applies. If you two got divorced before you turned thirty, the prenup means he'd still get a portion of your inheritance once you had access. See, it even mentions inheritance as known assets."

Erin's scrunched up her face. "That doesn't seem right."

Megan nodded. "I agree. That money has nothing to do with him."

Erin shook her head as her face went blank. "That's not what I meant. How could he have listed my inheritance? He doesn't know about it. I never told him."

CHAPTER 47

It was one of those moments when the room was so quiet we could have heard the proverbial pin drop. Even the normal constant buzz of the overhead lights seemed to have gone silent. It was the type of noise one usually grew so accustomed to that they forgot about it until it wasn't there.

I glanced up at the lights. Their brightness hadn't changed, and they weren't flickering either.

No one else seemed to notice. Sarah stared toward the table where Erin and Megan sat.

"You never told him?" Sarah asked as if unbelieving.

"Nope. I was still trying to digest it all."

Megan's eyes went wide. "That's a big red flag to me, then."

Telling him wasn't the only way he could have found out. "Larry gave you documents about it, though. Could he have seen those?"

"They're still in my desk at work." She turned back to Megan. "Could he just be covering his bases? Like if I did win the lottery?"

Megan sighed, then straightened the papers in front of

her. "I guess it's possible, but like I said, that language it more used in wills, not prenups. My gut says no. Let me head into my office, and I'm going to check a few things. Do I have your permission to discuss this with others there?"

Erin nodded. "Whatever you think will help. Thank you for meeting me this morning."

Megan tried hiding a yawn as she answered, "Of course. I'm sorry you're having to deal with all of this. You should be excitedly prepping for a wedding, not worrying if your future husband has ulterior motives."

As she gathered her things, I hurried into the kitchen to grab a wrapped Monday muffin for Megan. I returned as she was sliding Erin's paperwork into her bag.

Megan zipped her bag closed. "In the meantime, do not sign these papers and do not make any indication that you will be signing them."

Erin pointed at the bag, a small smile on her face. "Well, I can't sign them since you have them, but message received loud and clear."

Megan let out a loud breath and closed her eyes. "Right. I'm glad you know what I mean."

I walked over to her and stuck my hand out toward her with the muffin on it. "Here. One for the road."

"Is that a Monday muffin?" Her eyes glistened with both hope and exhaustion.

"Sure is. Looks like you could use one."

She snatched it up. "Oh, do I ever. Piper is going through a sleep regression, so what little sleep I do get is interrupted many times."

"I don't know how you do it." I had a hard enough time being woken up for just a few minutes at night be it from Saffy jumping off the bed or an unexpected ghost showing up. "Mom must have some sort of superpower."

"It's certainly something." She was already unwrapping the muffin from the plastic wrap. "Thank you for this. What do I owe you?"

I held my hand up to stop her. "Absolutely nothing. You have a good day."

Megan's shoulders fell with relief as she got through the wrapping, and she took a bite. Mouth half full, she turned to Erin. "I'll be in touch."

With that, she was out the door, already bringing the muffin back to her mouth. Maybe I had a new market for Monday muffins. Tired parents.

I chuckled quietly to myself before realizing that both Erin and Sarah were looking at me.

"Sorry, I was thinking about muffins."

Sarah rolled her eyes in amusement. "Only you."

I wanted to say something like how I was pretty sure Megan was thinking about muffins now too, but with Erin there, it didn't seem right. By the time Megan got to her desk in the law office at the other end of Main Street, her mind would be properly awake and ready to focus on Erin's problem.

Megan wasn't the only one in need of a baked good. "Would you like a muffin, Erin? Maybe a scone? I should have asked."

"That would be wonderful, yes, thank you."

While Sarah grabbed Erin a muffin from the case, I plopped down on the chair next to her. "How are you holding up?"

Erin shrugged. "I really don't know what to think. It's just a lot, you know?"

I placed my hand on hers as Sarah walked over with a muffin on a plate. "How about something to drink?"

"Coffee is fine. Do you have anything to put in it?"

"Half and Half, and sugar. I can grab milk from the fridge if you prefer that."

"No, the other stuff is fine." She broke off a piece of her muffin and popped it into her mouth. After a moment, she said, "Well, it looks like I won't be going home tonight either. But what excuse can I give him?"

"Don't you have people coming for the wedding you can hang out with?" Bryan asked as he pushed through the door holding a tray full of muffins. "Your mom? Your cousins? They should all be here soon."

"It would be good to spend more time with them," Erin admitted.

"Your mom would love it. Bet she'd let you crash in her hotel room, no questions asked."

She contemplated this. "A real bed does sound nice . . ."

Sarah brightened. "Oh, what about a bachelorette party?"

"I had one of those after the shower. Saved everyone an extra trip."

At that moment, Lily came out of the kitchen with another tray. "What about one with your *real* friends?"

Everyone turned to look at her. Erin sat staring, eyes blinking.

Lily's gaze darted around, pausing for a split second on each of us in the room. "What? You know how easy it is to hear when you're close to the door. Doesn't do much good if you want to keep something secret." She continued around Bryan and then Sarah to the case closest to the window. A mischievous grin crept across her face. "But I'm serious. And we don't have to call it a bachelorette if you don't want to."

When Erin remained quiet, Lily added, "You know we're a lot more fun."

"She's right about that," Bryan said, his smile matching Lily's. "And I have a plan."

CHAPTER 48

I was not told the plan. All I knew was that it was supposed to trick Travis into revealing what a bad guy he was. I didn't have to do anything but show up. They didn't want me knowing the plan to influence how I interpreted any of the interactions between Travis and Erin or the ghosts or anything like that.

As they planned, kicking me out of my shop—okay, not really, they discussed the plan while I made my deliveries and grabbed lunch—I took care of business and then made my way over to the park next to the bakery.

I plopped on the bench next to Arthur. He'd taken his hat off as he approached, and he leaned back, looking at the sun almost as if he was letting it warm his face.

"You look like you're on a mission." He chuckled as he straightened to face me. "When are you not lately?"

He had a point. "Do you still feel the sun?"

Letting his head fall back once more, he answered, "No. But I remember what it feels like. Sometimes that's good enough. That's not what you've come out for, though."

"No, but I was curious. Despite being able to see ghosts

my whole life, I'm finding there's so much I don't know about the spirits who remain here."

"That's what happens when you ignore a gift for so long."

"Is it? A gift, I mean." Was this the same thing as what Miss Susan had meant by a blessing?

"Do you not think it is?"

"At times, I would have said no. I've lost friends over this. Sleep too." If seeing ghosts was a blessing, the loss was the cursed part of it. "Ghosts wouldn't leave me alone when I was younger, and they weren't all like you."

Arthur arched an eyebrow. "Like me?"

"Yeah, you know, nice."

He held up a hand. "Say no more."

"Now, though, I like what I've been able to do. To help free ghosts who have been trapped. To solve the mysteries behind their deaths. Or in some cases to let them know they've died." I told him about Cindy Bug. "She got me wondering. Is there some sort of census on the other side? Are the people waiting for you over there aware that you're dead on this side and that something is keeping you here? Or do they assume you're still alive? What about the people who died after you? Are they looking for you up there?"

"Well, I would imagine they would know at least some of us down here are passed on. Edith for example. Anyone waiting for her has to know that she wouldn't live to be two hundred years old."

I nodded, a sigh escaping. "But is there a way to check to see if someone isn't there when they should be? Like ghosts who may not have chosen to stay here but are?"

He looked at me over his thick, black-rimmed glasses. "What are you getting at?"

"Remember me asking you about people who make

ghosts do things? What if what they could do was to force them to stay?"

"You mean trapping them on this side?"

I nodded. "Or anywhere really."

"For what purpose?"

"In the case of Anita? Probably to keep her from Erin. Erin's adamant she didn't cross over, wouldn't cross over before the wedding."

"Who would do something like that?"

I shrugged. "Anita didn't like Travis. So we're thinking Travis or someone who wants the two of them to be together. I'm starting to wonder if Travis can see ghosts. You know Alice can. And so could their father."

Both of Arthur's eyebrows rose. "I knew Oswald in passing while we were both alive. He helped fund a new football field for the school. Even got the Phoenix Foundation to match his donation. Never gave me any indication that he could see me after I died. But we know it's easy to ignore that which we don't want to see."

I knew he meant that last statement for me. I'd been here for almost five years, and for four and a half of them, I hadn't spoken to Arthur. At first I didn't think I could. With him and Bardi out here every day, it took several months for me to even realize he was a ghost.

Nodding in acknowledgment of his comment, I asked, "Is there a way to know for sure? You sent me Chrys when I needed to know about the north woods, but I assume she's fully crossed over now. Do you know of anyone else who could go between and check if she's there?"

"I can ask around. Don't you know of anyone living you could ask? What do you call them?" He thought a moment. "Psychics. Mediums. The real ones. Like you but someone who can talk to the other side as opposed to you and Alice who focus on who's here."

"I don't know if I focus on anywhere. It just happens."

He looked at me, brows pinched slightly. "Have you tried to do it yourself?"

"I don't think I'd want to." That seemed to be crossing back into what Gram had protected me from. As if that would invite bad ghosts to me. "Can't what I do be enough?"

He shrugged. "Only if you feel it's enough. Ask Alice. That team she's a part of might have someone. But I'll get back to you when I can."

"Thanks, Arthur. I appreciate all the help you've been giving me."

"It's nothing you haven't been doing for others."

I stood and said my goodbyes to the ghost and his dog, hoping that he'd be able to come through for me once more.

When I walked back into the bakery after lunch, Erin, Bryan, Lily, and Sarah all looked like they'd been caught with their hands in the cookie jar.

"We're just wrapping up," Sarah said. "Sure you don't want to go grab another marshmallow rice treat?"

I chuckled. "You know me so well, but I'm good with the one I already have. I'll head back into the kitchen for another few minutes." When Lily looked at me, I held my hands up to proclaim my innocence. "And I promise I won't be close enough to hear the last of your plans. But on that note, call Alice and get her involved."

Erin cocked her head to the side. "Why Alice? I don't know if she'd get behind the idea of this."

"Then don't tell her. Invite her. She is a part of your

wedding party." Plus, it would give me an opportunity to ask her about finding a medium. No matter the outcome of this case, knowing of one would probably be a good thing.

She looked at Bryan, who nodded. "I'll call her when we're done," she replied.

With that, I headed back into the kitchen. I'd been hoping to save my marshmallow rice treat for later, but my nervous stomach about whatever they were planning had turned munching on it into a necessity.

As I pulled the chair we had back there to my workstation so I could sit and have my dessert, I could only hope that tonight would bring us the answers we were looking for.

CHAPTER 49

We met at Double Aitch, and I was immediately on edge. I hoped that whatever they planned wouldn't cause any trouble for Carter's staff. Even more so because we did business together, and causing a scene could damage that relationship.

Sarah leaned toward me. "Seriously, don't worry. Nothing's going to happen right now. This is all about setting the scene and making the rest of the night not seem so suspicious. Besides, Erin wasn't comfortable about anything happening while her mom was here."

"And after?"

"It's nothing bad, I promise." She raised her fingers in a scouting sign. "On my honor as a familiar."

"Then why couldn't I be a part of the planning?"

"You're too nice. You don't even like taking part in gossip, and all you're doing is digging for it. You don't add to it." She gave a small shrug as a waitress, Lichelle, one of the local teens in Heartwood Hollow and sometimes babysitter to Ivy, set our drinks down in front of us.

"You all have a good night," she said, effectively ending

our conversation. "I'm on my way out but grabbed the drinks when I saw how many of you there all were."

That was probably an understatement. They'd had to push together four tables for us all, nearly half of what they had in the entire restaurant. "Thanks, Lichelle. You have a good night too."

She glanced at Erin, a knowing grin on her face. "And congratulations to you. I'm sure your wedding will be beautiful."

Erin thanked her, but the smile that accompanied it didn't reach her eyes.

Once Lichelle had walked away, one of her cousins turned to her. "What's the matter?"

"You getting a case of cold feet?" asked another.

Erin's smile was shaky. "Something like that."

Her mother patted her arm, then went into how she had felt before marrying Erin's father. She had meant well, but it did nothing to lift Erin's mood.

A folded-up paper triangle landed on Erin's plate.

Everyone looked as she reached for it, their gazes full of curiosity about what the note said. She opened it and shook her head, crumpling the paper into a ball.

He quickly wrote something down on another piece of paper and folded that too. The note hit Erin's glass of water. Her cousin commented on his aim, sending small giggles around the table.

When Erin opened it, she snorted a laugh. "No." She crumpled up that paper too.

But Bryan wasn't done. He had another tightly folded paper triangle ready. Like the first, this one landed on Erin's plate. She eyed him skeptically as she opened it, and as soon as it was open all the way, her eyes went wide. "Oh no. You have got to be kidding me."

Bryan nodded his head slowly. "Oh yes. That one."

This time, Erin's cousin was ready. Before Erin could crumple the paper, she grabbed it out of her hand. "Oh, you have to do this one."

"No way."

The first cousin showed it to their cousin sitting on the other side of her. "But this is such a fun song!"

Lily made a grabbing hands motion, and the second cousin passed it over. Lily let loose a loud laugh I'd never heard from her before. "Come on, it will be just like high school. Do you remember—"

"Oh, I remember," Erin said.

Finally I understood. "Karaoke?" I whispered to Sarah, and she nodded. "That's what you didn't want to tell me?"

"There's more, but that's where we're heading."

Then Becca grabbed hold of the paper from Lily and gasped when she saw the song. "I remember that night too! So much fun. Who are you kidding, finest moments? It was awesome?"

"I bet you can still rock it," Bryan added. He waggled his eyebrows at her. "Come on. Just like old times."

Erin looked up at the ceiling before giving Bryan a long hard look, but a smile soon crept onto her face. "Fine," she said, drawing out the long *I* sound. "But I get to pick one out for you, and you can't say no."

"Deal." I'd never seen him look so satisfied.

Part of me felt Bryan was hoping to use tonight for more than just Travis's downfall and that it was a risky move on his part. But the ever-present matchmaking tingle between these two stirred in a way it hadn't as they continued to banter through appetizers and into the main course.

It was a short walk around the corner to the Bailey, one of the local bars in town. It was also home to karaoke night each week as it had been for nearly thirty years, a fact prided upon by the bar. They'd purchased one of the first karaoke machines in the county, and a newspaper article about it hung in a frame by the stage. The original machine had since been replaced by newer technology, but the enthusiasm for karaoke night among a solid subset of the Heartwood Hollow population had not waned.

I'd come here a few times when I lived on Main Street, something to do with Steph and Alex to get out of our small apartments and have some fun. I'd never sung, though. There were enough rumors going around town about me, I didn't need to fuel them with how poorly I sang. The only song I'd mastered—out of necessity more than anything else—was Happy Birthday, and *mastered* was a stretch.

I sat in the back corner booth with Sarah, Alice, and Becca. Lily pulled a chair up to the end of the booth to join us. The rest of the group, including Bryan and Erin, who were sitting next to one another, took up the booth in front of ours and the two tables next to them. Fortunately we'd gotten here early enough to not be scattered across the bar. The bartenders were still coming around to take orders. My club soda with cranberry juice would probably be my only drink tonight. It was rare for me to have anything other than tea or water, although the bakery's partnership with the cider mill had upped my intake of apple cider these last couple of weeks.

"You wouldn't happen to know of any mediums, would you?" I asked Alice across the table from me. "Real ones."

She raised an eyebrow at me. "You need help talking to dead people?"

"I can only talk to ghosts. I need someone who can talk to people on the other side."

Alice took a long sip of her drink. "This have to do with . . ." She pointed over her shoulder to where I could make out the back of Erin's head.

I nodded. "We never figured out for sure if she's here stuck somewhere or over there." I recounted my conversation with Arthur.

"So you're hoping a medium would be able to tell you if she's there."

"If she's not there, then she has to be here somewhere, right?"

Alice pulled a face. "Why didn't we think of this before?"

"We wanted to assume she was right about it all. But what if she isn't?" Just because she'd come to me that night didn't mean she wasn't crossed over. Chrys had been able to come and go between here and there. Others probably could too, especially with the energy that had been poured into an object that had once belonged to them.

"Yeah. I know of someone." She took another swig of her drink. "I'll get you their number ASAP."

"Thanks." Alice's willingness to help me settled the small, lingering concerns I had about her involvement. But there was one other issue to contend with. "How much do you know about your mom's abilities?"

"Not a lot."

"So how do you know that she saw ghosts?"

She took a swig of her drink before answering. "My dad. Mom only ever told me that she could do things too and that she'd show me someday. She said she wanted me to be a kid first before we got into it all. To not worry about what we could do. That I could explore it when I was older." She sighed. "That she'd help me. So much for that."

"What's with all the questions? Don't get me wrong, I'm good with answering them, but I thought we were here for a bachelorette party. Time and place, ya know?"

"Sorry. It's just— I learned something last night that I think you should know." She said nothing but raised both eyebrows, prompting me to continue. "Your mom couldn't see ghosts."

She sputtered. "Of course she could. Only the women in our family can."

"Is that something your dad told you?"

It took her a moment to respond. "Yeah."

"So your mom's mom?"

"Died before I was born."

"So she could see ghosts?"

Alice drew her lips to the side. "I'm not sure, actually. I assume so."

Hands clasped, I lowered my arms so they were flat on the table. "I think your dad was lying to you."

Her head jerked slightly back. "Why would he do that?"

Next to her, Becca snorted. "Because he's your dad."

The comment seemed to strike a chord with Alice. "You're right. It would be just like him." Her face hardened, and she took another sip of her drink.

I spun the thin straw around in my glass, focusing on the ice cubes swirling around the bubbles. Guilt ate at me for having to reveal the truth, for what it would do to Alice. But it was the right thing to do.

Alice brought the glass bottle down with a *thunk*. "But why?"

"Because he's the one who could see ghosts. Not your mom." Alice and Becca sat silently as I recounted how I'd learned this information. At one point Alice's grip on her bottle tightened, and Becca placed her hand over Alice's other hand. After a moment, Alice's hold relaxed, but Becca's hand remained. When I was done telling them what I knew, I apologized.

"Don't be sorry," Alice said before glancing at Becca. Her face softened. "I'm not. I don't know why my father lied. Part of me doesn't care. A lot of good came out of me leaving home as soon as I could. Who knows what would have happened if my father had tried to develop my skills."

"No show, that's for sure."

Alice was quiet a moment. "Maybe that's why he was always so against it." She shrugged. "Maybe if I ever get a chance to ask his ghost why he lied, I will. But it doesn't matter now. I wouldn't change anything. Thank you for telling me."

I nodded, giving her a sympathetic smile. The truth wasn't easy sometimes, and if her standing up to get a refill of her drink after a long swig was any indication, it mattered despite her saying otherwise. No doubt, she was still processing it and maybe would be for a while.

But with that out of the way, I would hopefully be more able to concentrate on the evening and whatever was supposed to happen with Bryan's plan.

We'd been here for over an hour, many of us taking turns singing with the early slots in karaoke night as others started to filter in. It was fun. Even Sarah got into it. I had no idea she could sing, never mind do it so well.

Eventually, the DJ for the evening called up Bryan and Erin, and I wondered what part of Bryan's plan this was as he whispered something in her ear. She playfully pushed him as they walked laughing up to the stage. Then the music started, and I recognized the tune of a sweet duet from *Beauty and the Beast* about having feelings for one another that hadn't been there before. It wasn't a typical karaoke tune, but it was cute, especially considering the couple.

"They sang this in their high school musical," Becca said.

My eyebrows rose so high I could feel the pull at my ears. "Bryan was in a high school musical?"

Lily nodded. "Only because of Erin. She was nervous to try out by herself. They were letting people audition in pairs. So he did it. Don't know why she was so worried."

"Wow. Was this the song on the paper he tossed at her?" This had to be a move on his part to remind her how good they were together. And judging by the tingling emanating from the two of them, it was working.

"Yeah."

"They're so cute together. I have no idea what she sees in my brother." Alice thunked her bottle onto the table, her head still turned so she could watch the two sing. Then her eyes widened. "But it looks like we're going to find out what my brother thinks about them in a moment."

She pointed to the door.

There stood Travis, his gaze scanning the tables.

CHAPTER 50

"How did he know where we were?" I asked.

Alice shrugged, but Sarah nudged me in my side.

I glanced her way and found her looking back with one eyebrow raised. Oh, this was part of the plan, and I'd played right into it.

Travis's gaze searched the crowd. I wondered if he was confused as to where Erin was. He didn't acknowledge the rest of us at all. Then he must have recognized Erin's voice, and his gaze darted to the stage. A flash of annoyance registered as he took in the scene in front of him.

Erin stumbled in her wording but quickly recovered. Bryan paid him no mind, all his focus on Erin and the song. Had Bryan realized Travis was there?

When the song ended, everyone in our group clapped, seemingly releasing Travis from his sour expression. Had anyone else noticed?

Erin approached him with a shy smile, and he planted a kiss on her head. It seemed sweet a first, but then Bryan looked his way, and Travis caught his gaze. He put more pressure on her head, turning it possessive. Erin shifted and grabbed his hand, then pulled him toward the tables.

She tried pulling him into the booth with her, Bryan on the other side, but he slipped out of her grasp and stepped over to Alice. "Didn't expect to see you here."

"It is your fiancée's bachelorette party. Of course I'd be here. I'm in the wedding."

He contemplated this a moment. "And Bryan?"

"Her friend and the one who encouraged her to come out for the night while her family is in town."

Beside me, Sarah stiffened. Had Alice just given too much away?

"Ah," Travis said with a single slow nod. "So where's her mom?"

"Karaoke isn't her scene," Sarah answered. "But Erin is going to meet up with her after this."

He turned to her. "I didn't realize you two were friends."

Sarah shrugged. "I was invited along, and karaoke is fun, so I couldn't say no. Are you going to sing?"

Erin spun around to face us in the booth, her eyes wide. Excitement laced her voice as she asked Travis, "Are you really? I've never heard you sing."

He looked stuck for a moment, a real animal in the head-lights sort of expression. Then he plastered on a smile. "Sure, why not. Anything for you, right?"

Alice rolled her eyes. It didn't seem like she was buying his act. She looked up at Erin over her head. "I've never heard him sing either."

Travis snorted. "Probably a good thing. So how do I sign up?"

Erin was already sliding out of the booth. "Oh, let me go pick something."

"Please go easy on me," he said with a wink.

"I think I have just the song." She rushed off toward the DJ, and Travis turned to watch her movements. He didn't take his seat until she was back in the booth.

I glanced at Sarah. She shrugged, her mouth puckered to the side.

"What was that look for?" Alice said, calling out Sarah. "He not supposed to know Bryan planned this because it will make him jealous or something?"

"Or something," Sarah said.

I, however, couldn't handle the pressure. So this was why they didn't tell me the plan. Alice and I leaned toward one another across the table. Barely above a whisper, I said, "He's trying to show her that Travis isn't the guy she thinks he is."

"Oh," she sounded surprised, but not upset. Nothing like the reaction to my telling her about her father. "Well, good luck to him. Sorry I said anything, though Trav's never been dumb."

After a few more songs, it was Travis's turn. With bravado —I wasn't sure if it was false or not—he walked up to the stage. The music started playing, but I couldn't gauge his reaction to it. He was too turned toward the screen displaying the words.

"He's not half bad," Alice commented a few lines into the sappy love song. She picked up her bottle but set it back down after looking inside it.

And it was true. Travis wasn't doing poorly, but it also didn't look like he was enjoying it all that much either. He had at least turned more to the crowd, becoming less reliant on the words scrolling on the screen.

When the song was over, most people clapped, and Travis dipped his head slightly. He crossed the bar, weaving his way through the tables, then plopped into his seat. "Why'd you pick that one?"

Erin pouted. "I assumed you'd know it since it's our wedding song."

"But now I'm going to have that memory running through my head when I hear it."

Erin leaned over and kissed Travis quickly as she slid off her seat to let Bryan out. "And in a few days, you'll have a better memory of that song to replace it with."

Bryan walked toward the stage as the next singer performed. When that song was over, the DJ called Bryan's name, and he took the mic.

As the music started, I realized this was Bryan's last stand. The crooning song about not being able to help but fall in love was his attempt at getting her to notice him. The matchmaking tingle that I could feel from the two of them rushed through my system as he poured himself into his words.

"I did not know my brother could still sing like that!" Becca said as she stood to watch him, turning and kneeling on the booth's seat cushion.

Erin whistled at one point during the performance, turning some heads toward her, and Bryan kept singing as the tingle pulsed stronger in my system.

But like always, something was missing from it as it had from the beginning. They were a match, no doubt, but all his love couldn't make Erin realize she felt the same. Her side of the match was occupied by Travis as well. If he hadn't been in the picture, I was certain she and Bryan would have found their way to one another by now without my help.

The guilt struck me to my core. What if I had been giving Bryan false hope, so sure of all my matches getting together and having their happily ever afters? What if this had all been a matter of timing? What if they weren't meant to be together right now but they would be in the future? And how was that fair to Travis either, that I'd been a part of some scheme to test him? I didn't like him, he had proven to be outwardly possessive and a bit shady regarding the prenup and insurance policy, but I couldn't do more than help Erin when she requested it.

And suddenly Bryan was back at the booth, spilling his drink on Travis. I'd missed exactly how it had happened, but judging by Bryan's expression, this had been planned too.

I held my breath. But despite being soaking wet, Travis didn't react.

"Maybe it's a good thing you didn't get to drink that, Bry," his sister said, breaking the silence among our group.

"Yeah, maybe," Bryan finally said, deflating a little. "Sorry, man."

Travis said nothing, holding his hand up by his face, palms out to stop Bryan from saying more.

"I'll go get some napkins," one of Erin's cousins said as she rushed out from the booth. She returned a few moments later, a whole roll of paper towels in her hand.

Once Travis was sopped up, he stood. "I think I'm going to head home and get cleaned up. Have fun with your mom tonight." He pressed a firm kiss against Erin's head as he held onto her arm, then turned and marched out of the bar.

Erin watched him leave before glancing up at Bryan, who was still standing there with a mostly empty drink.

He gave her a small shrug, but his eyes said so much more. But what else could he do? His plan had failed. He hadn't proved that Travis was a terrible guy. And if he wasn't now, what if he wasn't when it came to Anita's ghost either?

CHAPTER 51

The next morning Erin, now as confused as ever, stopped into the bakery while her Mom had her hair appointment just off Main Street. It was part one of getting ready for the maybe still happening wedding. Erin didn't seem sure.

"One lemon poppyseed muffin, please," she asked Sarah behind the counter after she explained what she was doing. "Promised Mom a snack before we get our nails done."

Bryan came out from the kitchen, his face lighting up as he saw Erin perusing the cases. "Hey, Rin."

"So now what?" she asked, turning to him and putting her hands on her hips. "Because all that showed me was he's a pretty nice guy, and that's kinda one of the reasons why I'm marrying him."

"You can't marry him, that's what," Bryan said quickly.

Erin lowered her chin and glared at his statement. She crossed her arms. "And why not? Your plan failed, Bry. He walked in on us singing together. Nothing. You spilled beer all over him and nothing. Absolutely nothing happened last night that would indicate to me that he's some evil guy that I shouldn't be involved with. So why, Bryan? Why shouldn't I marry him?"

He rubbed the back of his neck. "Because I love you, that's why."

The tingling concentrated in my stomach felt more like an electrical storm than what I regularly experienced. Gone were the butterflies that regularly fluttered in my stomach near matches. They were hiding from the storm. It felt volatile. Like it was coming alive.

"You what?" She sputtered into laughter. "Come on, Bry. That's not funny." She thought he was kidding? Had she really never realized until now?

As big as Bryan was, at this moment, I'd never seen him look more vulnerable. He seemed almost smaller. His shoulders loose, rounded. Posture at a slight slouch. His eyes rounder, sadder. "I'm not laughing. I've loved you since we were kids."

Erin grew quiet. It seemed to take forever for her to ask, "Why didn't you ever tell me?"

"I did try. More than once. Starting with the prom. You were so busy focusing on who your crush at the time was dancing with that you didn't see what was right in front of you. Me. We would have been perfect together." He ran his hands through his hair as he took a step toward her. "Still would be perfect together."

"Bry . . ."

He reached for her hand, and she gave it willingly. His dwarfed hers. "Please don't marry him, Rin."

She stared at their hands before she looked up at him. "I don't know what you want me to say."

"Say you won't."

"I can't say that." She pulled away from Bryan's grip. "I'm

supposed to marry him tomorrow. I've been with him for years."

He searched her face. "You've been my friend for years longer."

"Yeah. Friends. And we can still be friends."

Bryan shook his head. "I don't know if we can be. All these years I've stood by hoping you'd realize that what everyone else said about him was true. He's no good for you. He's not a good guy. Your friends . . . your *real* friends didn't like him. Your grandmother didn't either. You told me as much yourself."

She took a step back. Pain etched her face. "So what are you saying, you're no longer my friend?"

Bryan let out a frustrated noise that sounded almost like a growl. Knowing what he was now, maybe it was. "I'm saying I wish you would open your eyes. I love you Erin, and now that the wedding is almost here, I don't know if I can stand by and watch you go through with it."

She furrowed her brow. "And it's supposed to be my fault that you stood around waiting all this time? You're supposed to be some sort of take-charge . . . guy."

"I am." He rubbed the back of his neck. "With other stuff. But with you?"

"With me, what?"

"You make me vulnerable."

"And that's not a good look for you, is it?"

Bryan shook his head. "That's not it at all."

She sighed hard. "Then what is it?"

"I thought I'd be okay if you were at least in my life. But now? Now I know I won't be. You're supposed to be mine. You say nothing happened last night with Travis. But you know what I saw?"

"What?" She crossed her arms.

"I saw a man who was jealous. Possessive. He didn't even remember that was your wedding song!"

"He didn't say he didn't remember."

"He didn't have to. First the embarrassment over having to sing it. Then the surprise of being caught off guard that he should have known that song. It was obvious to anyone who could smell him."

"How convenient that it's something only you can do."

"Then ask Becca. She'll tell you. You don't pick songs randomly, Erin. You never have. He should know that about you. What else doesn't he know? What don't you know about him?"

She seemed to deflate a little as the moments passed. Bryan had hit at the heart of all this. Why had Travis done what he did with threatening conservatorship, then the prenup and insurance policy?

Finally, she answered, "I don't know. I just don't know."

"Well, when you do know, you know where to find me." Bryan took the two steps he needed to get to Erin, then gently pressed a kiss to the top of her head. Unlike Travis's kiss last night, there was no pressure to this kiss, no claim of possession. Bryan didn't have Erin.

But she did have his heart.

As he walked into the kitchen, Erin wiped her face. She walked over to where she'd put her bag when she first got here. It had been a while. I wondered what her mom was getting done at the salon or if she was meeting Erin here. When Erin turned around, tears still welled in her eyes. A few minutes away from here and the situation would probably benefit her.

Alice sauntered into the bakery at that moment, a business card in hand. She took one look at Erin and beelined toward her. "What happened?"

Erin shook her head in reply.

Alice hugged Erin. How could anyone have thought Alice didn't like her almost sister-in-law? "Whatever it is, it will all be okay. Wedding stress is intense. I swear, if I ever get married, I'm eloping. Skip all of that ceremony nonsense." She turned to me. "Sorry. I'm sure it's how you make a lot of your money."

"No worries. I know they're not for everyone."

Alice let go of Erin—who was now fully crying but trying to collect herself—before approaching me at the counter. "Seriously, is everything okay?" she whispered.

I swooshed my hand in the general direction of the kitchen, and she nodded. "Got it. Sorry if I ruined anything last night."

"Nah, I don't think you did." Travis was either smart and knew to be on his best behavior or had nothing to hide and wasn't a bad guy.

"So . . . I heard that with whatever is going on with Erin's grandmother, you suspected me at one point." Heat rushed into my cheeks, and she cracked a small smile. "No worries. I get it. You had to consider all your options. I'm the same way when I do my investigations. I might know something is or isn't haunted, but either way, I have to rule out every scenario that could recreate a client's experience. Honestly, that's what would make you a great investigator. Offer still stands if you ever want to come out with us."

She stuck out her hand to shake, then took notice of the card still in her hand. "Right. Here. This is a bona fide medium. If you want to know who's up there, this is who you should go see."

"Thanks." I took the card from her with plans to call as soon as the shop was empty, then shook her hand. "And I might just take you up on that offer. Should probably learn a bit more about everything I can do."

She nodded. "Great. I'll keep you updated with whatever we have going on around here. You probably can't do much traveling, can you?"

I shook my head. "Between the bakery and my cat . . ."

"No worries. If it weren't for my awesome neighbor who takes care of mine when my roommates and I are away, I would be hesitant to travel too."

Behind Alice, Erin grabbed her things once more. "I'm going to go see if my mom's done with her hair." When she came up behind us this time, her eyes had dried and her face had returned to its usual complexion. The few minutes to collect herself had helped. She no longer seemed on the verge of tears.

Alice turned toward her. "So will I see you tomorrow for the rehearsal dinner?"

The question made my insides twist. Her answer could change everything.

Erin sighed. "I—"

"You may not want to answer that until you hear what I have to say," Megan said as she strode into the shop. With the door already open to let in the warm breeze and let the bakery smells out to lure more customers in, there'd been no noise to announce her arrival.

Erin jumped and spun toward her lawyer. She stood, back straight and almost frozen in place. "Why? What did you find?"

"Travis knows about your inheritance." Megan hiked her satchel up on her shoulder. "And he's already tapped into it."

CHAPTER 52

I had to stop my jaw from dropping.

Erin showed a bit more restraint. She turned her body with every step Megan took toward the counter, her tongue set into her cheek and her jaw tight. "Come again? He did what?"

Megan thunked her purse down on the counter next to the registers. "He's already made a withdrawal against your inheritance."

"How did he find out about it?"

Alice's eyes widened as she scrunched her lips. "My brother has a lot of connections. If you had something hidden from him, there's no doubt his people would be able to find it."

Erin shook her head. "But I didn't even know about it until the other day."

Alice gave her a sympathetic look. "Doesn't matter. You know that he stops at nothing to get over things he considers obstacles."

"So what, he views me as an obstacle to money? But it's

my money." Erin turned to Megan. "You said that he already took money out of it. How? When?"

"When he first filed for conservatorship before we got the injunction."

Now Erin's jaw dropped. "What?"

Megan pulled some papers out of her bag, then flipped a few pages into the stack. "You can't access your inheritance until you're thirty. But if something happens to you before then, others can access it, namely your power of attorney. It's supposed to be for your care and related expenses—"

"The conservatorship."

Megan nodded. "Given how quickly we got the injunction—"

"How much did he take?"

"A thousand."

Alice snorted. "That's nothing. No doubt a test to see if he could do it."

Erin wheeled on Alice. "You think he'd do it again?"

"He wanted control over your finances, didn't he?"

Alice nodded.

I cleared my throat quietly. "You didn't even know you had this money coming to you until after this happened."

Angry tears rimmed Erin's eyes. She nodded. "But why?"

"My brother's lifestyle has never been cheap as I'm sure you've realized. Even in high school, he was always asking our dad for more money. And our dad always caved." She rolled her eyes. "Never did for me, but that's another story. I don't think our stepmom has been as generous since Dad's passing."

"So you're saying he's out of money? It's his job to deal with finances and budgets. How could he run out of his own? Why wouldn't he tell me?"

Alice shrugged, and her tone turned soft. "Kinda makes

you wonder how much you really knew about him after all, huh?"

"Never knew what you saw in him anyway," Becca said as she walked into the shop. "I never liked him. Neither did your nonni. Some people can't change, she'd say." She looked at Alice. "You were taking a while. Thought I'd come check in on you."

Erin turned toward Becca. "I thought she was referring to your brother, telling me to choose the . . . safe option, no matter who it was."

Becca raised an eyebrow at her. "Then you clearly forgot the second part of that."

"Which was?"

She smirked, a small chuckle escaping as she did. "And what's the fun in that?"

Erin's brows furrowed, and a tear escaped onto her cheek. "Seriously? You're not going to tell me? Look at me. I'm a mess."

Becca placed a hand on Erin's shoulder. "You really think I'd do that to you? That *is* the second part. Some people can't change, and what's the fun in that?"

"Thank you." Erin pulled Becca in for a hug. "I didn't remember. You all were a lot of fun."

"Still can be." Becca's voice was quieter but still able to be heard. With a final squeeze, she pulled out of Erin's hold. She turned to me. "Can I go talk to my brother?"

I waved her toward the door.

She walked into the kitchen and clapped her hands upon entry. "Okay," I heard her say as the door swung back closed. Hopefully she could help calm her brother down. I could feel his frustrated energy from here.

"I need to head back to the office," Megan said. "I'm glad I caught you, but I'm sorry to give you bad news. It's not easy finding out something like this. And I am trying to track down exactly where those funds went, so if you want to follow up with me later to see what your options are, please do."

"Oh, I will," Erin replied, a new level of determination in her voice. "You better believe it. And thank you."

Megan nodded to the three of us before turning around and heading back out the door.

Once she was safely out of earshot, Erin sighed loudly. "I don't know how, but he definitely did something to my grandmother."

Alice nodded. "No doubt. If he's willing to do what he did to you to get to your money, no telling what else he'd do if he thought she was standing in his way."

Thoughts of the beverage board coming back to me. How quickly the problem arose and how quickly he'd taken care of it. Had that been a test the way Alice said the smaller withdrawal of Erin's money had been? I gulped. We had to get to the bottom of this fast.

CHAPTER 53

Erin strode back into the bakery a few hours later as I was hanging up the kitchen phone after speaking to the medium. As I walked back into the shop to greet her, she plopped down into a chair at the table where Alice had set up her laptop. She'd been working there quietly since Becca left for an early lunch with Bryan. I was happy to see them reconnecting.

Alice peeked over her screen. "How'd it go?"

"Mom took the news surprisingly well. She'll break the news to the rest of my family once I tell Travis. In spite of what he's done, he should hear it from me. And then I'm going to find my nonni. But I don't know where to look."

I wiped down the top of the case where I kept the candy. "She could be anywhere. In the last few months, I've seen ghosts anchored to hairbrushes, tiaras, and a knife." I hoped the information would help her think of a possibility. "But she is here, because she isn't there. The medium just told me as much." And more, though that was a conversation I'd need to have with Alice later.

Erin's eyes widened. "What about the boxes?"

The hair on the back of my neck prickled. "The boxes?"

"He still collects boxes?" Alice asked. Erin nodded. "Wow, he's been collecting them since he was a kid. Began with this carved wooden one that he got right before our mom walked out. It was so weird. He carried it around for days after she left. Finally Dad couldn't take it anymore and took it from him. I don't know what Trav finally said or did, but Dad gave it back to him. It stayed on a shelf in his room until I moved out, and likely beyond that."

I pulled out a chair and sat next to the two of them. "Sounds like your dad was pretty tough growing up, huh?"

Alice scoffed. "Yeah. And Travis didn't fall too far from the tree. Why do you think I left?"

Erin's shoulders fell. "Why didn't you warn me about him if you thought he was that bad?"

Alice gave her a look. "Would you have believed me?"

Erin said nothing, and given everything I'd been told, it seemed likely that Erin knew the answer. She wouldn't have. Especially not when she thought Alice didn't like her, no doubt a falsehood that Travis let continue . . . if he didn't somehow start it in the first place.

"The good thing," Alice continued, "is that you've figured it out before you've gone and gotten married to him. And you have me as a friend now."

Erin could only muster up a half smile in response. I imagined having a new friend was nice, but it likely did little to ease the sting of a romance gone wrong. Especially one that had been as serious or long-term as Erin's had been.

I folded my arms onto the table. "So the big question is, how do we get into the house so we can check out the boxes?"

Erin thought a moment. "Well, I haven't told him that the

wedding is off. I could say I need to talk to him about some final details or something. Alice is in the wedding party. Now that he knows we're friends, it's not off base that she'd come with me for whatever it is. Plus, she's his sister. It used to be her house too."

"Not that I regularly go visit," she quipped, but she seemed satisfied by her inclusion nonetheless.

"You could say you're curious about the kitchen renovations after hearing me talk about them."

There was still one other person who needed a reason to be there. "What about me?"

From behind the counter, Sarah shouted, "Last-minute muffin testing!"

We all brightened at this. "It's not usually something I make house calls for, but how would he know? I'll say it's because it's so close to the wedding." I smiled back at my familiar. "Can you be on standby in case we need backup?"

Bryan pushed his way out of the kitchen. "Count me in too. I'll be close should you need me to barge in to help."

"Thanks, Bry." Erin looked up at him and smiled shyly. The tingling stirred my insides in a way it hadn't before, and I smiled. About time.

Alice clapped, breaking the hold their gazes had on one another, unlikely aware of what she was interrupting. "So when do we do this?"

I made a face. "Tomorrow? I don't have many muffins left for this ruse."

Erin drew her lips to the side as she contemplated our next move.

"I can whip some up right now," Bryan offered. "No time like the present."

Sarah grinned. "Eager much?"

The corners of his mouth turned up as he gave an exaggerated shrug.

"I agree with Bryan," Alice said. "It's time to see what my little brother is up to."

CHAPTER 54

We stood outside the house Erin had been calling home for the last several years. I looked up at the gray two-story Colonial and felt nothing. I wasn't a locater like Larry, but I could understand why he'd had trouble figuring out if Erin was here or not. There was no energy coming from this house, and until this moment, I hadn't realized what that meant. Even without realizing it, I'd been able to feel energies coming from houses. Not in the sense of ghosts or who was inside, but a feeling the house gave off. Warmth, love, welcoming, that sort of thing. Even the house that others said gave off the creepy vibes a few streets away stirred something within me. This house had nothing, and the hair on the back of my neck stood on end as a result.

Erin sighed hard and shook her arms. "Let's get this over, shall we?"

"Let's." Alice put a hand on Erin's shoulder and briefly squeezed it.

Although I couldn't see Bryan, the tingling told me he was around. I'd driven here with him but dropped him off a block away so he wouldn't be spotted. He said he'd hide in the tree line that bordered one side of the property. My other backup was in my pocket. Sarah. Waiting in the bakery for me to call no matter the outcome.

I adjusted the box of muffins in my arms one more time. Half were still warm, whereas the other half had all the muffins we'd pulled out of the bakery case. "You can do it, Erin. We're here for you."

Erin reached up for the door handle, then twisted the knob to let the door swing open.

The house's energy smacked me in the face as I entered. To go from feeling nothing to feeling something, even though it still seemed muted to me, was jarring. Even weirder was the moment when Alice pulled the door closed behind her and I lost all sense of the tingling connection between Erin here inside and Bryan outside nearby. Gone. Not even a trace. Was this what it was like to feel normal? Some sort of match-making tingle always followed me around wherever I went, even if it was no more than a buzz. In town especially. But even out in the woods or down on the beach. I'd always thought it was a part of me. Now, with the feeling cut off, how much of that constant feeling was me and how much was everything—and everyone—else?

We'd entered the living room, full of clean lines in shades of gray and white, aside from an old wingback chair and ottoman that, while gray, had a floral pattern. Given the tradi-tional appearance of the house's exterior, I hadn't expected the inside to be so modern. The wall to the right was missing its top half and now provided bar-height seating at a counter overlooking the kitchen. It and the rest of the visible kitchen countertop was quartz. It sparkled where the afternoon sun coming in through the window hit it. This had to be part of the recent kitchen renovations Erin had mentioned. She'd said Travis wasn't into crystals. She probably hadn't considered the countertop when I asked. Was he aware of how much energy it could hold? Maybe that was why the energy in here was so different, as if the quartz was keeping the energy inside the house from ever reaching outside, same for the cell signals.

The quartz wouldn't allow us to get a call out. There'd be no backup. We were alone in here. Hopefully we could handle whatever would come our way.

I continued to look around Travis and Erin's house. The gray and white color scheme expanded into the kitchen and the adjoining dining room. But where were the boxes?

"Trav? Where are you?" Erin called.

"Erin?" He sounded surprised. Footsteps sounded from down the hall around the kitchen corner, growing louder as Travis approached. He stopped short when he saw the three of us standing a few feet into the room. "Oh, you brought other people. What's going on?"

"It's a muffin emergency," Erin said animatedly, putting her history of performing in her high school drama club to use. She took him by the arm and led him to the couch across from the recliner. "Alice stopped off at the bakery to get a few goodies for us to eat while the girls and I got our nails done, and Joanie had a few new flavors. She's been holding out on us regarding our post-wedding brunch."

I tried to look sheepish as she waved me over.

"So I begged her to come here so that we could have a second tasting," Erin continued. "Thankfully, she said yes. I think you are going to love some of these."

The leftovers from today would be good at least. I'd had no input to what Bryan was throwing in the batch he made. My only caution was that he had to make them edible because Erin or Alice could be trying them, too, and that bad muffins would tip Travis off to something being amiss. Bryan had given me an ingredient list so I could update our supply counts, but I had yet to look at it. If I read something that didn't seem right, part of me would still have a hard time serving it. A matter of professional pride even given the circumstances. I couldn't let the knowledge come between me and what we were here to do.

Travis smiled as if enamored by his fiancée. Maybe to some extent he was. Or he made a fabulous actor. More like he was in love with the money he'd have access to if he could manage her finances.

I crossed the room and then set the box down on the coffee table in front of them. "We took the liberty of cutting them into quarters for you while we were at the bakery to make things a bit easier for the tasting," I said as I opened the box to reveal a dozen muffins. That wasn't entirely true. I'd never have cut them ahead of time for anyone else's tasting. We didn't want Travis to have a knife within reach if things didn't go well with this ghost hunt.

"You didn't happen to bring plates, did you? Or napkins?" Travis chuckled, sounding amused with himself.

Erin playfully pushed his leg. "We have those silly. Be right back." As she stood, facing me and away from Travis, she rolled her eyes. Spell completely broken. She returned a moment later and handed both Travis and Alice napkins, keeping one for herself.

When she was situated back on the couch, I pointed to the muffin closest to me in the upper corner of the box. It was the side with the flavors I knew. "This one here is a lemon ginger muffin with chia seeds instead of poppy seeds. It's a warm, spicy spin on a summer classic."

The three tried the muffin and spent a minute or two commenting on the flavors before we moved to the next one to repeat the process. At the third muffin, I began squirming as if I needed to use the restroom. After the fourth muffin, I apologized and asked if I could use the bathroom.

Erin pointed down the hallway. "It's the first door on the right."

"Thank you. This really is so embarrassing. I never do this. It's—"

Travis held his hand up to stop me from saying more. I scooted off in the direction of the bathroom, which put me on a direct path toward Travis's box collection.

At least three dozen boxes sat on floating shelves installed at various heights on the wall opposite the bathroom. It made for an interesting visual, the boxes appearing to hover on nearly invisible shelves. Some boxes seemed old, others newer based on the condition of the wood or the style of carving. Some had gilding, and others had tiny crystal accents, but if they were being used how I thought they could be, the decorations on the outside didn't matter.

I hadn't expected this many boxes. How would I know which one to open first?

Moments passed, and as planned Alice came in search of me.

"How's it going out there?" I asked her quietly.

"The first one Bryan made wasn't bad. Butterscotch and chocolate chip. How's it—" She glanced up at the wall, and her mouth dropped open. "Wow, that's a lot more than the last time I was here."

"People's collections grow over time, right? This could be nothing . . ." Although I didn't want to be wrong and have to start our search over, part of me still didn't want to believe what could be inside them.

"Or they could be full of ghosts. Only one way to find out." She reached for a box.

I stopped her hand. "Wait. We should try to find Anita first."

"And how do we do that?" She pointed to the wall using her hand, accidentally tapping one of the boxes. It shifted slightly.

"That's it."

"What's it?"

"Erin said one of the contractors hit the shelf and a box fell off. It was chipped. She'd had to repair it." I briefly explained having seen Anita's ghost one night. "Maybe that damage had been just enough to let her ghost escape."

"Good idea, but I should head back. Travis will start to suspect something if I take much longer." She ducked into the bathroom, and the sound of the toilet flushing broke the silence. "Bought you another minute as you wash your hands." She took off toward the living room as I checked the first box. No damage.

I was halfway down the shelf by the time Erin came to check on me. "That's the box that broke the other day," she whispered, pointing to the one I was about to grab. It was a light wood with delicate scrolled carving.

"If we're right about what he's doing with these"—and we had no alternatives at this point if we were wrong—"I think it's the one your grandmother is in. Where's Alice?"

"Distracting her brother."

Made sense. I picked up the box. My fingers trailed along a rough line on the back, and I flipped it over. A glue line from Erin's repair work ran diagonally near the corner. There was more on the side. A whole chunk must have popped off.

I glanced up at her. "Are you ready?"

She took a deep breath, tensing as she did, then nodded sharply once before glancing behind her to check that we were still in the clear.

When her focus fell back onto the box, I opened it.

There was nothing inside.

CHAPTER 55

A spark of light flashed between us, and there was Anita standing in the same outfit I'd seen her in the night she'd come to me, but this time she was solid. Whole.

Erin gasped and threw her arms around her grandmother's back, bending them up between her grandmother's shoulders to pull her closer. "Nonni!"

"Oh, my sweet *patata*. I've missed you." The woman did the same with her arms, and the two clutched each other as if their lives—or afterlives—depended on it.

Something crashed hard in the living room.

"Travis, stop!" Alice yelled.

"Move," Travis bellowed before there was a thump. He charged down the hallway, and Alice scrambled behind him, holding her upper arm. "Drop that box."

Erin wheeled around, and Travis's face fell as his gaze darted between her and Anita next to her. He recovered quickly, and he plastered a smile on his face. "Oh wow! Your grandmother's back! She always said she'd be back for the wedding."

We were right. He could see ghosts. But had he realized he'd let his big secret slip?

"There isn't going to be a wedding. How could you do this? Locking Nonni in a box and keeping her from me?"

"Is that what she told you?"

"She didn't have to. I opened the box and now here she is. Why, Trav?"

"I did it to protect you!" At least he didn't try to deny it.

Erin scoffed. "Protect me? From what?"

"She doesn't have your best interests at heart."

"And you do? All you ever wanted was my inheritance. I don't know how you even found out about it in the first place."

He laughed sardonically. The jig was up. "I have connections. Of course I had them look into you when we first started going out. I was surprised they found anything remotely like an inheritance. And that you didn't know about it? Score."

Erin's exterior cracked slightly. "Did you ever care for me?"

He made a face as if to say, are you serious? "You were fun. Nothing more. There were worse people to have to pretend with, I'm sure."

"Why wait so long?" she yelled. Anita placed her hand on her granddaughter's back to comfort her.

"Just waiting for the opportunity. You think they would have let me file for a conservatorship if we weren't serious with one another . . . if I didn't have a document already granting me power of attorney?"

"That was from a trip years ago."

He tsked. "Always give something an expiration date if it's not meant to be permanent."

"But where does Nonni come into all of this? And don't say to protect me because I know that's a lie. If anything, it was to protect you!"

Travis held out his hands, wrists together. "Guilty as charged. Take me in." Then a Cheshire smile spread across his face. "Oh, that's right, you can't. No one would believe you."

He raised the pitch of his voice to one that mimicked Erin's. "Officer, I want to press charges because he was holding my grandmother's ghost hostage."

Erin's hands balled into fists as Travis laughed, and she shook as she stood there. Anita shifted her hand so it was on Erin's shoulder, almost as if holding her back, though I doubted she would have held on had Erin gone after him.

"That still doesn't tell me why you captured Nonni, made me think she'd left me. I might never have found you out had I not gone for help in locating her."

Travis glared at me momentarily. "I knew I should have done more than set the beverage board on you."

So he was guilty of that. Bryan was right about the knight in shining armor act.

Travis shifted his gaze back to Erin. "It was a risk I had to take. Anita found me out. Was going to tell you everything I'd done. Sure did surprise her when she realized I could see her. Just a little too late to do anything about it, though." He grinned wickedly.

Travis had been so focused on Erin and her grandmother that he seemingly hadn't noticed his sister.

"So who's in this one, Trav?" The wooden box Alice held was small with a painted floral lid.

"Don't open it," he yelled, worry lacing his voice, but it was too late.

Like with Anita, nothing was in the box, but there was a

sudden flash, and before us stood a man in dress slacks, a button-up shirt, and a tie with a knot twisted haphazardly so the tie didn't stand flat against the shirt.

The ghost looked around as if to get his bearings.

"The math teacher? Really, Trav? Who were you protecting from him?"

Travis snorted. "The whole ninth grade."

Travis's voice drew the attention of the ghost. The ghost rushed him, passing through Travis and continuing into the living room. A loud crack reverberated through the house as the ghost opened the door and then stumbled backward.

"Mr. Bingham! Are you all right?"

"I think he hit the ward," I said, placing the box Anita had been in back on the shelf.

"The what?" Alice glanced back at me. "Oh, never mind right now." She took a step in Mr. Bingham's direction, but he waved her off. He charged the door again, and this time, something shattered. What type of wards were on this place?

Alice grabbed another box and opened it before it was fully off the shelf.

"No!" Travis yelled like before, but he had made no attempt to pass Erin, Alice, and Anita. He rubbed his chest, and I wondered if he'd ever had a ghost go through him like that before. It was an odd sensation, the fleeting emotions and thoughts of someone else entering one's body.

Like before, a spark flared and revealed a ghost. This one was an older woman, a shawl around her shoulders.

"Alice?" the woman asked, a warble to her voice either from non-use or age. Perhaps both. "You've grown."

"Mrs. Mason?" She glanced over the woman's shoulder at her brother. "Mrs. Mason. Really? She used to make us cookies on the weekend."

"And make us itchy sweaters. She hated when my toys ended up in her yard. Yelled a lot."

"That was Mr. Mason. Is he in here too?" She shifted Mrs. Mason behind her protectively, saying, "It's going to be okay, Mrs. Mason."

Travis shrugged.

I placed my hand on Mrs. Mason's arm. "Please, let me help you." I wanted to guide her away from here, but she waved me off as Alice threw open the lid of the next box.

After the spark revealed an older man, Alice said, "At least you put them next to one another."

Mr. Mason passed directly through Travis as he approached his wife. The two ghosts embraced, then hand in hand, headed toward the living room, but not before Mrs. Mason could say "Shame on you" to Travis. The Masons turned toward the door, and this time there was no cracking noise to accompany their exit.

At that moment, Bryan rushed into the house. "What is going on? Who are these people coming out of the house and disappearing?"

Erin stepped toward him. "Those would be the ghosts Travis has been keeping locked up for who knows how long. Including Nonni."

Bryan looked at Anita, and for the first time, Anita let go of her granddaughter as she stepped toward Bryan.

He blinked repeatedly as if not believing his eyes. "How is this possible?"

"It just is," I answered.

Anita hugged Bryan then, and he seemed to relax into her. "It feels so real."

"That's because it is, *il gatto*."

He pulled out of her embrace and searched her face. "You know?"

"A little hard to hide a family with six kids like your-selves." She caressed his cheek. "I never minded. Everyone deserves to live in peace."

He smiled. "That's relative with my family. We were noisy."

"You know what I mean." She hugged him again and looked back at her granddaughter. "Why are you two not together?"

Erin blushed. "A really big misunderstanding. I don't know what I was thinking." She looked back at Travis and her look of disgust morphed into one of slight concern.

Alice and Travis stood locked in a stare down. "So what, you've been able to talk to ghosts your whole life like me?"

"See them, talk to them . . ." He glared at her, seeming proud almost. "Trap them."

"Why didn't you ever tell me you could do all this stuff? Why pretend when we were kids?"

"And ruin my secret? Oh, dear sister, it was much more fun this way, knowing I was more powerful than you as you paraded your abilities around on the internet."

"Is that so?" Her hand hovered over the next box, and she raised an eyebrow at him in challenge. "So, Mr. More Power-ful, should we try another one?"

Travis lunged for her, but Bryan was faster. He pushed Travis against the wall and held him there.

"Should have known you weren't far away. You've always been Erin's pet."

Bryan growled and for the first time, Travis looked genuinely concerned.

I slipped my hand into my pocket. With the wards broken, it was time to try calling Sarah. I pulled the phone out just enough to activate the screen and press her number that was already on the display.

"Hello?" came her voice.

I didn't answer as Alice opened another box. "Mr. McGovern?" she said curiously when the ghost appeared. She glanced at her brother. "Dad's business partner? Why him?"

Travis sobered. "I had to. You think I had a choice once Dad learned what I could do? He couldn't have the ghosts of those he killed running around town. Said they'd never leave him alone."

"You're saying Dad killed Mr. McGovern?" Travis nodded. "So what, you were Dad's accomplice?"

Travis snorted. "More like his cleanup guy."

My stomach churned at the implications. At what Travis was likely made to do for his father. I almost felt bad for him. What would he have been like had circumstances been different?

Alice pursed her lips a moment as she considered this. "So the Masons?"

Travis said nothing at first, but Bryan leaned into him. Travis relented after another moment. "Also Dad. He and Mr. Mason had a dispute over some trees at the property line. Dad wanted them down. Said they were a danger to the house. Mr. Mason refused to see eye to eye. One day, their argument turned heated. Don't know how it happened, but Dad killed Mr. Mason. Mrs. Mason saw, so she had to go too."

"And Mr. Bingham?" Alice asked.

Travis grinned wickedly. "Deserved it. Tried to fail me. Dad wasn't going to let that happen. I'd never have gotten into college otherwise." He glanced at Erin, and his lips curled into a smile. "Never would have run into you either."

And there went any trace of pity I had for him.

Bryan adjusted his stance to press harder into Travis. "Rin, you don't have to be here for this."

Anita squeezed her granddaughter's hand. "Come, why don't we go catch up."

Erin gave one last hard look at Travis and then nodded. As she led Anita back toward the living room, someone knocked on the door.

"Hello?" came the male voice. "Heartwood Hollow PD."

CHAPTER 56

I knew that voice. "Seth!"

"Joanie?"

"We're down the hallway."

Erin pointed toward us as Seth came around the corner.

He surveyed the scene. "What is going on?" He grabbed his radio. "Come on in."

A moment later, his partner, Oliver, appeared. "Should have known a cat was involved."

I took a step forward. "Bryan's helping. He's detained the real criminal." If Oliver knew about Bryan, what was he? Did Seth know? "Mr. Ellison has admitted to helping cover up several murders, officers."

"We heard it all."

"How?"

"Me," Sarah said from the doorway. She ran over to me and gave me a big hug. "I'm so glad you're okay. Seth and his partner walked into the bakery right after you all left and were still there when you called. When I realized what was going on, I put the phone on speaker for them to hear it too."

"And we came right over," Oliver said.

"You could have let me out of the back seat, you know." She put her hands on her hips. "Thank goodness you have a sliding partition. I had to shimmy through it. Ripped my apron."

"I told you to stay put. It was for your safety."

Seth cleared his throat. "Enough, you too. We have work to do."

Over the next several minutes, they cuffed Travis and began taking our statements, starting with Erin, who said she wanted to press charges against Travis for stealing from her and "whatever else he could be charged with for leading her on all these years."

With Travis cuffed and Oliver watching over him in Travis's office, Bryan had taken a seat next to Erin and Anita. Alice was in a back room I hadn't seen, giving her statement to Seth. I stood leaning against the quartz countertop with Sarah. I let the quartz's energy flow through me, keeping me grounded. With the situation de-escalated, my nerves had decided to make themselves known. My knees shook.

"Should have thought to bring some cookies," Sarah said. "Why don't you sit down?"

"We have muffins." I pointed to the box on the coffee table.

She ran over to it and pulled out a quarter before returning to me. "Here."

I'd just popped the last piece into my mouth when Alice came out from the room and Seth beckoned me toward him.

"First, are you okay?" He asked when he closed the door behind us.

"Yeah. I had some muffin. It's no cookie, but it did the trick."

"What happened? For real. Everyone is hiding something

from me. Expect it a bit from the cat, but you won't lie to me, right?"

"The cat," I started, weighing the implications on my tongue. "How much do you know?"

"Enough."

Not good enough for me. "What are you?"

He sighed. "A wolf shifter."

"Does Courtney know?"

"Of course she does. So why don't you start at the beginning and tell me what you are and how you got to be involved in whatever all of this is."

My statement lasted longer than any of the others had. But there was a lot to tell. Not just about this case but about me and how Erin had known to come to me in the first place.

When I was done, Seth said, "You need to tell Courtney."

"I should have told her a long time ago."

He nodded. "She'll understand. You should have been there when I had to tell her about me." He thought a moment. "But she can tell you that story. Let's get you back out with everyone else and we can wrap this up."

Seth opened the door for me and I returned to Sarah by the counter. Alice had taken a seat in the old wingback chair. Bryan sat chatting with Erin and Anita, one hand over hers. Seth diverted to Travis's office, and he and Oliver exited a moment later, sandwiching Travis between them.

We all stared silently as they led Travis out the door.

Once the patrol car left, Alice and I returned to the wall of boxes along with Sarah. One by one, we opened each box, hoping to be able to identify the ghosts and assist them in crossing over.

It wasn't that easy. Some outright refused to believe they were dead. Based on their clothing, others had been dead longer than we'd been alive, opening up a load of questions I didn't know if we'd get the answer to. A few accepted it and moved on. Most left the house of their own volition, some running.

"I promise I'll track them all down," Alice said after the fifth one had taken off without us getting a name. He wasn't the last, and by the tenth one, I promised to help her if she needed it.

Finally we were down to the last box. Alice grabbed it.

I put a hand on hers to stop her. "Before you open this one—"

"I know."

"It's just that the medium—"

"This was the box my brother kept with him after my mother . . . It was the box he had the last time I saw my mother. I know."

I gave her an encouraging smile as I nodded.

This time when the box opened, there was no spark.

Alice sighed as if resigned to not knowing for sure what had happened to her mom.

Then a tiny pinprick of light appeared between us. It grew in size and vibrance until a woman stood between us.

A sob caught in Alice's throat. "Mom!"

The woman turned toward her daughter, her arms outstretched.

No words were needed between mother and daughter as they held on to one another for several moments before I slowly backed away to give them some time together. Wiping tears from my eyes, I retreated to the living room where Erin sat talking animatedly with her grandmother.

Bryan had moved to the window.

"You okay?" I asked.

His shoulder rose slightly. "It's weird. Her talking as if on the phone but having the other person sitting right there."

"You can no longer see her?"

He shook his head. "I could for a few minutes, but she slowly faded into nothing. Erin kept right on talking."

"The energy surge must have passed."

"Is she going to disappear completely?" he whispered.

"She shouldn't. Hopefully it will be as if she never left at all. Would you like to see her some more?"

His eyes widened as his brows rose. "You can do that?"

"Happened with Ken and me once in the middle of dinner."

He snorted quietly. "That must have been a surprise."

"You don't know the half of it. So do you?"

He nodded, and I held out my hand. As soon as he took it, he let out a breathy "Wow."

Anita turned to him, smiling. "Nice of you to rejoin the conversation."

"It's good to be able to see and hear you so that I can." He lifted our hands. "Thanks to Joanie."

Anita smiled. "Yes, thanks to Joanie." She stood with an ease that would have defied her age had she been alive. She appeared older than Gram by several years. "I haven't been able to thank properly you yet."

"I'm glad I could help. How are you feeling?"

She gave me a lopsided hug, made difficult by my holding on to Bryan, then kissed my cheek. "*Molto bene.*"

"Very good," Erin said from behind her grandmother.

I smiled at Erin for the translation before returning my focus to Anita. "Was that really you who came to visit me that night?"

The woman released me from her hug and nodded as she

sat next to Erin once more. "I felt this swell of energy, as if someone had opened a window on a breezy day. It was just enough to partially escape the box. And that's when I found you."

"That must have been the day the contractor knocked the box off the shelf," Erin explained. "I glued it back together that night. I'm sorry. If I had known, I would have left it."

Anita patted her granddaughter's leg. "But you didn't know."

One thing was still bothering me. "What I don't understand is how you could have made it through the wards."

"I can answer that one," came a voice I didn't know. Alice's mother emerged from the hallway, followed by her daughter.

"Two ghosts now," Bryan whispered in awe. "I see them, but I still don't know if I believe it."

While still holding on to him, I maneuvered my hand out of his grasp so he could take Erin's hand. "Let's try something."

I let go of Bryan, and he plopped down next to Erin on the couch. "They're gone again."

"Had to try." Guess I was the only one with that ability. I'd have to ask Alice, but she didn't seem in the mood to experiment. She'd stopped crying, but tear-stained streaks ran down her face.

Alice smiled weakly as I approached. "Joanie, this is my mom."

Helen held out her hand, and as I took hold of it, she covered mine with her other.

Behind me, Bryan said, "And now I see one of them again."

His comment made me smile, but it fell as I focused on

Helen once more. "I don't really know what to say. It's good to meet you, although I wish it wasn't like this."

"I understand and wish the same. So how about hello?"

"I can do that. Hello. So what were you saying about the wards?"

"They were put up after the one box fell."

"How do you know that?"

"I helped Travis put them there. Let's sit, shall we?"

She settled into the wingback chair, and Alice pulled its ottoman up next to her mother. I went back over to Bryan so he could fully participate in the conversation.

"So about the wards," I prompted.

"Travis told me to. When he was younger, he used to let me out of the box and talk with me. I tried to reason with him, to tell him he could let me go and I'd stay, but it was always back into the box I went. As he got older, our time together became less frequent. I don't know how much time passed between those occurrences. My only way to judge was based on how much older he looked. Then finally he stopped. Until what I assume was not too long ago. He demanded I ward the house from the inside. I didn't want to, but he'd changed, and I couldn't go against him."

"What do you know of the other ghosts he kept?"

She shrugged. "Aside from a few that Travis mentioned by name, only that there were others."

"So nothing about the older ghosts? The ones that had to come years before you?"

"I really don't know," Helen replied. "I'm sorry."

We were all quiet for a while. No doubt we were lost in thought. I was still thinking about the older ghosts. Could Travis have been related to the person Arthur had told me about? It was the only thing that made sense to me, that these older ghosts had come from whoever had powers like Travis before their passing. Maybe we'd never know, and I wasn't sure it mattered now that the ghosts were free.

Eventually Helen sighed, breaking the silence. "This used to be my favorite chair. My father would sit here reading the newspaper when I was a child. The moment he'd get up, I'd take his seat and pretend to read. Once I was able to, I did read."

"Surprised Travis kept it given what he did," Bryan said.

"I'm not. He never wanted me to leave. That's why this all happened, to me anyway. Why would he get rid of one of my favorite things from the house I grew up in?"

"It was the one thing he never let me touch," Erin confessed. "I snuck onto it once when he was gone, but I felt guilty and never did it again. It's really comfortable."

"So it's true?" I asked Helen. "You wanted to leave?"

"I did." She looked at her daughter. "And I wanted to take you both with me. Get you away from your father. He changed when he learned you had special abilities." She glanced down the hallway. "Though I guess he always had a dark side I didn't know about until . . . after."

"Momma," Alice began, "did Dad . . ."

Helen nodded. "And then Travis put me in the box so I would stay. I don't think any of us realized he had powers until then. At the time, I believe he thought he was protecting me, though my being free would have been better for him." She caressed her daughter's cheek. "Better for you. It changed him, knowing what your father did, knowing what he himself could do."

Alice looked at her mother. Her cheeks were wet once more. "Why didn't you ever come see me? I was right down the hall and left wondering where you went for years."

Helen leaned into her daughter and wrapped an arm around her side. "Travis refused, and I couldn't. He had total control, though I don't think he ever fully realized that."

Alice nodded but said nothing. No doubt she had more to think about.

But I still had a question. "So what comes next?"

CHAPTER 57

Erin waltzed into the shop trailed by her grandmother, wide grins on both their faces.

The sight warmed me inside. I hadn't known her long, but I'd never seen Erin this happy. "Hello, you two. It's been a few days since I last saw you."

Erin dug something out of her purse, then held it out. Keys dangled from a small metal loop. "I've come to return these."

I held my hand out, and she pressed them into my hand.

"Thank you so much for finding me a place to stay when I needed it most."

I'd have to remember to call Russ later to return the keys to him. "I'm glad I knew of a place."

At that moment, Bryan, Ken, and Ivy walked into the shop. Ivy skipped across the floor and around the counter, stopping to give me and then Sarah a hug.

Ken walked over and kissed me. "Thanks again for watching Ivy while I help them move."

"Of course. We'll head over to your house when you call to say you're home." I shifted my gaze to Erin once more.

"And you're sure you're ready? You could have the apartment as long as you need."

She peeked up at Bryan who had come up behind her. "I'm sure. I had a good couple of days with my mom, cousins, and my friends, and after they left, I had a couple more days to catch up with Nonni. Although she's great company, when she wasn't there, I took the opportunity to sit and reflect and exist with just myself. And I came to the conclusion that I do not like to live alone. I thought I'd have to get a cat or something, and then I realized"—she leaned against Bryan's chest—"I already have one."

Bryan squeezed her shoulders lovingly. "I cleaned for her and everything." He chuckled. "She won't be able to say a pack of wolves lives there anymore."

I hadn't seen him this happy before either.

"I'm so glad things worked out for the two of you." The matchmaking tingle caused by the two of them had never been stronger. I turned to Anita. "And will you be staying long?"

"That depends," she answered, her grin breaking out into a wide smile.

I cocked my head to the side.

"I said I'd stay through the wedding. We'll see how long it takes before he asks her." Her shoulders rose and fell in silent laughter. "With as long as it took for him to finally tell her how he felt, it could be two days, two weeks . . . hopefully not two years."

Erin snorted lightly before leaning back into Bryan, who was none the wiser about Anita's comment. "I hope not."

"All right, should we get back to moving?" Bryan asked.

I turned to get a packed pastry box from the back counter. I plopped it on top of the case next to me. "Not until you take this. Some fuel for the job. I call them moving muffins."

He picked up the box. "Thanks, Joanie. Guess we'll all have enough energy to power us through the rest of this in no time."

After we waved our goodbyes to Erin, Bryan, Anita, and Ken, Sarah turned to me. "I'm heading to Leafs. Want anything?"

Ivy hopped in place, fists raised at chest height in excitement. "Fruit tea, please! And a marshmallow rice treat.

"One for me too," I added. "And a chai tea."

Magically by the time my tea reached a temperature that was cool enough for me to drink, no one was in the shop, which allowed me to sit at one of the bakery tables with Ivy as she colored to keep herself busy until closing time. Sarah pulled up a chair too, even though she'd finished her coffee already.

Things wouldn't stay quiet in Heartwood Hollow for long, they never did, but in as I sipped my chai, the peaceful moment we had right now was enough.

WHAT'S NEXT?

A matchmaking baker for the living and the dead.

Matching people with the ones they were supposed to be with had been a part of my entire life. But helping ghosts find their happily ever hereafters hadn't been on my radar until a few months ago. Between reuniting them with loved ones or solving their murders, I've assisted several spirits now.

So when I discover a ghost attached to a teacup used for tea services at the inn, I'm determined to help free the spirit. Only she doesn't want to move on, she wants to stay. And she wants to help the inn.

But to convince the innkeeper that the ghost even exists, never mind wants a job, is going to require a little help from some of my new friends.

Teacups and Typtology, **Book 6 of the Mixing Up Magic series, is coming soon.**

ACKNOWLEDGMENTS

I once joked that someday I would just copy and paste an acknowledgements section from an earlier book into the latest book without making changes because they all sounded the same. Well, things have changed a lot since the last time I wrote one of these, so I can promise you that this one isn't a result of copy/paste.

A huge thank you to those of you who have waited the two years since Potluck and Powers came out for this one to follow it. I could not have predicted the course of my publishing career if I had tried, and I am so grateful to all of you. But no matter how long you have been waiting, whether you found my books in 2019, last year, last month, or last week, thank you for being here now.

Thank you to my friends and family who have also been waiting, whether for the book to come out or for me to stop saying that it was coming eventually. It's finally out! Now you get to listen to me talk about the next book. But in all seriousness, thank you for your unwavering support, whether you read the books, share my posts about my books, or tell everyone about them.

Thank you to anyone who has had a hand in this series over the years. From Frankie at Real Indie Author for the initial spark that led to the creation of this series. To my editors past and present. To Molly and the OG team at WhiskMys during the short time these books were with the publishing house. To Melony at Paradise Cover Design for my photorealistic cover variation. To Paisley Press Books for sticking with it. To author friends who have let me bounce ideas off them or just been an ear during bouts of writers block. This series wouldn't be the same without any of you.

And that includes you too. Thank you to *you* for reading this book.

ABOUT THE AUTHOR

Rosie Pease is a native Rhode Islander but has lived in Vermont, New York, and Ohio. She uses the places she's traveled to as inspiration for the settings of her cozy mysteries, pulling the theater from one, the cider mill from another, the river from another to create a fictitious town that feels familiar.

She collects Funko Pops of the Harry Potter, Hunger Games, Doctor Who, DC TV, and Marvel variety, with a few others thrown in for fun. Her desk is a mess, but she can find everything on it, so it works for her as long as things aren't falling onto the keyboard as she writes.

When she's not crafting cozy mysteries, she's playing with her daughter, hanging out with her husband, or being amused by her two crazy cats.

Come find Rosie online:
Website: https://rosiepease.com
Facebook, Instagram, Twitter, and Pinterest:
@WriteRosiePease

ALSO BY ROSIE PEASE

The Matchmaking Baker

Coffee and Calicos

Sweets and Santa

Mixing Up Magic

Cookies and Curses

Scones and Spells

Weddings and Witchcraft

Potluck and Powers

Muffins and Mediums

Teacups and Typtology

Purrfect Travel Companion

Catastrophe on the Road

Catastrophe in the Kitchen